Only Strangers Here

Noel Howard

Published in Ireland by Orla Kelly Publishing.

By the same author:
Ballinacarriga Kilworth - a house, a family, a village (2020)

"Ballinacarriga's chequered past is meticulously documented." **The Irish Times**
"... an accomplished piece of research." **Irish Examiner**
"A fascinating new book..." **The Corkman**

Noel Howard moved from a teaching career in 1973 to work as a social care worker and manager in the Irish juvenile justice system until his retirement in 2008. He lives in Kilworth, Co. Cork.

To Lucy

In the little world in which children have their existence, whosoever brings them up, there is nothing so finely perceived and so finely felt, as injustice.
(Charles Dickens – Great Expectations)

Only Strangers Here

The wind, uncharacteristically biting for late April, had both men huddled on the platform. Others sought the shelter of wall or doorway, muttering about the lateness of the train, a regular conversation piece that even strangers were at ease sharing.

Without a word to each other, they glanced intermittently down the long track glinting in the sunlight. Nothing else held their attention, though not even the faintest sound heralded the train's arrival. At intervals, one removed a watch from his pocket with practised hand, despite the station clock being only a few feet from where he stood. Their silence was infectious, anticipation caught in the chill of the wind's embrace. They might have been waiting for a funeral.

To the motorman, seeing the train and the belching smoke before he heard it was nothing new, an experience gleaned from his many trips to the station. His companion, Rev Field, the rector, silver haired and bespectacled, questioned by a shake of the head this minor phenomenon of sight before sound.

When it finally reached his ears and those of the others, the sound was adequate compensation for the long, predictable wait. He edged closer to the track as did the others, their numbers increased by latecomers. The train bore down and halted.

The rector and the motorman were given pride of place on the platform. A policeman from the town discreetly placed himself at the crowd's edge, though none present paid him much attention. Curiosity rather than duty perhaps, had brought him. Today was not any day. It was the last day of April, 1911, and Edward Sheldon, the most sought-after King's Counsel in London, was bringing his wife of a few weeks home.

The rector, policeman and motorman were all there in what might be termed official capacities to ensure that the newlyweds were appropriately welcomed. Then it was the three mile drive from the station to the village of Shandrum, beyond which Woodlands stood. Mrs Sheldon's new home was an impressive building set in a magnificent riverside estate at the foot of a range of low hills, wooded and dense.

The rector was least certain as to why he was there. He was not enamoured of Edward Sheldon, though they had what might be termed a working relationship, as pastor and parishioner. Yet, as one of his congregation and a beneficial one at that, Field finally decided it appropriate to be there to welcome him on such an auspicious occasion.

The decision had not been an easy one, however, and Field had argued with himself all morning, before finally summoning up the courage to be at the rectory gate when the motorman passed through the village on his way to the station. That courage was aided by his insatiable curiosity, something which he had never managed to overcome. He just could not wait to see who had considered it worthwhile to marry Edward Sheldon, a man not given to public expressions of emotion.

Field would go further and claim he had seldom seen the man smile. But now, as he stepped from the train, an unmistakable look of triumph was evident on his cold, handsome face, which did not go unnoticed by those present.

Scanning the crowd, he identified those of relative importance, pausing, theatrically it seemed, before motioning his wife to join him. Field was taken aback. Sheldon, he saw, had not waited in vain.

Victoria Denham Lynd, now Victoria Sheldon, stepping off the train behind her husband, a man of no little stature and importance, quite overshadowed him. Or so thought Field, confirmed by the crowd's reaction. Her face, intelligent and spirited, would play temptingly on any man's mind. He watched, as her dark eyes ran quizzically across the crowd and the surroundings before turning, not quite beguilingly, to her husband's self - satisfied face. Introductions were made, appreciation expressed, congratulations extended. Field watched, as she nodded, smiled and responded impeccably to each greeting and remark. He could see she had made an instant impression, confirmed by the sidelong glances and whispering among the crowd.

Pleasantries concluded, Edward, Victoria and Field made their way toward where the motor stood waiting. A porter helped the motorman load various items of luggage, but not without difficulty, as room in the motor was scarce. Field, feeling more uncomfortable now, wished he had never come as two bags were awkwardly packed in at his feet as he sidled into the seat next to the driver. He now felt an intruder in this very public scene and tried to understand why. Had it something to do with the arrival of his newest parishioner?

He waited impatiently as Edward and Victoria settled themselves into the back seat, and the motorman, with a glance to see that all was in order, pulled away from the station's shadow and out into the sharp sunlight. The onlookers melted away.

At a steady pace, the motor was soon in open country. The road suddenly dipped, and their attention was drawn to the castle. Through a break in the trees, across the river, it stood, immutable, almost forbidding, its slitted windows eying the surrounding countryside. They crossed over the mill bridge, making a right turn before beginning the steady upward ascent by the castle gate and turning into the village. Field, still feeling uncomfortable, almost unwanted, prodded himself into saying a few words to the newlyweds in the back seat.

"A castle, a mill and a river. Not much different to an English country scene now, is it?"

Edward mumbled something from behind him. Victoria answered, quite genuinely, Field felt.

"Really beautiful, almost enchanting."

*

Snee, the village constable, stood impassively at the barrack door. The motor, slowing as it trundled into the village, allowed the passengers to observe the constable's demeanour at closer range. Making little effort to disguise his boredom, even on a special day such as this, he condescendingly offered an informal salute as they passed.

Servile recognition thought Field.

The constable's attitude was the exception, however. Long before the motor's arrival, its sound had alerted the villagers. The women, many discreetly sheltering in doorways, were there to catch a glimpse of Sheldon and more particularly, the woman who married him. Children, more adventurous, stared shyly from chosen vantage points. The men, most of whom had gathered outside Maguire's shop and public house, shifted self-consciously, pretending indifference until the motor had passed. Then, as if by a signal, their heads turned quickly to see what they had feigned disinterest in a second before. Their curiosity was hardly satisfied, however, as the motor moved away to the outskirts of the village. Too quickly gone, mused Field to himself, as the car approached his own gate.

He and a few more would not have forgotten the stately carriage that had brought the Sheldons, at a moderate, easy pace through the village before the arrival of the modern contraption. Progress indeed, Field sniffled to himself, as the motor thankfully halted. Muttering a goodbye, he stepped, unsteadily and awkwardly, on to the road.

For Victoria, as indeed any visitor to Shandrum, the scene now before her was more pleasing to the eye after the long, uninteresting village street. The road widened considerably. Observing the rectory, as Field alighted, she saw it set back in a well-appointed garden, carefully tended, with spring flowers in abundance and hints of those that would grace it in the summer.

As if deliberately and strategically placed, the house slightly opposite Field's was that of the priest of the parish,

Father Kerley. Greying and lengthened by galvanised extensions at either end, it contrasted sharply with that of the rector's. No evidence of flowers here and the pathway to the front door was neglected and overgrown. The garden and surrounds bore ample evidence of the priest's intermittent forays to give what the villagers referred to as "the jungle," some semblance of order.

Just along the road were the two churches. On the rectory side the spire of the Protestant place of worship rose amiably to a respectable height. Opposite, the "chapel," a solid and larger edifice was set back from the road on the priest's side, with the parish school just beyond. One might be forgiven for thinking that church and chapel were keeping an eye on each other.

Almost unnoticed by Victoria was a far less conspicuous building, situated between the chapel and the priest's rather ramshackle residence. She thought it quaint and not unlike a typical English cottage. It was thatched, overrun by a trail of roses that would no doubt be spectacular in season. Wildflowers, as if untended, rambled in all directions. Taking pride of place was a new crop of bluebells.

Waiting for Field to take his leave, she watched as two children, perhaps eight or nine, came gaily down the chapel yard, hand in hand, sharing some childish joke. Conscious of the motor and its occupants, they walked close to the chapel wall, almost hugging it. Shyly averting their gaze for a moment, they now stared, unable to resist the temptation offered by the sight of the important occupants of the motor.

Then Victoria noticed something most unusual. As they neared the thatched cottage, the girls almost instinctively moved out onto the road, giving the cottage a semi-circular berth until they were back again at a point where the low wall of the priest's house began. Edward, she noticed, had seen what had happened as well.

"Is it some kind of ritual?" Victoria asked him. "It seemed so natural for them."

Edward hesitated before answering. "It's very interesting, darling, that you are barely here and have just become privy to one of Shandrum's more peculiar customs. Not an endearing one, I might add, but one that has a very definite cause. They, like most others here, have, as they see it, a very good reason for what you call a ritual and it's an apt description, now that you put it that way. It all has to do with religion, or lack of it, I suppose." He paused again.

"Come now Edward, what's going on? Why did they do that? There's hardly a ghost in there."

"No, not a ghost, though I daresay a ghost might be more acceptable here. If you must know, and you would have found out anyway, the man who lives in that cottage is our resident village atheist. Fellow by the name of Golden, better known as 'The Pagan.' Yes indeed, that's Joe Golden, ... a definite thorn in the side of the clergy and that includes our own dear rector." Edward nodded in Field's direction, who was by now out of earshot and almost at his door. He turned and gave a listless wave in the motor's direction.

While all this was going on, Victoria was conscious of the motorman and how intently he had listened to the snippets of conversation. Expressionless but not missing a word. She couldn't help feeling that Edward's answers to her questions about the girls' behaviour was rather cryptic and grudgingly given. Then, she surmised, he might just be tired after the long journey or have simply been anxious to get to Woodlands and introduce her to her new home. Just as the motor was about to pull away from the rectory gate, the occupants' attention was drawn to a movement at the side of the cottage. A bicycle appeared, pushed with ease by a tall, lean figure. Victoria saw that the man was about Edward's height, maybe around the same age. Beside her she noticed that Edward stirred uneasily and instructed, rather than hinted to the motorman, that they should be on their way. The man wheeled the bicycle onto the road and closed the small timber gate at the end of the path. He was now only a few yards from the motor and quite deliberately seeming to ignore Edward and Victoria, he nodded to the motorman before mounting the bicycle and cycling unhurriedly away and up the village street.

Edward could not conceal his irritation at this quick turn of events. Staring straight ahead he spoke crisply to Victoria. "That's him, The Pagan, you've seen him now so I think we should take you home." They were soon at a turn on the road, known locally as the dangerous corner, and the beginning of the long, high wall that bounded Woodlands.

*

Approaching the gate lodge, the motor slowed. The road ahead rose sharply. Inside the lodge, the motorman's son, fair-haired and freckled, was engrossed in a newspaper, lost in the detail of whatever he was reading. Familiar with the motor's sound he was roused out of his reverie as it approached the gate. He bounded out the door. Seeming to ignore the motor and its occupants, he opened the huge double gates. The ease with which he performed this task indicated he was well used to it. Only then did he satisfy weeks of curious waiting, wondering what she would look like in reality, the woman who had married Mr Sheldon. Completely different, nothing like he had surmised. Even different, he thought, than any of the pictures he had seen of her in the grey wedding photos in the Illustrated London News.

He felt himself blushing furiously as his father turned to Victoria. "Mrs Sheldon, this is my son."

Look at her clothes. No one in the village like that except maybe Mrs Swan and she never looks at me. That smell now. Perfume but not like Miss Hartley's at mass. Different. Her fingers so long. Better say what his father had told him to and not to be shy. Look at her face and not at the ground.

"Welcome to Woodlands, Mrs Sheldon," What else, what else? Yes, say it, just say it. "I hope you and Mr Sheldon will be very happy here." Throat now dry, shivering even in the sun. But I said it, it's done now. Said what I was told.

He moved away from the motor's side, not expecting her to say anything in reply to his rehearsed greeting. "Well, that's the kindest greeting I've had all day. And right at my own doorstep. And what age are you?"

"I will be 13 in October ... I was born in 1898."

She was going to say something else but her husband's demeanour, stiff and disinterested, made her think better of it. As the motor pulled away, she waved at the boy, and he raised his hand and hesitantly waved back. Sheldon didn't like her talking to me. It was on his face. He often has a face like that.

He followed the motor to where there was a turn in the avenue, watching the new arrival take in the whole sweep of house and gardens before saying something to Sheldon. Whatever it was, it seemed to improve his humour. Standing at the corner, unnoticed by everyone else, he watched the servants come down the steps, ready to greet the master of Woodlands but more especially his wife. Even Meany came struggling around the corner from the garden. How well he heard the motor and he supposed to be deaf.

She's getting out now, the lovely clothes, the boots and again the thought of the perfume. Nothing like it. There's the boss now at her side. How could she like him, such a sourpuss? A laugh would crack his face, Joe said. Even though he never gives out about him otherwise. She's up the steps now, nodding and smiling at the servants, husband just behind her. At the door he lets her go first. Must be the right manners. She turns now, just before going into her new home for the first time and looks back across the wide expanse of gravel toward the wooded hills beyond and to where the meandering river carved out part of the boundary of the large Woodlands estate. All there for her to see.

Gone in now and the servants disperse, talking over each other and the subject of conversation is obvious. The first of many he thinks and all about her. The first thing she'll see inside is the big painting of Old Sheldon. You couldn't miss it. It's a portrait, his father had told him. The motor starts up again, to be driven round the side and unloaded, until needed. His father never finished, though, and he could be called at any hour. Always something to do or somewhere to go. And they all say in the village that he has a bobby's job. It's not. Look at Constable Snee above at the barrack. Walks around all day, wherever and whenever he likes.

Not a sound anywhere now. She had come and gone in a few minutes. And to think she made me forget all about the paper and the Titanic's launch. It would be a year, the paper said, before it would set sail. A ship that will never be sunk, Joe said, before adding that he had seen one of the biggest tankers ever built sinking somewhere off the coast of Africa. Had he seen Mrs Sheldon? The whole village was out to see her but that didn't mean Joe would be. Only one way to find out. I hope he didn't see her. It'll be my surprise. For once.

*

With a glance backwards at the house he turned and headed for Joe's. The road always quicker but you're seen by all. Did he mean it, Joe, when he said it would be our secret and ours alone? Surely someone else would find it at some time. Maybe not. They had measured it, hadn't they? Walked and timed the two routes. Woodlands' gate lodge to cottage by the road nearly a quarter of a mile. Lodge to cottage by the path nearly twice that. But safer. No chance of Father Kerley jumping down your throat. Watch him, Joe had warned him. He had written down the distance and time in a copybook in Joe's. Double but safer.

A rotten, miserable day it was when they had measured it. "Necessity the mother of invention," Joe had declared. Nearly sick at the thought of it now. Even after a year. Would it ever be forgotten? And to think that he almost got away. Nearly escaped him. But he misses nothing, Joe had said, and he has his spies in the village. If only I'd stayed closer to the wall, he'd never have got me. And I heard him giving out so much to Father as I got nearer. And the big hairy hand grabbing me over the low wall and standing me between the two of them. But I knew Father was mad at him. His fists clenched, like going for a fight. Then the priest. Off again about Joe. Spits flying out of his mouth. Veins running down his forehead. New word that would need the dictionary or better still, Joe, better than any dictionary sometimes. Demon. Lucifer. Soul destroyer. Reprobate. All tumbling out of the priest's mouth at the same time.

Staring at me. "This village knows, your teacher knows, your father knows, the aristocracy knows, and the aristocracy's rector knows we'd all be far better off without him here. And you, young whippersnapper, be in no doubt about it. He will lead you into the depths of depravity. Do you hear me. Be certain sure of that. Keep away from him."

Finger jabbing into my chest. Like a clown pointing in all directions. Back towards Woodlands at the mention of aristocracy, back across the road when he mentioned the rector and at the cottage about Joe. Depravity. Another for the dictionary. Hard to remember them but most he would have heard before.

Bending down now, eyes blazing into my face. Face purple and blotchy. Veins running all over his head. Snakes. But no snakes in Ireland. All sent away, banished the right word, by St Patrick, dear saint of our isle, in 432. AD 432. Get that into all your thick heads, insisted Slyne, the master. One of the most important dates in Irish history. When will Father tell him to stop squeezing my arm? I'll cry soon if he doesn't stop. But I won't. The last thing I want to do in front of the two of them. Be a man and don't give in.

Father moving between us. "I think, Father, he knows what you mean, but how many times have I told you, the man in that cottage, as you well know, has been a friend of ours for years like his mother before him? That's all it is. And he wouldn't harm a fly, the same man."

The big hand stops squeezing. No more of it maybe. But that will drive him mad, saying Joe is just our friend. See him now, standing straight as a die. Six foot two, Joe said. But no man that big that he can't be knocked down. What's he going to say next?

"My man, I am entrusted with preserving the moral fibre of this parish as I've done in others before now. Now don't think I will fail in that. That man is not to be trusted and your child is in moral danger. And I'm not the only one that says it. He spends too much time in that cottage. A blind man could see that. This is regularly brought to my notice by those upstanding people in the parish who have nothing but your boy's interests at heart and that of their own children. I'm sure you know what that means."

He's gone now. Dust rising behind him. Marching off like a soldier to pester someone else or talk to his cronies.

All that more than a year ago and it was only like yesterday. He remembered every time he took the path. No need for proof anymore. Longest way round safest way home and it would have been that way last year if I'd only bent lower along by the wall as I got beyond the chapel and closer. Nearly there now. Mind the crooked stones. Easy. Look now and then over the wall and you're just at Joe's. A funny smell somewhere. The castle behind you, only two fields away. Sometimes when the light was a certain way you could almost reach out and touch it. A different path from Joe's back door took you there. But forget about that and the smell. Did he see her?

"Did you see her? You know I did, but did you? She's like a princess. But Sheldon didn't like stopping, you could see it in his face. And do you know what she said? She said what I said was the best welcome she got. Now. But did you see her?"

"See what, who?"

Why won't he answer me? He surely knows what I'm talking about. But sometimes other things on his mind. He must surely have got a chance to see her. Wouldn't he have heard the motor no matter what he was doing. Could have looked out the window, anyway.

"Follow me," he said. He went out the back door and towards the shed. The terrible smell was now stronger.

"Look in there, now."

He opens the door, wait for the light. The stench is now awful. A sheep, head all rotten, its belly torn open, thrown on the floor. Maggots everywhere and the sound of flies. Worse than the two dead cats on St. Patrick's day. They were hanging on a nail over the backdoor. But not rotten and torn apart like this. Joe's eyes flashed.

"I suppose they think this'll worry me. The bloody hypocrites, the bastards, with their Hail Mary, Holy Mary, yes Father, no Father, morning noon and night."

"Tis the League again, I suppose."

"Ah, sure it is, but it's him of course, next door. Where he leads, they follow. Eegits, one or two of them intelligent and that only makes them more dangerous. Wait there."

Joe went back to the house and then returned with two pieces of cloth. Tying them across their faces, like cowboys robbing a bank in the stories, they set to work. He held open a worn sack while Joe shovelled what was on the floor into it. All this made the smell worse if such was possible. Not a word from Joe. Was he thinking of the priest? Or maybe it was her he was thinking of. Surely, he had seen her.

*

He had come to Shandrum at the beginning of the century. His reputation was there before he arrived. Ostensibly, his move to a new parish was a routine diocesan one. The old canon was in poor health and Fr Kerley would be his replacement. Nothing unusual in that then. But again, not unusually either, rumour had it otherwise. And with very good reason.

Though coming from the far end of the diocese, the new priest's reputation was firmly established as the prime mover behind the formation of a small but effective group known as The Irish Freedom League. It was one of a number of splinter groups that had come into being after Parnell's death in 1891. His death had brought disillusionment after his efforts had failed on Ireland's behalf. And of course, his reputation as an adulterer was grist to the mill for anyone who wished to adopt a more radical agrarian approach on behalf of the Irish peasantry. "The League" as it became known in Kerry and Cork spread propaganda and engaged in sporadic attacks on landlords and the aristocracy. "Ireland for the Irish," the league's motto could often be seen scrawled on the walls of landlords' Big Houses in different parts of the two counties.

Its most spectacular achievement or atrocity, depending on one's point of view, was, just at the century's turn, the burning and looting of Killaskey House, on the Cork - Kerry border. There were two consequences to this event. The most publicised was the return to England of Sir Reginald Edgar, the owner of the burned-out mansion, leaving a large number of local people out of work.

Rumours abounded as to who bore responsibility for the outrage. Less well publicised was Fr Kerley's move to Shandrum from Killaskey a few months later. The Cork Examiner, in early January 1901, under the heading "Diocesan Moves," gave a list of priests who were assigned new parishes and among them was Fr Kerley. No one was ever held responsible for perpetrating the outrage on the Edgar mansion.

Few in his old or new parish, however, believed his move was routine and, there was a strong belief, that this time his enthusiasm for the cause had gone too far. It also gave rise to complaints at various levels with a number of deputations calling on the bishop to publicly denounce the burning. He did, but of course it was a general condemnation assigning blame to no one in particular. There wasn't the slightest hint that one of his priests in Killaskey had anything to do with what had happened. A few months later, on a cold and snowy day in March, Fr Kerley duly arrived in Shandrum from Killaskey, many miles away at the other side of the county.

The move appeared to have been effective and the priest's patriotism dampened. But not for long. A few months after his arrival he became aware that Shandrum had its patriots too. A small group, of some standing in the village, had come together under the influence and respectability of the new priest. Never far from the surface was subtle support for the League's aims in the village and beyond.

Woodlands, the Sheldon home, was occasionally mentioned as a possible target though the priest was at pains to point out that time needed to elapse before any action might be taken. His reason, never openly voiced, was that it would be too much of a coincidence if another gentrified house was attacked and any association with responsibility for such an action laid at his door.

Woodlands, therefore, did appear to escape the worst of the League's excesses and unsavoury activities. The reason for this was not alone the priest's cautious reticence. Woodlands, an obvious symbol of the aristocracy, was seen quite favourably by many in the village and even more so than similar Big Houses in the surrounding area.

Old George Sheldon, Edward's father, was a somewhat benign, if eccentric, landlord and the main beneficiaries of this were the locals. Some would aver that he was more shrewd than enlightened in his dealings with the local tenantry. Whatever his reasoning or disposition, he took a number of actions which were of great significance locally and enhanced his reputation far beyond the walls of Woodlands.

Much to the chagrin of his landlord neighbours, he had often pleaded on behalf of poachers, sheep stealers and rabbit catchers, even when their actions had taken place in the grounds of Woodlands or the river that flowed through it. When new reapers and binders had replaced traditional methods of harvesting and meant men losing their jobs, such new-fangled machines did not find their way to Woodlands. This, despite Old Sheldon's friends in other local estates ecstatically praising their worth and savings. He resisted the temptation to pander to modernity. For this he suffered the scorn of his friends and the admiration of the locals. Indeed, such was the high regard in which he was held that he merited a ballad with the dubious title, "The English Irishman."

One of the most remembered gifts to the village was a plot of land for a hurling field, made available in one of Woodlands' fields. "Sheldon's Field" became the envy of every town and village for miles around, a model for other places to emulate.

Many of Old Sheldon's goodwill gestures were passing into folklore by the time his son brought home his new wife. They were not forgotten by all, however. Another deed not forgotten by a dwindling band of the older villagers was famine relief, in the form of soup and bread at the gates of Woodlands, over sixty years before. Memory of his munificence did not however find its way to the children of Shandrum; certainly not to the boys, whose master, Slyne, had little time for the Sheldons or those of their class. "A dwindling breed" was his analysis.

Though Old George's son, Edward, was to spend less and less time at home in Woodlands since his father's death, the house and estate still provided work for locals. For the priest then, Woodlands and the Sheldons posed a particular kind of challenge in that they had the favour of many who might otherwise be ill disposed to a less benign type of landlord. Fortunately for him though, there were a number of individuals in Shandrum who did not depend on Woodlands and the Sheldons for employment or their living. After ten years in the parish, Kerley loathed Sheldon and all he stood for, to the point where he had made some inroads, and could now depend on some of the more influential lackeys in the village to support and indeed act on his particular brand of antagonism. Woodlands, he surmised, might not always be as safe as it appeared if circumstances were to change.

If Sheldon and all he stood for presented the priest with an ongoing problem, another one, much closer to home, palpably proved to be more infuriatingly intractable. Practically every single day. That was the presence of The Pagan, right on his doorstep. A more hateful, despicable and intransigent adversary the priest had never encountered and that was saying something.

The Pagan, Golden, was coldly and provocatively defiant, and any man with no respect for God or church was highly suspect. But doubly suspect was someone who, by common consent, and the priest's definite belief, had an undesirable influence on an impressionable child. More darkly hinted at was where would this influence lead. Those who despised The Pagan and those who feared him, looked for answers to their priest.

*

As she looked out her bedroom window on her first evening in Woodlands, waiting for Edward to dress for dinner, Victoria recalled the sequence of events that had brought her there in the first place.

At 31, the prospect of marriage to an Irish landlord and celebrated lawyer might for some have been a most appealing prospect. Not so for Victoria Denham Lynd, writer of widely read children's stories, and whose suitor for many years was not a man but the suffragette movement.

The movement, gaining strength and some political support in the early years of the century had a lot for which to thank Victoria. Her independence and determination were felt from behind the scenes rather than in public, and she was highly influential in pushing the movement's onward march by what she wrote in papers and pamphlets. When necessary, she was no coward either and took her place when the movement faced down politicians and the law on the streets and at public events.

She had first met Edward Sheldon in 1905 when her

brother, Harold, an up-and-coming lawyer like Edward, had brought him for a weekend to the Denham Lynd country house in Eastleigh, Surrey. She and her mother had always thought of Edward and her brother as being particularly close. On social occasions they often eschewed the company of others and appeared very much at home in their own company, something surreptitiously commented on occasionally. That was not all, however.

Victoria recalled a summer morning when she had to take an early train to London. Walking along the corridor from her room and turning a corner she came upon Harold emerging from Edward's bedroom. She hung back and not noticing her, he slipped quickly into his own room.

She was aware of what her mother on occasion described as "other kinds of love." Such a view intrigued Victoria and her education in this area was enhanced by one of the suffragettes' leading lights and a woman she admired. Quite casually, one evening coming back from a march, while discussing men, Victoria had lightly broached her acquaintance's romantic life. She received the confidential, and somewhat shocking reply, given with a half smile, "where men are concerned it's women for me." It was an aspect of life, among so many others, that her time in London and her involvement in the movement opened her up to. She remembered the same woman, when confronted by one particularly belligerent politician at a town hall meeting, whispering to her as he resumed his seat "if he only knew we know that he is the father of his granddaughter." Victoria's interest in the meeting faded as she worked out that conundrum.

As Edward's star in the legal world rose and much of his time was spent in London, the visits to Eastleigh were a welcome respite from his hectic work schedule.

Harold continued to steer eligible men in Victoria's direction and had little difficulty in that. His sister, attractive, well-educated and fiercely independent would, he assumed, be any man's choice. And he was right. But he knew, as Victoria's mother did, that any man seeking her hand in marriage had to contend with another competitor.

At 26, on a family picnic, Victoria had watched, with horrified helplessness, as her then lover, Nathan Pilger, had drowned attempting to save a young boy. The boy survived, Nathan didn't. Stoically, she had endured but not without cost. Only she knew that when Nathan died, much of what she might feel for any man died too. Her self-reliant nature and her suffragette work had kept her sane for a short while, but her hidden grief persisted.

With her work, editing and writing for the movement, and protesting on the streets, she seemed to be coping. As if by delayed shock, she then cut her ties as the movement gathered more and more momentum and its demands on her grew. In effect, when Victoria lost Nathan, the movement lost one of its shining stars. A cause that had meant so much to her and in which she passionately believed lost its appeal, much to the disappointment of those at the helm of the movement. Her loss would leave a big chink in its armour although in time, the adage, no one is indispensable, proved that it would succeed, despite losing Victoria at a crucial time.

Though a woman of means, she had continued with her writing through it all and it gave her an income and social standing that few women, even of her class, came close to achieving. In the meantime, Edward Sheldon came and went regularly at weekends with Harold. She found him somewhat cold, even distant but never felt uncomfortable in his presence. Though an opponent of the movement to which she had given so much, she had many good - natured jousts with him and with Harold, knowing quite well that she would never win them over to her side.

A man on the move in the legal world, Edward had spectacular successes, leading, in 1909, at thirty-three, to his becoming one of the country's youngest KCs. His other preoccupation was his father's failing health. When not in London or Eastleigh with Harold, he was 'at home' in Woodlands. As his star had risen, however, these visits to Woodlands became less frequent, even as his father's health deteriorated.

Never short of female admirers, Edward's brusque, unsmiling exterior hid a certain shyness. Harold saw this Irishman, highly regarded and in much demand, as a perfect match for his sister, so much so that his mother had on occasion to warn him that his efforts at matchmaking were indiscreet. At times it verged on the unseemly, when what appeared to be his natural enthusiasm for his sister's happiness, became too evident. Victoria, knowing what she did, often wondered why. However, despite his eager efforts occasionally backfiring, he succeeded in Victoria and Edward being pushed, rather than drawn, together. His reasons were his and his alone and over time he had concluded would benefit his friend, his sister and himself. On a howling day in January 1911, with winter sun cutting through the windows, Victoria, in utter disbelief, sat across the drawing room table from her brother. It was for her a conversation and a year that she would never forget. She could never remember having a serious disagreement with Harold, though she was often the victim of his practical jokes. As he began, brushing a curl from over an eyebrow, it struck her how incredibly good looking he was.

"An ideal choice, highly respected with an assured career. You should see Woodlands, it's simply breath-taking. A paradise. The house and grounds and the whole estate are magnificent, and as for himself, well he is, you must admit, a most affable fellow."

She watched his face describe the man from whose bedroom she had seen him emerge on that summer morning.

"A bit serious, I might say, but that's our profession."

Speechless, she thought this was, indeed, one of Harold's practical jokes. If that's all it is why then am I laughing so nervously? This had been her only response to Harold's litany of platitudes about Edward. But then she knew, even though not wanting to admit it, he was talking of marriage. The nervous laughter subsided. A shrewd observer of the ways of men, she eyed her brother across the table, trying to make sense of how this ridiculous state of affairs had developed. But no, Harold was, she could see, deadly serious. No joking this time.

Seeing her puzzlement, he continued to outline any number of family, social and financial reasons why she should give very serious consideration to marrying Edward and move to his country estate in County Cork. Nervous and puzzled initially, she was now angry, believing a plot had been hatched behind her back and perhaps not by Harold alone.

"Who put you up to this, Harold? All so carefully rehearsed. Whose messenger are you? Mother's or the Ormsbys? She was referring to the two sisters, old friends of the family, who lived close by and who never ceased insisting that, as they put it, Victoria "should face the future." This phrase had crept into the sisters' vocabulary shortly after Nathan died and became an interminable refrain in the years following, particularly when Victoria's interest in men had seemed to wane. Vague as it might be, the insistent piece of advice simply and solely meant marriage. Victoria now furiously debated with herself as to how long this concerted effort to design her future had been going on.

"No one else is in on this, Vic. I'm serious, no one put me up to it. It's no one's carefully crafted plan, it's Edward's request."

"Edward's request?" This bizarre revelation only increased her confused nervousness as it alternated with anger. "This is one of your jokes, Harold, isn't it?" Again, before he answered, she knew it wasn't. Her throat tightened. What answer would satisfy her most?

"No, no it's not, Vic. I'm just trying to help you and help my best friend." She wondered had he some other, more personal motive but quickly came back to Edward.

"Help me, Harold. I hardly know Edward - you know what I mean – surely this coming down specially from

London … Explain," she pleaded, yet not wanting to betray her curiosity.

Waves of possibilities now swept through her as Nathan's laughing face was there before her again, as was his bloated body taken from the river. These two images came to mind time and again since his death and it did not surprise her, in the present context of Harold's presence and his message, that her deepest loss would emerge again. Torn between what she was hearing and Nathan's memory, she might well have walked out on her brother. But something compelled her to stay, to hear more. And then the absurdity of it all hit her again and she stood and glared at him.

"Do you have any understanding of what you're doing, Harold? Coming here from London and asking me to marry Edward. Where is he? This is hardly the most romantic or auspicious way to the altar!" Somehow, the word romantic and Edward jarred. It was hardly a word she would use to characterise him.

"Who would believe it?" She almost spat the words, accusingly, at Harold. "To be asked by your brother to marry his best friend. No one else I hope is aware of this so-called proposal?"

"No, no one else knows. Haven't I come right from the station? Mother doesn't even know I'm here." His tone was now almost one of tired impatience, that his sister would misinterpret his best intentions, even if she was right about Edward using him as an intermediary. She sat down, drumming her fingers on the table. So few answers to so many questions. Questions from past and present.

The few moments could have been an hour, there in the sombre January afternoon. What had just transpired was to her so beyond belief. Yet, she should have known Harold would not have come from London on a weekday were it simply to play some grotesque joke. It was then she knew, as did Harold observing her, that she would not say no to the inexplicable proposal. Her brother's gaze, now impenetrable, assessed quite rightly that any further protestations of disinterest would weaken. It would be something that would, over time, preoccupy her. Why did she not say no?

My God, she thought, am I going to become Edward Sheldon's wife? Just like this? She remained seated, her nails now biting into the palms of her hands. Shouldn't she be happy?

Harold stood up and came round to where she sat. "Look, Vic," he said, "no one will ever hear of this from me if you decide to say no. Not even Mother. I'll make some excuse for my sudden coming. I have done my part, kept my promise, strange as it may seem to you, to Edward. He will be here the weekend after next and will of course ask you formally. I don't have to tell you what my wish is. You know that only too well. After Nathan, even before him, all I wanted was and is your happiness. But don't do anything just to please me."

She saw his concern, she would give him that, yet realised it came after he knew she had succumbed. He touched her on the shoulder as the last sliver of what was left of the winter sun splayed across the drawing room table. As if understanding that she wanted to be alone, he closed the door softly behind himself, leaving her to ponder on so many uncertainties about her own future but also Harold's.

But it was not the future she had time to dwell on now, staring across the lawn as the cold January night came down. With its coming came Nathan too, as often before, teasing out what might have lain ahead for them had the river not taken him. He first inspired her to write, telling her that in the simplicity of a child's story can be found much of what the world pursues and seldom achieves. In the lighter moments they invented plots and characters that peopled her books and made her name a household word.

Now, darkness descending on another day, she formed other words, her lips moving in in apprehension and uncertainty. Not words of some child's fertile imagination but words that she thought she would never utter, Mrs Edward Sheldon. What would Mother say?

*

Before Edward Sheldon ever brought his wife home to Woodlands, the boy's father had always been known as the motorman. Before the arrival of the motor and its novelty to the village he had been the coachman, like many others found in similar positions in the Big Houses across the length and breadth of the country. Though the term 'coachman' had a certain common anonymity, not so 'motorman.'

The sound of a distant motor might be heard in the village and on occasion one might be seen, a rare sight. Where many in Shandrum had speculated on when, if ever, he might bring a wife back to Woodlands, even more of a novelty it seemed was the arrival of a Rolls Royce landaulette in 1910. The coachman became the motorman, technically as well as in name, by reason of his spending a week in Manchester to familiarise himself with every detail of Woodland's latest acquisition. Everything appeared to be in place for the motor's arrival except the weather. The muffled sound in the distance alerted the onlookers. This time it was a case of heard before seen.

Snee, not prepared to be impressed, stood at the barrack doorway with Cleary, the sergeant. The motorman, looking neither left nor right, stolidly steered the gleaming monster down the muddied street on a day of steady rain. Edward, looking almost regal, sat impassively and barely nodded through the rain at those with whom he was familiar. They were few. As if to reward those who braved the elements, he shouted something in the motorman's ear as they reached the outskirts of the village. The motor was deftly turned around and paraded back up the street, allowing those gathered there a second look. For some it was a gesture well meant to satisfy curiosity. Others would see it as Edward's way of letting them know just who their betters were. Here was the consummate example of that.

Standing in the shelter of a large umbrella, Field stood at the rectory gate, as curious as anyone else but a victim of mixed emotions. What he considered to be fiendish mechanical contraptions would bring havoc to the serenity of the village and the wider countryside. Yet, he secretly nurtured a wish that he might someday be carried in it to savour the convenience it might offer. Surely Edward would offer at some point? He hoped so.

Having given the villagers sufficient exposure to something they would never sit in, Sheldon again gave the driver an instruction. The eyes of the villagers followed, and they were about to move for what shelter there was when the rector became the object of their attention. As it slowed to a halt, Field moved back toward the gate, an instinctive gesture of protection. The motorman smiled, but not unkindly. Edward even seemed momentarily amused. Eager not to appear unenthusiastic, Field moved around the motor, his jaundiced eye examining it from different angles.

"Truly magnificent, Edward, though you know my views on such contraptions as this."

"You'll have to see what it's like, no matter what you think, but we'll find a better day than this one, perhaps." All three looked against the grey, unrelenting clouds.

"I would be delighted, Edward. My only concern would be safety."

The motorman smiled again. Edward managed what might, in less amenable circumstances, be construed as a sneer of derision.

*

Inside the schoolroom, Master Slyne's bark brought their attention back to his imposing presence and the blackboard. Their eyes had been drawn to the school windows, too high to afford a view for what they had been waiting all day. The dull approaching sound, music to their ears, was one they would remember long past their schooldays. The first motor in Shandrum. Like a long - lost smell, a particular colour splashed on a canvas, the arrival of the motor and its indelible imprint on their memories, would be one they would associate forever with one special school day, long gone but not forgotten. The master's all-pervasive influence went only so deep that day. Their bodies were at his command, but the sound outside was battering at their imaginations. The teacher's face betrayed open contempt at the motor's sound. In the classroom, his absolute domain, he lorded over all but not the clock behind him on the wall. The hand had climbed past the finishing time. As if to confound it, the master whipped his watch from his pocket only to return it instantly. He picked his gold tipped pen from the desk and with a stare, cold and bitter, told them to go, desperately trying to ignore the surge of anticipation as they bounded towards the door.

Usually, he would turn left from the school gate and head for the gate lodge at Woodlands while the majority headed toward the village street to then spread out in different directions. But today the crush carried him forward toward the rector's gate and the object of everyone's attention. There was the gleaming motor, its glittering newness undulled by the rain, even if the wheels bore evidence of the street's mud.

Edward isn't happy, the boy could see, much more used to surveying Edward's face than the other children. He's impatient. He wants to get home, but the children only want to look at it. He'll have it forever. The rector seems to understand their curiosity. Father, not impatient like his master, waiting for the word. It must be very hard, learning to drive it. So many things to know. Now the boys are looking at him. Jealous, but it's better than being pushed and shoved because of Joe. He's somewhere, watching all this, I know. But not among those still observing from up the street, out in all the rain. Sheldon is talking to his father. His father beckons to him in the crowd of staring classmates. He wants me. I'll push through them, they won't stop me now, he tells himself, safe in the presence of his father. Different when they have me alone but different now. Look at their faces. They're beaten this time.

Be careful stepping in, father had said. The inside, so dry and even warm. But he wants to be gone, away from the jealous eyes on the outside. Sheldon gives the word. The jostling crowd of schoolboys stand back, cowed by the motor's rumble. He looked behind at them now as they followed its progress until lost to view around the dangerous corner. Just then he noticed a figure arriving where the children were. It was the priest.

Back at the rector's gate the children huddled, only now realising how wet it was. It was as if they had committed a mortal sin. The priest did not have to say a word, just swung his umbrella in their direction. They scattered hastily for home, heads low against the teeming rain that swept down the street. It didn't prevent them moving away from the cottage as they approached. They had little choice as the priest stood and watched.

The Pagan's door opened. He came out to survey the now almost empty street. The master was determined to wait in the schoolroom until the motor's sound had faded. Had he not, then he would be forced to witness the children's reaction to seeing it. More particularly, perhaps, he would have to give some level of acknowledgement to the rector and the motor's occupants, loathe as he was to even contemplate so doing.

Slipping his pen into his pocket, he banged the door shut and opened his umbrella with purpose and defiance, only then noticing The Pagan standing at his cottage gate. He certainly wasn't about to give any recognition there and he loped toward the village, giving the cottage a wide berth, his scowling face half hidden by the umbrella. The Pagan, just as deliberately ignoring the master as he passed, continued to look up the street as the last few adults sought shelter to reflect on the day's event. They would draw their own conclusions.

*

"Well, you seem to contradict one of your opinions of a few years ago anyway. And to think you were involved in telling the women of the world what they should and should not look out for in their choice of men."

"Mother, don't bring all that back to haunt me, please."

"Well, one of the first pieces of gospel from your beloved suffragettes was 'Do not marry at all,' if I remember."

"If you must know, I did argue strongly against that, but we had to let it go because Lady Pritchard, who had two disastrous marriages, threatened to withdraw any further monies for the cause unless she had her way. And, as we well know, money talks."

Her mother opened a drawer and pulled a pamphlet from it. It brought with it a poster which fell to the floor. Victoria remembered the day she presented it, her creation, to those who led the movement. She picked it up and looked at it again. Its striking message could not be argued with and it would be a common sight throughout the land. "Convicts, Lunatics, Women," written in black. Below it in blazing red was the punchline "All Have No Votes." She replaced it in the drawer while her mother read from the pamphlet in her hand.

"You have at least done well to avoid the… here they are, 'Beauty Men, Flirts, Tailors' dummies and the Football Enthusiasts.'"

Victoria smiled, knowing what was coming next.

"And let's see now, you haven't come to tell me that you've been approached by any of those. Were you really involved in drawing up this claptrap? 'Look for a Strong Tame Man, a Fire-lighter, Coal-getter, Window Cleaner and Yard Swiller.' They are the desirables, dear, almost from your own mouth. Find it hard to think that Lady Pritchard agreed to that."

"No indeed mother, look, all that was a very long time ago; you know who I've come to tell you about. Little brother will have told you."

Her mother threw the pamphlet back in the drawer and typically, there was no small talk.

"Not a man I would marry, dear. But then, I'm not asked to marry him, am I? I wonder what father's view might be, were he alive, on this?"

Victoria was rocked by her mother's typical honesty. It never surprised. She and Harold had grown up with it and its advantage was that you were left in no doubt as to how her mother felt. Her honesty had cost her friendships over the years or as she said herself, "well they are hardly friends if they can't accept the truth."

Since Harold's visit, Victoria had staggered from bouts of disbelief to that of impending inevitability and back again. She foundered in a swell of doubt and apprehension before admitting to her mother, with trepidation, what was bothering her.

She knew her mother would tell her what she believed her daughter needed rather than wanted to hear. While her honesty could devastate it often led her daughter to soul searching and a realisation that her mother's view of situations was, all in all, a lesson in reality, whether her daughter, or indeed anyone else, agreed or not.

She had hardly slept. Fitful bouts of disturbing dreams turned to nightmares, with Nathan's handsome face turning into Edward's sombre image, always moving towards her, yet distant and inaccessible. At other times, Edward was there, clearly visible but never close and certainly devoid entirely of the heady passion her dreams of Nathan had previously conjured up and in which she revelled.

She took her mother's blunt appraisal of the situation as a starting point. It certainly put the ludicrous fiasco of Harold's proposal into some perspective.

"Why not a man you would marry, Mother?"

Even as she asked the question, she knew the reasons were as true for herself as for her mother. Yet, somehow, the die had already been cast. Harold had seen to that.

"Perhaps, Victoria dear, I should never have said that. If I had a penny for every time I should have held my tongue I'd be a millionaire twice over. I just meant we are all different. I'm sure you know what I mean or perhaps not.

It's something to do with his …lack of…intensity. Even in his zeal about the law there is something dispassionate, as perhaps there should be. But marriage is a different thing. Even in my honesty I have never sought to offend you, dear, but I somehow strongly feel the potential for passion appears to be misplaced if not …"

She hesitated and then continued, "if not missing completely."

They both laughed, a short cackle at first and then a longer, uncomfortable, shriek that tailed off with a hint of momentary despair, something she didn't allow her mother to notice. Why am I laughing, she asked herself? But one question had been answered. Her mother had confirmed her view of Edward. But then was it always right to judge every man on what she had found with Nathan?

It was her mother now at her most practical and indeed considerate. There was something of Harold in how she could be at times, something she had experienced when Nathan had been taken from the river, his hair a tangled web of slime across his face. With figures running, everywhere and nowhere, her mother was suddenly at her side, wondering what could she possibly say. She said nothing, preferring to wait until alone with her daughter. That night, sitting with a still inconsolable Victoria, her mother took her in her arms and spoke.

"My darling, you have lost him. All you have lived for, the dream, your dream has been taken away from you by this horrible twist of fate. You will look for answers you may never get but remember one thing. You had your dream for a while, a little while, I know. How many can say that, that they had their dream for a little while. Life can and will go on."

Victoria felt those words were meant for her mother as they were meant for herself, but she was incapable of responding. That was all of five years ago and it seemed that the conversation of that horrible day was now about to continue. To somehow play out against a different backdrop.

Now, with her view of Edward so trenchantly delivered, her mother expanded on her attitude to the proposal. It sounded like Harold all over again. From a woman though, it had a different, pragmatic tint of meaning, nuanced and understanding. Waiting until she had Victoria's undivided attention, she went on.

"I will give you the same advice as I got when I was about to marry your father. If you wish to marry, and not marry for love, whatever that is, let him know it without any shred of doubt. It gets rid of all kinds of complications, practical and otherwise at a later stage. You have always said there will never be another Nathan."

"If you can live with this man and take all the advantages that go with it, then don't say No. It could after all be a steppingstone to something else. And who can ever know? And don't ever forget that you can still continue to write, you've made a success of that and what it gives you is not to be frowned on. And anyway, money will never be a problem for yourself or Harold. Your father, who had his faults, made sure of that. That's probably agreeing with Harold but for very different reasons. Reasons that are not very fashionable, but I have seen too many miserable women and too many self-satisfied men in my time, emerge from what had been entered into, without a shred of understanding as to what marriage really means."

They sat without the need to say anymore. Not always had these two women agreed but Victoria was not about to argue with her mother's appraisal of men. Not for the first time had she marvelled at her grasp of the essentials in the face of the conventional.

For years Victoria knew her mother was aware that not all trips to London were to attain the suffragettes' holy grail for women. It was to attain it for herself as well and Nathan became that holy grail. Her mother never adverted to the fact that Nathan and her daughter were lovers. In a certain sense Victoria felt she was aided and abetted by her mother and a potent example of her ability to detect and pursue what was worth having and accept that for her daughter. Even at great risk.

There it was, then. The staid, sensible, successful lawyer and landlord and the outrageous, full-blooded, rebellious Nathan. The memory of one and the opportunity, as well as the challenge, of the other. Nathan had challenged her at every turn on the hideous pretensions of her class. Edward Sheldon offered her a place to espouse even more what being a part of that class meant and what it offered. And as her mother said, a steppingstone. That phrase lingered as if it were a challenge in itself; the steppingstone went hand in hand with marriage as did "and who can ever know?"

The conversation with her mother led Victoria into a pact with herself. Yes, she would never love Edward as she had Nathan, but she would marry him. Nothing in Edward's behaviour towards her suggested his motivation for marrying her was anything other than hers would be. She never detected anything about him to conclude otherwise.

She was ready then for Edward Sheldon and what all that implied, known and unknown. He would have his answer, the one he wanted to hear. But it would not be all as simple as that. If he wanted her hand in marriage, he would have it, though not solely on his terms.

What she did not know, and could hardly be expected to, was Edward's real reason for his proposal, delivered so awkwardly and bizarrely through Harold. It was hardly what she would consider convenience.

*

More familiar though it was now, a year after the motor made its appearance in Shandrum it was still an object of curiosity. Its sound and sight punctured the otherwise monotonous existence of those who inhabited the long straggling street and the outlying areas.

Field, by now partial to the occasional lift, had revised somewhat the contrary view he had held up to now about such inventions. Lured by its practicality and indeed its luxury, he was unable to banish entirely the twinges of guilt he still felt about his gradual conversion. It proved to him that even the strongest conviction can with time be shaken, if not reversed. He concluded that it just might have to do with his advancing years. Such a matter in former days he would have constructively discussed with Old George Sheldon. Not so with his son, however, absent more often than present and seldom disposed to conversation.

All the more so then was Field's surprise at Edward's attitude after service one Sunday in early January, one of the few weekend days that he happened to be at Woodlands. There was a lightness to Edward's step, an unusual exuberance in his bearing, as he greeted Field. Such greetings were almost always perfunctory, as if something obligatory had to be dealt with for appearances' sake.

Edward's dead fish handshake did little to make the rector feel otherwise. Indeed, he had heard it mentioned in the village street one day that Edward had, as the wag put it to uproarious laughter, "the personality of a trout." Edward, much to Field's amazement, told him that he hoped to have some news of importance later in the week if a meeting at a country house went according to plan. His clarification that the meeting was one of a personal nature, led Field, with little speculation, to one conclusion. A woman, or more conventionally, a wife. Field assumed that once Edward had imparted this information, he would make his way to where the motorman waited. But no, he waited for the rector to respond, his lawyer's eye for interpretation scanning Field's face. Taken aback at Edward's news and the stare for an answer, Field lamely wished him every good luck "with whatever it is."

A fortnight later, the sound of the motor brought him to the gate and as Edward passed, he waved and smiled at Field. This totally uncharacteristic greeting cemented Field's view that Woodlands would soon have a woman and whatever transpired had gone in Edward's favour. As the motor was lost to sight it suddenly struck Field that perhaps his own journeys in it might soon be few and far between, if he was right about a wife in Woodlands and changed circumstances, not only for Edward but for the house and perhaps, for the village. How drawn he had suddenly become to material things of the vain and vulgar kind.

Two things then came to mind. Perhaps Edward, after all, is human. He quickly banished the thought, ashamed that such a harsh judgement about another human being should pollute his mind. Less quickly to be banished was the second thought. Why had the League never attempted to go after the motor? It was a perfect target. Was it because the priest was so preoccupied with The Pagan that he had no time to rally his troops? At the word "Pagan" he winced at the damning nature of the word. He always believed that even pagans believed in something.

*

High above the village and its surroundings they charted the motor's progress by sound and sight. From the castle top they had a magnificent view and had little difficulty in picking it out as it left Woodlands. Going through the village it was lost to their sight but once it turned at the barrack under Snee's disinterested gaze, they could follow it again by sight. Down the hill, passing by the castle gate, it would come to the bridge and cross the river before drawing away towards the town.

While the progress of the car scene was being played out, the boy looked at Joe in the hope that he might consider "going through the nightmare" once more.

"Ah c'mon, I never fell yet."

Better not tell him I stand up on the ledge between the battlements all the time when I'm here alone. He'd curse and swear and tell me he'd kill me. "You'll be the death of me as well as yourself, just wait and see," he'd say.

"Here so, quick or they'll be gone. Christ, you'll be the end of me, frightening the life out of me. There. Steady, I'm telling you. Here, lean back, not out. Here, get down, I don't care whether you saw it go over the bridge or not. I don't want to be the cause of killing you. Now, wouldn't they love that. They'd say I pushed you. I could see him above on the altar, delighted. Well, I'm not giving them that chance today anyway."

They turned away after he had caught the last glimpse of the motor and as if by arrangement, they saw the priest coming towards the castle through the bushes on the riverbank.

"Give us this day our daily walk. Will you look at the get-up of him."

The boy strained, leaning out over the parapet, but could see nothing unusual in the priest's dress. Absent from school, the last person he wanted to catch him was now making his way towards the castle up a narrow pathway that zig zagged between the limestone rocks that dotted the immediate surrounds. He would skirt the castle and then head for home across the two fields to his own backdoor. They looked down, well hidden, as the priest's deliberate steps brought him closer beneath them.

The sodden ground between the rocks had him scrambling at times and for a moment he lost his concentration and fell. The boy sniggered but was not prepared for what came next. Joe put two fingers to his mouth and gave a long shrill whistle of triumph.

Scared now, he glared at Joe's laughing, jubilant face. As sure as God, he'll find us. More of Joe's playacting. Struggling to his feet, regaining his balance, looking round to find the source of the whistle. He looks towards the bridge. Maybe that's where he thinks it came from. Yes, he's certain. Or is he?

The priest stood in the castle's shadow. Directly above, they drew back at the least move but, high above him, they had the advantage. His face, darting in every direction came back to the bridge. He waved his stick in its direction, grudgingly accepting defeat, and walked away across the fields to his home. That's the end of that, the boy thought as they watched him approach the fence that separated the two fields at the edge of the village.

It was then that another piercing whistle rent the air and sent a squawking myriad of jackdaws out of the trees below and away across the river. Without a word they rattled down the spiralled stairs, Joe laughing, the boy terrified.

"He'll come back, I saw him turning, he knows now, we're finished. He's out to get you but it's me he'll get, and I not at school all day. Why did you do it? We had our fun with the first whistle."

Now they were out the door and the boy, ignoring which way Joe was going, made for the shortest way down between the rocks and away from the fields toward the bridge. He was intent on putting as much distance between himself and the pursuing priest as possible, certain now that Kerley would not be thwarted a second time. Joe could look after himself.

Falling and scrambling down between the rocks obsessed by what he would say if he was caught. Oh, Jesus, he'll get me. That big bony hand again, the vein filled red face. Oh, my God, I am heartily sorry for all my sins. Not daring to look behind himself he heard the running steps of the priest behind him and the shout of triumph – "got you now."

He turned to face the priest. It was Joe, his features contorted with laughter. He took the boy by the shoulder and brought him round the rock the castle stood on and said "look, he's gone, beaten." And then he laughed again. The fields were empty, no sign of him. He looked up at Joe, furious and relieved.

*

Familiar with Eastleigh's hospitality, Edward went to his usual room to change. Tired, having come back from Woodlands and dealt with an intricate case at the Old Bailey, he was anxious to speak to Victoria, sooner rather than later. Buoyed up by Harold's assessment of the situation, his lawyer's instinct did not allow for a firm conclusion until the matter was dealt with fully. Too often in his practice he had seen assumed certainty thrown into a humbling defeat. If the answer was no, he would forgo dinner and return to London, perhaps never to return to Eastleigh again.

He would tactfully avoid Victoria's mother before his conversation with her daughter. One formidable woman was enough to deal with on an occasion such as this. His watch told him he still had an hour. Should he meet her now or wait. He would wait. He had said six and he would stick to that. Rushing things might be to his disadvantage. An hour's sleep might help. But sleep eluded him, and he knew the ordeal ahead was the reason. Strange that he could sleep at will even when involved in matters of life and death in the courts but not now. Women?

The unslept hour did, however, allow him to go over what had brought him to this juncture in his life. He contemplated the reason again that brought him to proposing marriage to Victoria Denham Lynd. How could a promise made to a dying father have so plagued his son and for so many years? Were Victoria to say no, he would doggedly pursue some other eligible woman, until the quest for a wife was successfully concluded.

He recalled the news arriving, the telegram passed to his desk in a crowded courtroom. The frantic rush home to Woodlands from London followed, helped by the trial judge acquiescing to Edward's plea that this news was, literally, a matter of life and death. Old Sheldon was clinging to life, awaiting his son's arrival.

Never had the motorman driven at such speed through the village. Meeting Field, praying solicitously on the stairway, Edward practically brushed him aside. Ten years on, now in the calm of his room in Eastleigh, he recalled the consequences of his rapid dash from London. Had he been fifteen minutes later he would not be where he was now. No promise would have been extracted. Nor would his father's dying snippet of shattering information ever have come to his ears.

So near death but still lucid, Old Sheldon would strike, almost heartlessly, at his son's soul in the few minutes that remained before he went to meet his maker. His plea was simple and understandable. It was that the Sheldon name, associated with Woodlands and Shandrum for five generations, would not die. It was a plea that he wanted an answer to, one that might satisfy him in his last moments. Edward, tired, not knowing what was ahead of him, his mind racing, lied deliberately to his dying father but calculated that he deserved one last consolation on his deathbed. Yes, he had a fiancée in London, he would shortly be making marriage plans and yes, the Sheldon name would continue. The lie, blatant but kind in the circumstances, visibly changed the quizzical, haggard face in the bed. Edward, alerted by a low cough, looked around the room and realised he had forgotten that two others were present, never mind Field on the stairs. Cranitch, the local doctor and a good friend of his father stood in the shadows with Nurse Prout. Prout, Edward knew by reputation, was efficient at her job but far more so as the village gossip. She had seen many a dying soul, rich and poor, on their way and had gleaned much that found its way around the neighbourhood as "the gospel truth," a phrase she used regularly, especially if some dying secret was worth repeating. Everything Edward had said would be safe with the doctor but not with Prout.

From his bed came his father's bony fingers, pulling at his arm.

"And there's one more thing …"

Unable to conceal his annoyance, Edward dismissed Prout "until needed." She bustled her way out of the room and in view of what followed, Edward was never so glad that he had got rid of her. She had heard enough but not everything. Cranitch, detecting an added distressing croak in the dying man's voice moved closer to the bed on the opposite side to Edward. Just like the nurse, Cranitch was no stranger to deathbed scenes, but nothing prepared him for what a visibly agitated George Sheldon said to his son before closing his eyes. A last burden, momentous in its implications, was not taken to the grave.

Edward lurched towards the doctor, his face pale and his eyes staring in disbelief.

"Did you hear that? Why did he have to tell me something I would never have suspected in a thousand years? It would have been better had I never made it. And to think I never knew. This changes everything."

"Edward, here my man, take this," and Cranitch poured a generous measure and pushed it into Edward's hand. Unused to alcohol as he was to women, Edward swallowed. It did little except leave him spluttering in despair into Cranitch's face.

"But this changes everything. How many know this around here? Maybe half the county knows it?"

Cranitch steadied Edward before saying anything.

"My man, you're wrong. The two responsible for it are now dead. This is not common knowledge, only two people know. And one of those is not outside the door."

"Who are the two?" Edward pleaded, anticipating some new revelation.

"You and me, we alone know it and I don't need to say it, but it won't pass my lips. You have my word. And don't forget where you might be if she had heard it." Cranitch glanced towards the door.

"She heard enough but I'm grateful for that one mercy at least."

Edward, impressed and reassured by the doctor's measured tone, turned back towards the bed. Was it his imagination playing tricks on him or was there a limp, mischievous smile on his father's face? Imagination or not, Edward would believe anything now as he refused the proffered second glass, despite the doctor's insistence that it would help him sleep.

Cranitch continued, "Look, I'll have to get her back in here to take care of a few things. Before you go, don't forget he was a good man. He'll be remembered long after I and a few more around here will be. Look at what he did for the place when he was laughed at by those of his own kind who should have known better. Some of them reaped what they sowed in one way and another, but that's a conversation for another time."

Edward stood and looked again at the shell of a man that was his father and then, before staggering from the room, simply motioning to the nurse and Field that it was over. They went inside the room and Edward made his way downstairs.

In the years following Old Sheldon's death the village waited for Edward's fiancée from London to arrive at Woodlands either as a visitor or a wife but that didn't happen. Nurse Prout's reputation for the "gospel truth" suffered a major setback.

Work and travel had taken over Edward's life soon after his father was laid to rest in the family vault in the village churchyard. No matter how busy he was, nothing could eradicate the promise made to his father. It was as if he was being held to ransom by his father's dying request. Haunted by that night he tried to initiate approaches to different women but to no avail. That may have had to do with his innate shyness behind the gruff exterior that hindered him socially and in any romantic pursuits. None of those that appeared interested in him as a highly eligible catch, and many an ardent parent pushed their daughters in his direction, had him even slightly interested. And in his heart he knew why.

Years passed and his work dominated, but his promise to his father surfaced regularly. This was one constant, and there was another, his regular visits to Eastleigh and his firm friendship with Victoria's brother, Harold. He sometimes wondered if their mutual interest in each other was evident to others.

Not surprising then that his unorthodox method of seeking Victoria's hand involved Harold. Now as the night of his father's death and what it involved faded momentarily, he realised that he had just five minutes before meeting the woman he had come to see.

*

"Victoria."

"How lovely to see you, Edward."

The greetings were nervously exaggerated as Victoria came through the drawing room door. She waited for him to continue.

"I hardly have to tell you why I'm here."

Embarrassingly, he pondered what to say next. She thought how interesting that the expert lawyer, dark and controlled standing before her, now struggled for words. He fixed his eyes on her and she waited.

"I have given this matter my most considered attention, Victoria, and I believe our mutual interests can be satisfactorily served if you agree to be my wife."

Coming round by the table's edge he moved closer, awkwardly dragging the heavy wooden chair toward where she had now taken a seat. Then, with some insistence he leaned over and took both her hands in his. She felt this first expression of intimacy to be rehearsed and predictable. The leaden formality was not lost on him either and he withdrew as she placed her hands on her knees before settling back in the chair. An image of Nathan invaded her teeming brain, but she now continued, even as the contrast could not have been more pronounced.

"Edward, you have been coming here for quite some time and we all consider you as one of the family. But I thought Harold was up to his practical joking or had lost whatever little sense he had. I'm sure you can appreciate how I felt. Despite all that, I too have given this strangely presented request my consideration."

Stung by the reference to Harold, he nevertheless leaned forward expectantly, his elbows on his knees and his hands joined as if in prayer. Shadows from the flickering lamplight, fitfully playing on the highly polished table caught his eyes and he shifted slightly.

With surprising composure, she outlined for Edward what her expectations were if she was to agree to his proposal.

"For both our sakes, Edward, it is important that we are frank about this and fully understand what is involved. Otherwise much, much more will be lost rather than gained and we may well end up extremely disappointed, even hurt. We are merely friends, Edward, not lovers. There can be no illusions about that."

Nathan's image resurfaced, diverting her slightly.

"No, Victoria, there can of course be no misunderstandings about matters that are of such importance." A slight impatience was evident as if he wanted this over and done with as soon as possible. She would not be hurried, and it occurred to Edward that the suffragettes had indeed lost an advocate of considerable resolve. It was when those qualities were brought to bear on himself that he realised the full force of her formidable nature.

"At my age I do know something of men and women, as I'm sure you do. For many, marriage can have different meanings. As your wife you will expect me to be mistress of your beautiful Irish home, if Harold is to be believed. You will expect me to be at your side on the many occasions that will arise socially and indeed, formally. You will expect me to bear your children. It is your intention, I assume, that you wish to have a family?"

"Why, yes of course, that is my wish indeed ..." he stammered, shifting uneasily in the chair and blushing violently. The subject of children, the very reason for all of this, had taken him by surprise but then he realised, as if for the first time, that the woman he wished to bear his children, had given the question of marriage no small attention. Her definite, precise and explicit presentation of her views would have done any lawyer proud. He sat, seemingly lost for words, tongue-tied by the woman sitting so confidently across from him. Like an adversary laying a legal trap she had taken him completely by surprise, almost to the point of fumbling humiliation. He stumbled on, hoping to salvage some degree of dignity from the situation he found himself in at the mention of children and Victoria's directness.

"Is there any reason why we...should not...have, ah, children?" He struggled to get to the end of the question and then looked away from her, visibly uncomfortable at the thought of where the conversation was going. Her next remark did little to help.

"Not that I'm aware of, Edward, but it's not quite as if a grand passion has smitten either of us."

She saw him wince at the word passion. Too explicit, she mused, for the eminent lawyer. Her eyes widened, laughingly, as she waited for an answer, looking him full in the face.

"Hopefully, Victoria, time will take care of all that. It should not be a worry to us now, should it?"

"It's not now I worry about at all, Edward, it's about sometime in the future when and if your plans for this marriage do not coincide with mine. Sharing the same bed may not lead to rosy faced Irish children running about the fields of Woodlands."

He wanted this conversation over as soon as possible but knew it wouldn't be. Allowing for Victoria's forthrightness of which he was aware, he never suspected that the intimate level to which matters were now going would have arisen.

He was left in no doubt by the clinical evaluation of what she saw of the possible consequences, or not, of their marriage. Why did this singularly beautiful woman opposite him have to appear more of an adversary than a potential marriage partner? For a moment it crossed his mind that, perhaps, he should be writing children's stories and she should be the KC.

"I think I know what you mean, Victoria, and it is important that our views are known to each other now rather than later. We cannot see into the future, nor should we try. I can now see, from what you have said that you have, indeed, considered all aspects of my proposal."

He paused, unsure of what to say next, and then, plucking up the last bit of courage he felt he possessed, after what had gone before, he sat back in the chair and stumbled through the words that he uttered.

"Can I take it … then that you are … willing to become my wife?"

In the flickering lamplight she answered.

"Yes, Edward, so long as we are clear about the conversation we have just had."

He leaned over and she thought he was about to embrace her, but he kissed her gently on the forehead and stood up.

"Well, the matter is done then," was the answer he gave and the peculiarity of it all struck Victoria forcibly. Nathan again came to mind. Could anything be as different as the two men who would feature most in her life up to now? Indeed, the matter is done, she thought as if it all was an ending rather than the beginning of something, as it should have been. With Nathan, there were always beginnings, the future beckoned and his infectious positivity made every day special. Today, as she made one of the most important decisions of her life it might as well have been a business transaction. Perhaps that's what it was after all.

Edward would be staying for dinner. Bruised as he was by the ordeal and glad that he had got the answer he wanted, he too dwelt on the strange, disquieting formality that characterised his marriage proposal. But it was done.

Before dinner began, Harold again became the go-between, and announced that Edward and Victoria had good news, their marriage would take place at Easter time, barely a few weeks away. This appeared quite a hasty arrangement to Victoria's mother and in other circumstances might appear unseemly haste. She looked at her daughter across the table and for Victoria, her mother's eyes said everything before she rose and proposed a toast to "the soon to be Mr and Mrs Sheldon."

*

Early May. She had only been here a few days. One thing had definitely changed. The harsh wind and biting cold that had greeted her as she stepped off the train was gone, replaced by early summer days. All the more reason that Woodlands did not disappoint her. Its ivied wall hid a spartan interior where the lack of a woman's touch was glaringly evident. For all that, she took to the house the moment she walked up the steps and into the spacious hall where a portrait of Edward's father looked benignly down. In the freshness of early summer whatever advantages the house had, and grounds beyond, were shown to full effect. Tonight, she would have the curious, critical eyes of Edward's friends and acquaintances to face. Not as though she relished the thought, but social occasions were nothing new to her. Here at Woodlands, her first formal engagement would be no different and she was not particularly apprehensive.

Disconcertingly, if not unexpectedly, one other fact was evident to her after a week of marriage. Edward might, without doubt, be an expert in the field of law, but when it came to women, he was a rank outsider. Victoria had determined that she would not be found wanting when it came to Edward's wish for a family but, despite her best efforts, Nathan's sensuous face kept intruding during Edward's amateurish approaches in the bedroom.

She realised that making comparisons were unhelpful but was not optimistic about what might loosely be termed, the more amorous aspects of her and Edward's relationship. The fact that he put off their honeymoon until before the Michaelmas law term in September, due, as he said "to getting you to Ireland" and "settled in," as he kept alluding to it, was, in her view, not a good sign. This, allowing for her conviction that had they gone on honeymoon it would, no doubt, not be as her mother said, "the flowering of a grand passion." This remark only brought Nathan's memory back and she was on the verge of saying so to her mother in one of her letters, but desisted. What help would that be?

*

"We are lords of all we survey."

From where they were, high up on the castle's rim, Joe's remark made a certain amount of sense. Here, in the twilight, no one was higher, except for the birds, and no human could now have the view of the village and beyond as they had. In Joe's words, they were either "lords of all we survey" or "kings of the castle." when they got to the top and safely away from anything that might bother them.

Earlier in the afternoon they had set the rabbit snares and later they would trudge, in hope and expectation, across familiar paths, in Woodlands' fields, to collect their catch. But tonight, there would be a special treat, one not previously witnessed by the boy. As darkness descended, they would watch from their perch as a procession of carriages bearing the party goers to Woodlands came from different directions.

The house was lit from top to bottom and towards that magnet came the invitees. Other lights, less spectacular, lit up the village and the houses tucked away here and there in the distance. Well-schooled by Joe, the boy could identify each of the houses and who lived there in the distance when candlelight lit their windows. Joe always gave a running commentary as if discovering something new.

"Ah, there's Kershaws for you. That's Ingrams and look, there's Liam Wallace, taking his time tonight. And will you look, O'Reillys, there's Talbots nearly beat him to it. Harty, nearly always last to light up." The litany continued and the boy turned again towards Woodlands.

Joe is playing some game again with me. Surely, he saw her the day she arrived. Didn't the whole place see her?

And all he says when I ask him is that "he's seen a few beauties in his time." So Mrs. Sheldon must be a beauty too. He won't tell me where or when he saw beauties. He tells me he saw them here, there and everywhere. But where is that I asked him? England? Far beyond that, he said. But he knows she's beautiful. Didn't he say that the night after she arrived when he agreed with father that Sheldon was a very lucky man.

And all those carriages now. All coming to see her, the Smyths, Sindons, Kingstons, Robertsons, Bressingtons, all there to see her and all dressed up of course. All day dressing up for it. She too. Satin, it always says satin in the paper. Lost count of all the trips father made over the last two days getting food and drink. Whiskey, gin, wine and sherry. Lovely names. Sherry from Portugal, Joe said. Nothing like Joe and Father drink. Nicer looking bottles. What none of them down there at the house in all their fancy clothes know, is that I shook her hand before any of them even got near her.

They watched as the carriage lantern lights moved to the steps and halted, momentarily, then another and another, doing the same in turn, before pulling away over to the side. The lanterns were put out until it was all over, and they were ready for the journey home.

Joe roused him from his thoughts. "I'd say that's the last of them now alright. All inside bowing and scraping and telling her what a wonderful place she'd come to. Ha, ha, if she only knew. You know the usuals will be giving out about the Irish and how she should watch out for some of them. Oh, names will be given, you can be sure."

Would they be talking about the Titanic? About to sail away in a year's time. Even now it's all over the papers. Wouldn't they be talking about that?

"Oh, you can be sure they will and no doubt some of those in there tonight or others they know might well be on it. You know it wouldn't surprise me if the centre of attention over there isn't lined up for a trip with himself on it, sometime in the future."

I told him that couldn't happen because Father is always saying Sheldon hasn't time to tie his laces, so how could he go off on the Titanic?

"Whatever about the Titanic we better go and see about the rabbits. Hope that crowd down there won't frighten them."

By a well-trodden and familiar path, they left the castle and river behind. When their circuit was finished, they would be back by the river again. A good catch in winter time would be around twelve, or maybe fifteen on a good night, out of the fifty snares set. At times during the summer nights the number caught might be less and that would disappoint the boy, but not the man. He would temper the boy's disappointment by saying that a bad night for the rabbits might be a good day for the fishing next day. Not always true either but the simple optimism helped somewhat, as they came upon snare after empty snare. Even though Joe seemed to depend on the money he got for the rabbits it never seemed to bother him too much. His father said to him one time that Joe "wasn't short of a few bob." He wondered where he got it as no one would ever offer him work.

Now they were over the wall and into Sheldon's land. How does Joe get away with it? Look at what happened to Jack Dwyer for hunting and fishing in Woodlands. Sheldon gave out to him at the wall and even when I came along, he kept at him. And then Father said he went to the barrack to complain about Jack. The stories then must be true about others not being allowed on to Woodlands, others yes, but not Joe.

Must be some reason because the day we were bagging the fish, Sheldon came along on his horse. Joe seemed worried though he stood his ground. I couldn't warn him because if I was seen then Sheldon might say something to Father. Then, a strange thing happened. Sheldon jumped down off the horse and looked into the bag that Joe had dragged from the mouth of the dam made with stones across the river. He looked into the bag and even helped Joe throw a few small ones back in. Talking, but I couldn't hear with the sound of the river but no shouting like with Jack Dwyer. Then Sheldon got up on the horse and galloped away, even turning to Joe and waving. Never saw me hiding and I waited for Joe to come across to where I was. Forgot all about the fish to find out what was said. Thought there was going to be a row.

"Oh, no chance of a row between gentlemen" he said smiling. "All he said was in the long run not to get caught."

"But you were caught!"

"Ah no, what he meant was not to get caught by anyone from the village. I suppose it's all because of Dwyer and others being complained above at the barrack."

"Maybe he's afraid of you!"

"You can be sure he's afraid of no one. Look at all the murderers and killers he has to face up to in the courts over in England. Don't you see about him in the paper sometimes? He's afraid of no one, boy."

"Maybe he's not but I still don't understand."

"Well, neither do I. Never look a gift horse in the mouth, they say. Did you ever hear that?"

Never did but before I could ask what it meant, he gathered up the bag and fish and turned for home. Whistling to himself. Never heard him whistle for so long or so loud. At his back door he stopped and said, "but I suppose we better be more careful all the same." A day I would not forget.

Thinking about it now as they came upon snare upon empty snare. Stopping now and then, the far away sounds of music from the house as the strains wafted on the light breeze and then were gone as they moved along. Silence between them until they reached a hillock. There before them was the house. Ablaze with light, the music now easier to hear. Big downstairs windows open. The coachmen gathered here and there talking and smoking, some with glasses brought out to them from the house. Outsiders looking in. Just like the two of us. Silence and then some chatter. A familiar voice with "The Last Rose of Summer." The rector. Hand on my shoulder, a signal to listen. And they did until applause greeted the rector's rendition.

"The sights and sounds of gaiety, indeed," Joe mused, "our sweetest songs are those that tell of saddest thought." Then off again to finish the night's work. Music always in the distance.

The rabbit run, always an exercise in anticipation, now became a jaded ritual and their hearts were not in it. Why, the boy didn't know.

*

No expense would be spared to celebrate the arrival of Edward's wife to Woodlands. The preparations had not been in vain.

Never had there been such a night, attested to by those who were lucky or fortunate enough to have been invited. The majority of those present were from beyond the village and not all were in the first flush of youth. It was not unknown for some of the Sheldon class to sell out and move back to England in recent years, aided by a government tenant purchase scheme. The effect was that some land passed back to those from whose forebears it had been taken. The imminence of Home Rule, the land agitation of the latter part of the previous century and its reincarnation in the sinister force that had become the League was, for some of the aristocracy, a beating drum whose message was that change was on the way and had to be faced.

Threads of such conversation and its ramifications or not, for those enjoying the gaiety of the night, would have come to Victoria's ears as she played the perfect hostess.

Field was one of the first to arrive. Graciously received by Victoria, he was again struck by her feminine presence, and it confirmed for him that his first impressions at the station, on her arrival, and on the drive back to the village from it, were not mistaken. The carriages, all arriving together for the appointed time, clogged the avenue and disgorged the visitors, showing off their summer fashion to any and every extent possible. They would pause for a while in the glow of the setting sun before mounting the steps to be met by their hosts. Invariably, as they entered, they would acknowledge the portrait that would not brook ignoring, that of Edward's father.

In the awkwardness of small talk Field was assured of more attention than he sometimes got after Sunday service, when it invariably seemed most of his parishioners gave the impression of wanting to be somewhere else.

Excellent food and wine as well as some more exotic beverages were served. Field slipped slowly but knowingly into a nonchalant haze, as tongues were loosened, and defences let slip. More than once the phrase "in vino veritas" came to mind. This allowed him to observe different members of his flock. Since he was, as it were, aiding and abetting in the joviality, he would try to refrain from judgement. The splendid surroundings, vibrancy and heady atmosphere brought to the evening was enhanced by the object of everyone's attention, the perfect hostess, proudly displayed by her husband, who, to be honest would be far more at home in a courtroom.

Even if the courtroom suited him better, Field and the guests had seldom seen Edward so haughtily alive, a glint of pride in every glance. All round it was obvious, Edward marvelling at the ease with which she circulated. As if she were wearing a mask, so adept was she in dealing with the guests, whom she had never met before but on whose every word she appeared to linger, with engaging ease, even if much of it was small talk.

Field realised that tonight he was witnessing the exception rather than the rule. Social occasions in Woodlands were ones he had enjoyed in the past even if there was the sense of an obligatory burden about the gatherings. Tonight, he strangely felt some incongruity in it all. It had, he had to admit to himself, something to do with the woman, as if she were ushering in something different above and beyond the regular, very ordinary atmosphere that pervaded such occasions in the past. Maybe, she was, because such occasions were rarer since Old Sheldon died. If what's seldom is wonderful, then here, he concluded, is its perfect expression.

He watched husband and wife closely, but Victoria more closely as she circulated effortlessly among the guests. And yet, for all her ability to blend appropriately, as demanded by her position in such a gathering, as Edward's wife in the first place and as Shandrum's newest arrival, Field felt at times that she seemed strangely out of place. Maybe it had to do with the uncertainty her class faced as hints of a new dispensation floated from Westminster about Home Rule and its implications. She just appeared too vibrant, too young and too healthy to immerse herself in a way of life that Field believed was on its way out.

He was stopped short in his meanderings when he noticed her making her way towards him, politely ignoring those between them. Had she noticed him being somewhat apart with his thoughts? Taking him completely by surprise, she called for attention, announcing that she had heard Rev Field was an excellent singer and she was now asking him to give one of his favourite renditions, a Moore's melody. The fact that this challenge had come out of nowhere and totally unexpectedly might give him the opportunity to decline. But no, Victoria waited, as did the crowd. Steadying himself, hoping he remembered the words, he coughed and began. But the wine had fortified him and after an unsteady, hesitant start, he gave an excellent rendition of The Last Rose of Summer. The applause, slightly overdone, he thought, had him bowing in appreciation. Again, the music began, and he was certain she would move away. She stayed, however.

"Who gave you all this information about my singing ability or lack of it?" he questioned, his curiosity, as usual, getting the better of him.

"Oh, I've only been here a short while, but I have my sources," she answered, smiling, without elaborating.

She then enquired about the parish, his friendship with the Sheldons and other routine matters of mutual, easy interest. Field was struck by the attention she gave him as if everything he had to say was important. After some further smalltalk she excused herself at Edward's beckoning with a promise that she would be back to him again before the night was over. Edward, for his part, glowing with a conceited sense of having acquired the prize possession, glanced in Field's direction with what he concluded was a grudging acknowledgement.

True to her promise, she did return later with an enquiry as to whether he wanted his wine glass replenished. "A little more than a little is by much too much" he retorted but she gave him little option.

"Evenings such as this in the past would have been nothing new to you." A statement more than a question and he answered accordingly, going even further when he saw again how he had her full attention.

"Indeed, and I've never emptied so many glasses. That's why I should keep my peace at what is almost the end of a beautiful night for you and Edward." But he went on, "I've never seen so many of my flock and those not, seem so happy, happier than I've seen them in years. And that, if I may say so, is to your credit, being the real reason why they are all here. It's not often, you see, that they get to enjoy the finer things in life, good food, drink, music and of course company."

"But there will be many more such celebrations. It's always easy to find an excuse." He should have agreed with her and left it at that, perhaps, but he continued, with the wineglass replenished.

"I've seen a lot of changes here in Shandrum, Victoria, and indeed many in this house. Edward's father was very well thought of by the local people, much more so than many here tonight would be. Those of the other persuasion here are, how should I put it, a rather mixed bag, and life getting more difficult here for many of your guests. It's not so much difficult perhaps as uncertain, just the way the country is going. I don't know what you think of politics, but this Home Rule business is bound to happen and where that will leave us all is anyone's business. Then again, there is a lot of good will, as I've said, for the Sheldon name here. However, maybe I've said too much. It's this of course." He raised the glass with a smile.

"No, you have not said too much at all. I actually met your Mr John Redmond some years ago when I was in a different situation. Politicians do what they have to do, and their promises can evaporite overnight. My knowledge of Irish politics is limited though, and a friend jokingly gave me some advice when she heard I was moving over here. She told me the Irish would, as she put it, "eat you without salt." They both laughed, conspiratorially.

"But I do know now who to come to when I need my questions answered," she said to Field, with a flattering glance.

A few were about to make their goodbyes and she joined Edward. A slow procession now began to make its way into the hall and out to where the coachmen were rousing themselves. A few hardy souls lingered for a while however, much to Edward's disapproval. Field noticed and he made ready to go. Rather unsteadily, he made his way through the hall, glancing up at Old Sheldon's portrait. Was that a wry smile on the lips of the old man? Definitely the wine's effect, he thought. Down the steps he went and towards the avenue. Passing one of the carriages about to depart, he heard what seemed to be the end of a conversation between two of the departing guests, one of whom was helping the other into the carriage. A conversation he wished he had heard in full. The last words said, with conviction and certainty, by the man now closing the carriage door were "well, if The Pagan thinks he'll better the priest, he should think again. Goodnight."

For Victoria, nothing the rector had said of the uncertainties of the future really existed or mattered. That she was a stranger in an alien land had not yet occurred to her. By night's end she had, with some effort in a few cases, managed to be the perfect wife and hostess. The expressions of appreciation, genuine she felt, made towards Edward and herself, left her in little doubt that for many the night had been more than worthwhile.

As music took over after the initial greetings and food and drink had taken effect, she found herself in the arms of strangers, not a few of whom were excellent dancers. She joined in their polite chatter but, as the music took her, she was back again in Nathan's arms as his spirited shadow hovered. Only a few present were of Edward's age so no rival there, if there might be one, was evident. A strange thought, she pondered, and she a married woman for such a short while.

Her obligations as hostess as the night began and the music struck up had naturally led her to Edward and she took him in her arms. She soon realised that she had to make all the effort as a circle formed and they were at its centre. To the applause of the guests, she led Edward, now clearly conscious that he was hardly a match for her dancing expertise, round the floor. His rather pained expression was broken occasionally by an attempted smile to suggest that he just might be enjoying this, but she was as glad as he was when the last notes sounded and they again went their separate ways to mingle among the guests. Then, for the second or third time, she caught the observant eye of the rector taking everything in from the shadows provided by the heavy curtains by one of the windows. He seemed ill at ease and she determined to seek him out, knowing from her enquiries from the motorman that he was considered an excellent singer.

As if to make certain that everyone had departed, Edward checked that the grounds in front of the house were clear. She met him on the steps with a drink for them both, but he showed little interest in prolonging things. As evidence that he was not partial to alcohol he downed the drink in one gulp. She had hoped he might linger and talk about the night to which she had contributed enormously, thereby enhancing his pride and standing. She pressed him.

"Are you happy with how things went? I have so many questions about so many of those who came."

"The expense was well worth it," he replied "but I have a mountain of work to deal with tomorrow, so I think I'll call it a night. You made a wonderful impression, Victoria, and I've no doubt all who came will be waiting for the next invitation."

With that he locked the door, handed her back the glass, and made his way up the winding staircase, leaving her alone to contemplate the portrait of his father, before she too would climb the stairs. To what? The son had little of the open expansive features of his father, caught so well by the artist. Not like father like son then, she was certain. And no Nathan Pilger.

*

Early summer had, unapologetically, encroached on spring with a searing vengeance. His father told him, having read Old Moore's Almanac from cover to cover, that the summer would be the hottest in living memory. Joe, however, was not impressed with such prophets. "Red sky at night, shepherd's delight, red sky in the morning, shepherd's warning," was his philosophy when it came to forecasting, as was, "any fool brings an umbrella on a wet day, but the wise man takes it on a fine one."

Whatever about Joe's meteorological pieces of wisdom, the early days of May were warm and hazy. This meant that the bicycle was in constant use and through scheming and contrivance the priest was outwitted time and again. Not so easily avoided though were the jeers and jibes of his classmates. With the master's covert encouragement toward his peers, he paid a price for his connection with The Pagan. "Pagan Boy" was often tauntingly hurled at him with the harsh brutality of the young. His father was aware that he always left for school without enthusiasm and occasionally commented on it, but got no response, and no school story was ever brought home to his father or Joe. He carried his misery himself.

The "Pagan's pedaller" as Joe's bicycle was referred to, was for the boy a means of escape but for the priest a further glaring example of the evil grip the boy was in. A game of cat and mouse ensued. Whether with Joe or on his own, when he awkwardly managed the adult's bicycle, the grim spectre of the priest was around every corner. Twice at the forest bridge he stood knee deep in water underneath it as the priest passed by and no doubt glared at the bicycle resting against the bridge.

Eventually, it was to be the pedaller that brought The Pagan face to face with Victoria Sheldon. The circumstances, in hindsight, were memorable if inauspicious.

By agreement he had met Joe just beyond the main gate at Woodlands where the road, known as the high road, rose sharply towards the low hills. Today they would fish in a spot that was not on Sheldon's land, but this meant a slow climb up the hill before a slightly worn path brought them down to the river and the fishing spot. It was a climb up the road to be endured rather than in any way enjoyed. The prize was the return journey and the glorious exhilaration that careering down the hill at a breakneck and frightening speed brought. Or as they both regularly joked, the journey into the valley of death. Twelve today. A great catch and easily known Joe is happy. The first time I got more than three with the rod. Plenty practice and it's all in the cast. How many times had he heard Joe's mantra. But he was right. Just like days last summer now, the sun a ball of fire and sure to be in our eyes on the way back, adding another terrifying twist to the journey. One time Joe nearly lost control as the sun, full in his eyes, stopped him from seeing a herd of cattle until the last minute and he wobbled all over the road before gaining control. Nearly ready now. Joe just as excited. Trying not to show it. Settled nicely on the carrier, the bag of trout in the right place on my back. Won't go sideways as we twist and turn. Starting off. Slow at first, Joe gets himself ready and then we're off. Picking up speed, but it's not until we get to Healy's gate that it really starts. He'll get into his stride. Terror then.

"Into the valley of death" roared Joe, "hang for all you're worth now, I don't want to look around and find you're not there."

Sometimes he looked under Joe's elbow but mostly he kept his eyes closed, the excitement too much for him as they swept by trees and hedges, glitters of light dancing on the roadway. Wanting as so often before, to shout go easy. No. Joe might think he's a coward. Am I? Even if I shout a warning Joe would only laugh and go twice as fast. He always feared meeting the priest on the road. What would Joe do? He'd be killed if he tried to stop the bicycle. Why would he stop anyway, even for the priest? He wouldn't stop for anyone.

This is it. Now passing Healy's. Oh my God, I am heartily sorry for all my sins. Never sin again, never.

"Jesus Christ, it's him." Joe's words were garbled but unmistakable.

He peered under Joe's elbow, barely allowing himself to open his eyes. There at the bottom of the hill at Woodlands' gate were father, Field and oh God, Mrs Sheldon. Not the priest, Joe, not the priest, it's the rector. How could he not tell? Joe, talking to himself, cursing, pulling on the brakes. He'll kill the two of us. I'm going to jump off, jump, jump.

And he did, bravely but foolishly. The bag of fish tangled in the back wheel as he tried the impossible feat. What the brakes could not do the bag achieved in a few seconds and the bicycle came to a sliding, shuddering halt, with bodies, bicycle and fish all scattered with the crudest of ceremony on the dusty road before the three helpless onlookers. Field, somehow mistaken for the priest by Joe, with the blazing sun in his eyes, moved back against the wall, incredulous at the scene before him, shaking his head in disbelief.

From where he lay spreadeagled on the dusty road, Joe slowly turned over into a sitting position, looked round and burst into laughter. Field, unimpressed by what he saw as this latest outburst of madness, moved behind the motorman as if seeking protection. What could be so amusing? Golden was pointing at the trout littering the roadway.

Field stuck to the ground behind Father. Nothing seemed to happen until Joe's bout of laughter was over. Father moving towards me. But she passed him out and lifted me. Sitting now. Knees and arms torn to pieces from sliding along the road but there is that smell again, her perfume, like the first day when she arrived. Can't see her, the sun in my eyes. Father bends. Lifting me up and in the gate. The welcoming, familiar smell of home.

On the sofa, so close, examining the cuts and bruises. Room crowded. Heat and sweat. Father looking on as if wondering what would happen next. But they're all here. Joe near the half-opened door, covered in dust, Field behind him. Where is she going? "Five minutes" to father and then gone. Joe opening the door wider to let her out. She looks at him. Her stride broken. Not even for a second. What kind of look is that? Only an instant.

Field, unable to find anything to do to make himself of some use, lamely offered Joe a chair. It was a gesture made as if to suppress, to counteract, what he too had witnessed in Victoria's fleeting glance at the man with his own cuts and bruises, but otherwise apparently unshaken by the tumble off the bicycle. He had just done what anyone else would have done by opening the door, but Field felt some invisible barrier had momentarily interrupted her stride out into the sun. If she had even said a word of thanks to

him it would have been different. But, no, she had just
gone, away without a word.

Refusing the chair, Joe declared that he was off to see to
the bicycle and retrieve the fish.

"A rinse of water and they'll be fine," winking at the
motorman.

"You'll be alright, will you?"

"As right as rain. And you know what they say about fellows
like me?" He addressed the answer to his own question
toward where Field stood. "You can't kill a bad thing."

With that he shuffled away, hobbling on one leg.

*

"The Pagan", Golden … whatever he was known as, had
merely opened the door. It was a natural gesture as one
would do for anyone. Only for the sun his face would have
been in shadow. But once the door swung open a shaft of
light caught it. A simple "thank you" was on her lips but
his look cut through her. Just keep going, she said to herself
and hurried away. The others could not have noticed, it was
a split-second glance. They might think her lack of response
to his opening the door odd but of no great significance in
view of her hurry to get help for the boy.

This then is the man with whom the villagers of every
hue and standing seem to be obsessed and at war. His
presence had certainly dominated the few moments of
chaos on the roadway even as he lay there. In the almost
comic confusion, they had watched, inscrutably, as he
drew himself up on his elbow and rocked the soft evening
air with a burst of unrestrained laughter. The only one
seeming unsurprised by this was the motorman, with the

rector lost for words while Victoria, straight faced, went toward the boy.

The sight of the fish strewn grotesquely on the roadway did not strike her as particularly amusing. Ignored for a moment as everyone tried to catch their breath, the child lay stunned and bleeding. She was at his side before his father got to him and they carried the pale shivering frame inside the gate lodge door. Then a few minutes of confusion as they made him as comfortable as possible.

The short walk to the house calmed her somewhat. Maybe it was my imagination? Why should there be anything questionable or unsettling in the fact that their eyes met, naturally, as she passed him by? Something in her felt that this first meeting with The Pagan was unreal, too immediate, not given enough preparation, as it were. But too immediate for what? Allowing for the circumstances it was a chance encounter, wasn't that all?

She got what she came for, and still preoccupied, hastily made her way down the avenue. He would still be there. Her footsteps quickened as the half open door was pulled back. Him again? It was the motorman, and seeing him brought a twinge of disappointment. She immediately scolded herself, guiltily, at such a thought.

Glancing round the room she had uttered the words before realising what she said.

"Has Mr Golden gone?"

Field seemed taken aback but she rallied, "Is he alright? He was hurt too."

The motorman's reply extracted her from Field's critical eye. "Ah, I wouldn't worry about him. He's off to see what he can do to fix what's left of the bicycle. As for this fellow here, well, I think he needs a bit of fixing too."

So soft, her hands. Opening his shirt. Freeing both his arms. Dusty, bruised and bloodied. His legs too. Leaning over, shadows on the ceiling from the sunlight. The perfume again. Ointment on the cuts. Wincing. No one had ever been this way with him before. Gentle, easy words. Not like the master's bark. So different, a woman. And not any woman. Her face so close now. Hair falling over her forehead as she bends. The pain, the soreness, the scrapes. Not thinking of them now. All because of her.

But now she's finished. Advising. Go to sleep and you'll feel better tomorrow. Rector and Father nod. But sleep will take her away. Suddenly gone. The rector and Father following her out into the sunlight. I'm glad the bicycle crashed. And Joe knows what she looks like now. Can't deny it. The way he looked at her. Just for a second.

*

She followed Field from the lodge and waited for him to speak, now that the boy's father, having thanked her, had turned and made his way indoors.

She pointed towards the village indicating that she would walk some of the way with him.

She wanted to hear his summation of the events, particularly since he had been so hesitant to get involved in any way following the fiasco on the roadway. His isolation had to have been deliberate. After all, he had been in the best of spirits before the bicycle came hurtling down the hill towards them.

His aloofness in what followed was at variance with the impression he had made on her the night of the Woodlands' party. Outwardly melancholic and somewhat tetchy, she had found him far less rigid on that night. The wine, no doubt? Was it alone responsible for the erudite and witty soul whom the party atmosphere and the effects of alcohol had shown in a new light?

"Victoria, it infuriates me. That child could have been killed earlier coming off that infernal bicycle. And of course, so could his guardian angel, if I can use that expression when I refer to The Pagan. I shouldn't be calling him that. Force of habit now, but a good one. He could have been killed too. Not that too many around here would decry his passing, I can tell you."

Shocked by this judgemental attitude, delivered so seriously, Victoria replied.

"That's rather harsh, I don't quite know what you are talking about."

"Well, if you must, it is simply this. Golden is a most undesirable presence here. Even more than that and more importantly, he is a dastardly influence on the motorman's son. In one way and another, it is preached regularly from the other side, if you follow me. As an unbeliever, he flaunts the perversity of his position in a most infuriating and damaging manner. It offends us all, even many beyond the village."

The conviction with which Field spoke intrigued her. With a willing ear, he continued.

"The priest, not someone I have to say I have much in common with except the gospel we preach, is incensed at the boy associating with someone of such an outrageous disposition, who appears to revel in his disbelief. Believe me, nothing good can come of it, and the motorman is either unaware of it or unwilling to correct this liaison. No other word describes it. A number around here think Golden exists just to test the faith of the whole village. You should see, as I do frequently, how arrogantly he ensconces himself in front of his cottage when they attend their service."

Unsure whether he might continue in this vein, she was tempted to encourage him. Caution might, however, be more appropriate. He must have taken her silence as an opening.

"Now perhaps you can understand my hesitation in getting involved in the wake of the events on the roadway earlier. Only a lunatic would come down the hill at that speed. It goes against my nature and my calling not to help in any such circumstances, but that man cannot be encouraged or accommodated in any way. This is not an approach I can adopt easily. It goes against my nature, but I am at one with the priest in it."

She responded quickly.

"I am new here and for that reason know little of what goes on in the village, apart from what my husband tells me. Not until this evening have I been in the presence of the gentleman you describe. I know the circumstances were unusual, but I noticed no discourtesy toward me or indeed you, for that matter. Were it not for the unfortunate accident I would not have the information you have given me or the benefit of your opinion. It does not appear to me that I need approach anyone else in the village for a different one in relation to Mr Golden."

The rector grimaced uncomfortably with a sharp intake of breath. She was surprised at her testy response to what he had said but then his words were damning.

As they walked it appeared he had accepted what she said for what it was worth. She had heard enough on which to ponder. And there was plenty. The man in the shadow who had caught her eye less than an hour ago a moral danger to the child she had just attended? But the rector was not finished.

"Perhaps I have said enough but there is another aspect to all this that you may not be aware of, and which does concern you, if only indirectly."

His tone was now advisory and conciliatory, and she braced herself for what might emerge next or where the conversation might lead.

"People in the village, ordinary decent people, some of whom have very little and who live by hunting and fishing, mostly illegally, are annoyed at the freedom The Pagan has where Woodlands is concerned. It appears he has virtual immunity when it comes to hunting and fishing within the walls of your land. I do not have to tell you that very little happens here that does not become public knowledge."

He paused, deliberately she felt, to emphasise the last point. Continuing, he outlined the case of a local man, Dwyer, who had been taken to task by Edward and reported to the police by her husband when found hunting for rabbits on his land. The bad feeling engendered by this had been directed more at Golden than Edward, presuming that Field was telling her the truth. Despite his animosity toward Golden, she felt a man in his position would not invent a story, especially seeing that she could check its authenticity with Edward. She sensed that apart from further painting Golden in an unattractive light, Field was alerting her to the fact that his apparent free rein to hunt and fish in Woodlands might entail some sort of backlash against Edward. She could understand, aware of the negative picture given about Golden by the rector that he, rather than Edward, might bear the brunt of the villagers' anger.

They had almost reached the turn that gave sight of the village and she said she would turn back towards home at that point.

She thanked him for his company and for the information he had made her privy to, even if that information left her somewhat troubled. Before leaving him finally, she said.

"Before I came here, Rector, someone told me not to dare attempt to understand the Irish. What you have told me, I suppose, confirms that, don't you think?"

This gave Field further opportunity and he launched forth again.

"Whoever it was told you that, was quite right. They are a difficult people, devious and utterly frustrating at times. Yet, we, our circle and the powers that be from afar that govern us, may have a few questions to answer about all that too. But do remember, the Sheldons, as I may have told you that night of the party, are very well regarded here. As for the subject of our conversation, I felt I had to

get across to you, to emphasise again, the presence of this
… Golden, this Pagan as they call him, has so antagonised
everyone that I feel it augers badly. Something is going to
come of all this and I, among others, fear for that child's
moral safety. Not only are they against Golden but the boy
is shunned as well because of this undesirable association."
Whatever the rights and wrongs of what Field had said,
there was a message there. His view of the boy's position
disturbed her. Whatever message the village reprobate
conveyed earlier in the evening perturbed her, but it
certainly wasn't because she got a sense of any kind of
moral depravity emanating from him. Then again, it had
been just a fleeting moment, and can anyone really judge
anyone regarding their moral integrity in a lifetime, never
mind a moment?

She had heard enough. Field had said enough. Bidding
him goodbye, she walked back to Woodlands along the
road, calm and still in the best of the evening's sunlight, left
with her own thoughts and plenty to ponder. One thing
was definite as she reached the gate lodge. Everything she
felt inside her contradicted Field's inferences about the
village pariah. She could hardly blame him for conveying
something to her that he, and from what he said, the
whole village genuinely believed to be true. Much more
disconcerting was Field's view that the situation could or
would not just carry on and that worried her.

She passed the gate lodge and on up the avenue. The Pagan.
Something in that title, so insultingly and aggressively
conferred, suited him. The Pagan. Its blunt forbidding
message, its hint of the foreign, the unknown, rested well

on his shoulders and his unsettling eyes. A man not to be meddled with, she assumed, even if only half of what the rector had said was true.

*

Master Slyne had made the priest aware, on more than one occasion, about the boy's absences from school. The terse note from the motorman excusing his son's absences usually said "sick."

The latest said "accident."

Field, innocently, rather than mischievously, had mentioned the bicycle fiasco to Kerley and regretted doing so immediately. The priest's face reddened as if the snippet of information only further emphasised the hold The Pagan had over the boy and how the villagers were being thwarted by them both. The incorrigible child of an ineffectual father was in the clutches of evil. Field again detected, as often before, how the connection of the father and child with Woodlands rankled. An object of novelty to many, the motor was, for Kerley a "bellowing British bulldog." Field found this reference disconcerting since he himself was now on occasion the beneficiary of the motor's comfort and convenience.

The relationship between priest and rector was seen by many of a more progressive nature as an excellent example of "how people should get on." Field found himself cast in a rather enviable light when others, in a similar position in surrounding parishes, mentioned his good fortune to have someone on the other side, pastorally, with whom he could get along. It certainly made for an easier life, and he was aware of some of his fellow rectors being barely on speaking terms, if not having even a more fractious relationship with their opposites, despite, as he often thought, talking about the same God.

Everything has its price however, as far as Field was concerned, and the outwardly cordial relationship with Kerley masked a deeper suspicion which he felt was mutual, though never expressed as such. He regularly found himself disagreeing with the priest's view but held his peace, believing that a man of Kerley's disposition was not open to counter arguments or differing opinions.

Of late though he found himself inclined to see where the priest might be coming from in terms of The Pagan's influence on the boy. Troubling and distasteful. It was, as if against his will, he found himself infected by Kerley's insatiable obsession with extirpating a hideous example of moral degeneracy. Thus his refusal to be of any help to Golden as he lay injured and momentarily dazed on the ground the night of the accident. Feeling he had to make some gesture when they got indoors, he waited before lamely offering him a chair.

The conversations he had with the priest were just that, conversations, with little personal connection or empathy. He tended to see his opposite as an overseer rather than a shepherd. What emerged over time and did not surprise him, was what might best be termed animosity toward particular members of Field's flock, with Edward Sheldon heading the list. Invariably Field had to remind the priest that the Sheldon family were highly respected by the locals and gave employment to a number of them and those who had gone before. The favouritism shown by Sheldon to

Golden, when others like Dwyer were taken to task and reported to the barrack, gave Kerley the perfect opportunity, however, to put a dent in the shiny Sheldon armour.

This latest outburst by Kerley on foot of the bicycle incident made Field even more exercised and, at the same time, somewhat perplexed about Golden and the boy. There were lingering doubts. At times he agreed with the priest's damning condemnation while seeing how questionable his attitude was. His sacerdotal guise regularly slipped, and Field firmly believed that mixing a moral crusade with a personal vendetta might not be the best way to deal with any problem, never mind this seemingly intractable one. The Pagan was now an enemy to be defeated and the boy an opponent rather than a wayward child needing to be rescued.

This worried Field. Even more worrying was his inability, deeply felt, to make any inroads into the priest's obsessive attitude. He was becoming an unwilling though effective accomplice as far as the villagers were concerned and as such was apprehensive about what might ensue. He felt a certain helplessness as the priest's position and authority appeared practically irrelevant in the face of The Pagan's facility to flout him.

Some relief however was gained because he had at least alerted Sheldon's wife to the growing animosity regarding the Pagan's freedom on Woodlands' property. At least that was something and he would bring that to the priest's attention if an opportunity presented itself. Most of the conversations with his counterpart took place if they casually met. Despite their proximity to each other, days and longer might go by without their meeting. Hardly ever had he crossed the road to knock on the priest's house and he could not recall when the reverse happened. He would, at the next opportunity, let the priest know about having alerted Sheldon's wife to the fact that The Pagan's preferential treatment was a cause for concern.

That opportunity came sooner than expected.

*

For days he laboured through every agonising movement until the beginnings of recovery. Far outweighing the pain, however, were the benefits that had come his way because of the fall from the bicycle. For one, he was spared the great torture of school. With summer holidays coming soon he would now have to spend less time surviving through each weary day, finding everyone, from the master to his classmates, intent on making life miserable for him. His father had done his share to help by writing excuses about sickness when he saw how agitated he was at the prospect of leaving the lodge each morning to walk to school. Well known to both was the fact that those days off school were spent with Joe. Watching the clock on such days he waited until he knew any stragglers to school were gone and then he made his way by the path to Joe's backdoor. His hope now was that he might spend more days away from school on the strength of the accident.

The other benefit was a constant supply of papers and magazines from Woodlands, with Mrs Sheldon's advice through his father "to improve his education when he finished studying his schoolbooks every day."

Thinking again about the evening of the accident and what had followed in the room when he had been brought in from the road and settled somewhat was what must have been clear to everyone. The rector had avoided any contact with Joe, not an easy thing to do in the crowded room. Though Joe was injured too, he got little attention, probably, the boy thought, because of how he had laughed off the whole thing. He sought no sympathy and got none but no surprise in that. With Mrs Sheldon gone to get the bandages Joe had gone a few minutes later.

More unforgettable though was a recurring and dominant impression. How close he had been to her as she dressed his wounds, with soothing words of attention. He drank in her nearness, her compelling warmth. For days afterwards, still in pain, he relived it all and dwelt on it as long as he wished. Out of everything had come something that was his and his alone. The other consequence was that now for him she was no longer Mrs. Sheldon, a title that dragged a sour picture of her husband to mind, she was now Victoria to him, his Victoria, though he knew he would never address her as such except in his own world.

That name and the recurring memory of the night could never be taken away from him, not even by priest or master. It was all his and his alone. A strange, exciting agitation plagued him. In some ways he could trace this disturbing turbulence back to the beginning, the very first day she arrived and shook his hand at the door of the motor while Sheldon looked on, impatient. The smell of her perfume.

Then, the smouldering feeling somewhere inside him, he had raced to the cottage only to come face to face with Joe's cool response to the mention of the new arrival as the smell of the rotting sheep from the shed took over everything.

In his meanderings into ecstasy, would come other less welcome visions to dampen the warmth of her memory. Try as he might he could not shut out the faces that haunted his days and nights, the master, the priest and the grinning oppressive images of those he thought should be his friends, his classmates. And somewhere beyond those were the sombre, critical eyes of the villagers. This was never truer than in McGuire's shadowy, rambling shop where he regularly lied that what he wanted was for his father and himself rather than Joe.

On the fringes of those forbidding faces was another. Even up to the night of the accident he always thought of the rector as a kind man. But now, Joe might once again be right. He noticed the night of the accident how Field had done nothing to help, beyond unconvincingly offering Joe a chair. One evening Joe and himself had watched through the cottage window as priest and rector stood on the road. The priest, jabbing his finger in all directions as Field listened, meekly nodding in convenient agreement. "Athnion ciarog ciarog eile" was Joe's comment and it was the first time the boy really realised what one beetle knowing another really meant.

A battle ensued in his fervid mind between those ranged against him, Joe and also his father if the truth be told, and Woodlands' mistress, his Victoria. Her messages about him getting better, asked through his father, were a consolation. Even more so, when he managed to struggle painfully to the front window at the motor's sound, was the glimpse he got of her as she was driven out the gates of Woodlands.

He also realised that it was the first time he could remember spending time in his own house and particularly in the small room that opened immediately on to the patch of grass in front of the lodge. When he was well, it was always to Joe's, not being able to get there quickly enough and not always returning home for the shelter of the night and sleep. On nights he spent at Joe's he slept on the old chaise lounge in the kitchen.

Though it was always there, catching his casual attention, now and then, he began to notice more and more, the sepia picture in a light coloured frame on the wall over the fireplace. "She died so that you could live" was what his father had told him on and off if it got their attention for any reason. He tried to make sense of what this almost stark message meant. Something about the word 'noble' fitted. Perhaps, as his father often added, "one day you will know what all that means."

*

With a slight limp and scratches on face, arms and legs evidence of what had befallen him, he was back to school, having extracted as much as he could away from it.

Hateful as every step was that brought him nearer the village and the school, he still had his secret. His and his alone and it would not be taken from him. Making his way to his place with little sympathy of any kind from the master, except a gruff "so you deigned to grace us with your presence now, did you. We were beginning to miss you. I hope you kept to your books while you were relaxing." His classmates smirked.

From the day on the roadside that he had stood, riveted

in the priest's grip as his father listened to the diatribe, school had become a greater ordeal than ever. And yet he knew he was ahead of the others at each subject. A fund of general knowledge acquired from hours spent in what was grandiosely known as the "parlour" of Joe's cottage had him more informed than his classmates, something that clearly irritated the master and worked often to the boy's disadvantage when Slyne, to use his own term, "took him down a peg or two."

Joe had every capital of every country impressed on him, as well as the longest rivers and the highest mountains, not just in Ireland, but in the world, locked into his brain. The daily paper from Woodlands, sometimes unopened if Sheldon was away in London, was read eagerly and commented on by Joe.

As he settled into the classroom routine, he could recall a happier time when he was the envy of his classmates. Joe had allowed him to bring into school a peculiar object that he had acquired at the International Exhibition in Dublin in 1907. That was the day the king and queen had visited because, as Joe laughingly stated, they knew he was going to be there the same day.

The souvenir, proudly displayed to the others in the classroom, was an object in the shape of a bottle that could be pulled apart to reveal a cigarette holder. This could then be attached to the bottom half of the bottle to make a pipe. He was further to inform his wide eyed, appreciative audience that Joe had seen something else at the exhibition, something that had a strange and lively name. It was called electricity. More than that, a man there had told Joe the day would come when every house in Ireland would have light because of it.

'Pagan Boy,' sniggered at him a hundred times a day was strangely the least hurtful. There was an unintended compliment and he bore it proudly, recalling Joe's "sticks and stones" phrase, to sustain that pride. Being identified with Joe, though it had its miserable consequences, set him apart. In their eyes he saw a streak of undisguised envy. The Pagan, Golden, whatever they called him, a man who as McGuire said, "attends neither church, chapel or meeting," outlawed and despised though he and anyone associated with him was, had a certain enviable standing. Thrown in for emphasis to the Pagan Boy references were reminders of his envied status, living inside Woodlands, his father's position and who he worked for, and the motor. The master, far from attempting to control this regular flow of invective, seemed easy with the boy's discomfort. Thus, childish brutality unrestrained by the master was allowed fester. Day after dreary day he watched the hands of the clock lazily move towards school's end. Then it was home, jostled and pushed as he made his way to the school gate and freedom, though not without the casual insults ringing in his ears.

Then, hardly waiting to throw his few schoolbooks aside, he was off to Joe's by the pathway. The cottage was a haven, within sight and earshot of the priest's house, yet safe and unassailable, where time seemed to fly, and night came too quickly. Some unwritten stricture had yet to be breached by the priest in that, despite the hateful contempt he bore his neighbour, he had yet to stand at the threshold of the cottage. The invisible but potent barrier that had the villagers digress, once they passed in front, served too, perhaps, not to allow the man responsible for the ritual to breach it himself.

Through the hours spent with Joe, he had learned much, though trying to understand what Joe had told him about the League and its latent appeal in the village, left him baffled. So striking was Joe in his telling of any story that he often found himself frightened and apprehensive as his version of history was told. Trying to make sense of what the League might mean, if given reason to act, he could not understand why there might be people in Shandrum who would gladly be rid of the Sheldons and their kind. Joe, to make the point about the League, painted a picture of what had led to its growth and not just in the village but in villages and towns in Cork and Kerry as well as beyond on different occasions. He would list the sad and lonely names from Ireland's past, conjuring up images of colour and heroism, though mainly misfortune.

O'Neills, O'Donnells, Cromwell, Kinsale, Aughrim, Sarsfield, the Boyne, Wild Geese, Tone, Emmet, O'Connell. These names found their way into the boy's mind. Joe's ramblings always led to Parnell, "the uncrowned king of Ireland," who, though a landowner with a big house in Wicklow, had won the hearts of the Irish people and a few in England too. What was a dream, almost came to be, and Parnell, without firing a shot, had nearly wrested the prize from the greatest empire on earth. But a woman was the fateful flaw, and because of her and the way he was hounded by the likes of Kerley, Parnell died of a broken heart. A vision the boy tried to conjure up everytime he heard it and the image of a broken heart and what it might mean was a regular puzzle for him. Joe had shown him in the paper where at least Parnell would not be forgotten. A statue was to be raised to his memory sometime before Christmas in Sackville St. in Dublin. "The least they might do for him" was Joe's comment. Inevitably, for the boy, strands of these impromptu history lessons filtered back close to home especially, and in some peculiar way, any connections with the League.

He could never imagine the village without Woodlands and the Sheldons, though he did not like the owner. Since she arrived of course everything connected with the house took on an added meaning. Could what Joe had said, so contemptuously of the League and its main influence, actually lead to trouble for Woodlands? How could anyone ever think of harming her, whatever they might think of her husband? Yet, knowing some of the League's members and how powerful they seemed to him, this dreaded possibility could loom out of proportion in his mind when what he knew of Ireland's story, as told by Joe, was remembered.

If they could dump dead sheep and rabbits in Joe's shed, they would surely be well able to do worse if they wanted. That was certain if unpredictable. It became a monstrous fear, wondering what would he do if she were to be taken away, hunted out from her new home and away from his life, having just become part of it.

*

Languorous summer days drew her away from her writing and along the roads and boreens, lush with summer growth and distinctive smells. She was slowly getting her bearings and it was difficult to actually get lost. Deferred to by the locals, while those that had been at the party night idled their chance meetings with small talk and advice on where the best views were, "but none as good as from the castle." Also detected by her was the question a few posed suggesting that it made no sense to walk when she had the luxury of the motor to go wherever she wished.

"Plenty of time for that when summer is gone," she retorted, being agreed with instantly as well as being advised about making the best of it, it wouldn't be here forever and when it broke that would be the end of it.

In Woodlands she added casual touches to the inside, but to her way of thinking, nothing major needed to be done to alter the dowdiness of faded grandeur that had its own appeal. Improvements, suggested without too much enthusiasm by Edward when he was about, could wait for her consideration when summer had run its course.

The rector's pointed analysis kept coming back to raddle her brain. Nor had the unsettling feeling experienced at the lodge door on catching Golden's eye gone either. In a peculiar, clandestine way she felt it linked her to the less charming aspects of life in the village as portrayed by Field. The eyes of the Pagan. They might have been laughing, even threatening, perhaps maybe cold? Even, dare she think it, inviting in some audacious, shameless way?

Edward was due and the motor's sound soon heralded his arrival. Tired after the journey from the blistering heat of London to be welcomed by the very same at home he rested for an hour. He grudgingly accompanied Victoria for a walk by the river as the evening respite from the heat made it more inviting. Distant and silent, he did little to offset the feeling that in the finish it was the lure of the summer evening, rather than being with her, that was the deciding factor. In vain she waited for some casual comment of enquiry or perhaps endearment after his absence. None came. His thoughts were elsewhere.

She would impose on his contemplation and found a response that was unexpected and enlightening. She briefly told him of the bicycle accident and her subsequent conversation with Field.

"It's really quite simple, dear. You must see how the rector and more especially the priest, feel compromised by the antics of this irritant in their midst. And of course, it's not just them, it's wider. He has to do very little to irritate their sensitivities."

She pounced on what he said.

"Apparently, he does cause offence in one particular way that has to do with you ... and me, I suppose, for that matter."

He stopped instantly and faced her.

"Oh, how?"

"It appears he trespasses at will and to his benefit. It seems he has the run of the place, this place."

"That's putting it a bit strongly, isn't it," he answered, irritated by the broadness of what she said. "Only you and I have the run of Woodlands."

"Come now, Edward, you surely know to what I am referring."

"I do, and the reason for what you so exaggeratedly call, the run of the place, is quite simple. A few years ago, I unexpectedly came across him with a catch of fish. It wasn't far from here, further down the river. We got into conversation, and I found him to be an amiable, intelligent individual, despite his reputation. That's it really and we parted on good terms. It perhaps might have been better, indeed, if I'd warned him off, but our amiable conversation didn't allow for it. I did of course let him know that both of us would benefit from his silence where the villagers were concerned. To reinforce that I told him, maybe a year, maybe two ago to be careful when he had our chauffeur's boy with him. You know how people talk. I know it probably annoys the locals but if it were not that it would be something else. That's just how they are, and I daresay, they seem to forget sometimes how much they have benefitted from Woodlands. I'm sure he's not the only one who trespasses here."

Something in his demeanour was different when he talked about Golden, something imperceptibly easy and connected. She had noticed it the very first day she arrived as he told her of his village status.

"You did report one of them to the police?"

"Dwyer, yes. He's a ruffian but to the villagers he's what they call 'a hard man.' I just wasn't going to let him, or the locals, feel they could take me for granted and I was simply making a point."

Giving what he must have felt was the last word on the matter, he moved to go on along by the river towards the hills, bathed now in the last of the evening haze.

There was little in what he had said that she could find

fault with, but the fact that he had mentioned the boy did give her an opportunity to probe a little further.

"What about the boy and Golden?"

Again, she detected an unease.

"What about them?" he reacted, a note of annoyance evident in his reply.

"You must know that there is much concern – Field says so anyway- about the influence Golden has on the child."

"What kind of influence?" he answered, his annoyance increasing.

"Well, if you must know, Field is no doubt that his influence is rather … how shall I put it … rather unhealthy."

He laughed derisively as if to dismiss any further comment about what she had raised. Unnerved, she waited. Then, realising that she wanted more than a derisory dismissal of what she had said, he continued.

"What will they think of next? Their hypocrisy and humbug never cease to amaze me. Field is in no doubt, you say, and we won't even mention his counterpart on the other side. Do you know something, Victoria, that man's mother, Golden's, could have rotted in that cottage and it wouldn't have cost them a thought. And that's what would have happened only for that child's father. He befriended her in the face of no little opposition, which is still there now."

He swung around, turned towards the village and gave full vent to his feelings, directed towards the cluster of houses from which smoke lazily rose in the twilight and from where lights had begun to appear erratically along the straggle of a street. He continued.

"Look, Victoria, you must realise something about this place or rather some of those who live here like the priest and rector, our good friend Field. They worry more about what is wrong than what's right. Golden is different, so they conveniently christen him The Pagan, skirt by his cottage and turn him into some kind of a monster. His friendship with the child is exactly what they want to destroy by suggesting, saying aloud no doubt, that Golden is this unhealthy influence. If the clergy believe that, or more obviously allow others and encourage them to believe such nonsense, you can see where it leads."

She was somewhat taken aback by the conviction in Edward's tone. He certainly knew where he stood anyway, and presumably, wanted her to believe likewise.

"I know from the child's father that he learns more from Golden, an intelligent man as I've told you, than from school. What's wrong with him spending his time with an adult and doing what any child would do in the circumstances, copy what he's doing, hunting, fishing and the like? I did the same with old Scott, a farmhand here years ago and it didn't do me any harm now, did it?"

Obviously, having never known "Old Scott," she didn't comment. What Edward had said with such forcefulness was, she felt a mixture of conviction and perhaps hope, that his view of things was the last word. Seldom had she seen him so loquacious. So much so that she decided to pursue matters about the boy, despite what he had said.

"But surely, while all you say seems sensible at one level, do they not have a point? He just doesn't drop in and out to Golden's cottage. It appears he spends more time in his company than that of his father, even accepting that his father is often away on his duties and sometimes at odd hours. Maybe he is after all in some sort of … moral..."

He didn't give her a chance to finish and as if despairing, threw his arms in the air and moved away from her towards the riverbank. He considered his reply, then answered.

"My dear, this is Ireland not the fleshpots of Egypt. I knew it would be only a matter of time before that paragon of virtue, Kerley and his right-hand man from our side came to such a conclusion. It's rumour and hearsay of the kind that gets people ostracised. Sometimes killed."

"Killed," she asked, incredulous at the word.

He came back to where she was standing and looked her straight in the eye.

"It's no use hiding my views on this from you. I don't trust that priest. In his odd dealing with me he has been smiling and obsequious or blunt; one never knows what to expect and he leaves me distinctly uneasy. His background is suspect. He is the focus, if not the leader of what is known around here as The League, a group of locals who should know better. They are at his beck and call."

"Edward, this is indeed a surprise. You now paint a very different picture of Shandrum than you did previously, when you and Harold had other things on your minds. Like getting me over here married to you, by hook or by crook."

His expression was that of a scolded child at this dose of reality with which he was now confronted. Quickly, however, as if turning what she said to his advantage and giving her a lesson in reality, his demeanour changed again.

"The last thing I want to do is alarm you. Let me, however, surprise you some more, as this may be as good a time as any to be perfectly truthful with you."

It was now evening's close, still warm. The murmuring river, quite depleted, echoed other summer sounds of night, vainly attempting to tranquilise the disturbing information her husband was about to impart. Flinging his arms in an arc that took in the house and far-flung fields, he paused at a point where for a second time in their conversation, he faced the village.

"There are those, Victoria, and mark you, I know who I am talking about, who would gladly see me at the end of a rope, preferably with our home in flames as a backdrop." He spoke calmly and evenly as if he were summing up in the Old Bailey.

"Edward, please," she gasped, recoiling at his graphic image.

"You began this conversation, Victoria, so now hear me out. Who are those I refer to you may well ask? Well, you have the priest and his cronies. I remember meeting him, it must have been two or three years ago, and intent on making small talk mentioned Home Rule. That was alright until I had the misfortune, or perhaps good fortune, because of what it told me about the man, to mention Mr Parnell and his efforts which I felt might not have been in vain. He rounded on me, his bluntness unmistakable, saying that adulterers should never be, nor would they ever again be allowed to represent the Irish people. He rounded off nicely by saying that this country would be best served by those who were loyal to their history and their god rather than their women. Now you can well imagine what his notions about the boy and Golden lead him to believe and concoct for his own ends and those of his allies."

Numerous questions searched for preference, but she desisted, dismayed and distressed by what she had heard. Her scant knowledge of the Irish question, as she had often heard it referred to, had her ill prepared for Edward's revelations.

Noting her obvious distress, he put his arm protectively round her waist. It was a departure from his lack of anything in the way of a demonstrative gesture. Leading her back the way they had come towards the house, he attempted to impress on her that while what he had told her was true, she should not be worried. There were many locally who respected and admired the Sheldon name. They were dependable should anything untoward ever happen.

More easily said than done she thought, unimpressed by this counter argument to all he had told her. Welcome to harsh reality, she said to herself.

Then, as they neared the house, out of nowhere came Nathan's face full of passionate idealism so seldom found, except in youth, yet untramelled by the raw realities of the angry world. How she loved so much about him. Why had she suddenly thought of him now?

The lonesome bark of a dog in the distance slowly brought her back to the present. They climbed the steps and paused for a moment to look back into what was now nearly darkness. Still in Edward's casual embrace and Nathan's memory, the look of The Pagan, out of nowhere, hit her again. From what Edward had said and her conversation with Field, he was a marked man, a target for anyone with any reason. Now, with no basis that made sense to her, she shivered for a moment at the thought of that look again. Edward, thinking she was cold, slightly tightened his hold and guided her indoors.

In some contradictory, unexplainable way she felt close to him. He seemed to sense that too and he drew her closer. The kiss was awkward, perfunctory. Were it not for ghosts more powerful, even at a distance, she might have been tempted to respond more intimately than she did. She was glad when he mentioned a nightcap.

*

"A jail, a jail."

The shout, begun by one or two in the hilly field that was the school playground, was soon taken up by others. Just another children's game and like so many just seemed to surface, as if from nowhere. "Jail," one of the more popular games among the older boys, sent a wild panic through the scattering children of all ages.

The object was simple, to surround as many of those unwilling or unable to resist and confine them to a corner of the playground where the chapel wall and the hawthorn fence met.

The jailers were always the older bigger boys. Like so many children's games, innocently boisterous on the outside, it afforded the bully a subtle and acceptable vehicle to reign supreme. The method of capture was well and truly understood, so much so that when the chant began, many of the smaller children, knowing their fate and seeing resistance as useless, ran to the corner out of habit. It avoided the ritual of them being dragged there.

Getting free was seldom achieved no matter how wily or sure footed the potential escapee was. It depended on the whim of the jailers. Occasionally the crude half circle might be breached, but that was seldom. The prerogative to release was only exercised when all were inside the half circle and under guard. The head jailer, generally Maguire, most popular or most feared, began pointing at those allowed to be let go. Once free they then joined in attempting to influence the fate of those still inside. Petty grudges, social standing internalised at an early age and other less obvious reasons, combined in ensuring childish justice was done. But of late the game had one target and one alone.

As the chanting began a jolting sickness hit him and his throat constricted. It was a feeling that had become more and more familiar as his status among his classmates had declined. Sidling as unobtrusively as possible, he made his way to join the ranks of the prisoners, most of whom were smaller and younger than he. He had learned the futility of resisting.

The noise and screaming pleas to be allowed free grew louder and for some turned to shouts of glee as one by one of the more favoured was identified and allowed past the guards. The whole process could last for the full play period or yet again a general amnesty was granted to the last few still inside and the whole roundup might begin again.

Today though, something was different and the nods to each other of the captors told him so. This was reinforced when those set free, normally scattered as far away as possible, now gathered behind the guards and waited expectantly. One by one each of those around him were allowed "escape."

He was now alone, the single prisoner. Eyes widened, greedy for novelty, the guards and those freed behind them stared at him. Then from a gloating whisper came a chilling chorus. His stomach knotted. Grimacing faces came nearer, confident in their power and his vulnerability.

"Keep the Pagan Boy in jail," they chanted. With military precision the mob advanced, then drew back, only to surge forward again. McGuire was in command and his huge frame towered over all.

Dwarfed by the surging, chanting mass, his mouth and lips dried as his tongue madly searched for sustenance. Rivulets of sweat trickled from his armpits. He could see how they recognised his plight with relish. Out of nowhere to add to everything, the putrid smell of the maggot eaten sheep invaded his nostrils. Joe came to mind and thinking of him seemed to forge a rage inside him. The pale, fearful frame had become a bundle of pride and he ran, flailing and kicking towards them. This doomed to fail attempt, to burst through his tormentors, only delighted them more.

Maguire and an ally, flaunting their inflated status, tackled him and a third boy joined in. In this lurching human vice, he was dragged into the centre of the hilly field and landed on his back, surrounded by the delirious crowd. From somewhere a grimy set of rosary beads was produced and Maguire pressed the crucifix to his face. Blocking out the sky the strongest among his captors jostled for a vantage point.

His face contorted to deny their savage demand as the figure of Christ met his lips. "Say The Pagan is the devil. Golden is the devil. Say he is the devil and we'll let you go." "No," he struggled, throwing back a scream of defiance. "No, No, I won't." Again and again, he roared at the smothering heaving mass of bodies, energised in some contradictory way by his very weakness. He wanted to spit but something stopped him from using such a vile act of self-protection. Rolling his head from side to side he managed for a moment to avoid the imposition of the cross. Enraged at his resistance and frustrated by his unwillingness to condemn The Pagan out of his own mouth, his captors lost patience. At Maguire's instruction someone grabbed his hair from behind and yanked his head still. Now they would try again.

"No. No. No" he screamed. Maybe Joe would hear.

"What have we here?" A clipped, cold voice commanded immediate attention. But it was not Joe. The master's face now took everyone's attention, as the crowd pulled back, their gloating insolence giving way to sheepish looks of feigned innocence.

"Only playing, Master," Maguire, the spokesman, volunteered with a scowling grin, as if aware that he would hardly merit correction, let alone punishment. They waited for the master's next move.

Muddied, bruised and shaking, he lay where they had left him. Uncertain whether to remain where he was or not, he searched the master's face for some signal.

The familiar "line up" catapulted him to his feet. A line formed and he made to take his place. The master had other ideas, however, and he stiffened under the grip. Mouths gaped as his classmates anticipated the spectacle continuing in some other form. They were not to be disappointed.

His feet barely touching the ground, he was paraded in front of the line, pushed forward by the master. Deliberately or not, the march stopped in front of where Maguire stood, his brutish, dancing eyes glowering in expectation.

Waiting for absolute attention, the master had little difficulty in instantly getting it. Loosening his grip, he stepped in front of the line, leaving the boy standing, alone and isolated. The master turned to the line of children and delivered three throaty, sneering sentences.

"Never forget this. Tell me your company and I'll tell you who you are. That is why this thick bucko here is the author of his own misfortune." As with most of the others, he was uncertain of what the words meant but not so the tone. Joe would know the meaning. For the others, it barely mattered, except that they were exonerated. The perpetrators went free, emboldened to put him through the same or worse ordeal again. That might well come at school's end, but he would escape if another trick, learned from harsh experience, worked. He would seek refuge until their patience ran out.

The clock reached three and with it, dismissal. The threatening glances and whispers told him his plan needed swift execution. Bursting through the jostling crowd of young and old, in a mass of confusion, he made for the open door. This time, with the element of surprise he managed to evade those intent on grabbing him and raced up to the chapel door and pushed it open. Whatever their intent they would not defile the house of God.

Welcome, always, the heavy, simmering smell, from the worn pews subject to years of the fumes of candles, incense and humans. Kneeling, a few seats back from the altar. The refreshing feeling. Safe, unassailable. After school, they never stayed too long, with other duties calling. It would soon be safe to cautiously check as their voices became fewer, their vigil abandoned.

Lapsing into reverie, muttering in the direction of the huge hanging Christ above the altar. Mumbling prayers. The begging kind. Keep them away from me until the summer holidays; Joe, himself and his father safe. Never let Joe or me fall off the castle or father crash into the dangerous corner. Make Fr Kerley sick or send him to a new place. The master says no matter what we pray for we get from you, dear Jesus. The boy in Cork. Prayed for a football. Got one from an uncle in England who was supposed to be dead but turned up alive after many years. My mam and Mrs Golden. Maybe down there in Purgatory. Take them up to heaven with the angels. Poor Mulcahy. Keep him away from the asylum. Not mad, only different. Joe said.

Open the door. Is the coast clear? Looked up the aisle towards the altar. Would Joe ever see the inside of this place? Even when he died? Years and years away and the priest would be dead by then. Did not betray you Joe in the hilly field. No. Against all their strength and power. Standing still. Never let me betray Joe. You, dear Jesus, were betrayed. There in the garden. Judas. Mind the Sheldons especially her and never let the League do anything to Joe. Next year don't let the Titanic sink. Joe says it will never sink.

*

The snares had all been set and they lingered in the dense heat of mid-afternoon. Usually, it would be straight home after the snare setting but today the heat kept them in the shade of a tall oak, one of many on the stretch of river that bounded Woodlands. Swarming sounds of bee and bird drenched the day. Looking lazily across the river toward the hazy hills, observing everything and nothing, not a word passing between them.

"What does the author of your own misfortune mean?" It was said on impulse.

"Where did you hear that one?"

"The master said it the other day to one of the lads."

Conscious of Joe's ability to prise information out of him, he had no intention of reliving the ordeal of the jail. He was just curious yet knew it might not take much to pour out the whole story to Joe.

"Didn't I tell you about Napoleon and the march to Moscow?"

"Oh, yea, you did but what has that to do with an author and misfortune?"

He recalled the night by a blazing fire in Joe's cottage, the winter wind invading every cranny. Joe had painted a picture of flags, maps and generals with Napoleon as the centrepiece. Warned by his advisors that it would be impossible to reach Moscow during the Russian winter, he was not convinced. When a trusted friend then told him a second time that it would be impossible, Napoleon replied that the word "impossible" did not exist in the French dictionary.

Now, as they lounged in the heat, Joe would again describe the advance and then the disastrous retreat from the outskirts of Moscow. His description of the soldiers dying in the freezing snow sent a shiver through the boy, despite the heat. And they were hardly dead before their clothes and boots were taken off them by their fellow soldiers, desperate to get away. And to think also that Napoleon could feel the heat from Moscow burning a few miles from where he was stationed, a beaten man.

Joe always ended his stories with a flourish, and he was back from the frozen tundra to the boiling village summer. Though he had forgotten the original question that gave rise to the retelling of the story, Joe had not.

"Now you can see how Napoleon was the author of his own misfortune by not listening to those who knew better. He made a fool of himself in the long run."

He tried to apply the logic of Joe's story to his own situation and what the master had meant after his ordeal in the school playground, blaming him for what happened, not those who had jailed and jeered him. He remembered the first time Joe had told him the Napoleon story. He said to Joe that the master had told them one day that the great Napoleon, after all his victories, had said the happiest day of his life was the day of his first communion.

"Knowing Slyne, he probably made that one up," was Joe's retort.

He was on his feet then, indicating it was time to go. Sorry he had ever asked the question, the boy rose slowly, letting Joe move on, playing for time. With leaden steps and head bent he reached Joe who had stopped, waiting at the first fence. Joe lowered his face and looked the boy in the eye.

"Was it yourself he said it to, was it, the bastard?"

The truth would have to be told but how. He was about to blurt out something when his eye, looking across the fields over Joe's lowered head, noticed movement along by the orchard wall. Puzzled by the boy's hesitation, Joe turned to see what had taken his attention. A small grey cat picked its way along by the wall and they then saw the object of its interest. She sat in the shade of the high wall, her parasol upturned on the grass. As the cat got nearer, she didn't react, dozing as she was in the shade that was fighting a losing battle with the heat.

Joe motioned to him, and they advanced, crouched, until they reached the fence that went from the orchard wall down to the river. He watched the expression on Joe's face as the cat reached where she sat. Crouching instinctively, knowing that she would wake when the cat disturbed her, they waited. Joe was on one knee, as if ready to move at a moment's notice and the boy took up a similar pose.

The cat stopped, then nestled close to her before climbing on to her lap. Drowsily, she moved at the cat's familiar feel. The watchers crouched lower, fearing discovery. Her fingers ran along the cat's back as he stretched to nuzzle close to her neck. Then it retreated and settled cosily in her lap, encouraged by familiar hands. Soon they were both asleep, but the watchers, breathing more easily, still waited.

Joe stood up, slowly, carefully. The boy waited for some indication of what to do next. Another signal told him to stay where he was, and Joe knelt again. Was this to let her not be disturbed or was it fear of being discovered? Without a word or a movement, they stayed and watched, oblivious to the merciless afternoon sun. He knew some irresistible urge would draw him closer somehow to where she lay were Joe not there. It was as if Joe was lost. Not a muscle moving, his eyes standing out on stalks, beads of sweat on his forehead, his tongue glided slowly between his lips and his neck, taut and lean, wrenched as he swallowed. A slow unsatisfied gulp.

Looking away from Joe, he concentrated on the sleeping form, threatened and excited in a swelter of quivering disturbance, hating the cat and the privileged position it had so effortlessly achieved. If only he were alone. Greedily, he wanted this sight for himself without the dominance and dilution of anyone else's presence.

Somewhere in the distance, the village he guessed, sounded an impatient bark. Though the cat and woman hardly moved from this intrusion, the far-off sound shook man and boy out of their locked, hypnotic staring. He could have stayed forever. They stood and Joe pointed lazily towards the river but not before turning back to where the woman lay, still asleep.

"Jesus," he muttered. Somewhere, somehow the boy understood. They would retrace their steps towards the river, circling so as not to alert the sleeping form, now so utterly at ease. Then the path home. Napoleon, Moscow and the master forgotten about, replaced by a more immediate, enthralling image. They plodded on in the heavy heat, hardly noticing, their thoughts elsewhere but not for sharing. Absorbed in what they had seen, it all made words superfluous.

They neared the back of the chapel wall. Hardly aware of where he was, he was suddenly pushed to the ground as Joe's powerful arm came round him. Yet another signal not to move. He felt the man's breath in his ear.

"Are you bloody well deaf, are you?"

Plagued by other images, he had heard nothing. Joe pointed over the wall towards the chapel grounds. The boy peered, still guided by Joe's grip. The priest and the master were at work.

"The hanging gardens of Babylon," muttered Joe.

The master, with a rake kept his distance as the priest, wielding a scythe, took furious swipes at the long grass. The master was shaking his head in disbelief, at the reaper's handiwork, which left the ground he had covered in irregular grass clumps. Signs were made by Joe. The instruction was clear. Head held high he strode towards the cottage while the boy crept along by the wall, out of sight of priest and master. Their respite would have been welcome had it been anyone else but The Pagan.

Now at the cottage back door and out of sight, a grin of connivance was shared. The enemy outwitted again. The boy, looking back from a safe, unseen position where master and priest stood, saw both in deep conversation. That they had outwitted them might have been victory enough for Joe, but no. He put his fingers in his mouth and gave a taunting, provocative shriek of a whistle. Priest and master froze. The priest made as if to drop the scythe. The master put a hand on his arm and said something which seemed to calm him, before they both got back to work. What had he said? The boy glowered at Joe. His reward was a smile of mischievous complicity

*

"It were better for that man that a millstone were tied around his neck and he were drowned in the depths of the sea."

He ended the sermon, if one could call it that, with the same biblical reference with which he had begun. Long before the finish, the mass goers, gripped by the ferocity of their priest's diatribe, were in no doubt as to the object of it. Well used to the priest's dramatics on the altar when it came to the sermon, the boy's mind was elsewhere. Only when his father shifted uncomfortably next to him did he realise that today something was different. He listened. Not even a cough was heard as row on row listened, absorbing every sentence. As if given a licence, not a few cast streaking glances of curious satisfaction toward where he and his father sat.

Mulcahy, who was supposed to be mad, sat two rows up and to the left from the boy and his father. Not fully understanding all that was being delivered from the altar it was clear that The Pagan and anyone associated with him were at the receiving end of today's sermon. But Mulcahy had a strange, passive look on his face and when others nodded at the priest's words, he didn't. Instead, he looked around at those nodding before turning back to hear what was coming next.

"The hand of Satan is in our midst, with time not for God but the corrupting of the young. Evil in our midst must be rooted out."

Heads nodded as his father, fists clenched white in impotence, moved closer as if to protect his son.

"Those who betray their God will betray their country. Look at the famous Mr Parnell, seduced by a woman into adultery. His campaign came to nought and so will its aftermath. If your hand is a cause of evil, cut it off."

He saw an axe glint in the summer sun and take Joe's hand off at the elbow before a cheering crowd in the village square. He squirmed at the intensity of the priest's word about the foul wickedness in their midst. Then the priest hesitated, as if the attention given to him was not enough. His hesitation wasn't necessary. He lowered his voice for full effect and came round from behind the lectern, standing closer to the congregation, on the altar steps.

"Where has this come from? Where has this corruption that stalks our village and our children come from? You know and I know now it was a bad day for all of us when he came back to bury his dead. No, we would have performed that duty and left him to wallow in whatever cesspool he was, far away from here. But a bastard son came back into our midst."

Uneasily, they shuffled, some glancing again in his father's direction. The question of Joe's legitimacy, an ongoing cause for conjecture in the village, had now been mercilessly introduced into the house of God.

The priest's words about burying Joe's mother raised unexplained possibilities in his mind. I will ask Joe.

Something had always stopped him at the last minute when he was on the verge of asking Joe about his mother, but now he might have a reason, a good one, seeing that it was mentioned in the sermon.

His father's fingers were still clinched and white, gripping his knees. If they could only run out of this cauldron of hate, then they would. But no one would ever stand up to the priest in the house of God and do something like that, certainly not stand up and leave in protest. But thankfully, the sermon was almost at an end.

"The day will come when the name he bears will no longer foul this parish. God is not mocked. Now do not forget what I said at the beginning when speaking of the most unnatural evil the word of God condemns. It were better for that man that a millstone were tied around his neck and he were drowned in the depths of the sea."

He paused again, the attentive faces waiting to see if something else would follow. It did and an audible gasp greeted it.

"Protect your children."

He turned back to the altar. The congregation stood, some shocked, some mesmerised but many comforted by the novelty of what they had heard. A sanction had been given to exorcise the demon in their midst.

The boy rose before his father, who haltingly and slowly got to his feet, as if his hesitation was a sop of defiance. All eyes were towards the altar, but the boy noticed that Mulcahy had turned back toward where his father reached a standing position. He shook his head in his father's direction and turned back to the altar.

"Credo in Unum Deum…" the priest went on. The boy had never seen the sea and often wondered what it looked like, but now he conjured up an unnatural image of Joe with a big stone around his neck rambling round the village asking where the sea was. This kept playing on his mind until the crowd made its way back from communion, their sombre judgment finding its way toward where he knelt with his father.

Consolation of a sort came out of nowhere and the prospect of the school holidays, now only a few days away, tempered what had gone before. The thought of getting away from all that school involved now raised his spirits, even if the long summer days might be crowded in uncertainty. Maybe the priest's words would be forgotten as just as the words of the Sunday sermon were often forgotten.

In nomine Patris et Filii… It was time to go. His father took him by the hand, making his way quickly, pushing his way through the crowd that slowly edged towards the door. This was unusual as the boy never remembered him rushing from the church before. Father and son were now among the first to the gate and the boy was propelled away from the village toward the gate lodge and home. As they got further away his father loosened his grip and the boy struggled to keep up. Normally, this would be a leisurely stroll after mass, with plenty of time to drive Victoria to service. Today was different and his father strode along with purpose and intent as if to get as far away as possible from what he had heard. Half running in his wake, he gave a look over his shoulder. His heart jumped with fear and exhilaration. Yes, there as usual, at the cottage gate, seeming now more defiant than ever, stood Joe.

He wanted to tell his father to look back but didn't. He would know anyway. Today however, Joe's regular post mass stance might well mean something very different. and the departing crowd, passing by the cottage, seemed from a distance to give it a wider berth than usual.

*

Each Sunday's routine was predictably sacrosanct. With mass over, father and son walked back home and then the motor brought either one or both of the Sheldons to Field's village service. In recent years there had been a noticeable decline in the congregation. This reality did not go unnoticed but was hardly ever mentioned as if it might somehow cement the fact that the landlord class was beginning to decline. Field himself, fortified by what he had drunk, had given the reasons to Victoria the night of the party.

Having arrived at the church, the motorman usually sat in the comfort of the motor for the duration of the service if the weather was inclement. Otherwise, he ambled among the gravestones by the side of the church or might have a quick word with The Pagan. There was a time when he occasionally went to the cottage and had a cup of tea. Recently such visits didn't take place for reasons mutually accepted, though Joe had been slow to accede, telling the motorman that it was "letting bigotry rule." He agreed, but in the boy's interest they grudgingly accepted that it was the best thing to do and avoid, as the motorman said, "adding fuel to that particular fire."

When the service ended, Field usually spent some time

greeting those who emerged from the church and then it was back to the blessed relief of the rectory. The after-service routine had changed, he felt. There was a time when carriages were parked right up along the village street and back towards Woodlands. He often spent twenty minutes or half an hour chatting with those fortunate enough to be driven to church and back again. Ironic when he considered his counterpart's situation; yes, the odd carriage here and there for Sunday mass but the majority walked, with some lucky to possess a bicycle. The priest spent little if any time conversing with those who congregated outside the chapel gate and strode past them with nods of recognition. While the women made their way home, the men chatted, observed and then sauntered up the street and fanned out from there towards the frugality of their cottages or Maguire's public house.

Field was convinced, even without Home Rule, that the day would come when his successors' worshippers would be counted on the fingers of one hand. His mind accepted all this, but it was often with a heavy heart as he trudged across the road to the echoing sound of the Woodlands' motor invading the stillness of the morning air. Certainly, no increase in worshippers there. While Sheldon's name regularly graced the pages of newspapers, he was seldom at home, his wife an ornament to convention, His meteoric rise to the top of his profession seemed guaranteed, but at what cost?

For the boy, one of the week's highlights was the lunch from Woodlands brought back by his father when the churchgoers were deposited, and the motor parked. Food came daily from the house to the gate lodge, but the Sunday lunch was a special treat. It was another enviable advantage enjoyed because of his father's position, something of which he was often snidely reminded.

Still smarting from the sermon, the frown on his father's face told him that the matter would not easily be forgotten. "Now they're all bloody well against us."

He threw the food on the table in dejection and anger while casting his cap aggressively in the direction of a fireside chair. It spun to the ground at the fireplace.

"Who? What?" the boy questioned, puzzled as to how things could be any worse that after the priest's outburst.

"It's Field below. He's after telling his crowd the very same thing without the roaring. But it's the same story anyway."

He knew his father often heard bits of the rector's sermons as he wandered among the gravestones.

"What did he say? Are you sure?"

"I only got bits and pieces, but it's all the same as far as we are concerned. We'd nearly be as well off out of here, do you know that? As well off maybe out of it altogether. Go on, eat something."

Hungry, yet slow to eat, they picked at what was before them. His father's forehead moved as he ate, a shroud of troubled and troubling ridges. What did he mean that they might be as well out of it altogether?

Somehow, despite his father's clenched fists in the chapel and his angry face now, he was not afraid. Joe would make sure everything would be fine, he had no doubt about it. He always had answers and he would have an answer for this.

"I'm certain she knew there was something wrong when I picked her up, but you should have seen the way she looked when she got into the motor after what she'd heard from Field."

His words were directed at the boy, yet it seemed his father was speaking as if alone.

"And then there was your man, brazen as brass outside the cottage when we left. His usual carry on. Playacting. As if he was the new king. You'd think he ruled the whole bloody place. Ahhh… I just don't know."

He watched and listened, wondering what Joe would have to say now that they were after reading him from the altar. Unable to fathom the full extent of the ill will and spite of the grownups around him, never mind that of his classmates and the master, he followed each movement of his father's face with limited sympathy.

After all, there was only one rotten week of school left.

*

Her writing continued, intermittent and erratic as summer heat won every battle. With Edward absent she was obliged to substitute on some social engagements, and this slowly gave her a greater knowledge and insight into the lives of others of her class. Field was right. Children were few among their class and the majority of those she visited were older than either Edward or herself. A musty weariness characterised many of their genteel homes, their preoccupations and their routines. Victoria was a welcome novelty into their lives.

Just a few, predictable topics dominated conversation on these visits. The weather inevitably and now and then the

Home Rule question, the king's coronation, the launch of the Titanic. But, whatever the conversation or extent of it, talk invariably turned to The Pagan. His reputation was further afield than Shandrum and views varied as often as they were similar. She was to find, however, that Field's sermon had added an understandable gravitas and a new dimension to the conversations' tenor.

She had accepted an invitation from Lavinia Chapman, long-time friend of the Sheldons and described by Edward as a "drunken relic lurking on the fringes of gentility." Edward looked visibly relieved the night of the party on being informed that Lavinia was indisposed. Ostensibly, it was just a routine visit on the basis that she had not been able to attend the party.

The visit necessitated the motor and it brought Victoria the five miles or so to a house that had seen better days. Overarching trees and branches almost reached inside the motor as it trundled up the pot holed avenue, shrouded in darkness despite the sunshine. Were that not enough to suggest that better days were behind it, one look at the house confirmed the fact that Lavinia was either too poor or too disinterested to make even basic changes or improvements. Despite the faded grandeur it still retained a certain character.

Two other couples, The Bressingtons and the Kingston-Halls were present as well. A fine meal was followed by a good wine. Small talk dominated the conversation over the meal before they adjourned to the drawing room where Lavinia's liberal distribution continued, increasing in pace rather than slowing down. A gaunt, imposing lady, Lavinia eventually posed the inevitable question to Victoria. Her intent was clear, what information might she glean about "that strange creature they call The Pagan." "He's been causing quite a stir for some time. Indeed, after our good rector's sermon recently they may be calling him something else, I daresay. I've come across him on that bicycle thing with the child in tow and he's made that road into the village a death-trap. He seems civil enough from what I've seen of him though he does rather look through you. You have seen him, I daresay, Victoria?"

Taken aback at the rather precise assessment of Golden, Victoria thought some of the others might add to what Lavinia had said but they settled back, waiting for an answer, as if this had been planned. Knowing The Pagan matter would surface at some stage she also knew she had drunk too much and too quickly. Her reply, once she had begun, immediately seemed like a betrayal as she told them about not having met Golden, except for the bicycle fiasco, and giving a short description of what had actually happened. The others, well aware of what had happened that evening with added embellishments, now had it again from a witness to it all.

Sniggers of merriment came from Edwina Kingston-Hall especially when Victoria mentioned Field's presence. Her husband, in an attempt to cover up for his wife's inebriated tittering, gravely interjected that what he had heard only confirmed what he thought of these infernal machines, "deathtraps on wheels," that would soon have the king's highway overrun with disastrous consequences. He then went on to motor cars only to realise that he was sitting with someone who had arrived in one.

Lavinia, knowing little about bicycles, was not about to have the conversation steered away from more interesting matters.

"Death traps indeed Robert," she nodded in agreement to Kingston-Hall, but immediately turned back to Victoria.

"But tell me Victoria, what do you think of this fellow, now lucky to be alive and the child lucky too after that horrendous tumble. Surely, it's not wholesome, as Field quite rightly pointed out at service, for the motorman's boy to be so often and so blatantly in the company of such an eccentric non-conformist? It has created an atmosphere, you know, and very much so on the other side. That priest, Kerley isn't it, must be beside himself, even if I've little sympathy for him. You do know he was a fomenter of dissension in whatever parish he was previously in?"

Nods of agreement all round at Lavinia's description of things, left her in little doubt that Field's intervention had Golden outlawed and suspected on all sides. Guilt welled up in her when she thought that her contribution had perpetuated this scandalous gossiping in a most irresponsible way. The Pagan's look from the night in question came back into focus. He could have been sitting opposite her.

John Bressington, took up the conversation with a sombre and serious contribution, suggesting that Golden had always appeared to him to be a "decent enough chap, even if a bit unconventional. And are we sure that what our pastors say is true?"

Kingston Hall's wife, Constance, was about to add something but Victoria got in quickly, glad that a degree of balance had been brought to the matter.

"I couldn't agree more John, live and let live, I say. Our rector is not God, and his counterpart most certainly isn't either."

A giggle all round had Lavinia finishing off her glass at speed, while fetching another bottle.

She went on, rather unsteadily, but in no doubt as to what direction she intended to take the conversation.

"That may be so, Victoria, but I have always had the utmost confidence in Field's observations and advice. He had been approached by the priest and a very lurid picture painted. Very lurid. He just had to speak out at the service, and it would have been a dereliction of duty not to have done so. That child, spending so much time with this man of such … such dubious moral standing. It doesn't bear thinking about. I've heard about this sort of thing among the locals when Alfred and I were in Alexandria. Quite revolting. It makes me wonder what the Empire has given the world after all. We seem to have failed in influencing the natives in so many places."

Nods of agreement but this time not so enthusiastically, with Bressington, shaking his head and again beating his wife to getting in with an opinion, sceptical of Lavinia's analysis of the Empire's influence and said so.

But Victoria was less interested in the Empire than Lavinia's twisted innuendo about The Pagan, so definite, so assured and backed up by Field's sermon and her view of him. As Bressington went on to list the benefits of Empire, Victoria remembered Edward's sane dismissal of the general populace's view. Perhaps he was right with his practical, no nonsense attitude toward life in Shandrum and its people, so heavily influenced by their pastors. She missed him now, the perfect antidote to Lavinia's ranting. Stung by the next remark, she was glad it steered things away from the Pagan, but only to an extent.

"You should ask Edward, my dear, about things around here and I daresay in the rest of the country. It's not as secure as it seems. We know you must miss him and it's unfortunate he's away so much. But such an important job, that's where the successes of the Empire are evident. In the pursuit of justice, and there should be more of it, like here. But you must indeed miss him so much. I nearly wasted away when Alfred was posted to Khartoum after we were married. I should have gone with him from Alexandria but was told it was too dangerous. And so it was, costing him his life eventually, a life spent in the service of others but leaving me nothing."

She was lost for a few moments in a haze of memory and Victoria noticed the two wives looking despairingly at one another, fearing that Lavinia would launch into a long monologue about her dead husband and the life he and Lavinia never had.

To pre-empt this, and for the first time in the discussion, Constance Bressington, a wily pert faced woman, added her own view. It did little to assuage Victoria's growing anger and frustration. She turned to Victoria.

"They really can be quite impossible here at times, you know. Troublemakers are not in short supply and the rector has no doubt that this League or whatever it's called is still waiting to strike a blow for God and Ireland. That's what they have on some rag of a banner, I hear.

It's getting quite intolerable, I tell you. And to think Parnell contended that they could rule themselves. As I've often said to John, it makes one glad to be old and you know what, at times we seriously think of moving back to Norfolk. We wouldn't be the first to move away back home."

Strange, Victoria thought, isn't your home here?

An uneasy interlude followed with Victoria still stung by Lavinia's reference to Edward's absence and troubled by what Constance had to say. Constance wasn't finished.

"Perhaps Edward might have a word with that child's father, the motorman. I believe he's a reasonable individual and I am sure he has some control over his son's movements. And indeed, Edward might take that other individual to task about his trespassing on Woodlands' property. He's now so reassured that he's doing the same elsewhere so it's becoming a wider problem. But I will say no more, maybe I've said too much, Victoria. Sometimes it's impossible to avoid the obvious."

Streams of fading sunlight signalled the beginning of the close of another hot and humid day. Bressington, less drunk that any of the others present, herself included, may have sensed Victoria's irritation. His attempt to pour oil on troubled waters did not succeed.

"I am not so sure, Constance, and we've disagreed on this before now. Everyone knows and you know I am less enthusiastic leaving here than you are. Sometimes I think our rector isn't always right even if his intentions are good. There is room for all of us here even if there are less of us than them. I'm inclined to think this League thing is just a few hotheads looking for diversion. When they get their Home Rule they will still be creating some sort of trouble. Never satisfied, I say. Laws do not change people like that."

Edwina Kingston-Hall, obviously aware of Bressington's views, ran a hand through her hair. She had said little all evening and now suddenly rounded on him.

"John, you surprise me. He does know, he has to know what's going on."

Her words were barely audible above the approaching sound of the motor. Never so pleased to hear it, Victoria made haste to leave. It was not lost on the others. The wine had taken its toll on all, except Bressington. Slowly Victoria rose. Overly eager to escape from all she had heard, she awkwardly knocked her wine glass across the table. Kingston-Hall, in a despairing lunge to catch it hit two more glasses and the result was they shattered on the floor. It brought the night of the bicycle and the fish to mind.

Lavinia, in response to the glasses shattering was to carelessly dismiss what had happened and, with words now very definitely slurred, interjected.

"Don't worry, Victoria, don't worry John, they're only trinkets anyway. We won't be needing them much longer around here, it seems to me. Betsy Pender will clean all that mess up in the morning."

She was really addressing Victoria, who in other circumstances, might have taken the words as kindly said. She sensed, though, a hint of mockery, even foreboding, in Lavinia's words.

They all moved unsteadily out into the twilight where the unkempt front had them stumbling to gain a foothold. Forced goodbyes were exchanged with promises to meet again. Victoria, feeling quite drunk but not wanting to show it, quickly made her way to where the motorman waited, facing away from the door in the avenue's direction. He greeted her and she sat in, hoping he would leave at speed. Lavinia had come to the side of the motor looking first at the imperturbable face of the motorman and then fixing her lean, intoxicated gaze at Victoria. Had a carriage, coming to take the Bressingtons and the Kingston-Halls home not just made its way out of the trees on the avenue, forcing the motorman to wait for room to pass, Victoria would have been spared Lavinia's parting salvo.

"God bless the King, and hear now, my dear, mind that pagan fellow."

The motorman surely heard but his impassive expression gave no indication that he had. The motor pulled away. She turned to see Lavinia floundering in the direction of the others and their carriage.

"Bitch," Victoria whispered to herself, realising she could find little sympathy for one of the Empire's forgotten relics, old, alone and drunk in her crumbling big house in an alien land.

The glow of twilight and the softness of what had been a perfect summer day was lost on her.

*

Those he could depend on were numbered easily and quickly. They were the ones who mattered, not the illiterates in the cabins at the village edge or beyond. They might have their place, if necessary, but only time would tell. For success he knew he could depend on the master, the shopkeepers and Cleary. Dwyer, publicly warned about trespassing on Woodlands' property, would be a useful ally, with a point to prove. "Holy Mary" Beglin could always be depended on.

He was smugly content that his recruiting of Field had worked. The opportunity to persuade him to accept the evil in their midst and preach about it, presented itself when Field had knocked on his door one evening, with a few papers in his hand.

"It's this Ne Temere business," Field said, shuffling some papers for Kerley's attention. "A mixed couple and the father of the bride on my side is proving resistant, saying Pope or no Pope, decree of 1908 or not, he wants his daughter married in my place. I explained to him but to no avail. Can we talk about this?"

The priest, alert to what advantage he might gain from this meeting, saw his opportunity and obsequiously invited Field inside to a comfortable, if untidy room with papers, books and the like everywhere. Numerous framed religious pictures and photographs adorned the walls and mantelpiece. The atmosphere, though, was cosy, if somewhat stifling with the summer heat. Immediately a whiskey bottle was produced. Field recoiled, but anxious to make the object of his meeting - some way to placate one of his flock - succeed, he accepted the proffered drink, a generous measure. All he wanted was an answer to his question and he would be gone.

Slightly unsure of himself, he drank back the measure and instantly felt more confident. Kerley, master in his own domain, took a measured sip and sat back. Field presented his problem and unexpectedly he got his answer and quickly, but not before that answer betrayed the priest's anathema of mixed marriages. It was like he was reading from a script. Having said his piece, he advised Field to persuade the Protestant father to allow the marriage to take place, as Catholic teaching demanded, in the Catholic church. This to be followed immediately by a similar ceremony across the road with Field officiating. As far as the priest was concerned the ceremony in his church was the valid one and the couple could do as they pleased after that.

Still somewhat uncertain as to how amenable the father of the bride would be, Field considered the pros and cons of the priest's suggestion.

"It's how you'll tell him, Rector. I've seen this before. Get him on your side or rather his daughter's side. It's her big day and if he wants to believe that what takes place in your church is the real wedding then for him it is. So long as my man is ok with it, and I know him and he will be, then we're all happy. There now, a problem shared is a problem solved."

It may have been the whiskey, but Field now readily fell for the solution offered. His sense of relief was obvious, and he found himself settling more comfortably into the chair. So much for getting an answer and going.

The priest, building on the advantage gained, ignored Field's protestations, and reached for the bottle again.

"Wouldn't it be wonderful, Rector, if all our problems could be solved as easily as that one?"

"I couldn't agree more, but maybe our problems are small compared to what we read about in the papers, wars, pestilence and famine here and there. Then we have our Home Rule problem and the question of where it will all lead. It's a sad and weary world, isn't it?"

Field picked up his glass and raised it to his lips. As he did so he noticed a faded photograph in a frame on the mantelpiece. Not really knowing why in particular it took his attention, he asked the priest about it.

Kerley finished his drink and replenished his glass.

"Ah, isn't it interesting that you should pick that one. If you only knew the story of that picture, you'd know a lot about me."

He stood and took it down, passing it to Field. It was the picture of an eviction, with a tumbledown house in the background and a family group in front of it, bedraggled and frightened looking, with a priest beside them and a policeman to one side. Pointing to one of the children, a boy of seven or eight, holding a bag, the priest said, "who do you think that is?"

Field examined the picture more closely and then it dawned on him. He looked at the priest and back at the picture, then back at the priest again.

"Is that really you?" he asked, clearly noticing a resemblance.

Taking the picture and placing it back on the mantelpiece, the priest replied. "Indeed, it's me. All we had was a potato plot. That picture holds the story of my life."

Intrigued, Field waited for some explanation. It came, measured and calm. In its telling, Field surmised it wasn't the first time the same story had been told.

"That's west Cork. I came home one day from school, and they were pulling the roof off the house. A shack with a few spuds and turnips attempting to grow in the bit of a garden we had. It wasn't much but more than many others around had. And of course, most of all, it was home. Everything had been planned and that's why the picture was taken, by an American photographer travelling around Ireland. I heard afterwards that he paid the bailiff, a godless reprobate known by all in the district, to let him photograph the next eviction to take place. They staged the eviction so the American could get his photo. But for us it wasn't staged, it was real, and we were left on the side of the road despite what Fr. Malone did to try to stop it. The bailiff got his thirty pieces of silver, the police did their job, and the American got his photograph, which by the way, found its way into newspapers all over America and eventually back across the sea to these parts. I can remember my mother crying while my father, a proud man, seethed with rage and anger but was helpless to do anything with the force of the law backed up by the police ranged against him."

Field was staggered by the relevance of the story to the life of the man sitting opposite him, sipping his whiskey, gazing again at the picture, as he must have done a thousand times before.

"And what happened?" asked Field, drinking too fast now but eager to know what brought the child in the picture with the school bag to where he was now sitting.

"It was the poorhouse for us only for Fr. Malone, a Christian and a patriot. He was my inspiration. He gave us a roof over our heads when no one else helped us and pledged to me that if I 'did my books' he would ensure I could be like him, a priest who put God and country before mammon. He was true to his word and because of him, I'm here today, a priest of God and a testimony to a good man, another priest of God. My pledge to him the day I was ordained was that I would be true to what he stood for - God and country - and, by God I have been and will be, bishop or no bishop."

It was only with those last few words that the calmness slipped, replaced by a grim determination. Throughout this history lesson what struck Field most was how different the excitable, gesticulating priest that the parishioners knew was from the man who had just told him his life story in a nutshell.

Mesmerised by the picture and its incarnation before him, Field was easily open to a third whiskey, even though he knew he had had enough.

"Now Rector, let us drink to what we have and where we have come from. But maybe, your journey here may be just as interesting and more so, than mine."

Field laughed, feeling humbled in the presence of his village counterpart and declared that his story couldn't match his "by a country mile."

"Ah now, nothing as dramatic as what I've just heard, very normal and routine. My path mapped out in a way, even though I didn't think so, as God works in mysterious ways. Father, a rector in Dublin, me an only son, Classics in Trinity, taught for a while but something drove me towards the church and my father drove me more. And sometimes, after thirty years in this place, I wonder, do we make any difference at all."

"Well, there's one difference we can make," the priest quickly replied, sitting up in his chair and leaning towards Field.

"We can make a big difference here in this village by rooting out the excuse for humanity that is in our midst, and you know who I'm talking about."

The man who had so graphically told Field the story of where he had come from, was now on the edge of his seat, suddenly catapulted into action. He proffered another drink, but Field had had enough, too much in fact. The priest went on and Field felt himself being drawn, unwillingly and worryingly, into some conspiratorial plan with which he was far from happy.

"Parishioners are coming to me regularly complaining of his malign influence. Whatever your and my differences may be, we are no doubt agreed that the good book doesn't lie and I'm going to vigorously use it next Sunday to finally speak out in the hope that he no longer exercises his heinous influence on an innocent child. No one knows what goes on in that place of his. It's unnatural, a child spending more time there than in his own home with someone who hasn't an iota of godliness."

Feeling he needed to make some response, Field was about to make a reply when the priest dealt what he now believed to be his winning hand.

"No use, Rector, in me performing my Christian duty if I am alone. A bird never flew on one wing and I, and the good people of both persuasions here, need a united approach on this. I don't have to tell you that people around here, good people, not troublemakers, view him the same way as I do, a danger not only to that child but to their children too. That's why we can't stand by and allow this suppurating sore to fester any longer. We must at least speak out. I've done it a number of times without being specific but to no avail."

Field knew where this was going. A combination of drink and the priest's convincing logic delivered an urgency he himself could never conceive of mustering. He had forgotten why he had crossed the road an hour ago. He then remembered the seemingly intractable problem of one of his flock which now seemed trivial with Kerley's swift solution. From there it had now come to a situation where he felt he had to reciprocate, though the thought of where that might lead left him in an uneasy quandary.

"A concerted effort by the two of us on Sunday may well have the desired effect. It will be a show of Christian strength that we should have shown long ago."

He tried, but again unsuccessfully, to replenish Field's glass before sitting back in his chair. He eyed him as if they were two children about to embark on a playground prank.

"I'm going to emphasise the millstone and emphasise it I will, I can tell you. Straight from the mouth of the Lord. Who can or will argue with that, tell me? Now, what angle will you take? Nothing wrong in the words, a show of unity and all that, coming from both sides of the divide. The main thing is that we are seen to lead those who come to do their weekly duty. Nothing less can be expected of us."

Pleading for time to consider what his approach might be, he sought "a period of reflection to see how best to address his congregation."

That was enough for the priest. He had played his cards and won.

In a celebratory gesture, he picked the bottle up again and persuaded Field to "have one for the road." This time Field's protestations were in vain and as he took another measure his eyes went again to the picture on the mantelpiece. Just above it was something he hadn't taken particular notice of, a mirror with a crucifix on top. Only then did he notice a reflection in it and he turned to see another picture, not a photograph this time, but a painting hanging over the door. With a rising sun behind her, a figure, more a girl than woman, striding forward, unfurled a flag. It read "Ireland for the Irish."

Rather unfortunately, Field commented, "Well, I have no doubt when Home Rule comes and that looks very likely, it will be Ireland for the Irish, won't it?"

The priest, as if a button were pressed, reacted, his face reddening.

"Anything contaminated with the assistance of an adulterer will never satisfy me, I can assure you. That profligate, Parnell, tainted it all by his carry on and any principled Irishman would reject the gains of an adulterer of the landlord class and his lackeys who sullied the name of his country and its people. I see they're putting a different face on it these days, Smith O'Brien and Redmond, but

we won't buy it, under any guise, no, by God, we won't."
Shocked by this unexpected outburst to an innocent
remark, as he saw it, Field got up, put down his glass and
steadied himself, before turning as if to make his way to
the door. The priest stood in front of him, as if to face
him down. It was however to ensure he didn't leave the
house with his mind changed about their agreed plan, to
denounce The Pagan from the altar.

"With that said, Rector, and I know the architect of this
Home Rule was of your faith, but at least he had one.
Now, let us not forget about this character next door
who not only has no faith but scorns those who have any,
especially on Sundays, taking up such a deliberate stance
at his gate in all weathers when our flocks attend their
places of worship. It's just the get up of him, sneering
at those who worship their God. And that's without
mentioning that child, another story, scandalous as the
fleshpots of the Empire."

He saw that Field had been ruffled and he would ensure
that he would not leave the presbytery with a changed
mind about denouncing the evil in their midst. From
Parnell to the Empire's fleshpots, he now moved to regain
any ground lost in what he had earlier achieved.

"And while we're at it, what about his poaching and
trespassing all over the place and our man in Woodlands
below attempting to bring the full rigour of the law to
bear on poor Dwyer by reporting him to the constabulary
above. And then to rub salt in the wounds he lets that
wretch next door do as he pleases and with the young
fellow in tow."

Field put his hand up and waited for a moment before replying.

"I will tell you that I have brought that matter to Sheldon's attention ... in fact I made it my business to acquaint the new mistress with the feeling of unrest and bad feeling being engendered by the freedom allowed to ... our friend next door."

He saw the priest relax somewhat but at the mention of the term "friend" in the same context as The Pagan he saw that Kerley struggled to accept any diminution in the reference. He did, however, restrain himself and took for granted the rector's hesitation in having a different attitude and a milder approach in his language than himself. He wasn't happy with that, but he would hold his counsel.

"And what had the new lady of the manor to say when she heard about it?"

"Concerned, but of course and quite rightly she stressed the fact that she is very new here and had been told before she ever came that we ... the Irish, are difficult to understand. But she did undertake to let himself know and maybe that might have some effect. However, if you were to ask me that would be a hope only. She is, though, a woman of strength and principle. She deserves time to adjust to things that must be very new and puzzling for her."

"Keep after her about it, the more often you let her know what people around think the better. Aiding and abetting The Pagan doesn't go down too well, as you know."

Field had had enough. He left his half-finished drink where it was and made to leave. Kerley followed him to the front door and said, before opening it, in a tone, conspiratorial and insistent. "I'm sure you won't forget that on Sunday, now. Let us pray it bears fruit."

"I gave you my word." Then he was gone, shuffling somewhat from the effects of the whiskey and hating himself for having succumbed to Kerley's insidious generosity in the first place and subsequently agreeing to publicly condemn the man in the cottage to his flock the following Sunday. At least the mixed marriage issue might not be the problem he had anticipated and that, at least, was something. Yet only a sop.

Waiting until his visitor had closed the gate, he then closed his own door, standing for a moment with his back against it, satisfied that a vital ingredient had been added to his and the League's armoury. This particular triumph he would share with a small coterie of those whose aims were similar to his own, not just where The Pagan was concerned, but everything remotely connected with him. He would have preferred to have waged a successful campaign against The Pagan on his own, but had, however, agreed with the master, that getting the rector involved gave the matter a much wider audience with the net also spread wider. The Sheldons should be dragged into the whole thing no matter how resistant. Doing so might ultimately compromise them in some way. That was of particular satisfaction, the Sheldons and all they stood for being the very antithesis of what the League stood for, "Ireland for the Irish."

*

The remnants of the League he had managed to rally over time, much as had happened with his previous parish.

Aware that Woodlands and its occupants were well thought of but representative of all that was anathema to him, he believed that a few trusted henchmen were all that was needed, to target the enemy. And that enemy was clearly a slap in the face to all those who had some conscience about the evil in their midst and anyone who helped foster it.

He was particularly satisfied that Field, by referring to the eviction picture, had given him an opportunity to prove his credentials and clearly show that his opposition to The Pagan and the landed gentry had a firm foundation. From poverty, to eviction, to education, to the gift of the priesthood, he had travelled a hard, demanding road to where he was today. How could his stand be otherwise after the indignity his family had suffered? He had not only survived but had profited from that ignominious experience.

As he poured himself a nightcap, he thought of the connections that were fundamental to any course of action to be taken. The Pagan, the child, the motorman and the Sheldons. Even if Sheldon was absent except for infrequent visits, it was a godsend in that it gave rise to the term "absentee landlord" and all that implied. The arrival of a woman on the scene might alter that perception, but only up to a point. He had learned little about her from the conversation with Field but enough to know that she was not ignorant of The Pagan's status; and her husband giving him free rein to literally have the run of the benefits of what Woodlands offered in terms of hunting and fishing. It was common knowledge that besides Dwyer, unfortunate to have incurred Sheldon's wrath, there were those who poached wherever they could but at least didn't have carte blanche to do so.

The motorman was another story and had its history. As coachman in Woodlands, he occupied a routine position. His relative prosperity, living in the gate lodge and the beneficiary of what came with that, was envied by some. In a strange way, the arrival of the motor and its driver's promoted prestige and status, created further resentment, something that the priest did little to dampen. Where many in Shandrum had little, it was as if the motorman's function, still essentially the same, had slowly placed him on a pedestal.

For the priest however, it was not the motor's arrival in the village that changed much of his attitude toward its driver. Rather it was the fact that he had befriended The Pagan's mother. That continued to irk him. Coming back to the village with her bastard son, from where the nuns had looked after her, was one thing. Flaunting the result of her iniquity without contrition for all to see was another. Her godlessness had passed seamlessly to her son and she resented every minute that son had spent in school and chapel. One thing to be said for the motorman, at least, was that he persuaded her to have her brat educated and given the sacraments until he took off, as soon as he could, for God knows where, England it was presumed. Fortunately, he stayed away until she died. He was to replace his mother though, in the long run presenting a far bigger challenge.

His mother rejected priest, church and any semblance of religion. A half mad recluse she turned out to be, feared by the children, as her son would be, and only allowing inside her door the motorman and his wife while she was alive and then his son.

Warned of what to expect from "the holy terror" as she was described to him when he arrived in the village, he recalled his one attempt to make her see the error of her ways and come back to her God. It was his first challenge in his new posting, and he relished it, partly because a few of the villagers implied it would be a test of how successful he might be in establishing himself in his new parish. Getting the madwoman back to the church would be a feather in his cap and an indication that he was someone who got things done when he set his mind to it.

The minute she opened her door to him she spewed a foulmouthed tirade of abuse, including the words "where was the priest when I needed him?" Shocked at the level of invective, he tried to speak but she was having none of it. Knowing he was being watched by some of the villagers he tried to regain some ground but before he got any further, she turned into the hallway only to return in an instant with an enamel dish of dirty water, fully intent on letting him have the full contents. He turned to get away but not before she showered his retreating head and shoulders.

It was an inauspicious start to his ministry, and the guffaws from the village at his humiliation didn't help. He made as quickly as possible for his own door. That, however, was a long time ago and he had regained his banished honour over time, though he never again tried to reform The Pagan's mother. His escapade was often referred to with raucous laughter, especially in shop and public house when boredom or drink intervened to break the monotony of simple lives. Over time it was added to and suitably embellished as when Cleary, the sergeant, smirked at him one day as they finished a conversation, and she was casually mentioned. Though Cleary was now a trusted ally he never forgot his remark. The sergeant was careful that it was attributed to someone else, in this case, Mulcahy, an easy target because he was perceived as mad. "Sure, Father, Mulcahy said it was the contents of the po she threw at you."

Still smarting as he thought of it, his consolation now was that with Field as an ally, the two-pronged attack on his nemesis would prove successful and the village would be rid of what the mad woman had spawned. Those were his thoughts as he sat for a while and had another drink. Bleary eyed now, his eyes came back to the photograph of the eviction, making a connection between past and present. The godless scoundrel of a bailiff, proudly standing after his evil deed and looking straight ahead, could just as well have been The Pagan at his gate every Sunday, mocking those who worshipped their God.

The day was done, the glass was empty, the drink finished but not his determination to speak as never before on Sunday. It would avenge the many wrongs that those of the calibre of the bailiff and latterly the half breed next door visited on the poor and innocent. He would not be found wanting and he prayed with every fibre of his being for the strength he needed before drifting off to sleep.

*

Standing for a moment in the blazing sun he heard Nurse Prout holding forth.

"We'll be dead from drought, I'm telling ye. Sure, wasn't there a man in Ballyhooly last week who had to shave himself with lemonade."

A burst of laughter greeted her remark, and he knew by the sound where it came from even before he went in. Definitely from McGuire, the shopkeeper, and yes, it was his blotched face, red with the exertion, that greeted him. Also, there was Constable Snee, whose reaction to the nurse's story was a suspicious smile.

McGuire's expression changed immediately as the boy, cautiously eying Snee and the nurse, asked for "small loaf and a quarter of tea."

McGuire looked to Snee and the nurse before replying with a sneer.

"And who might that be for now? The Big House, I suppose?"

"No," the boy replied sensing something that made his stomach churn, "it's for Mr Golden."

"Well now your MR Golden, as you put it, will have no more from this shop. Did you hear what the priest said last Sunday?"

He looked at Snee who stood, sombre, shifting from one leg to the other while Nurse Prout, beak faced, waited to see what would happen. Not quite certain of what to do next, he looked back at McGuire.

"He doesn't believe me," McGuire bellowed, "he thinks I'm joking. Do you think I have to write it down for your MR Golden?"

His blotched face reddened even more, and he looked towards the front door where a few had gathered and then at the open door leading to the public house, where the faces of a few seasoned drinkers had appeared to witness the scene. It was easy to see whose side they were on.

"Well, me bucko, one thing you haven't learned from Master Slyne is how to listen. You better listen to me then because I'll tell you for the last time. Tell your MR Golden to scoot off somewhere else because he won't get anything from here, and with good reason, do you hear me?"

No one moved and a heavy, sinister silence hung in the air. Then the constable, with a look the boy could not fathom, walked to the door without a word. A path was cleared for him through the bunch of onlookers that had now swelled from the one or two there when he had last looked.

He looked towards the nurse in the vain hope that she might somehow change McGuire's mind while at the same time knowing clearly that was not going to happen. She snorted and said to McGuire, "I wonder what his poor mother would have thought of all this." Then turning to the boy, she added, "and she died bringing you into the world. Look at the way you're after turning out. Tell me your company, indeed."

He backed away from the counter, helpless in what he could not understand, except in its foreboding. Joe will go mad. He turned and left. No path was cleared for him, and he had to bustle his way through those at the door and into the glare of the sun. Bolting for the cottage, one or two of the the crowd jeered in his wake.

Joe stood with the teapot in mid-air.

"What's wrong?"

"No bread, Joe or anything else," he hoarsely replied, his throat dry.

"Why?"

"He wouldn't give me anything. Because it was for you."

"The bastards, the dirty rotten bastards. This is a new one, now it is."

His words were more in inevitable resignation than in anger. Lowering the teapot on to the table he looked in the direction from where the boy had come.

"Did he say anything else?"

"Just roared at me."

"Anyone else there?"

"Just the Constable and Nurse Prout but others were in the bar."

"Ha, the sheriff and the Bell Telegraph together. No wonder the brave McGuire shouted. Protected by one and certain the whole country would know it in half an hour. Nice timing alright."

On another day Joe's allusion to Nurse Prout as the Bell Telegraph would have them laughing. Not today.

"What will we do now? Maybe I can get the bread and tea in Creighton's."

"You needn't mind. You can be sure the other fellow's sermon may well have done the same for Creighton, if what your father says is anything to go by … but we'll see the next time we have a catch." Creighton, the butcher and grocer, whose shop was frequented more than Maguire's by Field's flock, was considered a better run business than

Maguire's, with his main income coming from the public house attached. Creighton always took the bulk of Joe's rabbit catch.

McGuire's face came back, and he burst into tears. Joe walked round the table to where a red floral towel hung on the back of a chair and threw it towards him. It reeked of sweat and soap. Drawing it across his face he soaked in its familiar pungency and waited for Joe to continue.

"Don't mind the whole bloody lot of them. We'll cycle to town. That's what we'll do. They won't refuse our few bob there."

With no tea to hand, Joe scooped two cups of water from an enamel bucket by the door. They drank the lukewarm, brackish water, emptying both cups in one motion. It did little to assuage their thirst.

"Ah, that heat beats all, doesn't it? Well, we'll give the town a go and then, when we catch a few tomorrow night, maybe we should give Creighton a try anyway and see how things lie there," said Joe. It was, the boy felt, said more in hope than any sense of it working out. Not sure about Creighton, though, either.

*

Field watched her elegantly stride down the dusty street. Those she passed deferentially nodded to her or gave her an odd word of formal greeting, the weather dominating the simplest of exchanges.

The uncomfortable sense of subservience towards her gave her a distinct feeling that she was getting something more than she deserved, something she hadn't earned. She recalled Edward's outline of their own position here, respected or envied by some and sternly begrudged by others. And very hard at times to distinguish who fell into any of those categories.

Since the evening at Lavinia Chapman's, her view of Field was somewhat compromised, portrayed as he was, possibly exaggeratedly, as a purveyor of gossipy knowledge, something she loathed in anyone but more so in a man of the cloth. And his allowing himself to be actively recruited by the priest was disturbing. She would say a few perfunctory words when she came to his gate and move on. Making a few weakly sounding remarks about the lack of rain, she pointed to his garden, now showing distinct signs of the constant daily heat and its effect on his grass and flowers. They looked across at Golden's cottage. While it too showed signs of the drought, it looked just as she had thought before, a doll's house from one of her children's stories.

Their musings were interrupted by shouts of jubilation. Let loose from school, not for the day but for the summer, the scholars tumbled out onto the roadway. Their jostling exultations ceased for a moment when they saw her and the rector, unexpected intruders in their new-found freedom. With shy civility they appraised her from head to toe. Field thought to himself how she must have looked in their eyes, stunning in appearance and dressed so elegantly, adding to her mystique.

The rag taggle bunch made their way towards the village street, every one of them giving Golden's fairy-tale cottage a wide berth. Soon they were converging on Maguire's shop, eager, if they were fortunate enough to spend a few pennies in celebration of school's end, and whatever lay ahead.

In the midst of it all, she had forgotten him. Excluded from the running, shouting mass that had preceded him he now emerged. There was no lightness in his step, no sense of longed for release in his gait. Without looking in either direction he turned to begin his journey home, alone and dreary, until he got to Woodlands' wall and seemed almost obscured by the welcome shade.

She quickly bade goodbye to Field. Hurrying forward, she soon caught up with him, with nothing to indicate that he heard her approach. Playfully, she tapped him on the shoulder, bending slightly to greet him. He jumped in fear, a few pieces of paper scattering from his bag onto the ground. She immediately regretted what she had done as confusion, mingled with relief, gave way to a shy smile when he realised who it was. She picked up the sheets of paper. Their eyes met again but now he was looking intently over her shoulder back towards the village.

She turned to see what had taken his interest. The children at Maguire's door stood watching. Field was still at his gate. For a moment, the scene was transfixed. Then the master emerged, loudly banging the school gate shut, not for the day but for the summer. Unaware of anything around him he strode, head down, to the priest's doorway. His arrival had broken the temporary lull. The chattering children moved away from Maguire's shop door and Field moved away from the gate. She watched the scene, frozen in time a moment before, now disintegrate. She turned back to the boy.

He had, however, gone on and again she hurried to catch up. He plodded on as she walked behind him, allowing them to still avail of the shade, a waning, faltering barrier as the sun beat down incessantly. He took an odd backward glance towards her and beyond her as if expecting something or someone to be following them.

Then they were at the gate lodge. Turning to go in he was stopped by the hand she placed on his shoulder. This time he didn't jump and stood dutifully.

"School is over and you're free for weeks. Isn't that wonderful?"

A concessionary smile encouraged her to go on and she leaned forward, slow and easy, to bring their faces directly opposite each other's.

"I think I know why you were so glum just now. It's because you didn't want them to see you with me. You think they'll jeer and make fun of you, isn't it? Boys are just like that, but it's no harm."

He fidgeted and shuffled in the dust, his troubled face making no attempt to hide what he was thinking. Then he blurted out.

"I have no friends. They all just hate me."

"No friends?" Come now, you must have some friends out of all those boys I saw just now?"

"It's all because of Joe, Mr Golden, you know. He is my only friend and it's all because of him and what they say about him. Even the priest and rector, last Sunday."

Tears appeared and he motioned with his eyes toward the village, not knowing what next to say. The confused picture of fractured innocence stood, pitifully, before her.

She felt outraged. Golden's behaviour was indeed giving the boy as a hostage to fortune. The evidence, bedraggled and numb, was standing there, dwarfed by the gates of Woodlands behind him and the festering tensions of the village facing him, unseen because of the turn in the road but torturing him, nevertheless.

She reached out and held him in the shade of the great wall. His childish, angular frame, resistant for an awkward moment, convulsed against her.

*

It had been a day of agitation and suppressed relief for him. Sneaking glances toward the clock. Egging the big hand forward.

"Mind yourselves now for the summer, do ye hear me?"

That was the signal, the master's grudging, dismissive warning.

He tried as usual to get to the door before as many of the others as he could. If necessary, the refuge of the chapel would be sought but he hoped that today, the last day of school, the others would be less interested in him than making the best of the beginning of the holidays. In their eagerness to escape the others hemmed him in.

A growl from the master halted him.

"You, wait."

In the streams of sunlight angling through the rising dust from the classroom floor he stood and waited, not knowing what to expect as the others half ran towards summer freedom.

"You better watch yourself for the summer, do you hear me?"

"Yes, Master."

Certain that something else was to come in explanation, he waited. The gold lettering on the master's pen glistened in the sunlight as he replaced the top and ceremoniously slipped it into his coat pocket as if it were a badge of honour. That done, he waved the boy in the general direction of the door without another word. A cold, deliberate dismissal.

It was this he couldn't forget when she touched him on the shoulder. His relief at seeing who it was had quickly given way to the sickening realisation that they were being watched from the village. At another time her presence would have been ecstasy but not then. She would not understand, and he left her where she stood, watching the village scene they had left behind. He shuffled on by the wall as she caught up with him and followed.

The mention of Joe at the gate. She understood. The first touch. Awkward but then his taut and frightened fame fell forward into her arms. Too soon it was over. But it had driven the master's cold and vaguely cautionary admonition out of his mind. The smell. Her arms closing around him. Her hair against his face. Past gone. Only now. No more school. The summer ahead. Everlasting.

The avenue's wide sweep took her away from him, though something told her he was still watching. She pondered his innocent, confessional outburst. His ongoing misery was directly related to Golden's friendship and the perception in the village around that. His blubbering admission brought her face to face with the intolerable burden placed on him by that friendship, with Golden oblivious to it. He was hardly so callous a man to ask that a child endure insult and isolation simply because it served his own exclusive pattern of protest. It was understandable that the child would try to fight his own battles and maintain his independence. But the weight was too great for him to bear, were he even an adult, submerged as he was by the odium of his peers, tacitly endorsed by teacher, priest and now by rector. In other words, a young child was at odds with the whole village, caught between Scylla and Charybdis. And it was to her alone he had opened his child's soul.

At the door she concluded that this state of affairs was an outrage. No child should be victimised simply because the adults around them chose to pursue a course of action for their own particular ends, no matter how noble or glorious in their own eyes. Something of the old rage and indignation that had her aligned with the suffragettes now welled up in her again. Could she stand by, smugly protected, and allow such a monstrous situation to fester and perpetuate itself with any number of serious outcomes? Maybe after all, Golden had some unholy interest in the child but the very thought, hideous in what it conjured up, chilled her, leaving a sweet, sickly taste in her mouth.

*

"I knew it, I knew it. I should never have asked you to go. Well, we really know where we stand now. I should never have asked to bring that catch and have you put through the same thing again with that so and so."

Joe's piercing words of self-criticism greeted the news from Creighton. It was evidence, if needed, that Field too had played his part in turning the whole place against him, seeing that Creighton was a regular at Sunday service.

The boy regularly took the rabbits to Creighton's long, low ceilinged shop that always reeked of blood. This constant intrusive smell, the boy always surmised, must have affected Creighton, a man of dour and moody disposition.

As he slung the rabbits onto the counter, he knew something was different, as Creighton emerged from the butchery to where the groceries were. The routine was simple. Creighton served others if they were present and then carefully counted out the coins for the rabbits. Then a piece of meat was slowly and meticulously wrapped.

Looking first at the rabbits and then at the boy, Creighton drew himself up to his full six feet, his head almost touching the low ceiling.

"Tell that blackguard he can keep what he's poached. We all know where they come from, don't we?"

His enormous fist came down on the counter, making the boy jump and lunge for the door, but the butcher's thunderous roar rooted him to the floor, half in and out of the shop. Creighton swept the rabbits off the counter and the tangled mass lay at the boy's feet.

"Now get out with that wretch's ill-gotten gains and don't darken this door again."

The finality of the butcher's words found a deep spot in his belly as he bent to retrieve the twisted knot of heads and legs. He wanted to get away from the rancid smelling shop. Outside the door, in relative safety he stood looking back into the darkness at the butcher's glowering face. He shouted.

"The Pagan, he'll get you and Maguire for this."

It came out before he knew it and he got a certain passing satisfaction from what he had said but didn't know why or where his threat had come from. And it was the first time he had ever referred to Joe as The Pagan.

Creighton made as if to come round the counter but stumbled. As the boy made his escape, he heard a string of threats from the shop. His escape was not that easy because he had the rabbits over his shoulder. Slowed down by this he had to run the gauntlet of those who stood at their doorways to see his burdened journey down the street to the cottage.

Joe knew the outcome immediately and quickly bundled child and rabbits in the door. He felt totally safe once the door closed. The luxury of the room's dry, embalming smell blotted out the blow just received. The scattered papers, books, ornaments, faded photographs seeped security and familiarity, caught as they were in the soothing sound of the ever-ticking clock and the heat of the day. Joe fumed in silence.

"God blast the whole lot of them. Get out the bicycle and we'll get rid of them in the town. 'Twill take a bit more than that carry on to get rid of me."

The emergence of man and boy from the cottage was perhaps expected as the doorways were still occupied, with few more having gathered at Maguire's doorway. The Pagan, deliberate in barely concealed rage, pedalled the bicycle along the street with the boy on the carrier holding the rabbits in a sack.

Shielded by Joe's frame he glanced nervously from side to side, wishing they were past Creighton's in case some madness might bring him lunging from the shop with a butcher's knife to finish off Joe and maybe himself. By the time they passed Maguire's the drinkers had swelled the numbers at the doorway.

Everything eerily silent in the heat as the bicycle left a trail of swirling dust behind it. He expected someone to shout something at Joe, but no one did. Maybe they were all afraid of him. That was until they reached Creighton's doorway and a shout from the darkness rent the stillness and brought all eyes to where the sound came of Creighton's salvo.

"Ha, ha, there's nothing for you in this village, me boyo. Your goose is cooked."

Flinching as Joe slowed, and it looked like he might get off the bicycle to reply to what had just been said. Just then, a few of Cremin's scrawny dogs, lured perhaps by the smell of the rabbits, made a lunge from an alleyway at the opposite side of the street. It took Joe's attention for a moment, and he growled in the dogs' direction. They slunk away as by then the bicycle was well past Creighton's and they were now at the barrack door.

Snee stood there, statuesque and not quite grim. Joe ignored him and as they turned away from the village towards the castle gate. Snee was smiling, he thought. What could it mean? Was he laughing at Joe and everything that had taken place? Settled down now. Towards the mill bridge at speed. Ten minutes to town.

Snee watched the bicycle and its passengers slip out of view, taking with them one of the few diversions in the drab routine that was his lot in this outpost that he barely tolerated.

From the streets of London to the village of Shandrum was the hell he had to endure for the foreseeable future. Had he withstood the attractions and temptations of the seamier side of London life, he might still be there. Consorting with some of the more disreputable individuals of both sexes meant his dismissal was a mere formality. A senior officer, Mackey, with whom he got on quite well, offered a lifeline, though he stressed the matter of his rule breaking was an open and shut case.

Somehow, through an ingenious number of procedures, which he never understood but willingly agreed to, on Mackey's advice, Snee found himself one of a select, notorious few, banished to the more remote fringes of Empire. Even in this he was lucky, as some less fortunate than he, found themselves in such far away outposts as Palestine or India, in the hope that they might learn a lesson and more easily conform to the standards of their calling. Shandrum had the honour of getting Constable Snee. How often had he thought that it was more of an outpost that any far-flung shore of Empire? Of necessity, the reasons for his posting were known only to Cleary, his sergeant. One or two remarks over the years left Snee in no doubt as to which of them had the upper hand, not just in rank but in knowledge.

Now, as he took a stroll down the village street, trying to avail of any sliver of shade, he was conscious of a change in atmosphere. Animosity towards The Pagan, always evident, had turned more ominously sinister. Kerley, Field and their cohorts had used the pulpit to strike a serious blow. Word had come to Cleary, passed on to Snee, that a boycott was to be one weapon used in the hope that it might send a message to Golden, the motorman and his son. But not only to them but to Woodlands, facilitators of The Pagan's extracurricular activities, denied to others. More pressing on Snee's mind was Cleary's vague suggestion that the boycott might just be the beginning, an opening shot in a campaign that yet might lead to other measures. He sought more information but didn't get it from the sergeant.

To Snee's mind, The Pagan was not the satanic monster portrayed by the clergy and some of their influential backers. His reason for this belief, not always the ideal for a man in his position, was a matter of instinct rather than fact. And instinct also told him that victory for either side might not come easily.

*

"Victoria, I wouldn't dream of it. Maybe the father, yes, but Golden, definitely not. In fact, I must tell you directly that contacting him, in any fashion, is out of the question and invites consequences of a serious nature, I have no doubt."

"But Edward, it's not the child's father that's the problem, I've explained. That poor innocent is going to continue suffering indefinitely unless someone, with nothing to gain, alerts Golden to the harm his association with the child is causing. I could suggest you take the lead in this, if necessary, and see him yourself."

"Please, Victoria, I haven't the slightest inclination or stomach to get involved in this situation. None whatever. If those who should know better allowed those with different attitudes to live their lives, such trivialities would not take on the enormous proportions things like this do. That's it as far as I'm concerned."

Ruffled and annoyed at Edward's disinterest in something of great concern to her, she was struck by his wanting nothing to do with Golden, despite his having the freedom to benefit from their property, denied to others and causing understandable bad feeling locally.

Were Golden not mentioned, Edward would have dismissed any reference to the boy as just another irritant beneath the consideration of someone in his position. Adamant that she not embroil herself in a local squabble, he prepared to deal with correspondence on his desk.

"Edward, this is not a trivial matter…"

Both just then noticed someone approaching on the avenue. Edward groaned when he saw it was Field.

"What does he want? Can he not let us know if we are available to him and set a time? One never gets a minute here."

His words were subtly chiding her, not Field who was a convenient distraction for Edward to make his point. She was now in no mood to accommodate him without some plan of action on the child's behalf. Both waited, stone faced, until the rector was ushered in.

Beads of perspiration dotted his forehead and he apologised for arriving unannounced. Courtesies were exchanged and Field turned to Victoria to announce it was Edward he had come to see. She crisply informed both that she would be in the orchard.

Sooner than expected Edward joined her, indignation etched in every feature.

"It's our friend again," he said, his tone somewhat more conciliatory despite his evident annoyance.

"Who?" she asked, not sure to whom he was referring.

"Golden."

"Oh, that's a coincidence, isn't it? Is something further wrong that brings the rector to our door?"

"To put it simply, it appears I am the only landowner who allows this gentleman to fish and hunt where others can't. It now appears your Mrs. Chapman found him and the boy wandering through her fields the other day. According to Field she was informed by Golden that if he can hunt and fish in Woodlands, surely he can walk through her fields."

"Served her right too."

"I know it serves her right, my dear, I'd have been tempted to say the same myself, but don't you see it's another stone turned against me. Lavinia, that crone, just like her, let Nurse Prout know and you know it's probably news in New York in an hour. As if it were not my business, and mine alone, who hunts on my land or for that matter does anything else on my land."

"Well, you can't blame them for that, for being the way they are. Isn't that what you've told me from the beginning?"

"I know, but Field and a few more like him know too that I can hardly appear to be disloyal to my fellow landowning class. But leave that for a moment. There is something else."

"Oh, what now?"

"Field informed me also that the shops in the village are

refusing Golden's custom. Boycotting is the word used for it around here, apparently."

"But that's utterly despicable, Edward. Can they do that?"

"Perhaps yes, perhaps no. They're doing it anyway."

"Can't you see why Field came just now. It's all part of a plan. If you forbid Golden to fish and hunt here, he will have nothing, though I daresay he is a resourceful character. But he will hardly survive if his every means of living is taken away from him."

He did not answer immediately, and she hoped he saw the dastardly web that was slowly, but effectively, woven to get at Golden.

"What are you going to do?"

His lips twitched in a mischievous sneer.

"I'll do what I have to do. Enough to keep that bag Chapman, our esteemed rector and his prompter parishioners satisfied."

"And what's your grand scheme? This is deadly serious."

"Well, if it is I am not going to make it any more serious. For your part, all you have to do is continue to enjoy this glorious summer and not worry about storms in teacups. That's all there is to this, my dear. Just think, this time next week I'll be in the middle of a case where a man killed his mistress to convince his wife he loved her. And here we are talking about rabbits being caught. There has to be a sense of proportion, don't you think?"

She was about to react to his patronising playing down of what she saw as a matter of grave importance when he put his hand up to stop her and calmly said, "Here's what I'm going to do."

*

Their foray to the town had not only given them heart but exhilarated them. It was as if the more time-consuming trip was an immediate answer to Maguire and Creighton. It proved so easy to walk into Rice's shop in the town square, ask for what you wanted and be served with civility and thanks for your custom. Joe was right, his money would not be refused there.

Even more cause for celebration was Joe's success with Kelly, one of the four butchers in the town. The boy waited, holding the bicycle and watched as Joe entered the shop and engaged Kelly in conversation. Whatever was said ended with Joe shaking Kelly's hand and returning with a broad smile of satisfaction.

"God never shuts one door, but he opens another. Our Mr Creighton won't be too happy when he realises that a town butcher knows on what side his bread is buttered." Pointing back through Kelly's door, Joe went on, "it will mean a longer journey with the rabbits, but we'll get over that. He'll even give a penny more for each one. What do you think of that?"

The boy's face lit up and lit up more when Joe said, "Come on over the bridge and we'll celebrate with a drink. We're dying with the thirst and we're not the only ones." Even though Joe would haggle for every last penny the boy always noticed that he never seemed short of money, even when the rabbits yielded little.

Soon they were standing outside Green's public house and Joe went in, returning with a bottle of porter for himself and a lemonade for the boy. In the broiling heat they sat against the long windowsill without speaking, satisfied that their expedition had been a successful one. The few possessions in the hempen sack hanging on the handlebars was evidence of that. He noticed that occasionally a suspicious or critical eye was cast at them by passers-by who obviously either knew Joe or knew him by reputation. After all, the village was only a few miles from the town.

"Time waits for no man," was Joe's signal that they should be on their way and soon the town was behind them. Joe struggled in the heat and as they approached the village at the mill bridge, he dismounted as usual, and they began the walk up the hill. Turning the corner at the castle gate, they both ambled leisurely towards the village. Just then, ahead of them, Snee came out of the barrack and took up his usual position.

Joe stopped for a moment to rest, the boy thought, but soon realised he was also considering something as he looked in the constable's direction.

"Let you take the bike and go ahead; I want to get the law's view on what's happening here with our custom not wanted by Creighton and Maguire. Just curious. You take care now and watch the bag doesn't make you wobble. I'll be after you in a few minutes."

At the barrack door they parted. He mounted the bicycle with some difficulty, leaving Joe and Snee at the door. He wondered what the outcome would be but wasn't hopeful. He trundled forward, awkwardly moving his weight from pedal to pedal and swaying from side to side. Maguire was at the shop door and shouted to someone inside.

Sensing that all was not well, he pushed forward as fast as he could, passing Creighton's and nearing Maguire's. If he managed to get past that he was safe.

But Maguire's shout brought the priest's gaunt figure running from the shop door. They straddled the street. Not without difficulty, they brought the lumbering bicycle and its passenger to a halt. A juggling struggle ensued as he was thrown forward between the two men and landed in a heap on the dusty street. His first thought was for Joe's few messages in the bag and half dazed, he scuttled to retrieve them, scrambling toward where the bag lay.

The priest's scrawny hands dragged him to his feet as he retrieved the bag. Maguire's towering frame stood by. Figures appeared from inside the shop and out of doorways, attracted by the commotion.

Catching him by his threadbare shirt the priest bellowed, "Where were you, boy?"

"In…in…the to…town he stammered," his lips dry and quivering.

"For what?"

"Mess…messages, Father."

"Who are they for? C'mon now, don't waste my time."

He squirmed and turned away before answering.

"J…Jo…Mr Golden," his voice barely audible above the gathering crowd.

"Mr Golden, indeed. Mr. Is that right now, MR Golden." Laughing derisively at his answer, he looked around to draw others in the crowd into the circle of contempt. He beckoned to Maguire. The shopkeeper, unsure of what was being asked of him, saw the priest nod towards the shop door through the crowd. It was the priest's walking stick and Maguire made a move to get it for him. Before he had a chance one of the women snatched it and brought it to the priest, half bowing as she backed away.

He grimaced, fearing a beating in front of the whole village. The priest brought the round handle of the stick under his chin, jerking his head upwards, forcing him to stand on his toes.

"Weren't you and your father told in the house of God to keep away from that devil of a man because he's doing the devil's work?"

The stick jutting into his dry, thirsty throat made it impossible to answer. Locked to attention all he could see was the church spire rising above the priest's shoulder. "If you don't keep away from that degenerate, you'll never darken the door of our church again. Do you hear that?"

Only one word he could not understand. He must remember to ask Joe. His legs were weakening, and the more pressure exerted by the priest the more difficult it was to hold on to the bag. It fell from his grasp onto the dusty street, lying in a miserable heap. He noticed a classmate snigger as he peered through a gap in the crowd of adults. "Holy Mary" Beglin, red-faced, eyes dancing, also came into sight. No need to wonder whose side he was on.

Turning his attention to the bag, the priest took the stick away from under the boy's chin and hooked the bag by the two straps, lifting it, as if a trophy, high into the air. He then let it fall with a grin, as if he had just won some hard-earned victory. The contents scattered at the boy's feet.

"Quick, Father, look!" shouted Maguire. So intent on the circus of cruelty playing out before them, no one noticed The Pagan arriving on the scene.

"Outa my way!" Joe shouted, his voice surging in rage.

No one dared hinder his progress as the crowd parted to let him through. Too interested in what lay on the ground, the priest heeded Maguire's warning too late. Joe, his face raging red in the glare of the summer sun, caught the priest by the shoulder, swinging him roughly away from the pedestal of power and attention he so unquestionably held in the middle of the crowd. On his way backwards the priest tripped on the bicycle and fell, sprawling awkwardly into the dust.

There was silence as Joe picked up the priest's stick, hesitated and then with a roar of rage threw it, twirling high into the cloudless sky, over the heads of the crowd. Shielding their eyes from the sun, they followed its path until it came to rest at the forge door. A horse, tethered outside, pawed the air in fright.

Maguire, urged on by Beglin and galvanised into action by the undignified heap that was the priest on the ground and the flight of the stick, stepped forward, fists clenched. The circled crowd moved back instinctively, waiting with curious apprehension for the fight that must now surely take place.

Deep throated whispers urged Maguire on. Joe moved towards where the boy stood and brought his arm around his shoulder, cradling him to his side. A murmur of disapproval from the crowd, its low hissing tone unmistakable, rippled in the direction of man and boy.

Joe looked Maguire in the eye. He had been rendered motionless for a moment by his adversary's protective gesture towards the boy. Silence. The priest looked, from where he lay, towards friend and foe.

"Don't do anything Jack," said Joe, his words uttered with a definite, almost easy familiarity. "You have done enough already."

Stung by the reference to the boycott, Maguire stepped back, and to redeem himself moved to help Beglin assist the priest to his feet. Taking his hat from a bystander, he turned to where Joe and the boy were salvaging the few items that had fallen out of the bag. A brown paper bag had split leaving a cone of sugar formed on the road.

As if he had all the time in the world Joe knelt on one knee and scooped up what he could of the sugar that was free of dust. But the priest was not finished. His words, unrehearsed, stunned even his most ardent followers so laced were they with ferocity.

"You have desecrated the temple of God by striking a priest. And you have fouled the mind of this rogue of a child … and I daresay … his body too. You are a running sore, and your iniquity and degradation will no longer…"

Joe moved towards the priest, eyes straight ahead, his gait slow, almost intimate. The onlookers, including Beglin and even Maguire, pulled back again, uncertain what The Pagan might do.

"Father, if I struck you as you say I did you'd still be on the street there and not giving me a sermon on what you know nothing about. As for the child, I've met a few of your lot in my time and all I'll say is maybe he's a lot safer with me than the likes of you."

A shuddered gasp of horror came from the crowd. The priest seemed incapable of movement, seething at what he had just heard, transfixed where he stood at such an unheard-of implication. He looked around him, his lips quivering, searching for what to say until he noticed someone standing a few yards away from the crowd.

"Constable."

Heads turned away from the scene that had so intently had their attention up to now and settled in the inscrutable face of Snee. The priest continued.

"The safety of this man, and make no mistake, the safety of this child cannot be guaranteed as long as individuals are allowed to act like savages in this village. A Christian people will not allow or tolerate what has been said and done to their priest in sight of the house of God. With the disgrace of what has happened here just now there is only so much people will take."

By accident or design the priest had managed to switch the crowd's attention on to itself. Nods and murmurs of assent greeted what had been directed at Snee, the law now called upon as a convenient ally.

He shook the dust from his clothes before adjusting his hat. Something was missing. On a parent's instruction a willing, barefooted boy ran to the forge and delicately picked up the stick from near where the horse stood. Dusted down, complete with hat and stick, the priest now more suitably arraigned, brought a semblance of normality to things. He turned again to the constable and awaited a response.

Attention, for a moment, now turned back to The Pagan who appeared to have little interest in what the law might have to say. He lifted the bicycle from the dust and tested it for any damage. Nothing seemed amiss and with the boy at his side, he pushed his way through the crowd and set out for the cottage, leaving behind him a scene of confusion and doubt. In disarray, the crowd's attention was divided between the departing man and boy, the priest and the policeman.

"I have heard and seen some of what happened here today - some and only some of what happened after my arrival. Any complaint you have, Father, can be made at the barrack. I am now on my rounds, but Sergeant Cleary is there and I'm sure he will deal with the matter as he should."

The caustic clarity of Snee's words were clear but confusing to those who stood around the priest. What did Snee mean? Some in the crowd looked towards Maguire who had emerged with very little credit in the eyes of those present.

"I hope, Constable, you have noted what our priest has had to put up with here today. That tramp gone down the road there is well named. The pagan savages outside in Africa would have more respect. He's touched, I'm telling you, and a danger to God and man. Touched."

"I have noted all, Mr Maguire. I have never been to Africa and don't know how the clergy are treated there so maybe now, I could have a box of matches."

Maguire saluted the priest and slouched towards the shop door. In the doorway he turned and in the crowd's hearing, said to Snee, "People won't stand for it, I'm telling you, they won't."

The priest, watched by the crowd, turned for home and saw the rector at his gate, taking in as much as he could at that distance. Hesitating at seeing his counterpart and with an about turn the priest headed up the street towards the barrack, those in the crowd touching their foreheads as he passed. Heads were shaking, opinions shared, some gesticulating to add weight to whatever they wanted to say. In their leaving they watched the lone retreating figure until he reached the barrack door.

Looking back down the street at the dispersing crowd and, as if between two minds as to what he would do, he paused for a moment and surveyed what he had come from, the street now all but deserted. A small girl wandered into the scene where he had been humiliated. She bent over, watching incredulously as a steady stream of ants arrived from nowhere to stake its claim to the remains of the sugar. In her fascination she watched the mesmerising creatures, crawling under the scorching sun, gain what they could from the day's events. She could hardly be aware it was the day that everything changed.

Shortly afterwards the priest emerged, head high against the sun's glare as the sergeant bade him farewell. Whatever had transpired in the barrack appeared to have restored his outward dignity and he strode purposefully down the street. A lean solitary dog, searching for shade, followed the angular strides of the priest as far as Maguire's front door. Maguire greeted the priest and quickly ushered him inside as the dog turned, sniffed the dry summer air and ambled back to where he had come from.

*

Edward's solution to Golden's trespassing was practical and his lawyer's mind considered it quite ingenuous. For the moment at least, it would keep Lavinia Chapman, the rector, the villagers and last but not least, his wife, happy. Before leaving for London, he had instructed Meade, the handyman, to make up a number of signs to read "Trespassers Prosecuted - Police Notified." Meade, an intelligent if excitable jack of all trades came back with a sample for Edward. The sign read "Trespassers Persecuted - Police Notified."

Edward looked at the sign, noticing the mistake and then looked at Meade, standing to attention, waiting for approval to go ahead and make the rest. The mistake and its implications as it read touched whatever peculiar semblance of humour Edward possessed and he smiled at Meade. About to point out the mistake he saw Meade smile too and then break into a laugh, delighted that he had caught his master out.

"Ah, sure sir, I thought that might make more sense to sort out The Pagan. Persecution rather than prosecution might work better on a fellow like that. I'll make up the rest as you instructed. I thought you'd notice I was only joking!"

"Get them up as soon as you can and let Mrs Sheldon know when they are in place. You'll need eight or ten and put most of them on the trees on the way into the village where they'll be seen. Now I had better be going or there will be persecution to face me."

Meade had by day's end erected ten signs around Woodlands and on his way home called to tell Victoria that the job was done. He alluded to the heat and added that it must have affected the whole village. When she inquired as to what he meant she hardly expected the outline of what had transpired outside Maguire's, or in Meade's words, the "murder" that had taken place. His graphic account concluded with his assertion that "Father Kerley had put The Pagan in his place and then went to the barrack to report him. And rightly so, I may say, that Pagan is a tramp. We should have nothing to do with him. He'll ruin that child."

When Meade was gone it occurred to her that, with Golden's custom being refused in the village shops, the signs around Woodlands might now be seen as another well-planned element of opposition to The Pagan.

This all brought back the boy's tear-stained face and shivering frame, as well as Edward's stricture not to get involved. She went back inside to her writing, but this evening had little heart for it. Always an invigorating and rewarding exercise, she found her efforts after an hour frustrating, and she put down the pen. What, she wondered, had happened in the village? Meade had barely mentioned the boy, concentrating as he had on the two main protagonists, priest and pagan.

The sound of the motor arriving back gave her an idea. As the motorman came from round the back of the house from where he had parked the motor for the night, she asked him in, with a promise she would not delay him. The glow of the evening sun rendered the grounds outside a panoply of beauty and peace that stretched to the river and further away to the hills. They both stood admiring it until she broke the silence.

His analysis of the problem was as simple as it was impressive. If, for a moment he feared in any way for his son's safety, he would lay down the law and forbid his child to have any contact with Golden, difficult as that might be to enforce. In as discreet a way as possible she suggested that maybe what was being said about Golden was true. Only too well was he aware of what was being said and he made reference to what was said by the two clergymen.

"Joe is like a second father to that child and the rumours are not true. If they were, I would be the first to teach him a lesson and one he would not forget. The final promise I made to that boy's mother the day she died was that I would keep our son safe. I will do that, and I don't need the clergy, the League or anyone else to do it for me."

Golden being referred to as Joe for the first time by anyone in her company added a new, more personal angle to her perception of someone she had only ever heard of as a problem. The more he spoke the more she recognised his strong and lively oneness with the man in whose company his son spent so much time. Glad of the chance to speak to a willing and genuinely concerned ear he elaborated on his own situation. His job in Woodlands and his relative prosperity were envied. He had no illusions about Golden's position in the village and in every word he spoke there was loyalty. That would not easily be weakened, she knew. "After all, Joe's mother while she was alive was the only mother my son knew for a few years as a baby. Now she might have been a bit strange, and who knows with good reason, but she was a good and kind woman, not that many around here would give her that."

Casually uttered, the words took her by surprise. The introduction of another into the close-knit trio of two adult men and a child was completely unexpected. It was as if some unknown and hidden area of great significance had been dredged up in a single sentence or two. He saw in her reaction the need to elaborate. There was a hesitation in his voice, an awkwardness at times, very different from his straightforward view expressed a few moments before. Touchingly, he spoke of the Pagan's mother. Shunned by the villagers, paralysed as they were by an implacable ignorance and dearth of forgiveness, she had raised her son until he too left. Afraid that he might for some reason decide he had said enough, her eyes pleaded for some explanation. It came immediately but with some unease which he could not conceal.

"She was not married, you know. Joe is a bastard son."

Again, the words introduced another new, revealing aspect. He moved quickly to tell her how, with her son gone, she had lived out her life as an alien, unaccepted even then when the cause of the villagers' spleen had vanished. The residue, and her fierce reaction to the priest calling at her door was a perceived blight on the normality that passed for village life. A reclusive, living example of a sin that could never be expurgated. When she died her son filled her shoes, albeit with a far more consistent, provocative resistance to priest and people.

He finished off by saying, rather pointedly, she felt, that "I learned a lot from her about things very few around here know about. But look, I've said enough."

Through the window they noticed the boy approaching. Obviously in search of his father who might normally be at home by now. This interruption meant the conversation was at an end and the motorman seemed relieved. He had begun to speak so readily about the problem that confronted himself, Joe and the child. More wary when talking of the past and the Pagan's mother, he had, she thought, almost logically stumbled into telling her of a tarnished past, that he might well have avoided were the conversation to begin again.

The boy made to go around the back where the motor was and where he assumed his father was. Surprised when she opened the door, he blushed, as if he had come upon some secret liaison. At least it was not the crestfallen face she had seen on the last day of school.

"Joe and the priest had a fight on the street and the messages were all over the place."

He told of what had taken place, seemingly forgetting what he had himself been subjected and concentrating on Joe, the priest and Maguire and what Joe had done with the priest's stick. His father listened to a story very different to Meade's version, given earlier to Victoria. She knew whose version was nearer the truth.

Looking towards where the motorman stood, and with a hint of mild collusion, she said, "can I take him for a few minutes, there is something I would like to show him?"

The motorman nodded and headed down the avenue while the boy, arms dangling by his side, waited.

"Come," she beckoned.

Across the tiled hallway under Old Sheldon's portrait he was led, expectant but unsure and apprehensive. Despite his father's position he had rarely been inside the house. Now he followed and there it was again, the perfume, catching him in a throaty swelter. Then through the library door to a world of books, everywhere, floor to ceiling and strewn with abandon on tables and shelves.

She sat him down, his sweaty bare legs sticking to the leathered chair that dwarfed him. Walking across the floor, she stooped and scanned the titles of books along the lower shelves. Nimbly, she picked out what she had been looking for and turning back to where he sat, caught his steadied look. She came from the side and placed a hand on his shoulder. Flinching in a naturally awkward response to this unexpected gesture, he settled to its light embrace for as long as it lasted.

She handed him the book. It was the picture on the cover rather than the title that took his eye. A boy, lazing in a hammock, lost in thought, gazed at a river flowing from distant, wooded hills. Above this scene of enchantment was the title, The Coral Island and the author's name, R.M. Ballantyne.

"Now let us see how well you are able to read."

She opened the book at random and again placed her hand on his shoulder as if to encourage him. Leaning forward attentively, he coughed in readiness at the task before him, recalling the many times Joe made him read from books and papers at the cottage. If only he could see all the books here. Hesitantly he began but improved as the random lines grasped his imagination and only stumbled at the odd difficult word.

But there was no pity in the breasts of those men. Forward they went in ruthless indifference, shouting as they went, while high above their voices rang the dying shrieks of the wretched creatures as one after another, the ponderous canoe passed over them, burst the eyeballs from their sockets and sent the lifeblood gushing from their mouths.

O reader, this is no fiction. I would not, for the sake of thrilling you with horror, invent so terrible a scene. It was witnessed. It is true, true as the accursed sin that has rendered the human heart capable of such diabolical enormities.

The last two words tested him, but he mastered them to his own satisfaction.

"You read excellently but I don't quite know whether this is a book you would like. You might be awake and scared at night after reading bloody scenes like that one."

He had never heard the word bloody used other than as a swear word and it took him by surprise to hear her say it. He would not let himself be deprived of the book.

"No, I'd love a story like that. And Joe can help me with the big words, he's very good at reading and has loads of books. Not as many as here though."

It was the mention of Golden that overshadowed even the appeal in the child's eyes. For him there was no Pagan, no demonic monster, just a man who would help him read an adventure story and enjoy it. Contemplating his upturned face, she thought of the forces ranged against its innocence about which he could only understand in some muddled, childish, simple way.

"I know you like Mr Golden very much, but you know too how lots of people in the village and even the rector and your own priest do not seem to like him. And just now you've told me about what happened today. Now they will hate him even more and then what will happen to you?"

He turned away, his gaze falling along the wall of books across the table from him.

"Don't know," he shrugged.

"Maybe you should stay away from him for a while and spend your time in the lodge at home."

At this he became suspiciously alert. She noticed but continued.

"Maybe after your holidays you can then go back to school and things might not be so awfully horrible for you. The priest would not be angry then with you and your father."

She went on, conscious that she was treading on dangerous ground, especially in view of the earlier conversation with his father. More than that, she felt guilty of what she was trying to engineer by playing on the boy's emotions and introducing more conflict and uncertainty into an already fraught situation.

He listened, as he would out of respect, but the rigid frame, dwarfed in the huge chair told her clearly what he must be feeling. She knew her suggestions were a gross betrayal, and he knew it only too well. It was too much, adding another layer onto what faced the innocent before her. After all, he would hardly shun The Pagan for her and certainly not for the priest. Their eyes came back to the book again and it broke the awkward silence.

"Very well then. I want you to have this book as it's a wonderful story for boys. I know because I read it a long time ago at home in England. It will not be too difficult for you especially if Mr Golden will help with all the strange and mysterious words."

Deadly anxious to be at one with her now that she had set things even again, he smiled enthusiastically. She pulled back the heavy chair and he got up, detaching himself with difficulty from the leather. Recognising his sheepish embarrassment, she moved ahead of him to the door. It opened with a long complaining creak.

"It's just the heat, every door is creaking in this house."

They were halfway across the hall towards the front door when she turned, completely taking him by surprise. He jumped backwards. Leaning forward she looked into his eyes.

"You are a very brave boy."

The words were said thoughtfully, almost reverently. She then flicked a finger under his chin, playfully affirming. Face to face, they were locked for a moment into what had just been said.

Am not brave at all. Can't say that though. Won't say it. Her neck. Near. Front door creaking open.

Twilight approaching greeted them, warm and muggy, the smell of flowers, the thrumming sound of insects all around. Holding the book to his chest, he thanked her and ran off down the avenue, glancing back once to wave. She waved back and watched him disappear.

*

He sat in Joe's cottage "parlour" engrossed in the book. Then, with no warning the door burst open and in strode the priest, a huge crucifix in his hand.

"Where is he?" He shouted.

Joe was suddenly there out of nowhere.

"You, out now and fast."

Holding the book, he jumped from the seat as commanded and ran to the door, the priest's menacing stare propelling him. He pulled the door shut and then went to the window to look in. Joe was kneeling, trembling before the priest who held the crucifix in the air and brought it crashing down repeatedly on his head. Joe did nothing, just knelt trembling on the ground as the blows seemed to make him shrink.

He rushed back to the door only to find it locked. He kicked and kicked at it, powerless and fearful, screaming to be let in.

Then Field was coming across the road and up the path, quickly catching him by the shoulders to pull him away from the door.

"It's alright, you're alright."

His father sat on the side of the bed, rocking him gently. Sweat trickled down his body and he gasped for air, grateful to know what he had dreamt was just a nightmare and not the reality he faced in its unfolding. The heat was such that he pushed his father away to get more air. He looked around him. On the floor lay the book, carefully laid there after he turned page after page before sleep overcame him.

"What was the dream about?" his father asked.

Living again each moment, he told it in detail. Joe would never tremble before anyone. Hadn't he stood alone on the village street and braved the priest, Maguire and the rest of the crowd?

His father listened, smiling at the absurdity of what he was being told. His reaction soothed the boy's fevered brain and by the time he had finished they were both smiling.

"Will you tell Joe?"

"Of course, I will. Can I get a drink of water now?"

"I'll get it for you, and you can go back to sleep."

Sleep came but only after what he had dreamt played over and over in his mind.

*

She had risen at seven, the morning sun blazing across the room, heralding another scorching day. After a light breakfast she set to with her writing and by ten was satisfied that she had made far greater strides than in the previous days.

Her writing desk overlooked the front lawn and as she got up to get a drink she looked out on a splendid scene. About to turn away from the window, her attention was drawn to the corner of the avenue where a figure on a bicycle heaved and panted in the morning sun. She waited until Constable Snee had reached the front door and then went downstairs. One of the servants had answered the door and soon Victoria stood before the policeman. Sweating profusely, he removed his helmet. He saw the quizzical look on her face.

"Mrs. Sheldon, a rather minor matter brings me. I hope you can afford me a few minutes."

"Certainly, Constable, come in. I'll get you something to drink. It's incredibly hot again today."

"Thank you kindly. Yes, this weather has us all hot and bothered and the papers say they are dying of drought on the continent. And, of course, you have heard about our two unfortunates found dead way out beyond the mountain. No other reason for them dying but the drought. Old age didn't help, of course."

Edward had told her of the two elderly people found in their cabins.

"Our own Nurse Prout - you may not know her - tells us that men are shaving themselves with lemonade in Ballyhooly. Don't take that as gospel though, the same Nurse Prout is what one might call in my line of work, not the most reliable of witnesses." He smirked rather than smiled, giving little away.

"No, I have not made her acquaintance. I'm sure when they are shaving with whiskey she'll have a field day."

Victoria, embarrassed by her silly attempt at humour, led him to the drawing room and a seat, which he more than gladly accepted. The ice had been broken and she waited, intrigued at what 'minor matter' had brought him.

He took out a small jotter and leafed through a few pages and was about to begin when a servant arrived with a jug of ginger beer and two glasses. She poured and they both drank, she delicately, the constable with a long gulping sound, looking across the rim of the glass as if inspecting her. Part of his job, a learned routine, she supposed. He finished the last drop and rather delicately this time, smacked his lips in appreciation.

"A life saver, that," he commented as she refilled his glass.

She thought of the many policemen she had faced on the odd suffragette demonstration, in which, on occasion, she had been coaxed into taking part. Never feeling intimidated, even by those at the highest rank in the force, she rather felt they would much prefer running after common criminals rather than facing a brigade of well off, educated women, fired with the zeal for reform in favour of all women, as they invariably put it. But that was all very far away now, in the morning quiet of Woodlands and Constable Snee's presence.

He began, shifting slightly in the chair.

"I am aware that your husband is away, but I have been instructed by my superior, Sergeant Cleary, to bring a matter of perhaps minor importance, as I've said already, to your attention. It concerns a local man, Mr Golden."

He paused, quite deliberately, she felt, to gauge her reaction. She reddened slightly. It was involuntary and she was annoyed with herself in allowing it as it surely did not go unnoticed by the man opposite her. But she maintained her composure.

"And what is the problem, Constable?"

"A complaint has been received from a Mr Dwyer, another local man, about which you may not be aware. This gentleman was formally cautioned by me on foot of a complaint by your husband. The grievance was," here he consulted the jotter, "yes, that Mr Dwyer was caught 'trespassing on private property.' In fact, he was found fishing. Now, and this my reason for my disturbing you this morning, the same Mr Dwyer has submitted a list of dates and times that Mr Golden has been observed not only fishing but returning with catches of rabbits from Woodlands. In other words, doing the very same thing as said Dwyer, but as my Sergeant was told," here he again consulted the jotter, " 'getting away scot - free and laughing at the rest of us.' "

The constable's voice had lowered to give his final words a touch of feigned gravitas. There was, she knew, a very simple answer that would quickly have him on his way without perhaps any more ginger beer. This was a matter for Edward who would be back at some point, and she should not have been imposed on about something that was her husband's business. But no, that would be as undignified as it would be of little value. She would, hopefully, get some elaboration and at least satisfy her curiosity and learn a little more. Better play the innocent. "If this is, as you said, a matter of minor importance, why could it not wait until my husband arrives back?"

"May I?" He beckoned towards the pitcher, and she leaned over to pour but he reached the drink before her and offered to fill her glass. She declined and he patiently filled his own, raised it and noisily swallowed. He looked into the empty glass for a moment and then replaced it on the tray.

"Mrs. Sheldon, you are absolutely right. The reason I am here is because my superior, the sergeant, wishes it to be brought to the attention of, as he put it, 'the attention of Woodlands.'" "As he said to me," and here he knew he was contradicting what he had earlier said about his knowing that Edward was not at home, "we are not to know when or when not Mr Sheldon is at home. Of course, I can always make a point of returning when he is here, but today I am simply carrying out an instruction, ours not to reason why and all that, as you will appreciate."

"You noticed the signs on your way here, no doubt. I think we can reasonably assume they should take care of this "minor matter" as you call it."

The point was not lost on him, she could see, but he kept his formal composure and reached for his helmet, pushed the chair back in place and faced her.

Not an unattractive man, she thought, yet strangely at his age, maybe in his early 40s, not married, she had heard.

"Very well, Mrs Sheldon. Indeed the signs may be enough to satisfy Mr Dwyer and others. Whether they have the desired effect or not, well, we'll just have to wait and see."

"And do you think they will have the desired effect, Constable?"

He pushed the two glasses together on the tray, as if she might have somehow trapped him, and looked across at her, breaking into a smile, genuine she thought, not forced. "If I could answer that question Mrs. Sheldon, I would not be just a lowly policeman in a little village like this. I'd be running the force."

She smiled back and she felt there was a connection of sorts, uncertain though she was as to what precisely that might be. But it brought another question from her.

"And Mr Dwyer's friends?"

The question was pointed, and they both knew it.

"Perhaps I should not have mentioned them at all. Let us hope matters will sort themselves out. And yes, the signs on the way in here and around the rest of Woodlands may have the desired effect."

She knew he didn't believe his own words but what else could he have said? He looked slightly more defensive after saying what he had then than at any point in the conversation. He sighed and she almost felt regretful for having asked the question. But then again why not?

"Many thanks for your time, Mrs. Sheldon, and for the drinks. I would have preferred to have met you in more auspicious circumstances. But you or I have no control over things like that, do we? I hope these matters which others see here as most important do not intrude on your first few months here in Woodlands. But I won't delay you any further. And remember, if there is anything that I can be of assistance with, do call at the barrack or send for me."

The night before in the twilight she had watched the child skip down the avenue, a picture of innocence; and this morning she watches the constable, his duty done, his instruction obeyed, cycle off assuredly in the sunlight.

Now alone, she had plenty of time to dwell on where things now stood or didn't. This latest move was engineered, she was certain, to further isolate Golden. As for the signs, that would be seen as Woodlands' contribution to the cause. Golden could hardly see it any other way. How was he to know that the signs were simply Edward's tame, if outwardly significant, response to what he saw as a local squabble and an irritation. From what Edward had said he had no intention of preventing Golden from what he had always done, with a blind eye turned. And yet Edward had said it might have been two years since he had suggested that Golden be discreet. Look at all that had happened since, much of which she had probably never heard of and if recent events were anything to go by, then the future seemed ominously unpredictable.

Edward's stricture about not meddling came back to her. The hypocrisy of it all infuriated her and she wondered again if somehow Golden should be told, for his own sake as well as the boy's. But how? What? Tell him to take more care when he hunted and fished? Silly that, the whole village had an eye on him now. It wouldn't work. He'd take it probably as a welcome new challenge.

She was in turmoil, thinking again of the boy, really the most important element in all of this hatred and subterfuge. Surely, he must be protected as Golden became more and more targeted. It was fortunate that school was out as no one knows what might have befallen him, were his classmates to be further caught up in some kind of revenge, as a result of what their so-called betters had articulated about the perceived problem in their midst, never mind the priest's humiliation on the street.

If the danger was as real as she felt for the child, she could hardly stand aside and see him dragged into a whirlpool of adult prejudices and their possible consequences. Lending him books and telling him he was brave would do very little to counteract the forces that inexorably seemed to be gathering momentum. And Edward's signs, however ostentatious, would simply add to those forces. What could be done? In many ways Golden could and must take care of himself but not at the expense of an innocent child. A phrase of Harold's, her brother, came to mind. 'A man, if he's a man, must fight his own corner.' She went back to the drawing room. The masculine, sweaty smell still lingered. And so did she, before rousing herself and purposefully getting back to her writing. But it bested her, every attempt to capitalise on her earlier hours' work seemed to fail. She put down the pen.

*

Crumpled sheets of paper thrown away in frustration attested to her failure. It must be something very important, he thought, as he sat and watched her with pen poised for another attempt. Her head, bent to the task, brought her features into sharp relief. The sunlight glanced off her burnished hair. It all seemed so long ago now, the first day he had met her. Unknown to either of them was the stark reality that both were faltering on the fringes of a darkly crowded future.

Always thinking of her. Day and night. No one to stop him. His thoughts only. Drifting in every direction. And no one knew. Her tongue on the envelope before closing it.

"You will be very helpful and take this, carefully, with no one to know, to Mr Golden."

Joe? Why write to Joe?

She rose to give him the envelope and as she moved away from the chair, he noticed her previous failed attempts lying crumpled near the fireplace. Still holding the envelope, she bent to pick them up. He moved to help her but too late. As she stood up, she misjudged the nearness of the mantlepiece overhead. Her head hit the streaked marble with a thud, and she cried out, stunned for a moment. Instinctively he ushered her towards the chair.

"Is it bleeding?" she whimpered, leaning over for him to see, parting her luxurious hair at a point where she suspected the bleeding might be. From where he stood, he could see her bared shoulders but there was no blood on the crown of her head except a swelling that seemed to slowly form.

"It's not bleeding but it will probably be black and blue. Isn't that what happens?"

He stammered, desperately wanting to comfort her but not knowing how. The envelope was still in her hand, wrinkled and sad looking. Straightening up, she threw her head backwards with a grimace to settle her hair, wiped her eyes and settled herself before attending to the letter again.

"This is proving more difficult than I thought, for some reason," as she placed the envelope on the table and smoothed it. Her words were said with a kind of resignation, yet they helped restore a level of normality, for which he was grateful. The cause of the accident still lay at the fireplace, and he dutifully picked up the crumpled pages and brought them to the desk. She was about to give him the envelope when she had second thoughts. Peeling back the flap she removed the page and looked over what she had written, making sure he could not see. She set about rewriting it and he waited to see her tongue slide across the envelope flap again. She can't know. Couldn't know. What I feel. No one could. My secret. But something in the way she looked now. Maybe she knows. No, she couldn't.

He took the letter, blurting out, "I'll take it the backway, no one will see me."

"Yes, no one to know is important. In fact, what you are doing for me now is our secret, remember. And ours alone."

She again brought her hand to where she had hit her head. "Now you go carefully and don't fall. Black and blue for one of us is enough."

*

The cottage was empty. He assumed Joe was either putting down snares without him or gone fishing. The house was like an oven in the late afternoon sun. Still holding the envelope, he helped himself to a mug of water from the bucket in the kitchen before walking through to the parlour.

In the little hallway he noticed another letter pushed under the front door. Even at a distance he could recognise the word PAGAN, crudely capitalised. He lifted it deftly and brought it to the parlour table and set both letters side by side. One bore the elegant flourish Mr J. Golden, Esq., the other a dark and threatening scrawl. Acutely curious, and tempted to open the second envelope, he desisted and waited for Joe.

He searched the papers on the table for something to read. The words DID YOU KNOW caught his eye. He loved articles like this, and he moved the envelopes slightly aside and leaned over the page to read.

Did you know a fly will crawl to the top of a windowpane, fly back to the bottom and then crawl back up again? The order is seldom reversed. It is on record that a fly crawled up a windowpane 32 times returning each time to the same place.

This somewhat useless piece of information took his full and undivided attention. Then the faintest smell rose from the table. It came from the envelope he had brought from Woodlands and swiftly swept the crawling fly from his mind. He brought the envelope to his nose, closing his eyes and picturing again her tongue moving along the very paper he had in his hand. The backdoor latch brought him back to reality and the mystery of the crawling fly but without the slightest interest.

"These are for you," he said to Joe trying to appear casual. "One is from Mrs. Sheldon and the other, well, 'twas here when I came in."

Joe's curiosity was immediately evident even though he too tried to appear casual about both letters.

"Could be from the good old Kaiser himself or maybe the new King."

He held the letters, one in each hand, deciding which to open first. He picked the Woodlands' one. That didn't take long to read. As he had watched her write it, he watched Joe reading it. Then he opened the other one and his expression hardly changed. As often, when situations out of the ordinary arose, he began with a line and waited for the boy to finish it-

"If you can meet with triumph and disaster…"

Even before he added the next line, the boy realised how well it fitted the situation that Joe now found himself in and continued-

"And treat those two impostors just the same…"

"And how I wish I could. What do you think of the brave man that composed this piece of literature?"

Joe handed him the cheap school copybook sheet with its message smudged and hardly discernible. GOLD IS DEVIL SATAN WILL BURN SOON.

Looking to Joe, who had a stoic smile on his face he asked, "Who sent it I wonder?"

"Ah, it could be anyone of them. But whoever it was will have to think again, the cowardly bastard."

The boy now looked towards the other letter.

"The Lady of the Manor wants to see me about something. She didn't say what. You never know, I could end up with a fine job like your father yet. Now wouldn't they all like that?"

His casual couched dismissal of the message did not mask the expectation on his face. The boy was immediately jealous. The letter from Woodlands had taken the provocative sting out of the other's sinister message.

"When are you going to go?" he piped up, concealing the surge of jealousy that had just shot through him. "She might let you see the library, there's millions of books there, all over the place."

"Well, you probably want to stay and read your precious book, so I'll go to town and get a few things. There's nothing in the house and we have the rabbits tonight. I don't know when I'll go. Anyway, I can't be at everyone's beck and call now, can I. An important man like me that some here want to have sent to hell and someone else wants to have for tea and biscuits."

He drew himself up to his full height and stretched. He was about to tear up the letters but stopped. He turned to the nearest book at hand, a large bible out of which ribbons of every colour fell, and randomly placed the two letters between the pages.

"Oh, I want to ask you something out of my book."

He leafed through the pages and found the passage with the words *diabolical enormities* and handed the book to Joe.

"What does that mean?"

Joe read the sentence with the words to himself, moving his lips.

"Something like evil deeds. Now get the bicycle out."

He wheeled the bicycle from the shed round to the front gate and quickly returned to the corner of the cottage, eager not to draw attention to himself. Joe, lazily glancing to his right and left, as if he hadn't a care in the world, mounted the bicycle.

With his back towards Woodlands, he haughtily set off, in no particular hurry, through the village that didn't want him. The heat was almost unbearable.

With the house to himself he returned with anticipation where the bible was and found the letters. He read her simple message over and over again. Had Joe noticed the smell of perfume? Footsteps outside on the dusty street. He returned the letters to the bible, easing it shut. From a vantage point inside the window, he saw the priest passing by, having come from the chapel, perhaps. He had often watched the priest come and go from the same spot, knowing he would never be noticed. Every time he passed the cottage he never gave it any recognition. It might not have existed. Today, however, perhaps certain he was not being observed, he gave a momentary look into Joe's garden, a mass of flowers and plants, with what the boy determined to be a sneer of jealousy.

Diabolical enormities. Evil deeds, He was back to the book again. Only then did another word resurrect itself from the struggle on the dusty street of a few days ago. He took down a dogeared dictionary, heavy with use and age. It took him a while to find the word, uncertain about the exact spelling. Then there it was. Degenerate.

What was meant to explain puzzled him more. How, if what the priest said was true could Joe, in any way, be what he now read- *an immoral or corrupt person* or *falling to a lower moral, mental or physical level?* He looked up *corrupt* and then *immoral.* He recalled what Joe had said that so stunned the crowd, incensed the priest and had Maguire approaching Joe with his fists raised, ready for a fight. He wasn't long about taking them down.

*

In sullen, melancholy mood he sat, contemplating the empty fireplace not used for weeks except to boil the kettle or cook a simple meal. His head pounded as he relived the humiliation heaped on him by The Pagan on the village street. It cut him to the quick and more so because of the rapturous attention that had greeted his sermon and left him satisfied as never before.

But that moment of glory, that advantage, so easily won, was lost now and lost in a most ignominious fashion. The Pagan's sinister jibe about the child and his safety had stung at him again and again, unearthing a groundswell of anger that he had seldom felt, even in the days in his former parish when he had so hated those who had everything and who he had tried so valiantly to bring down. The silence that hung in the air at The Pagan's words, brought about not by himself but the vile instigator, he would never forget. Only a satanically inspired reprobate would utter such words in public, an obscenity to sully the reputation not only of himself, the priest, but the whole of God's holy church by extension. And yet he had walked away with his bicycle and the youngster by his side, like the king of the castle.

He looked at his watch, then the clock on the mantelpiece and then at the faded eviction picture he had talked to Field about. The bailiff's look of triumph was etched indelibly. A look of triumph after putting a family out on the road. Brave man indeed.

Back to brooding at the empty fireplace. One sliver of consolation was how he had persuaded Cleary, the sergeant, to take some action. Not much persuasion was needed. Cleary had called Snee in and in front of the priest told him to call out to the Sheldons about Dwyer's complaint. Snee had argued but Cleary pulled rank. No love lost there between the two of them and good to know whose side Cleary was on. The word would get round that one of the things to emerge from his visit to the barrack after the street scene was the sergeant instructing his subordinate. Without much persuasion and very quickly, the supine sergeant accepted his version of events, agreeing that what had transpired on the street was a disgrace but not unexpected from a blackguard like The Pagan. After that it was all "yes Father," "no Father." At least the law would be dispatched to Woodlands even if it was on foot of dredging up Dwyer's old complaint.

Maguire, he had to admit, was proving to be his most

efficient ally, first by instigating the boycott and leading it and then taking a stance against The Pagan by at least facing up to him on the street. A token gesture as it transpired but at least an effort at support. True to his affiliation with the League, Maguire persisted that Woodlands, inextricably linked with The Pagan through his association with the motorman and more especially the child. must be dragged into this. Cleary, with similar views, needed little persuasion.

Maguire and his cronies were aggrieved when the rumour about Sheldon getting married became a reality and more so when his wife arrived in Woodlands. Derisive remarks were traded about the marriage in the public house. "Who'd marry a man that can't smile?" led to "well, if he's back and forth to London as he always was, that will slow up the children arriving." "It might be the other way round, you'd never know, he might be faster on the job." A remark that was greeted with sniggers from the bystanders.

The spectre of children in Woodlands nagged at Maguire who always touted the notion that Sheldon would never marry and if he did, he'd sell up and move away. Now the opposite had happened, and Maguire was not a happy man seeing his prediction had come to nought. All he had to hang on to was Nurse Prout's crude attempt at humour in the shop one day when she wondered aloud "if he'd even know what to do with a woman." The remark was thrown out to chuckles of amusement with the riposte, "well, he's no son of his father so," this to even greater howls of laughter.

He eyed the clock again and his spirits rose slightly at the thought of food. Something brought Field to mind again and buoyed him even more, the thought that he had enlisted him in the fight against The Pagan was a particularly satisfying feeling. He had no link with Field, apart from their calling, meeting occasionally with a casual greeting. He despised him, as he did his dwindling congregation. Beglin had said once to him, when Field's name came up in conversation, "do you know father, all his kind will be gone soon," followed up by an allusion to no prospect of children in Woodlands.

He ate his meagre supper, the eye of the enemy again in his sights. Had The Pagan not arrived on the scene, with the inept Snee following, he would have made an example of the child for all to see. Blasphemous and sacrilegious, The Pagan's words and actions brought a new urgency to everything. The story of the incident had spread of course, and as he finished his meal it rested well with him that he had heard it back with various embellishments as to how evil in their midst had sullied the good name of their priest. No mention of course about what the innocent child had been subjected to, that was conveniently forgotten. Rather was it the case that not a few took a strong and strident attitude to what their priest had been subjected to, and that resentment could be built on. Sooner for that to happen rather than later.

A cup of tea finished his meal. Then a whiskey, his office and a wait for the company that should arrive after darkness.

*

He had kept her waiting. Two full days. One of the servants answered the door as another blistering day came to a close.

Taller, she thought, than her memory of the night of the accident. Stronger too, though his hands were gaunt, sinewy, contrasting with his powerfully simple face. The eyes that had so engaged her that night had lost nothing. His subtle informality was very different from that of the constable's not quite straightlaced pose. Very different from Edward too. Seldom had she seen someone so at ease in what must be for him a rather formal setting. She was about to ask him a silly question as to whether he had ever been to the house before, but he spoke first, without any formality and no apology for his arrival so late in the evening.

"Well, I'm here."

"Yes, you must be wondering why. By the way, Patricia let you in. You can depend on her discretion."

His gaze was disconcertingly direct; in her experience, most men found it practically impossible to maintain contact eye to eye and generally shifted their gaze to accommodate themselves. The exception proved the rule and that exception, up to now, had been Nathan. Leaning back in the chair her visitor waited for her to continue. The fading light played fitfully on his side face, confirming her earlier observations.

"I must be truthful. You may have wondered at any number of reasons I might have for asking you here. Some of those reasons you may have considered trivial, but you will eventually be the judge of that. I think it is often better to err on what one considers to be the side of caution and be wrong in so doing, rather than do nothing at all. Doing nothing very often creates more problems."

He gave her no indication that he had an opinion either way but persisted with his slow, steady gaze, listening carefully to every word she spoke. She continued.

"You are aware I am sure that there are local objections, to put it mildly, to the freedom you enjoy here on the grounds. Hunting and fishing. Legally of course you are trespassing."

She thought it sounded harsh to put things as bluntly as that when in fact all her preparation, in terms of what she would say to him, was to introduce the subject of the boy, however sensitive that might be. He listened, imperturbable.

"Some of our friends - landowners - are also upset that you presume on the very same freedom where their property is concerned. My husband has been approached about the matter, but due to his commitments in London, has very little time to do anything about it."

At this, he smiled for the first time, a slow, disarming glint of mischief in his eyes. She tried to ignore this, difficult though it was, and get to the point about the boy.

"You have, I am certain, noticed the signs with the police warning added. They are there because we had, I had rather, a visit from the constable on the basis of a complaint by a local man. As I understand it, this man was cautioned by the police some time ago after my husband had found him trespassing on the grounds here. In a roundabout way, what I'm saying is that you must know that your movements are being observed and noted. That applies very much to your fishing and rabbit catching here and occasionally, from what I hear, elsewhere as well."

She felt she had rather absurdly laboured the point which she might have come to immediately and with more effect. Nothing of course in what she said was news to him and his sultry smile and casual arrogance made her feel distinctly uneasy. She edged closer to the table, sitting sideways to it, glad of its support.

Why, she thought, did I ever send that stupid note that had him arriving in his own good time and almost acting like he owns the place? Edward's warning came back to her, but it was much, much too late for that advice to carry now. Anyway, the sobbing, tear-faced image of the child trumped any advice. Whatever way she felt she would come to the point, no matter how painstakingly, and say what she wanted to say.

"What I'm trying to say is …"

He barely motioned with his right hand. It stopped her. He stretched out his legs, crossing them at the ankles. His well-worn, dust covered boots were close to her own shoes, almost touching in fact. She might have flinched from this display of languid familiarity, and it occurred to her that she might well be the visitor and this his very own house, so easily did he comport himself. Sinking more comfortably into the chair, his head now resting against the dark leather, he looked directly at her and spoke, his tone deliberate and even.

"What you are really trying to say and why you have asked me here is that you, your husband and indeed everyone else would be much happier if I kept out of Woodlands and for that matter, a couple of other places too."

Surprised and heartened that his assumption was wrong, she immediately rushed to petulantly contradict him.

"No, that is not the case at all. Whatever about others, my husband and I do not want you out of Woodlands. That's his wish and I, a complete stranger here really, have no desire to disagree with him. You may continue as before. All we ask is … you just might be more careful. We are in a rather awkward position as my husband takes little relish in being taken to task on a matter that is his business and his alone. But we do have to live here."

Her words, assertively delivered, trailed off into silence.

"Your husband is right. His business is his alone. That's how it should be, but this is Ireland and this place here is Shandrum. Here, your husband's business, mine and yours too is everyone else's business as well. We're all tangled in the same web. And what a web it is."

She nodded, not really knowing why. His view of things was spoken with a reasonableness and conviction that hardly brooked contradiction. He had included herself as 'tangled in the same web' as he called it and if he did, it gave her an opening, that increasingly seemed a distant prospect, to broach the subject about which she had agonised over and eventually written the note.

"Well then, if we are all involved at some level, as you say, in what goes on around here, perhaps you should know the main reason I asked you here. Let's be clear, the trespassing is important in its own way, and you'll have to be careful. However, there is something else, something in my opinion anyway, of far more importance and about which only you can do something."

She noticed the slightest change in his demeanour, a curiosity, and she wondered if he had some inkling of what she was about to say.

"It's about the boy … the boy and you."

At least it was said now, out in the open. But how to continue. For once he came to her assistance and there was something enticingly familiar in his voice.

"Go on. You won't be telling me anything I haven't heard before."

She searched for the words, they came and flowed.

"That child adores you, I know it. It's all too much for him, overwhelming. Do you know he is being taunted, jeered at and bullied in school? He has told me this, cried to me that his life is a misery because of his association with you, something of course he does not want to give up. You know what the clergy have said about you and him; but it's not them I'm worried about, it's him. Soon he will not want to go to school, and the older he gets the more he will realise the reality of what's being said. He may already be about to stumble on it at his age, in some disturbing, misunderstood way. And that may well make things worse for him."

He listened to her every word with the same detached indifference as he had earlier displayed. At least now she knew why. She was telling him nothing new but somewhere perhaps she was acquainting him with an aspect that he was not familiar with; even the way the boy was being treated at school might well be news to him. That would be something at least. As to the even more serious implications, the jolting thought came to her that maybe the clergy were right. Maybe this was a foul monster lacking any sense of morality that sat so at ease before her? She drew back into herself and as if knowing what she was thinking, he moved towards the table, not that he needed to be more at ease, she felt, but that whatever direction the conversation was now to take was going to be at his discretion.

In view of what she had been thinking she should have recoiled. But she didn't. Rather it was an unspoken statement, a prelude to what was to come, obliterating the import of the vile thoughts that had just been playing on her mind.

"You are worried about that young lad. Well, that makes two of us but it's not a worry those out there have."

With a sweep of his hand, he angrily encompassed the village from which he had just come.

"Have you really been taken in by it all in what, a few short weeks? Hardly the Irish welcome that you might have expected or indeed deserved, because after all, even with short memories some around here do know that they've done well out of here, and not just by trespassing. But listen to me, a blind man would see that the youngster is a grand excuse because to the Men of God, I'm more than some sort of leper, just because I can do without them and their god. Ask your Mr Field about how the villagers give my place a wide berth when passing, as if they might be contaminated by some inescapable disease. Maybe you've seen it yourself. And the clergy have the cream of the crop here behind them. Oh, I could tell you stories, girl."

The words had spilled out, his earlier nonchalant composure diluted in the caustic analysis of his position. It was his use of the word 'girl' that struck home, however. Its familiarity as a local term was not something with which she was familiar. Its effect, a single word, was to cut away any doubt she might have about the clergy being right in attributing the basest of motives to his friendship with the boy. That moment would come back to her time and time again.

He now leaned more forward in the chair, his nearness drawing her in, an ally. She sat and listened.

"My mother died five years ago. I should have been here but that's another story. Who had she then? Priest and rector passed her door every day of every week. The weeds could have grown in the windows. She could have rotted only for the motorman and his youngster. When no one else called to her door they did, often with food from this very house. I have it all, in her letters. And yet they all, both sides, beat a path past her door to praise their god and make themselves feel the better of it."

"But why, what was the…"

His answer was to continue, evading any question and choosing to tell her what he wanted to at his own pace.

"You see, Mrs. Sheldon, I never knew my father."

He paused, not for effect but as if he too somehow was hearing it for the first time. So casually and disarmingly uttered, his words shook her.

"Oh, that must have been dreadful," she exclaimed genuinely, realising at once how trite it sounded. If he noticed or cared, he did not show it.

"It was far more dreadful for my mother though it wasn't all sunshine for me either."

Still feeling she should compensate for her remark at his disclosure, she asked, "were you too young to remember him?"

"No, it wasn't as simple as that even. The fact is I'm what's commonly known as a bastard."

Again, the casual offhand manner of his information was all the more effective for the way he delivered it. The dignified, unrestrained resonance of his words hung heavily in the brooding heat.

"Maybe you are telling me things you may regret later!"

"Plenty around here have more to regret than I have. You see, she could have sent me off to Cork or Dublin out of their sight. But she didn't and that's what really got to them. She wasn't ashamed of me and that made her a shameful woman. Ah, but she paid for it and so did I. You needn't tell me about that youngster and school. I went through the very same thing in the very same school presided over and added to by the very same master. When I was able to, I ran out of this place and that broke her heart, though she didn't blame me. She never blamed anyone in her life, except the hypocrites around her."

Absorbed by what he was saying, wanting at times to interrupt but unable to do so, she listened to the relentless story of his and his mother's misery spun out before her.

"I only came back when she died and would have been out

of here after she was buried except for what that paragon of virtue next door to me said in the graveyard, making sure those around him heard it loud and clear. Only for the motorman, her last few years would have been more miserable than all she suffered before. Do you know what the priest said to me? He's forgotten it, I'm sure but I haven't and won't."

"'Why don't you go now. You and your kind aren't wanted around here.' Those were his words, and they would have been his last only that the motorman came between us. But I told him, twice, that he would be gone out of here before me. I made sure his cronies heard it. Those who turned up at the funeral, not out of feeling for the woman who was dead or for me but no doubt aware that their priest would give me some kind of ultimatum and they wanted to be there for that. Not respect for a dead recluse but sheer curiosity. I would have gone, indeed had the return ticket booked, but what he said changed everything and I'm here to stay, until I have a reason other than theirs to go."

There was anger of a kind she had never experienced before. An anger more vibrant because it was subdued. Questions were doubling up in her head. In his telling she saw how he watched her as if testing her ability to sit and listen to the reasons the village was against him, and more importantly why he was against the village. What about the boy now after all he had said? It was as if he were forgotten. The Pagan, the outcast, unwanted and vilified by all around him, except the motorman and his son, now leaned closer. "Now what do you think of that? Do you know that I can't

get a loaf of bread or an ounce of tea here in the village?"
After all he had told her, the mundane reference to something so uncomplicated, yet so vital as 'a loaf of bread or an ounce of tea' brought to mind a phrase of her mother's and for the second time in her life she knew exactly what it meant. When she had told her mother about having fallen in love with Nathan, after asking a few routine questions about him and listening to her daughter's response, she replied with a knowing smile, "hmmm, he's certainly turned you upside down, hasn't he?"

Now, as night fell on her home of a few weeks, she tried not to betray any emotion beyond acceptance, her head shaking as she saw something of the very same look as the evening of the bicycle accident. Its exhilaration, dangerous and mesmerising, barely admitted to herself, had lain there since. Now, the self-same look tore through her. With images of past and present rampaging through her mind, he took her hand. The dark, voracious eyes of The Pagan locked her into his rebellious world, and led her down a path she might have imagined with Nathan but never experienced. Nathan, Nathan again, but, my god, it was never like this. She revelled in it.

By the time he left that night, the wind had come up, slowly at first, almost a gentle breeze but in a few hours had grown in a swirling fury. As she left him at the back door, neither could believe how strong and wild it was. They had never even heard it. She climbed the stairs in the afterimage of what had happened. That image then became an all-embracing glow.

*

Rain had been prayed for at every Sunday mass. Tales of drought, never before experienced, were bandied about as stories surfaced in the papers of animals and people dying in different parts of Europe due to the prolonged heatwave. It had happened in a townland of their village. Tonight, the wind rising seemed to herald a respite from weeks of sunshine; but this was a summer of one certainty, heat, heat and more heat. The rain couldn't come soon enough. The street was empty save for one of Cremin's dogs, hungry and scalded looking, crisscrossing the street in search of shelter from heat and stifling dust, built up over weeks, blown about and into every crevice.

Twilight edged towards darkness. As if signalled, a number of figures, bent against the wind's swirl, approached the priest's house. Not necessarily trying to elude detection, the onset of darkness helped. Not one of those making their way had anything to fear and why should they? Respectability was worn by each for different reasons because of the position they held.

Slyne, the master, Maguire from the shop and McSweeney, the strongest man not only in Shandrum but far beyond, were the first to arrive. "Holy Mary," Beglin arrived at the door together with Dwyer, a tough, astute bachelor, distrusted by all except the priest. At Slyne's instigation, the priest had suggested to Dwyer that he complain at the barrack of The Pagan's freedom, about which neither "God nor man," seemed to be capable of addressing. He needed little encouragement and was egged on by Beglin, the priest's right-hand man, there at his beck and call, the very antithesis of all The Pagan stood for. "He'll go straight up when his time comes" was a remark often made about him because of his religious fanaticism. He neither drank nor smoked, was first to every church event and last to leave. When Dunne, the old sacristan for over sixty years, eventually died, Beglin was going to take on the mantle; he had been promised as much by the priest on many occasions.

With the door slammed against the wind and dust they were glad to be inside. McSweeney towered over them all, even Maguire. Powerful in stature and temperamental by nature, McSweeney was known far and wide for his feats of strength. He collected pennies from amazed onlookers at fairs, hurling and football matches, races and circuses in return for performing feats of strength. Not a man to be crossed.

These were the nucleus of the League; they were the doers when a plan of action had to be executed. Their influence was powerful, made more so by the fact that Cleary, the sergeant, was as good as one of themselves when it came to turning a blind eye to their occasional activities, all in the cause of "Ireland for the Irish." Ostensibly opposed to the League, understandable in view of his position, he was a valued ally.

None of the group had much time for Edward Sheldon. Maguire especially got little from Woodlands and instead it was Creighton, "one of their own," who had the custom. As an employer of both permanent and seasonal workers, the benefits that flowed from Woodlands were real and often a bone of contention among the League members. The conflict was obvious – if the Sheldons and their like were rooted out, not a few in Shandrum were going to lose out. Yet, the antipathy towards the landowners generally, the very reason for the League's existence, won out over the economic benefits that might be lost when hard decisions had to be made and action taken.

Times were changing, of course, and many landowners among the aristocracy were beginning to sell up or consider it. It had always been rumoured that Edward Sheldon would be one of the first take advantage of what the state could offer him after the Wyndham Act of 1903. That rumour was seen for what it was, worthless, when Edward, instead of leaving, had arrived back last April and installed his new wife in Woodlands, something described as "a kick in the teeth" for the League.

A different issue, albeit related to Woodlands, brought them together tonight. The priest was encouraged by their punctuality and sense of urgency. All except Beglin accepted the proffered drink. It had barely passed Slyne's lips when he adopted the master's pose. It could have been the classroom as he surveyed the others before turning to the priest.

"Well, Father, what do you think we should do?"

Two hours later they emerged, more carelessly perhaps than they arrived and faced the wind that had increased in strength. Leaving, they shouted their goodbyes to make themselves heard. Beglin turned to the priest who was anxious to close his door against the dust and wind, but he couldn't go without a remark, "Great God Almighty, Father, isn't it a terrible night. May God and his Blessed Mother protect us all."

Animals huddled and gates rattled. Darkness shrouded their departure, but it did not go unnoticed. Field sat at his window and saw their blurred images emerge as he had seen them arrive. Despite the casual informality of their leaving, he detected a sense of purpose. A tight, sickly sense of foreboding grew inside him. About to leave his vantage point and go to bed, he noticed the light in The Pagan's window. He was hardly rabbit catching on a night like this.

*

Persisting long beyond his bedtime with the book, he was unable to put it down as his interest grew. Beginning the last chapter, by candlelight, in Joe's kitchen, he was oblivious to the wind raging round outside the cottage. He hated that the story was over, hated that he had come to the last chapter and its opening lines: *To part is the lot of all mankind. The world is a scene of constant leave-taking, and the hands that grasp in cordial greeting to-day, are doomed ere long to unite for the last time, when the quivering lips pronounce the word - "Farewell." It is a sad thought, but should we on that account exclude it from our minds? May not a lesson worth learning be gathered in the contemplation of it? May it not, perchance, teach us to devote our thoughts more frequently and attentively to that land where we meet, but part no more?*

His drooping eyelids told him it was time for bed. No sign of Joe. Sounds on the street alerted him and he ran to the parlour window just in time to see the huddled figures leaving next door. He heard the priest's door bang. Beglin, with his long and gangly walk, hurried away, the last to leave

As Beglin hurried away up the street, Joe came in the back door and closed it with difficulty against the wind.

"Jesus, what a night, why aren't you asleep?"

"Well, what did she want you for?"

The boy's words were innocent and eager. Joe fumbled about, attempting to tidy the table that never was tidy.

"What did who want?"

"Mrs. Sheldon, weren't you going to see her about the note and all that, remember?"

He pointed toward the bible on the windowsill as if Joe could have forgotten. He would know too that he had read the content of the Woodlands' letter at some stage. Following Joe back to the kitchen he watched him take a mug of water from the bucket and slowly drink it down.

"Are you getting a job there?"

"Curiosity killed the cat. You must be mad to find out and sure, why wouldn't you be? I'd be the same. Well, all it is about is that we must be more careful, you know, with the rabbits and that. Snee was out with her about Dwyer and the complaint if you don't mind. They were told above in the barrack that I can do what I like around the place, but Sheldon has told others to get out. The signs are up now, as you know but we've just to watch our step. That won't be easy with the eyes and ears of the whole place on us. The path to Woodlands is great. If we had to take the road we'd be lost."

"Was that all she said?"

"That's it, now. Anyway, I'm off to slumberland so you take up your position," pointing to the rugged chaise lounge.

Joe's mumbled answer made sense but something about it did not ring true. Apart from that he had another question that he was anxious to ask him.

"Now don't you think she's nice like I told you?"

"What are you asking me that for?" Joe answered, irritation in his voice.

"Yeah, sure she's a nice woman. Aren't they all saying that around the place?"

"But I was the first one to tell you the first day she came." Glad of the candlelight. Colour rising to his cheeks. Hated Joe. A special invitation. But I'll be there again. The perfect excuse, to return the book. Her image again. Strange. Joe lost to him. Now watching him. That look of his. Almost knowing what I'm thinking. Feeling. But he couldn't. Or could he? No, he could not. Never. No, no one else either.

"Well, I'm off. Blow out the lights. I don't know how we're going to sleep with this wind tearing around the place."

"So that was all she had to say?"

"That's it now, we must just watch our step, the two of us," Joe answered, quickly opening his bedroom door.

Out with the lights. One last look out at the street. Not a sinner. Never told Joe about the visitors next door. Tired. Watch his step? Why so long to tell him just that? All evening?

*

Though the wind buffeted at the doorway, she waited and watched him go out into the troubled night until he was lost to the darkness. Closing the door, she knew she would not sleep. She sat at her bedroom window reliving what had happened. In attempting to be rational she was dragged back time and again to every detail from the moment he arrived until he left. Luxuriating in what the village outcast had made her feel, dredging up a part of herself she thought extinguished forever, old memories, the inevitable comparisons with Nathan kept surfacing. The truth was there was no comparison.

Naturally, Edward hovered all the time at the periphery of her thinking, troubling her. His words, the very first day she had come to Shandrum rang in her ears, "You'll be hearing more about him." She had and much, much more. The demonised stranger, everyone's problem, it seemed, had swept away all the trappings and chasm of her class. Feelings, long dormant and untouched by Edward's clumsily ineffective approaches had surfaced unerringly from some unexplored far, forgotten place. She had felt unbearably helpless in his, The Pagan's arms, and something told her it was mutual.

Then the boy, the very reason for writing the note, was forgotten about as other wants and needs, other forces had taken over, driving everything else away, as if all else was just a distraction that couldn't compare with what had been engendered by The Pagan. Someone who could not even get a loaf of bread in his own village.

Then she wondered if the servants might have heard anything even though their quarters were at the other side of the house. One consolation was that the maid, Patricia, who had answered the door always seemed the essence of discretion. But then, she had only known her for a few weeks.

She left the window and readied herself for bed, knowing that sleep would not come easily, if at all. It did, in fitful bouts. What would happen now? She would not, could not stop wanting him. The word *magnet* suddenly took on a new meaning she had never associated with it before. Something had been set in motion, overwhelming, disturbing, but desirable in every fibre of her being. She knew that it was incapable of being reigned back.

What about others beyond Edward, the boy, the servants, the clergy, the villagers? Hadn't he told her that anyone's business was everyone's here? And he had told her also that nothing would satisfy them more than the knowledge of what had happened in the drawing room at Woodlands. Added to their long list would be "the icing on the cake," as he referred to it. Indeed, when twisted to suit their purpose, its value might well outweigh the monstrous suggestions made about him and the boy.

Making an adulterer of Edward Sheldon's wife would easily be trumpeted as a scandal too far, breaching some indefinable code of class and culture. No, Shandrum would not tolerate that. He had said something else to her, before she opened the door to let him go, placing his fingers on the nape of her neck and pulling her towards him. He told her he would go mad if he thought he would never see her again. Then he was gone.

*

Over a week had gone by. The storm and rain had made a minimal impact. The boycott was working. Neither Maguire nor Creighton had a single complaint about their course of action. Except for Mulcahy, "the madman," who took Maguire to task about one man's money being as good as another's. But then, Mulcahy could be conveniently ignored, bound, as it was rumoured, for the asylum in Cork where, as Maguire was quick to remind him, "they'll soften your cough in that place."

The Pagan, whose presence and money as well as that of the boy, his messenger, were unwelcome meant Golden blatantly pedalling his bicycle through the village on his way to town. His journey never brought a greeting, only sideways' glances, the odd scowl of derision but little more than that.

As with Mulcahy, there was an exception in the person of Constable Snee, lower key and less obvious.

"Mr Golden, Sir," accompanied his gesture of salute.

Without slowing, Joe gestured in mock salute, bringing his hand to his forehead. This most basic interaction was an exceptional breach of the new village code. Despite Snee's underplayed display of recognition, needless to say, it did not go unnoticed.

Just down the road from the village, the boy waited at the mill bridge, having gone through the familiar two fields that brought him to the castle and then the bridge. Joe slowed and he vaulted with ease on to the carrier and then they were away, in open country, towards the town. The same routine was followed on the way back.

Joe had, reluctantly at first, agreed to this. Going through the village brought jeers and remarks from children, mainly the boy's classmates. Some were of a nature the boy could not understand. The children were taking a chance and one glance from Joe had them scurrying away, fearful that The Pagan might take them to task. Meeting at the bridge was a necessary surrender but they both knew it wouldn't be long before that too was noticed. For the moment it worked.

The rain had threatened all day, black clouds flying low over the hills. Going to town was put off for this reason as the rain seemed imminent all morning and into the afternoon but by five Joe had made his mind up. The only difference was the terrible wind of the previous week had not whipped up.

Joe went out onto the street and came back with his decision made.

"Look we'll go, there's nothing in the house and maybe it will hold off."

They reached the town, visited a few shops at their leisure, purchased their meagre supplies and got ready for the return journey.

The battering, sweeping rain came so suddenly they barely had time to shelter in an archway in the town square. The scorching heat of the previous weeks, lasting forever it seemed, was replaced for the second time in a week by thunderous rain. It seemed to blot out the evening light and a brooding pall of semi darkness settled over all.

They huddled for over an hour under the archway while others joined them for a while and then hurried on, aware that there seemed to be no prospect of a let up as the relentless sweep continued unabated. Joe stepped out occasionally and peered away toward the north but came back, shaking his head.

A woman shoved two children, a boy and a girl, under the archway, hardly noticing Joe and the boy.

"I'll be back in a while," she told the children, "stay there or ye'll be drowned."

Hardly had the woman gone when the girl, whispering in her brother's ear, nudged him to look at Joe. Then they both pulled back sharply, and it was clear that they recognised him and had some inkling of his reputation. They began to play in the puddle that had formed a few feet away, intermittently glancing in Joe's direction.

Alerted by a sudden move from Joe, they stopped to watch. A snail had emerged from near the archway wall and made its way towards the street. Joe had moved to let it pass by his boot. They watched the snail make its way out on to the sodden street until it was at risk. A man hurrying by almost crushed it. Joe moved out on to the street and retrieved it, carefully placing it beyond the puddle and facing away from the direction of the street. As if aware of what had been intended, the snail set off in a new and safe direction. Joe stood with the three children, watching it.

Just then the woman arrived back to collect her two children, muttering about the weather. If there was doubt in her children's mind as to who Joe was, there was none in their mother's. Recognising him, she recoiled for a moment then grabbed the children and pulled them with her out into the rain. Her shrill departing words to them were clear.

"Don't ye know who that fellow is? Stay well away from him."

Again, Joe scanned the northern sky but knew the answer. "Not a bloody hope and we're nearly drowned as we are, and it nearly dark already. C'mon, we might as well be hung for a sheep as a lamb."

The boy made no reply. He was too miserable and hungry, dwelling on what the woman had said to her children and really all he could think of was the cottage and a fire burning in the grate.

Pulling their threadbare clothes around them they ventured out into the driving rain, Joe more definite in his stride, the boy less so. They left the square, plodded up the hill to the point where they would mount the bicycle. Here and there, light from windows on either side of the hill had the boy envying those inside, warm, dry and cosy. At last, they were on the bicycle and Joe settled to the task at hand with relish, shouting over his shoulder, "a shower of rain never killed anyone."

Soon he had gained a rhythm and the sky seemed to darken further. Rivulets of water soon travelled down and lodged uncomfortably in their boots. Hedge and trees on either side were no use tonight. Water everywhere. As they approached the mill bridge before making ready to climb the hill to the castle gate, Joe told the boy to stay with him and not go by the fields. No need for caution on a night like this.

Delighted at the reprieve the boy got ready to jump off for the walk up the hill only to be commanded by Joe, "stay put, we'll go for it, 'twill make men out of us."

Heaving from side to side with every pedal, Joe faced what would be a challenge on a dry day, never mind on a night like this. No one ever did it. Even Joe would be bested. Bend low behind his back. More shelter.

The hill was gradually conquered as Joe pushed the creaking frame of the bicycle and its two passengers toward the turn at the castle gate. Buoyed up by achieving the impossible the boy shouted, "we're nearly at the castle gate, you did it, Joe."

Without warning they were brought crashing to the ground by some barrier unseen in the rain and darkness. Joe, falling first, broke the boy's fall and he tumbled away in the mud with hardly a scratch.

"Jesus Christ."

Joe's shout was smothered as they lay on the ground, stunned by this sudden, unexpected dead stop to their journey.

"Are you alright?" he shouted at the boy.

But now other voices and other movements were heard.

"Get the rope off the road, lads. It did its job, we have him."

"Christ, the brat is with him."

"Ha, what would you expect? True to form."

Then he heard Joe's voice, a command, and he reacted like an arrow from a bow.

"Go as fast as you can, I'll give these bastards a run for their money."

He vaulted over the castle gate just as he heard McSweeney's reply to Joe's challenge, "oh you will, will you?"

Safe behind the pier. Listen. Go or stay? A dull thudding, almost jangling sound. Smashing up the bicycle. Shouting. Terrible words.

"Go on McSweeney, aren't you the brave man with your gang of guardian angels?"

"Shut up you dirty bastard."

The master's voice. Like every day in school.

"We can always use the sledge on you if you go on the way you are, insulting us and our priest. We all know you're a bloody degenerate. That's what England did to you, whatever cesspool you were in over there. Why don't you go away and get a woman for yourself instead of carrying on with a youngster? No child in the village is safe with you around. By the time we're finished with you won't be much good to anyone, woman or child."

Joe bellowed with rage but was soon subdued as his screams reached the boy's ears, where he shivered in rage and fear against the pier in the face of such overpowering and unexpected brutality being doled out in the pouring rain.

"Easy lads, we only have to teach him a lesson."

It was Beglin. Same as at mass. Voice from the chapel. Heard above all others praying. The dirty Holy Mary.

"That'll fix him for a while, boys. Don't forget the sledge and the rope."

With that they were gone, congratulating each other on a job well done, their boots sloshing in the unceasing rain. Then the groans.

"Who are you, you faceless bastard, back to finish the job, I suppose?"

"No, it's me Joe. What way are you, you're nearly killed dead."

"Oh, it's you."

The words faded and the prostrate form lapsed into silence on the rain swept road. In a frenzy of uncertainty, the boy instinctively tried to pull Joe to the side of the road. Impossible.

He knelt and spoke, not certain whether he was heard or not.

"I know what I'll do, I'll ask father to get the motor. He'll have to. You just wait there."

"I won't be going anywhere after what those sons of bitches have done to me."

"Aaagh."

The muffled cries of pain came in waves but by now he was gone, across the sodden fields to the pathway from Joe's to the gate lodge. He clattered on, soaked to the bone but that was forgotten as he could only think of Joe and how quickly the others had done their dirty work and were gone.

He pushed open the door and his father put aside the paper while the story, garbled in places, was blurted out. The mention of McSweeney and Slyne made his father wince. At Beglin's name he just threw his eyes up to heaven while getting his coat.

"I could see something like this happening, so I could. I knew it. Change your clothes and I'll be back … that's if it's alright with herself. I'll have to tell her."

Then he was gone, running out into the rain and up the avenue.

Pulling on a pants, a shirt, too small for him and a pullover that was too big for him, he waited for the rumble of the motor. Unbelievably, the rain had eased off as the motor slowed. He was nearly in the car door when he realised his father was not alone. She sat there with a lantern.

"Tell me what happened."

Her voice. Savage and serious. Never saw her like this.

Such a state. Tell her. Shout so she'll hear.

They reached the village and suddenly the car came to an abrupt halt. One of Cremin's dogs ambled into the glare of the lights and stopped. The boy jumped out and hunted the dog away. A voice, harsh and throaty was heard from an alleyway.

"Leave that dog alone, you there. He was here before that motor and maybe he'll be here when it's gone."

"Don't mind him. It's only Cremin," the boy said to Victoria as he got back in. He laughed nervously as the journey resumed, all three silent with expectation.

The bicycle, a battered tangle, was the first thing they saw as they came near and strained to take in the scene. Scattered all around were the few sodden provisions they had got in the town. Against the wall, almost as grotesque a sight as the remains of the bicycle, was Joe. She was out of the motor before it had come to a stop, rushing with the lantern to where he lay. She shuddered at the sight as "Oh my God!" escaped her lips.

The motor was being manoeuvred by his father to face back towards the village. She was kneeling with the lantern close to Joe's face and was whispering something into his ear. The Act of Contrition, maybe? Told in school. For anyone in danger of death. Maybe Joe was dying? But she's a Protestant. Joe. Well, everyone knows what he is. A Pagan.

The motor was now positioned as close to Joe as possible. Directing the boy to open the back door his father lifted the sagging, rain soaked frame and with Victoria's help they bustled Joe, reacting to each move and groaning with pain, into the back seat. This was not easily achieved. Victoria eventually managed to clamber into the back seat as well, motioning the boy to close the door and get in next to his father. He went round the back of the car and saw the remains of the bicycle. He quickly dragged it to the side of the road, throwing it against the wall where Joe had been. His father shouted at him to hurry on.

The journey had been a short one and not a few in the village wondered what its purpose was as it returned down the street. Before a latch could be lifted or a curtain pulled the motor had sped past.

*

In Maguire's, however, there was less uncertainty as to the purpose of the motor's journey. After the labours of the night, a job well done, McSweeney, Dwyer, and Slyne, in jovial spirits, were ushered by Maguire to the fireplace to dry the clothes they stood in. The fire had not been lit for weeks as there was no necessity but because of the rain, it now blazed.

The fiddle player in the corner, backed up by a colleague with a melodeon, had ceased playing as the door opened and the four swaggered in. Fortified by a round of drinks from Maguire's wife, the interaction of the four at the fireplace with the others in the bar alternated between hushed seriousness and joviality. With the arrival of Beglin, who had stopped for a moment at the priest's front door, a large bottle of lemonade was taken off the shelf and presented to him as if it were a trophy, with Maguire adding, wryly, "Mattie, you won't have something stronger?" Beglin turned to the onlookers.

"Wasn't it a fright of a night, boys, with all that rain. Good God Almighty, sure you wouldn't put a dog out in it. 'Twas wanted now though, wasn't it after weeks of that heat. Last Sunday's prayers were answered, you know, and it couldn't have come at a better time."

Raising the bottle, he joined the group at the fireplace and turned to the musicians.

"We won't interrupt ye lads, so strike now with a few fast ones. The night is young. Give a few belts of A Wintery Night."

The music started up again with gusto, allowing those around the fireplace to discuss the night's events without being overheard. The night indeed was a long one.

*

He had waited for a knock at the door. He had fallen into a kind of reverie from the heat of the first night-time fire he had lit in weeks. The terrible rain would leave everything damp and the fire would be company. When the knock came, he jumped and scuttled to the door.

"Just to let you know, Father, that things are alright."

Beglin winked as if to give clarity to his message.

"Right. Now go on over to the lads, ye must be drowned."

With that, he closed the door and returned to his sitting room where he poured himself a glass and settled back into his reverie before the fireplace. Sipping his drink, the picture on the mantelpiece, always a constant reminder, caught his eye. He began to hum a tune that led to a low lament before ending with a flourish of satisfaction.

O well do I remember the bleak December day
The landlord and the sheriff came to drive us all away
They set my roof on fire with cursed English spleen
And that's another reason that I left old Skibbereen.

O Father dear, the day may come when in answer to the call
Each Irishman, with feeling stern, will rally one and all
I'll be the man to lead the van beneath the flag of green
When loud and high, we'll raise the cry: "Revenge for Skibbereen!"

*

She knew the motorman had noticed. Even allowing for the terrible thing that had happened, she knew she was too interested, too full of shocked anxiety. Her offer, without reservation, to accompany him to the scene of the attack, she supposed and hoped, might simply be interpreted as genuine concern for someone in distress. She doubted though, even in the midst of desperately trying to appear detached, that the motorman would see it as just that. At least she had resisted making the suggestion that Joe be brought back to Woodlands, much as she wanted that. The untold complications of such a move were too evident to be dismissed. The thought of Edward, due back soon, confirmed her decision.

At first, she thought he was hardly injured at all, so diplomatically did the motorman request the use of the car. Once she responded as she had – she saw him watching her, missing nothing- he told her as much as he knew. So too had the boy in the car. Compared to his father's measured account, the boy's hurried, garbled story, given with conviction and terror in his voice, led her to believe they would be bringing back a dead body. There was a strange, contradictory sense of relief in that thought. He said he would go mad if he could not see her again. Was dying the same as that?

"Please don't die on me, I'm here with you now."

The words were not overheard with the noise of the engine. She was glad of the darkness and the sombre dullness of the rain, threatening again. Animals, she thought, seething with anger in every fibre of her being, would not do this to their own. How could they do this to a man she barely knew, yet seemed to have been known to her all her life? And what of the child, a witness to such brutality?

In the midst of her meandering outrage the priority was obvious. Somehow, they managed, and when she got into the relative privacy of the back seat, she was able to cradle his head in her hands. Feeling for his eyes she could not help remembering that they were the catalyst, that look, that had led to the first embrace and all that followed. Hatred and anger surged through her again. Her fingers moved through his bloodied, matted hair, along his face and neck, down under the soaking, sweat filled shirt that covered his heaving chest. No matter how gentle her touch, he reacted in pain, telling her at least he was alive. Believing he might somehow hear, she kept repeating the only plea that made any sense to her.

"Please don't die on me, don't die on me, Joe."

The words she whispered wrenched her back to another time. The terrible familiarity of the words had her back on the riverbank in Surrey when she had thrown herself, a weeping, screaming bundle of misery, on Nathan's body. Then, as now, her words were the same, but now, at least, there was hope.

Why were they stopped? Of course. They were at the lodge having passed by the village and the cottage. For a moment, the appeal of going to the house again tempted her but it would be sheer lunacy.

The boy was already at the door with the lantern. The haze of light it threw on the back seat and its occupants did not reveal the look in the boy's eyes, fixed and ungiving, taking in, as if for preservation, the sight he beheld.

Time could not be lost. Their combined effort carried Joe's complaining body down the narrow path to the lodge. A mattress was dragged from a room and Joe rolled on to it. The door was closed, the misery of the night was shut out. Not so its memories or its consequences.

The lamplight revealed the full extent of the beating he had received. The car was gone again, this time to get the doctor. It was this journey, in quick succession to the previous one, that brought questioning glances from those in Maguire's.

The boy, acutely aware of the attention Joe was getting, hurried about the house doing as he was asked. Much of what she asked for was given with shame and embarrassment. This was not the big house up the avenue and its limited supply of basic necessities was woefully exposed. She did not seem to notice this, however, and if she did, she gave no indication of it.

She sought his help to remove Joe's ragged, bloodied shirt or what remained of it. Close to her now he watched her face contort with every expression of his aching protest. Still not conscious, he grunted in pain as they heaved him sideways, back and forth to get the shirt off. It seemed she was scraping it off his skin, lodged with grime and blood. As best she could, she tried to wash it from wherever she could, all the time looking toward the village, as if to hurry the sound of the motor's return.

A stranger from it all. Shut out from everything. No matter how much I try to help. She in charge. Isn't Joe my friend? Her hands moving. Her hands. Tender. Kind. For Joe only.

The sound of the motor came through the night, jarring him out of his jealous preoccupation.

A pompous man, Dr Lehane had been an army doctor in India before coming back to the town to continue his practice after Cranitch retired. No one was allowed to forget his foreign stint of duty. The conversation with the motorman, as they got out of the car and came through the door, was about a tiger he had shot in Kashmir. She had moved aside as had the boy when they came into the room. If he noticed her, he did or said nothing to acknowledge her presence, so caught up was he in reliving his shooting exploits.

"I know this man and he'll live as long as Leary" the doctor announced, barely glancing at Joe's wounds. After a cursory examination of Joe's head and chest he motioned towards the motorman for help. In an instant he had Joe's boots off and finally his trousers removed and thrown next to the shirt on the floor. Woman and child flinched at this unceremonious, necessary procedure.

The motorman tried to alert the doctor to the fact that others were present. He never noticed, so intent was he on getting what had to be done out of the way before, no doubt, regaling him with another of his exploits.

First time. Someone naked. Look at Father. Trying not to let her see. Her face turned away. Angry and sad.

With a quick, propelling movement his father had him scurrying to get another sheet.

The light from the kitchen cast a leaden streak into the bedroom as he pulled a sheet from his father's bed. He stood for a moment behind the door, out of sight and watched what was taking place just a few feet away from him. The doctor, still oblivious to the presence of the woman, worked expertly and easily at his routine. His father still tried to shield Joe's exposed body from her. She stood in the shadows against the wall near the table, not stirring, her fingers pressed against her lips.

Her clothes too were muddied and soaked to such an extent that she might well have been dressed as any of the women he saw every day in the village or in the town. Yet her bedraggled state only added to her despairingly magnificent features, from which he could not avert his gaze, until his father looked towards the bedroom, and he hurried out with a threadbare sheet.

Finished bandaging Joe, the doctor returned what he didn't need to a battered brown case and rose, his job for the night done. It was then he noticed her. He jumped back a pace, startled as if he'd seen a ghost.

"My God, Mrs. Sheldon, I never even noticed you."

"Forgive me for not taking account of your presence. It must be the light here."

As if to compensate for his faux pas he curtsied affectedly and launched into a monologue about Edward's father, whom he said he barely knew but the only real gentleman he had met in his many travels. Woodlands was the envy of so many and the village had done well out of it. More drivel about how he had been recognised and honoured for his work in India by the Viceroy. This tested her reserve. She interrupted him saying that Edward and herself would be delighted if he visited them at some point in Woodlands. The boy watched, intrigued by the doctor as much as by Victoria's obvious annoyance.

Just then Joe shivered and opened his eyes. Slowly lifting his head, he blinked a few times, mesmerised by the scene around him. He shivered again and looked down to where the flimsy sheet barely covered him. As if seeing a ghost, the atheist half shouted.

"Jesus, Mary and Joseph, will ye look at the state of me?" He tried to drag the corner of the sheet more closely around him but roared out in pain. The boy laughed out loud, more from relief that Joe was speaking, and in some way back to himself, than at his vain attempts to cover his modesty. Victoria then stepped from the shadows and settled the sheet for Joe. The boy watched. Surely Joe had seen her already and yet, for a man who was seldom lost for words, he was now. The most imperceptible of smiles crossed his swollen lips and he spoke, low and intense, for her and her only.

"Thanks."

Without hurrying, she drew back to a standing position as the doctor was about to speak again.

"Perhaps then, Dr Lehane, you might at some point accept the invitation to Woodlands that I mentioned a moment ago. My husband and I would be fascinated to hear about your time abroad in the service of the Empire."

The irony was lost on him but not on everyone else.

"That indeed would be a most welcome pleasure. And there is much to talk of the Empire, whose influence and presence is dwindling in these parts."

"Indeed," she replied, barely tolerating his presence now and ushering him towards the door. He peered at the night sky now beginning to clear and announced that he would walk home now that the rain had stopped. He turned, bade good night and turned back towards the kitchen and Joe on the mattress.

"That man needs little looking after. A week or two's rest. There's good blood there. Did I say he'll live as long as Leary. No doubt about it but he will."

"Living as long as Leary" was a phrase the boy understood well. It referred to a man from the outskirts of the village who had lived in three centuries, having been born in 1797 and dying in 1902. The proof was there for all to see in the village graveyard and visitors often came to read the inscription on his headstone. He was too young to have remembered Leary, but Joe often said to him that he might equal Leary's record. He saw no reason why this might not one day be proven true. He had been born in 1898.

Now as the doctor walked out into the night sky the boy's mind, doing the sums, shot ahead to the year 2000, the year to aim for if he too was to have a headstone to equal

|Leary's. The two of them and Shandrum would then be more famous. Would he live for nearly ninety more years? Tonight, it seemed like a very long time.

With the doctor gone an immediate sense of relief descended as if an inveterate ear- splitting sound had been dulled.

*

Walking up the avenue by her side, he tried to catch a glimpse of her face in the darkness. The rain indeed had stopped, and the clouds were breaking up allowing a full moon to break through now and then. He was going with her to bring back what she termed "a few things that might be needed." They had left his father spooning tea into Joe's battered face.

He remembered her wistful goodbye to Joe.

"I'll be enquiring about you," she said and a nod from Joe, that seemed too casual, was the reply.

At the front door she stopped and considered going in but then, looking at her muddied boots, went round to the back entrance. He followed. Passing along the dimly lit corridor, servants' quarters on either side, they came to three stone steps and a door that he imagined would bring them somewhere round to the back of the main hall. She pushed open the heavy door and then, looking again at her boots, sat on one of the steps to undo them.

She sighed, tired and impatient as the laces gave her trouble. Seeing her difficulty, he blurted out that he would be able to untie them. Relieved, she rested her back against the door as he bent down to wrestle with the laces. With the first lace finally undone he slowly removed the boot, savouring his task as a heady smell rose from her stockinged feet. He breathed it in and wondered if she noticed. There was no indication that she did as she sat with her eyes closed waiting for the other boot to be removed. He lingered, taking longer than necessary, savouring the smell from her feet and her nearness. Did she notice?

The job finished, she rose, thanked him, and placed the boots on the bottom step. He then looked down at his dirty boots and slipped them off though his feet were not much cleaner after the night's events. He followed her through the great hall, and she turned to go up the stairs beckoning him to wait. |He followed her movement step by step, straining to keep her in sight as she moved, slowly as if in contemplation. Madly he thought of how close he had been to her.

Her returning footsteps alerted him and he had forgotten why he was there, revelling as he was in all that had happened since they came to the steps where she had sat to have her boots untied. Then the searing pang of jealousy that had shot through him when he saw her in the back of the motor with Joe's head on her lap and her hands holding his face.

Tall and erect she came down the stairs with a brown paper parcel in her hand. Then she led him back to collect his boots and they were soon at the doorway where they had come in.

"Take these few pieces home. Just to help out while Mr Golden is unwell. The doctor says he should be well soon." There was a tremor in her voice. He nodded and waited.

For what he did not know and there was silence for a few seconds before she broke it.

"You were very brave tonight and your father and Mr Golden must be very proud of you."

He felt he should make some reply, yet nothing was as important as being here with her at the door in the darkness, the wind and rain gone, the moon above among the scudding clouds and the flooded river's sound in the distance. Maybe she did know how he felt but then who could? No one could. Out of nowhere the scene on the roadway came back and the moment the rope across it had brought Joe and himself clattering to the ground.

"I know who attacked Joe tonight and broke his bicycle. It can never be fixed because they had a sledge. And they were laughing."

"Who are you talking about?" she answered as if reluctant to be drawn into what was now such an unseemly sequence of events, so serious no one could venture as to where it all might lead to after tonight.

"You couldn't have seen them in the dark and wasn't it raining as well?"

He could give her the names but then she might not know them.

"I know who they are and so does Joe. And another thing, I think the priest knows too."

She peered into his eyes.

"My dear child, don't say such things or we will all be in trouble. Such evil men will, somehow, be punished, I am sure."

She took him by the shoulders and drew him closer until his face was just an inch or two away from hers. Slowly and deliberately, she told him what he must do, what they must do.

"This must be our secret. Maybe all you know is true, but it is now very dangerous. Promise me you won't say anything until we have time to think about all this. Until your friend, until Joe is better. That will be time enough. Can you promise me that?"

"Yes," he answered, drawn by the comfort of her closeness and the pact she wanted to make with him. Her arms came round him in a hug that was momentary but gratifying. The parcel was between them, hindering the embrace.

"Now you must go, or they will be wondering what kept you so long."

The clank of the iron gate at the side of the house told her he was gone. She made her way to her bedroom, removed her soiled and muddied clothes, in some vain attempt to obliterate all that had happened and what the boy had told her.

After washing, she sat on her bed, assailed by the complicated and dangerous predicament she faced. The anger welled up in her again, as it had when she knelt beside Joe on the roadside. The attack, premeditated and brutally effective, had delivered its message. Who was to know if it was just a first step, a final warning? Maybe some unknown force had kept him alive when he might have been lost to her forever. Just like Nathan.

Thinking about what had transpired in the lodge she assumed that she had betrayed very little to anyone and felt all she had done could only be interpreted as an act of neighbourly kindness. Neither could sending a few pieces of clothing be misconstrued. She had resisted putting a note in the parcel, fearing that the boy or his father might come upon it by chance. How, she thought, could such another foolhardy idea have entered her mind? But then she knew how. The madness of love.

Then there was Edward and the spectre of discovery. She had dismissed out of hand every piece of advice he had given her. The unmistakable consequences kept coming back to her. For the wife of Edward Sheldon KC, George Denham Lind's daughter, the mistress of Woodlands, to be the lover of an Irish outcast and all that involved, would be the dream of every London editor. At least for the moment no one knows.

Another night of fitful sleep, roused by the memory of Joe, a physical wreck, lying on a mattress on a floor, with his bicycle, as important to him as the motor to Woodlands, smashed on the roadside. What a source of fascination that would be the next day for passers-by and those lured to where it lay with the curiosity of rumour and innuendo?

The sleep of others nearby was fitful too. Down the avenue, Joe's heavy slumber was interrupted by shouts and sighs of pain, warding off imaginary blows that peppered his dreams. The boy, too, twisted and turned to escape the phantom shadows that troubled and plagued his weary frame and would not be banished. Further into the village, the assailants, fortified by porter and back slapping for a job well done, slept perhaps more easily than any.

*

The previous night's rain, welcome as it was, might never have fallen as morning came with a hazy start that foretold another day of heat. Voices roused the boy from his sleep. It was Joe's he heard first, guttural and awkward. At least that was a good sign. Then he heard his father's voice.

He listened at the door having gingerly made his way there from the bed.

Both men were angry, not at each other but at what had happened. Glad that his father was firmly on Joe's side, he listened to Joe speaking as clearly as he could manage. Nothing disguised his contempt for the attackers. Their method, the rope, the numbers, the sledge, symbolic of the destruction they could cause, had done its job on the bicycle.

Seldom had the boy seen his father so agitated as he spoke names with a snarl. The priest was mentioned, as was the sermon and Joe's confrontation with him on the street. The words of condemnation used in the sermon and the threats made on the street had been acted on with a devastating vengeance.

"The hardest bit is the bicycle," Joe said.

"What are you bloody talking about, man. Look at yourself, look at yourself, a bloody mess from head to toe, nearly killed and all you can think about is the bicycle. Why should that worry you?"

"Ah, I don't know. I suppose it has something to do with himself."

He shrank back behind the door at this. Joe continued.

"Don't you know that a lot of them hated to see him on

it because it belonged to me. Anyway, whether they like it or not it'll be replaced as soon as I'm back on my feet. Rudge's have them in the paper. We'll see. They won't have their satisfaction for long, the bastards. They'll all be out to get me now that the brave head heroes have made the first move."

"Well, you have Florence Nightingale on your side anyway. It's not every woman that would do it you know."

He was uncertain for a moment about "Florence Nightingale" but then it came to him. He pictured her again with Joe's head on her lap and the same resentful surge came back. He waited for Joe to reply. It was his father who spoke next again, however.

"Look Joe, here's what I think and I'm going to tell you the truth. I'm afraid of what will happen. You know I see and hear a lot more around here than many of those who think they know it all."

"What do you mean by that?" asked Joe, easy and slow, yet with a defensive tone to the words.

"All I'm saying is that I know my own know and I won't say anything else about it. Only be careful, for Christ's sake, or we'll all pay the price and that includes herself too. A lot has happened in that house that too many don't know about."

"Like what now? What are you saying to me, c'mon, it's me you're talking to, out with it. Is it me you're talking about?"

Joe was agitated now, trying to lift himself up off the mattress but failing miserably and falling back with a scream of agony.

"Not at all, Jesus, Joe, will you watch what you're doing. You're an injured man so no more bits of bravery from you. And go easy or we'll wake the child. Will you look at the time, I should be gone ages ago. Lie down and take it easy now."

At this, he moved as quickly as he could and got back into the bed. He waited for a few minutes until his father was gone to get the motor and then got up.

Joe lay, half asleep, his face a twisted frown, emphasised by the bruises and scratches. Nearby was the parcel. Not wanting to rouse Joe he slowly tiptoed to where it was and slowly opened it, making as little noise as possible. Joe was suddenly awake, watching what was happening. They inspected the contents. Two shirts, socks, two sheets and a suit that had obviously belonged at some stage to Edward or perhaps, his father. The boy could not recall seeing Edward wearing it. Though not new it was in far better condition than anything Joe had or would want to have.

"I think you'll be wearing that suit because I won't," Joe said in a voice that sounded ungrateful.

"It's grand, why wouldn't you wear it?"

"Can you imagine what would be said if I paraded around in Sheldon's clothes. By God, that woman has no sense at all now, has she? Yet, you never know, it might come in handy for some state occasion."

He laughed but the effort caused more pain than the laugh was worth. The boy wondered what a state occasion meant. He added, forlornly,

"And the bicycle is finished."

"Indeed, it is and why wouldn't it be after that laughing hyena with the sledge. Jesus, I could put a knife through the whole lot of them. But as I said to your father, I'll have another one before you can say Jack Robinson."

"We'll just have to walk to town now that's all, I suppose," picturing each twist and turn from the village to the town.

"Well, I won't be doing much walking for the time being as you can see. But look, put on the kettle. We'll have a cup and face the day," Joe replied, as if he hadn't a care in the world.

By midday, the heat was predictably unbearable, like so many days over the previous weeks. Before leaving the lodge he opened all the windows and the back door. Its effects on the heat's stranglehold were barely noticeable and he left Joe in a welter of sweat.

*

She walked down the avenue as waiting had become unbearable. On her arm was a basket of food, outwardly giving a reason for the short journey. She knew such charity would soon become common knowledge but for now she hoped it would be seen as a gesture made to help someone in desperate circumstances. A man brutally beaten, she foolishly surmised could hardly be denied sustenance, even if some thought otherwise.

Picking her way along the avenue, she tried hard to give the impression that, really, she was taking a stroll in the sun and performing an act of charity on the way. She saw the back door and all the windows were open. Stepping inside, taking a while to adjust after coming in from the scorching sun, she saw the crumpled body.

He was asleep but it wasn't a peaceful one and his body twitched every few seconds as if swatting away some invisible foe. Rivulets of sweat stood out on his forehead. She got her handkerchief to wipe the sweat away, before taking a few moments to dwell on the luxury of being in his presence, and savour it.

Despite the marked and bruised body, it had for her an overpowering and irresistible wholeness. She desperately wanted to dismiss his protestations of pain as she touched him. Try as he would to respond, he could not. She told him to be still and not to speak. He obeyed.

"My darling Joe, I'm sorry. Don't move. I know I'm just being selfish, but all this is making me go mad. What are we going to do? I can't even stay here with you now because if I do suspicions will be aroused. I had to see you. Now I have to go but I'll try to come again tomorrow if I can wait until then. Can I wait that long, my love? But whatever happens, you are in my mind, all the time."

The words came out in a jumble, so much to say and so little time to say it. She rose to go and then knelt again to give him a long, languorous kiss on his swollen lips. He tried to bring his arm around her, but it was too painful. He lay back, giving her that look that had made all the difference. She should have allowed him to speak but she had to go, desperate as she was to stay.

At the gate she faced towards the village to give the impression that she had merely dropped in some provisions as she took her walk. Staying by the wall for shade she tried to put some perspective on things, make some sense of all that happened. But what in it all would make any sense? Edward again came to mind. Two letters had arrived that morning, both from London, one from her publisher and one from Edward. The publisher wondered where her manuscript was for her latest book, planned for publication later in the year. Edward's letter said a trial was going to last longer than anticipated but he would be back "as soon as circumstances allowed." She had little reaction to it, consumed as she was, by more immediate, pressing events. What had happened in the drawing room told her that Edward was very much at the periphery right now.

Approaching the village, her musings were interrupted by Field, his head covered by a wide brimmed straw hat. Outside his gate, he lazily drew a broom to tidy around it, even though it didn't need it. Like his garden it always looked immaculate. She would have preferred not to have met him but on the other hand saw the opportunity to let him know what had happened. Something for which he had, through his sermon, to bear some responsibility.

He listened, shuffling from one foot to the other, unaware of what had happened the night before. Having heard the motor coming and going, he had no idea why. He listened with increasing apprehension. She never mentioned the sermon because there was no need to, instead using the phrase "those who should know that what they say have consequences." That stopped his shuffling and he sheepishly replied with a lame justification "well, two wrongs don't make a right."

She saw little point in going any further or having an argument and was wary that she just might say too much.

He understood. She bade him a stiff and reproachful goodbye, before looking beyond him up the street, deserted in the scorching sun, and turning on her heel, back the way she had come. Field stood, shaking his head as he watched her go and then doing exactly as she had, looking the other way up the village street as if that offered him some answer to what he had just heard. All he could think of then was the sight a few nights ago, the night of the storm and the first rain, of the departing shadows from the presbytery door. A bad, bad business was his thought and yes, he too had played a part. Embarrassed and guilty now by his "two wrongs don't make a right," response to Victoria Sheldon's pointed remark, he looked again up the village street before quickly making his way indoors as if to escape from a bad smell.

*

He had gone back to the cottage at Joe's suggestion to see if everything was as it should be. Just as they had left it the evening before against the threatening sky, its familiarity was a welcome break from the frenetic events of the night. Yet he was restless, and he soon realised why. It was the bicycle. He wondered if it was still where he had pulled it in the rain against the wall.

He could have gone by the fields to the mill bridge and then come up the hill towards the castle gate where the rope across the road had brought them to the ground. To go by the fields now would be sensible but an upsurge of cheekiness took him over and he set out up the street. It wasn't that he was not apprehensive, but it was something to do with standing up for Joe.

The midday sun bore down, and he could have kept close to one side of the street where the houses gave a little shelter. But no, he would walk up the centre of the street. Apart from the odd look in his direction no one said anything to him. He strode on as the sombre grey of the barrack, bleached in the sunshine, came into view. Then a drink at the village pump and down to where everything, still so fresh in his mind, had happened.

Would the bicycle be there? Probably, because it was now of no use to anyone, just a battered relic that was once The Pagan's. He came round the corner at the castle gate and came to an abrupt and unexpected stop. Standing over the remains of the bicycle was Constable Snee. The courage which had made him face the villagers a few minutes ago now vanished when faced with the law. He could pretend he was on the way to the town so he kept as close as he could to the opposite wall and had almost got by Snee when the constable, without even turning his head said, "And what have we got here, young man?" Surely Snee must have known by now what happened.

"That's Mr Golden's bicycle."

"I know that but what happened to it?"

He moved the tangled remnant with the toe of his boot, a gesture that made the boy wonder how terrible it must be for a policeman on a day like this in heavy uniform and helmet. He wondered what he should answer to the simple question. Maybe he had just come across the scene after all. Imperturbable, he listened as the boy spilled out what had happened the previous night.

"So, they did nothing to you?"

"No, I escaped," he replied proudly.

"Do you know who they were?" Snee asked in the same deadpan voice.

How could he make sure he did not break his promise to her? He stumbled and stammered about the rain, the shouting and the curses but he was determined not to tell the names. Certain that Snee was annoyed by his evasions, he said as convincingly as he could,

"I'm not sure. I was afraid."

Strangely, rather than pursuing the names, the constable nodded as if to himself, almost as if the names didn't matter after all and pointed to something he had noticed in the grass, a few feet away from where the bicycle lay.

The bicycle bell had escaped the sledge. Snee picked it up and without a word, gave it to the boy. His face lit up at what was now his and had been so miraculously rescued from the mayhem

"I'll have to show him this. I'll wonder what he'll say?"

"And while you're at it you can give him a message from me," added Snee. He waited, the bell momentarily forgotten. "Tell him I'll be calling to see him when he's a bit better. Officially like."

That ended the conversation, and clasping the bell, he continued as he had first pretended down the hill towards the bridge and the town. Looking back, he saw Snee was still there, jotter and pencil out.

Arriving where he would normally meet up with or leave Joe, he wondered what would have happened had he left Joe last night and made his way, as usual, through the fields. It might all have been a different story and who knows what might have happened.

He hopped over the wall and sheltered in its shade. Peering against the sun towards the castle he heard the sounds from the mill and the murmur of the river, swollen after the night's rain. He examined the bell which in some peculiar way made up for the loss of the bicycle. Not everything was gone.

Time meant nothing and he had lost track of it, cleaning the outside of the bell on his shirt to a silver sheen until it sparkled in the sunshine. From where he sat, by allowing the sunlight to reflect off the bell, he was able to throw a spot of light down toward any bit of shade given by the trees along the river. He let it hover here and there but soon tired of the game and put the bell on the ground near him and closed his eyes.

What was she doing now? Hate the way she looked after Joe. Even with his terrible injuries. The three stone steps. Her boots.

His imagination accentuated every detail, every feature until he was lost in her imagined presence. The heat, the sounds from the mill and the river cocooned him in a shell of delirious privacy. Another image now invaded.

Coming down around the castle wall was the priest on his daily walk. He was later than usual; it was said in the village that you could set your watch or clock so strictly did he keep to the same time. From where he sat, he was well hidden, but the appearance of the priest had him drawing back against the wall with apprehension. He watched the purposeful stride.

He picked up the bell, holding it away from himself until it glinted in the sun. Slowly he engineered the spot of light down to the path where the trees now and then shaded the priest. He focussed on the priest's face, trying to get some reaction. For a moment, the priest ignored this irritation but the playing of the spot on his eyes soon annoyed him. He slowed down and the boy refocussed. The priest stopped and looked around, his annoyance clearly evident at this unexpected, unidentified intrusion. Setting off again he soon had to contend with the same problem.

Now I have you. Solve that. Detective Kerley. Like in the comics. Joe would love it. Pity he's not here.

Then the priest was out of sight as he passed under the bridge and would soon turn up the road to where he would come upon the scene from the night before. Would Snee still be there?

He froze against the wall as the priest's footsteps came nearer outside where he sat. Trying to make out the name of the song the priest was whistling, he waited until the footsteps began to recede and clambered up on the wall to watch him arrive where the remains of the bicycle still lay.

A glance was all it got as he hardly broke his stride, continuing round the turn where he was lost to sight.

*

Confined as he was, Joe's impatience grew daily.

There were advantages, of course, not least the constant supply of food and papers from Woodlands. The boy saw a side of Joe not experienced before. He knew it was the thought of spending so much time inactive and powerless that irked him most. He had bouts of rage and then fell into a deep sleep, punctuated by constant dreams, evidenced by his sudden movements and talking in his sleep which usually took the form of curses and threats. He would then wake and vent his rage against his attackers. Without being in any way specific he would simply say something about "playing a waiting game," "they'll know what hit them" or "if they think I've driven them mad up to now I'll find a few more ways." He was afraid to ask Joe what all this would entail.

Late at night when he was supposed to be asleep, he would creep to a spot behind the door and listen as his father and Joe talked, sometimes in whispers and it was often hard to follow the conversations. Certain things kept coming up. The bicycle and Joe's pledge to replace it as soon as possible; names, other than those of the attackers were mentioned as was the League; Woodlands came up too but both men seemed anxious not to spend too much time on that subject. He wondered why. Field and the priest were spoken of too, scathingly and dismissively though they could not be dismissed. Occasionally, both men laughed about the bell and how the glint from it had so annoyed the priest. He heard Joe use the phrase, less humorously and with contempt, "shining a light on darkness."

They were surprised that Snee had not visited, even though he had said he would wait until Joe was better. He questioned the boy at length about the meeting where the bicycle lay. All seemed puzzled that he had not questioned him more closely about who the attackers were. Their puzzlement would grow.

Victoria, beside herself because she could only visit

intermittently, knew even such random appearances at the lodge might rouse suspicions. Maybe that had happened already. The boy was not always absent, and there were only so many times Joe could send him away when she arrived, to see "how the cottage is." Guiltily and knowingly, she longed for the school holidays to be over. That luxury would be at the boy's expense, and well she knew it.

Their physical passion, hampered and limited by Joe's injuries and the possibility of discovery, gave their time together a frantic intensity that engulfed them in another world. A world of pampered, yet insane self-confidence, that they were somehow immune to what might befall any other two lovers in the same situation.

If anything, this existence on the edge of discovery made Joe recover more quickly and father and son were amazed at how the wrecked body of a little over a week ago, now was on the mend, brought on, they felt, by rest and the food being supplied daily from Woodlands' kitchen. So quick was his progress and genuinely not wanting to impose on the hospitality of the motorman, he announced one humid evening that he would return the following Saturday to the cottage. That was only three days away, the motorman argued, pointing out that though he had made great strides he was still injured and far from well enough to return home. His protestations met with stubbornness and obduracy. Joe was going, it was time and that was it. His return would be a reminder that whatever they had inflicted on him the night of the attack would not keep him "on the flat of my back for a minute more than necessary."

This meant that the boy could be dispatched the day before to make ready for the return. As if timed, she met him as he left the lodge and, rather lamely, asked where he was going. He told her about Joe and his plan to return to the cottage. This seemed to make her uneasy, lost for words, as they parted.

She placed the basket on the low table near the window. Adjusting after being in the sunlight, she had hardly turned from the window when his arms were around her waist and his face snuggled into the nape of her neck. She responded but without her characteristic enthusiasm.

"Is something wrong?" he asked, a hint of panic in his voice.

"I'm certain the boy knows about us."

"How do you mean knows?"

His disarming smile met her apprehensive eyes.

"Well, unless he's blind, at his age he's bound to be aware of something. I can see it in how he looks at one. All innocence and yet I have felt uneasy with him. Do you know what I mean? You were his age one time."

She had her head on his shoulder waiting for everything, no matter how it impinged on them, to be explained away, yet knowing it couldn't be.

"I know what you mean, I suppose," he replied, looking into her eyes, his slow, captivating gaze on the verge of momentarily shutting out all her anxieties.

"But sure what can he know about us? What can he really understand about you and me? It's no harm saying though, that all that has a lot to do with you, rather than me."

"Go on, explain," she asked, anxious to get another view while wondering if Joe's was necessarily the best or most objective. But then, whose would be?

"Well, I can see a lot in what he says and the way he talks about you. He's only a child that you've bewitched and I'm sure there's a few more in the village, not all boys by the way, that feel the same about you. Sure I was the same at his age about Harriet Esmonde. What's wrong with you is that you're too bloody lovely."

She flicked him laughingly on his shoulder.

"I suppose you're right. I always remember how Harold at that age used to act when the two Dukesons visited Eastleigh. He'd sit and stare at Charlotte for ages, even when eating. It became so embarrassing that mother had to throw him out into the garden at times. When he wrote from school, he constantly asked about her, trying to appear casual. Now whatever way we look at it, it's no great help that our young fellow feels the way he does or knows maybe much more about us than we think."

She waited for his kiss as he took her head in his hands. It did not come. Instead, he spoke, carefully and deliberately, as if the conversation and questions about the boy had made him see things more clearly.

"He, I think, is the least of our worries. It's those other lackadoos out there led by the two paragons of virtue. And what about your husband?" Then he kissed her.

"I don't want to even think of all that involves. And speaking of Edward, I almost forgot, I had a letter from mother this morning saying she is dying to see Woodlands and is planning a visit, 'soon' was how she put it. She would of course tell me to my face what she thought, and that, for you and me, might be a good thing."

He spoke again, stark and straight, saying the consequences were too complicated to wrestle with, in the little time they had. She trembled but loved how direct he was even though all he said seemed to have implications way beyond working out to any level of satisfaction. Where Edward's obfuscations annoyed her, it was refreshing to hear the truth spoken, no matter how unpalatable. Shades of her mother. All they had now was a doubtful present and for it the future would have to wait.

*

Why, nearly every day, did Joe send him back to the cottage? Yes, he had done all he had been told to and more. The only thing that he hadn't done was to chop the wood for the fire, used so sparingly and just for cooking as the long summer days dragged on. He had the place looking spick and span and even managed to put the piled-up parlour table in some kind of order. He had wound the clocks, delicately and carefully as Joe had taught him.

Now it was Friday, and the sticks were next. He got two axes, one large and one small from the garden shed, and began to chop the carefully arranged logs that were stacked against the wall. The heat was all around him, but he enjoyed the satisfaction of splitting the large logs in four and a few of the quarters into kindling.

Stopping for a rest he had a feeling that he was being watched. He turned towards the road and saw Snee at the corner of the cottage. He had arrived unseen and unheard. "Well, it's good that someone around here is doing a bit of work. You've a good job done there. I hope he's paying you."

The hint of humour brought a shy smile to the boy's face. "Oh, he'll be back tomorrow. I'm after getting the place ready for him."

"Is that so, now? And how is he at all?" The constable's voice was casually intimate.

"He's fine. Isn't Mrs Sheldon after bringing him down loads of food from the house."

Almost sorry he had said that, he continued, saying that Joe, apart from a limp, was nearly back to his best.

"You can't keep a good man down, they say."

The boy was unsure whether he was referring to Joe's health or the benefits of the food being brought to him from Woodlands. Snee now clambered over the small wall and came closer.

"Tell him I'll be in someday to see him."

He winked as he said it, leaving the boy uncertain as to what that was meant to mean. As if it were an afterthought, he added, "I'm glad he's over it."

Still unsure, the boy nodded.

"Duty calls, I'm off now and so should you be. He'll have enough in what you've done there for weeks. Do you know that people are dying from the heat over in London? That's how bad it is. You may never see another summer like this, you know. On the way to beating all records. Worse than Arabia or India. We might be better off living over in someplace like Siberia. I'm off."

He's right. So different today. Not like he was at the bicycle. All sort of serious. Nice that he talked to me.

About Joe paying me and all. The sergeant. Never talk like that. Knee his nickname. Boys genuflected behind his back. Just fun. He knew that. Heard them laughing. Playacting. The sergeant not like that. No. Snee that parents threatened their children with rather than Cleary. Why?

But back to the wood and he made two stacks by the back door. Joe would be pleased, and he'd like if his father could see it too. Satisfied with his work and Snee's compliments, he jumped over the wall into the field and took the pathway home.

*

"The last supper."

Joe smiled at his father's words.

Having eaten their fill, supplemented by a few bottles of porter and lemonade for the boy, they briefly reminisced about the events that led to Joe's time at the lodge. Their anger had not abated. But it was a celebration of Joe's recovery more than dwelling on what had happened. When more bottles were uncorked; it was time for lamplight as another long twilight brought the scorching day to a close.

Deciding to put matters of contention aside they talked of hurling matches, Mulcahy and his brother's plans to get him away to the asylum, and of course the weather and all the predictions that were as many as each person one met. The villagers were convinced that divine intervention, based on the prayers for rain at mass, had caused the two recent nights of rain. Joe's cynical laugh suggested that particular aspect of things didn't merit further discussion.

Mulcahy's donkey and cart rattled past the gate towards the village at the same time every night. It was not unusual to hear him later in the night singing or preaching to an imaginary audience as he made his way home. Though he drank in his public house he had a fractious relationship with Maguire, seen as somewhat on the fringe of village life. His nickname, Mad, attested to that.

The boy and his father had often heard him late at night when he stopped just beyond the gates at Woodlands. Jumping off the donkey cart, he stood and started talking loudly, sometimes to himself and at other times as if he were talking to a crowd. He had a fund of knowledge about world events. It was from him that the boy first heard of things and people he knew nothing about and that needed answers from his father or Joe. The Boxer Rebellion, Marconi's wireless, Peary and the North Pole, the Morse code or as Mulcahy put it, dot dot dash. He learned that Jack Johnson was the first black man to win the 1906 world boxing championship from what seemed like a running commentary on one of his fights. When he told this in school, the master asked him where he heard it. When the boy replied it was from Mulcahy, there was a burst of laughter from master and classmates, with remarks like 'sure he's mad,' 'he'll be off to the big house in Cork soon,' or 'sure the brother and himself are killing each other.'

He and his older brother who shared the small farm with him, were not on good terms; this was the reason that getting him into the asylum in Cork was well known to be his brother's intention, 'when the papers were signed.'

The motorman reminded Joe of how Mulcahy had not joined the nodding heads of assent in response to the priest's tirade in the chapel, to which Joe replied, "not mad, just different."

As the night wore on, so did the conversation. Any number of topics were rehashed, many not new to the boy but he still relished hearing them again. The more bottles that were opened the looser the tongues got. The boy could contribute little to the conversation except listen, lulled by the sounds of tales past and present.

Woodlands was mentioned as was old man Sheldon and his good deeds which were contrasted with some of the more notorious ones of other landlords. Having heard the same names and incidents trotted out as often before, the boy nodded off in the corner. The last thing he remembered was counting eight empty bottles at the fireplace.

*

"But Joe man, as sure as I'm sitting here it's the gospel truth."

His father's raised voice wrenched him out of his slumber, and he noticed that the eight empty bottles that were there when he fell asleep had now risen to twelve.

Joe had not yet replied to whatever 'the gospel truth' was and he waited, alert for his father to continue.

"It was the last thing she said before she died, and I've often told you she was in full control of her senses. I'm only telling you now because I'm not blind. There's more to this place than the lady up the avenue. You know I won't say a word but for Christ's sake man, be very, very careful."

He listened, furious with himself for falling asleep, He moved as quietly as he could in the corner and waited, spellbound trying to figure out what had his father raising his voice and Joe speechless. Joe, his voice trembling, muttered indistinctly to himself and then spoke.

"But that can't be true. Come here to me now, I know she always told me never to come back here, that I was better out of the place ... but God Almighty ... I never thought it was something like what you're saying."

Stiff from having fallen asleep, he moved again in the corner to make himself comfortable. At the sound, his father jumped, looking towards to corner.

"Jesus, I never thought you were there. Weren't you in bed I thought? Tell me what you heard us talking about."

The words were garbled, drunken but intense and meant from the heart. He answered, not untruthfully, that he had heard nothing and that he had been asleep until their raised voices woke him.

Relief covered his father's face and he motioned towards the bedroom.

"Off with you now."

Slinking off to bed he listened, as Joe, despite his upset at whatever had been discussed, told him to sleep well in preparation for the next day's return to the cottage or as he put it, 'return to base'. The drink had taken its toll on both men as they waited for him to close the bedroom door and he hoped a return to what they had been talking about. He listened behind the door but there was only a disappointing silence. Then from Joe came a single sentence that brought the night's proceedings to a finish and left the listener behind the door no wiser.

"Well, whatever you say, it can't be changed now, and do you know, maybe it was as well I never knew, maybe just as well."

He waited for his father's reply and when came it threw no light on the matter.

"By God, Joe, aren't secrets hard kept, especially when the few bottles are plentiful. Look at them, their mouths open, laughing at their handiwork."

A clinking sound told him the bottles were being gathered and he could hear them being pushed hither and tither around the fireplace before being put into a wooden crate and pushed away roughly in the back door's direction. He waited and waited for more to be said, but it was a vain wait. Settled in his makeshift bed for the last night, Joe mumbled goodnight to his father.

None of them had thought of or noticed, that in all their chat and talk, they had heard no sound of Mulcahy's donkey passing by, as usual, on his way home.

*

He was awake before the others and waited for what seemed like hours for some movement in the kitchen. Joe and his father eventually got up, looking the worse for wear and in little humour for talking. When the boy joined them, he saw that it was nearly eleven, and looking out the door, there was nothing to suggest that the day ahead was going to be cooler than the many that had already eaten up the summer days so far. After a hastily arranged frugal breakfast, they got ready for the return to the cottage.

Joe wore the tattered clothes, now washed, that he had worn the night of the attack. Washing failed to obliterate the evidence of the night's attack. As well as the clothes he wore being a testament to what he had suffered, Joe still bore some scars and seemed to have difficulty shaking off the limp. He moved a little less surely. Yet, when he stepped out along the path from the lodge and surveyed the scene around him, defiance was written all over his face. He looked up the avenue towards Woodlands, and for a moment, preoccupied, he was lost in another world. He couldn't hide that from father or son. Then he was ready to go.

"It feels I've been locked up all my life," he said, addressing no one in particular.

Of course, the motor was there for the asking to bring him home but there were many reasons why that would not be a good idea. Anyway, Joe had decided that the boy and himself would not take the pathway which would keep their return from the villagers unknown until they leaped over Joe's garden wall. But no, they would walk back along the road, heads held high and as he said, anyone who cared to watch would see that "you can't keep a good man down." Snee's very words.

He shook the motorman's hand, looked back up the avenue once more and commanded the boy to "lead on McDuff." The words were music to his ears as if something magical was lost and now regained. Joe could engender a sense of adventure in the most routine of activities, like the rabbit catching, fishing, or trips to town and always trips to the castle. But today was custom-made, a new kind of adventure.

The church and chapel loomed large before them, and Joe passed by each without as much as a sideways glance. His eye was on the street, and he made an extra effort not to let the limp show as they strode towards the cottage gate. Little did either know that so much was to happen that day, a sequence that brought everything almost to a point beyond understanding. And not just for them, believing as they did that they were coming home.

*

They went round the side of the cottage to go in the back door. The boy slowed, waiting for Joe to look approvingly at the two mounds of timber assembled with such care the previous day.

Something wrong. Wood stacked. Just as he had left it. But no. Something. The dead cats. The rotten sheep. The attack. Sick feeling. Danger. Throat dry. Joe just normal. Wondering what's wrong with me.

"Go on in, isn't it great to be back, after all?"

"Joe … I don't know … there is something wrong."

"What's wrong? Sure look at the great job you did. Don't be looking for too much praise, now."

The man stood, perplexed at the boy's hesitation who felt there was something ominously thick in the air; his throat constricted. But with Joe nothing was wrong, and he responded to the boy's hesitant "you go first."

Standing back as Joe opened the small red door, he swallowed again, his apprehension only increased by Joe, just so casual about everything. But then.

"Christ, you're right boy, there is something…"

An animal stench, accentuated by the heat, met them as the door opened. Waiting to adjust to the darkness after the searing brightness outside, they noticed not a thing was amiss in the kitchen, tidied and ready. They moved, drawn by the smell towards the parlour. A sickening fear ripped through him now that there was no doubt about what he had felt before they ever got inside the door.

Were it not so foul and sinister, what they saw at first glance was comical. Standing, almost filling the room with no room stood a donkey and cart. The donkey gave them both a baleful, innocent look. Mulcahy's. He knew immediately in his mesmerised fright and inability to make any sense of what they were looking at; his next thought was the image of a ship in a bottle that his father had once shown him in a shop in Cork. How did the donkey get in with the cart? A mystery.

Shaking now, his hand found Joe's as the full extent of what lay before them became clearer. Chaos. Everything ripped from top to bottom, papers, books, magazines cast in all directions, chairs and table upended and thrown against the wall to make room for the donkey. The soothing sound of Joe's two clocks, wound the day before, keepsakes of his mother, were silent, shattered on the ground.

In the mass of confusion on the floor something else met their eyes. The shattered glass obscured the carefree, smiling face of Joe's mother, making her image look grotesque. It was as if it had been placed there deliberately to be seen when they came in, though that was hardly the case. Looking from the photo to Joe's face, begging for some explanation, something to be said to take the terrible cut and edge out of the stinking air. The stench of animal dung seeped from walls, floor and ceiling.

He let go of Joe's hand and clumsily picked up the photo and tried to steady it on the mantelpiece. It stood for a moment and then tumbled forward on to the ground. He took it out to the kitchen and came back in to see Joe, who yet hadn't spoken, looking in the village's direction. Alive in its seething outrage, his voice grated through his clenched teeth.

"Someone up there will pay for this, by Christ, they will." The boy had expected the words to be loud, to be heard out on the street, to be heard next door by the priest. But they were low, coming from his belly, and barely audible. Desperate to say something to let Joe know how he felt, he tried to speak through dry and quivering lips. Words would not come and after Joe's seething warning he had never felt so afraid. Not even the night of the attack, not even in the muddied school yard where his classmates hurled abuse in his face, not even the priest holding his cane under his throat under the boiling sun on the street, never had he felt like now. It was almost as if Joe was out of control though he seemed strangely calm in another way. The heat in the room was suddenly almost unbearable. Sweat ran down Joe's face as he reached and patted the donkey's rump.

Waiting for the next move, more confused than ever at this riddle of destruction and hatred visited upon them, he watched as the last thing he expected happened. Joe slumped to the floor amid the sorry mess, looked around the room, then to the donkey and then to the boy. Despite his simmering rage, the big man's frame convulsed on the floor and tears ran down his face, a face barely healed from the night of the attack. The crying, the first time he had ever seen a man cry, oddly took away some of the fear that gripped him. He wanted to cry himself. Only a whimper escaped his parched lips.

Reaching out his hand, Joe, still sobbing, beckoned and a great arm came round his slender shoulder and he was brought close to the man's chest. In the midst of the foul-smelling chaos all around them, there came a momentary thread of peace. He felt Joe's chest heave and relax. Secure in the embrace, the hideous incongruity of what was all around them receded for a moment. Then looking from where he sat, he realised that he could not see the front door through the donkey's legs. Soon, he saw why. Something was hanging from the donkey's neck which neither of them had noticed. He moved from Joe's embrace and round by the cartwheel nearest him. The donkey shook his head with a flourish as the boy raised a large piece of cardboard from where it hung and read the toxic message.

Scrawled in capitals was what might be one or two words. To the boy it read as one, GOLDEVIL but on closer inspection he saw there a second D and it read GOLDDEVIL. Joe, dragging himself to his feet, had come round to see for himself. Expressionless he looked and expressionless he turned away, but not before patting the donkey's head and looking into the dumb beast's innocent, impenetrable eyes.

The boy had noticed one other object, the bible, and it lay seemingly untouched on the windowsill. He opened it and his heart sunk. The note he had brought from Woodlands was gone and all that remained was the other crude scribble that was the forerunner of the sign.

"They took it, they took the letter."

"What are you talking about? Letters are the least of our worries now."

"But it was the one she wrote to you. Remember, the day I brought it and the other bad one, this, was here."

"Ah, you must have missed it, here give it to me," Joe asked, now frowning at this new possibility.

He held the bible by the spine and shook it. All in vain and a despairing smile crossed his face. Whoever had wreaked havoc had done so with patience. Who could have known that the notes were in the bible when every other book was tossed at random around the floor? It meant that time had been taken and a method used. Patience had yielded a prized piece of information.

"Superstitious bastards," sneered Joe, "they hadn't the guts to touch it," and he put the bible back.

Not understanding what Joe meant the boy pondered on the imponderable. How did they get the donkey and cart into the house?

"How did they do it?" he asked, perplexity in every word. He raised his arms as he spoke, hoping this most elementary of gestures might possibly bring an answer.

"They did it the same way as we're going to have to get it out. C'mon, I'll show you, it's as good a place to start as any."

With devastation and the stinking, putrid heat all round them Joe still managed to get a kick out of teasing the boy through what appeared to be an incomprehensible puzzle. "Now look at it. Which is the easiest to get out, the donkey or the cart?"

"Well, the donkey, I suppose, but then what about the cart?" the boy asked.

"Right then, first things first so," Joe said, lifting the poster over the donkey's ears, casting it aside with disgust. Together they unharnessed the donkey from the cart and lowered the shafts on to the floor. Then, after a struggle to open the front door, the boy led the donkey into the small, flower filled garden, blistering in the sunlight. The donkey bent over to nibble at the parched grass, oblivious to the part it had played in such a well-executed plan.

He returned for the most formidable task that now faced them, the cart. He looked at Joe, then at the streak of sunlight coming through the front door. With a slow shake of his head, he indicated that it couldn't be done.

"What do you do with a big number that you want to make small?"

"You divide it or take away from it," the boy answered, not at all sure as to how a classroom question would get them out of the dilemma they faced. Insolvable, he thought.

"You're right. Now look at it again and tell me what has to be done to make it small enough to get out the door."

Studying the cart again, he followed the line of Joe's eye to where it rested on the cartwheel nearest them. All he could see were the brightly painted red spokes. There, in front of him was the pin that secured the wheel to the axle.

"I have it."

With a whoop of excitement that seemed contradictory in the misery all round them, he saw a way out of the dilemma.

"That's it, isn't it? You take off the wheels first and then maybe the rest of it can be turned on its side to fit out the door?"

A wink was Joe's answer. With difficulty they achieved what it must have taken a number of men to do the previous night. He noticed how Joe struggled and it was clear he was far from fully better as he groaned and moaned at each heaving movement.

The wheels were removed, one by one, and again with difficulty rolled outside to the front garden. As they got each wheel out, neither, as if by agreement looked about them. Knowing, without doubt but that they were there for the show at this stage, they wouldn't give the onlookers that satisfaction. Deep down they knew of course that their efforts and struggle was a spectacle, relished because of its novelty, and the word would now be all over the village.

The body of the cart would prove impossible for just the two to move. It would have to be angled on its side so that the axle bisected the open door and that demanded agility, strength and assistance.

"We'll never get it," the boy said after a few grunting attempts cruelly exposed Joe's less than usual strength and competence. The attack's effects were still evident. Their victim stood, angered and defeated. The boy felt that with Joe in the best of health, the task would be too great for the two of them anyway.

"I'll run back for Father and he'll help us to get it out."

As if not hearing, Joe looked again at the cart, then around the room and finally out the door. A mischievous grin and he said, "we'll need help sure enough. Do you know who you'll go and ask?"

It then dawned on the boy that the most logical person to get to help was Snee. That's what he's there for in a way isn't it and anyway he had said he would visit Joe. No harm for him to see what had been done in the dead of night. About to say the constable's name he suddenly realised something so elementary, so obvious, that he blurted it out as somehow stumbling on some great unrevealed truth.

"But that's it, Joe, it's him, that rotten bastard, Snee. He was the only one that knew you were coming back because no one else knew except me, and I told him that yesterday when I was doing the sticks. He's a traitor, as bad as all the rest of them. I'm not going to ask him for help."

He was suddenly defiant at the thought of the traitorous policeman and how he seemed so nice the previous day before setting off to give the information to the League, so they had time to plan their dirty work. The constable's sweating image again brought a sickening feeling.

"Hang on a minute now. It wasn't him at all I was going to ask you to get. But wait, what else did you tell him?"

"Nothing else that I can think of…anyway I told him enough, just what he wanted to know."

"Look here to me now and wait. We have enough to do here without trying to be detectives, even though there might be something in what you say. We'll do what we can here first, so now you know what you can do, and it might kill two birds with the one stone. Go across the road there to the Rev Mr Field and tell him I need his help for a few minutes. I know he's no Samson but between the three of us we'll manage somehow."

"But we can't ask him with the way things are," he replied, remembering his father's fury at the rector's sermon.

"Go on, I'm telling you," Joe leered, "won't it give him a chance to see what his sermonising achieved in the last week or two?

*

At the rector's door he was shaded for a few moments from the beating sun. He wasn't sure now about Joe's plan to kill two birds with one stone. And what would be gained by showing him the results of the League's latest act of bravery? He knocked and waited but no answer came. The rector did not have the same power as the priest. The master had told them that in school one day saying the rector was "presiding over a dying breed and soon will have nothing to do around here." He told the class they didn't even have a statue or a holy picture to pray to in their church and didn't believe in the Pope or Blessed Virgin. He was tempted to ask the teacher how he knew there were no pictures or statues inside the Protestant church if no Catholic was supposed to even look in there, never mind go in. He thought better of asking that question, though.

Another knock and again no answer. Maybe if he went back to Joe to say the rector was out, he might send him to the priest and then what. But no, he would never, ever, do that. A sudden spark of curiosity brought him round the path at the side of the rectory to a wooden gate that led into the garden. He pushed gingerly and it opened.

Now in a place he had never before seen, never mind been in, he looked around. Flowers everywhere and their smell forcefully hit him and left him wondering how the rector was able to have a perfect garden when evidence of drought was everywhere else to be seen.

He saw why there was no answer. Away at the very end of the garden, stretched out on a wicker chair lay the rector, a magazine covering his face from the blazing sun. He looked like a puppet with his arms hanging by the side of the chair and his legs spread out. Never had he expected to see such a sight. He coughed slightly, then more loudly to awake the slumbering figure. That had no effect. What next?

He could see clearly what was on the cover of The Illustrated News where a bold headline shouted, "New Information on Submarines." Beneath was a picture of a sailor with some kind of a microscope studying an emerging submarine on the horizon. It was an old edition and he had seen it a few weeks previously in the cottage.

Wondering whether to cough again or not he was suddenly frightened out of his wits. Without warning and with a yell that would have put the savages in The Coral Island to shame, the rector jumped out of the chair, very much awake, throwing the magazine up in the air.

"Aha, that fooled you my little man. There's no fool like an old fool and that I never intend becoming."

Immensely pleased that his trick had worked so well, he continued, "Always remember that things are not always as they seem to be. If you remember that, it will get you out of many a scrape. Now, don't tell me but I am sure I can tell you who sent you here. Now, I'm just going to do a little mind reading. You just close your eyes and think of the person who sent you and then count to three."

Surely, the boy thought, he cannot know who sent me. Yet after his pretending to be asleep trick maybe he did have some magic power. He did as he was told, thought of Joe and counted to three before opening his eyes.

"Yes, I have it. One person and one person only sent you, namely Mrs Victoria Sheldon, mistress of Woodlands."

The words were proclaimed with childish satisfaction and Field waited for the boy to confirm that what he had said was true.

"No Father, I mean Reverend, it was not Mrs Sheldon who sent me."

Somewhat crestfallen that his mind reading had not proven right he then said "Well, you know what they say, Homer nods." This meant nothing to the boy, and he would have to ask Joe as well as tell him that he had seen the rector acting as never before.

Apparently not wishing to have another go at mind reading, he asked, curiously, as to who had sent him.

"Joe, Mr Golden sent me," he volunteered awkwardly, pointing back over his shoulder towards the cottage as if Field wasn't aware of where The Pagan lived.

"Oh, and whatever would he want me for?"

"Because, sir, Reverend, something terrible has happened to him and the cottage and he's not strong enough after what they did to him below at the castle gate."

A sequence of expressions crossed the rector's face as he digested each detail of information. The uncharacteristic fun and humour that had so mesmerised the boy was now gone, well and truly. The rector seemed puzzled and somehow the boy knew why he might be. To gain some time he lifted the magazine off the ground, glanced at the cover and said, "have you seen this?" He was about to proudly answer that he had seen it but didn't get a chance "We think we have problems here but wait until we have to fight against monsters like that. That's the modern world. I just wonder sometimes what will they think of next? On land, sea and air, new inventions. Did you hear that two fellows in America went up in the air in some kind of a flying machine a while back? Machines, machines, machines."

The boy again was about to say he'd heard about the flying machines when Field seemed to be brought back to earth and asked, "what does he want me to do?" His tone definitely suggested he wasn't keen on doing anything for the village pariah.

He tried to explain as best he could what had met their eyes when Joe and himself came back to the cottage and especially about the donkey and cart. His description left Field completely baffled and uncomfortable but with his usual curiosity aroused. Why can't he just come over and see what has happened?

"Couldn't he have asked his neighbour ... the priest?"

The boy thought this was a joke and the words were barely said when Field shook his head and his comment trailed off into silence, "I suppose he would hardly do that would he?"

*

She had woken earlier than usual, racked by a crazy compulsion. Should she go to the gate lodge on some excuse before he left? She fell back asleep again and woke, instantly realising that that it would be folly and too obvious to the boy and his father.

No, she would force herself to wait and then later would walk through the village, nothing unusual, and this would bring her past the cottage. This simplistic plan brought a stinging desire that she was loath to banish. Yes, she would go around midday but how the time would drag until then.

She had a number of letters to write and that, at least, would take some time. The terrible heat sapped any bit of creativity where her writing was concerned but she realised that was making excuses, and she knew why, deep down.

She would face a blank sheet and try to put her mother off the thought of visiting. That would not be easy. It was, after all, holiday time. Her mother needed to be dealt with cautiously because of her innate ability to "read between the lines." In this case it would literally be true. Keeping to the mundane where possible and alluding to Edward's involvement in one of the year's more sensational divorce cases, with millions at stake, she rambled on about the weather and finished up by vaguely suggesting that a holiday in early autumn might be more appropriate. She reread it as other thoughts invaded, sealed the envelope and threw it to one side.

Then to a letter that had been brewing in her mind all morning, more appealing and more demanding to be written. If she couldn't be with him, she would put her thoughts on paper as a way of expressing what she felt. How incredibly easy to know that what she now began to write was really what she meant, with no restriction, no wondering how to phrase things, just a flow of undiluted passion committed to paper for one person and one only. It would be a letter never intended for delivery, it was to herself, written as if he were looking into her eyes and she into his. It was like all lovers' letters, meant for one alone. To an outsider it might seem outlandish, exaggerated, shot through with an intimacy that words could scarcely describe. Fortune had played into her hands, and she knew it. Shandrum's least favourite son had unleashed in her a swell of determination that would brook no opposition, even in an alien setting.

What she wrote was written with a vehemence and intensity never felt before. Wasn't it strange then that in its writing, Nathan's ghostly presence should tap at the edges of her imagination? Yet, it demanded no comparison, rather bringing a conviction that she had been doubly lucky. This thought led to a long, hurried outpouring of all she wanted to say about what a few weeks ago would have been impossible to even imagine. Left with a trenchant satisfaction, it was as if what was denied her for the moment, was for that very reason, even more acutely present.

Carefully she placed what she had written in the secret compartment of her desk. This brought Edward to mind, and she remembered the day, shortly after she arrived, when she sat here at the desk, that was to be hers, and he pointed. "Something you may never need," he had said, "but then one never knows." Indeed, she thought now. He had never entered her head as she wrote her words of love. Nathan, yes, but not her husband.

With parasol in hand, scant protection against the unforgiving sun, she stepped on air down the avenue. At the lodge she mused what it would always mean to her, small, squat and almost miserable looking though it appeared. Out onto the road, dry and dusty. It was here that she recalled the accident when she had first seen him sprawled in the blood red sun, invisible barriers between them, under the studied, defensive gaze of her pastor.

Darkly and uncomfortably, she realised their coming together had been through actual accidents, though she would not consider that savage attack as such. Even in the noonday sun she shivered as the images recurred, the rain, the child's sweaty, frightened face and the stricken heap, bloodied and beaten in the summer night.

With such a resurrected ghost, her step was now not so light as when she had set out. Approaching the village and nearing the churches, it was not the past events that she was forced to confront but a present one. She noticed that a donkey and two cartwheels stood outside Joe's door. Has he a donkey and cart? Could such a basic fact have escaped her? It evidently had.

Then her attention was drawn to two figures emerging from the rectory. It was the boy with Field, looking decidedly uneasy, following him. The boy, seeing her first and, taken aback, said something over his shoulder to Field who stopped and shook his head in disbelief. They waited for her, and Field's agitated look told her that she was not the most welcome intrusion at this time. Not wishing to appear uncivil he tried, as best he could, to steer her away from what she might come upon.

"Good day, Mrs. Sheldon. You appear to have happened upon a most unfortunate incident and one which I have not had the time to fully assess. If you would allow me, you can rest from the sun and all of this in the rectory. Once this unfortunate state of affairs is dealt with, I'll then be able to tell you what has happened. It's terribly unfortunate and upsetting."

"But what happened?" she asked, moving beyond Field and going through the gate of the cottage.

"Someone broke in here last night and I think I know who it was too," the boy volunteered. About to continue, he was interrupted by Joe coming out the door. Madly anxious to know what was going on, she blurted out "Joe, what on earth has happened now?"

She almost said "my darling" but something providentially prevented her and made her take stock of what she would say from now on. But the intimacy of how the question was asked by her was not lost on Field and it drew a look, critical and questioning. A bristling silence hung over the singular scene and the four caught in it. Along the street hardly a doorway was unoccupied. Clusters stood about, with the usuals strategically placed at Maguires for a grandstand view. And what a view it was that met their searching eyes. A donkey, The Pagan, the boy, the rector and the mistress of Woodlands, all standing as if ignoring the sun which beat down relentlessly.

Joe salvaged a degree of normality by seeming to ignore Victoria. Field, let so unwittingly into a secret haunt he had somehow always suspected as existing, strove to regain his composure.

"Rev Field, in a moment of need where does an honest man turn? Where in this place, where I am denied a loaf of bread by those who were once glad to buy my rabbits, eat my fish and welcome my help when they needed it, where am I to turn? You know more than most what the good book says … 'out of the mouths of babes.' Sure enough when I asked where I could turn, his nibs here had the answer. Do you know what he said? Do you?"

Perplexed by the way the conversation was going and The Pagan's performance leading up to where he was now at, the rector felt he was somehow being seductively groomed and reluctantly led down a path he had to take. Reluctantly, but curiosity growing as to where it would take him.

"The boy there, do you know what he said? He said we'll ask someone who is always there to help. And for a minute I thought he meant someone else. Old habits die hard, you know," Joe continued with a hint of mischief in his voice.

"But no - out of the mouths of babes indeed - he said the rector will help us. Could I say no to that? How could I and before I could open my mouth, he was out the door and over the road to you. Now come in and see what the upstanding citizens of Shandrum have done. The wild man from Borneo couldn't have done a better job."

Submerged by this barrage of flattery and rhetoric, the rector, as if hypnotised and ignoring the etiquette of ladies first, made his way to the door and Joe gestured for the boy to follow and then Victoria. In the short interlude, going from outside to inside the door, Joe looked around him and aided by the adjustment from darkness to light, audaciously took Victoria's hand and squeezed it. It didn't prepare her for what met her eyes. The small room, looking now like a dungeon, enveloped them in its bizarre odour, a sinister smell and sight of destruction.

Savages she thought and then uttered the words into the dank air. Field, as if shocked by the word, or more by who had uttered it, turned as if in reprimand. She stared at him but what he then said gave her some immediate comfort.

"Animals do not act like this towards one another. Why do we?"

Something on the floor looked vaguely familiar to her. Picking up the tattered half of the book she realised it was the one she had given the boy. He was now holding up the poster with the scrawl for Field and herself to see. Even in the stifling heat she shivered as the import of the message struck home. Field stared intently as if to confirm that the single word, the threatening scrawl, was as it read.

He then snatched it from the boy and tore it into pieces which fell randomly to the ground to rest in the debris. The boy watched their fluttering descent as Field, noticing the bible on the windowsill turned and looked at Joe, questioning the incongruity. He tried to open the window, but it stuck. For a moment he placed his elbows on the sill and stared out into the sunlight before turning back to the others, searching for some way to articulate how he felt.

"Mrs. Sheldon … er … ah, what can I … say … do about this despicable and outrageous … it's what happens when, whe … ah, what's the use? Where ignorance is bliss, it is folly to be wise." In a further gesture of helplessness, he threw his arms in the air, nearly touching the low ceiling. Then, turning to Joe, he said, "well what do you want me to do? You sent for me and I'm here."

She thought he meant how he would deal with this at service and maybe that's what he meant. Joe wasted no time in turning away from feelings to practicalities.

"Well, for one thing you can help me get this out of the way before Mulcahy comes along and blames *me* for stealing it. That would be a good one, wouldn't it but I'd believe anything at this stage!"

Field moved adroitly and as directed toward the shafts of the cart, and Joe went to the back, motioning Victoria to move away, back towards the kitchen door. Nearer to the front door, however, she went out into the sunlight. She was met by the shy stares of a group of children gathered across the road at a safe distance. Knowing and sensing that adult eyes were on her too, perhaps those of the priest next door, rage welled up inside her, making her oblivious to the searching eyes and wagging tongues relishing this latest event. An event that had been well heralded, she thought as she turned back towards the doorway, uncertain of what she might say or do if provoked, even in the slightest.

The huddle of children edged closer, their curiosity increasing. They would not be denied an opportunity to view what was to happen next. They would speak of it as old men and women. They would also speak of the fact that not another single helping hand came from the village. It was as if a pact could not be broken, even in the name of simple charity.

*

The boy marvelled at how anxious Field was to be of help. Though not a young man, his assistance meant Joe was able to direct operations. With a lot of heaving and shouts of encouragement, they slowly angled the cart through the door. In the finish, despite Field's best efforts it was Joe's strength, hampered though it was, that achieved success. She watched, realising then how it had been manoeuvred inside in the first place. Both men rested and then had to get the cart and wheels reassembled on the roadside. As this was going on she asked the boy if there was water in the house and he beckoned her round the back and into the kitchen, It was a very different picture than what she had seen on arrival. Rudimentary but clean, everything in its place and the boy pointed to the bucket of water. She looked around and got two glasses from a shelf, filled them and brought them round to Joe and Field.

With the wheels on the cart, Joe lifted the shafts, and the boy backed the donkey between them and what had faced them as the biggest job to get done was finished. Now it was back to the mess inside. Field, showing an unexpected burst of energy, proclaimed, "now to get things cleaned up."

"No, you've done what I wanted you for, more than enough and I'm grateful for it," replied Joe. "Anyway, I've plenty help to get this done and I want to look through what might be rescued."

Victoria was not sure if he meant she was part of the 'help.' While Field was present, she could justify being there. With him gone things might not be so clear cut but she wanted to stay. The guise of helping to clean up was worth the risk.

"If you insist then I'll go but I don't envy you the task you have ahead of you," and he hesitated before adding "in more ways than one."

He bade goodbye to Victoria, promising that he would see her soon and making a cursory enquiry about Edward while adding that the divorce case he was involved in in London was the best possible example of "human greed among those who should know better and entertainment for the masses. Why can't people put aside their differences and live together?"

Field's attitude and his willingness to assist someone with whom he appeared to be at odds, greatly surprised Victoria. A Pauline conversion was all she could think of, and she found herself, sneakily, admiring him. It also gave her a certain consolation that it was one of her own that had done the good deed and good deeds were certainly in short supply. Despite the reversal in his attitude, he was not about to take herself and the boy into his confidence on everything and he signalled Joe to come out onto the road with him, out of earshot but in plain view of the villagers. From inside they both watched as the two outside spoke, Joe listening and the rector gravely choosing his words.

Not wishing to be privy to the conversation taking

place on the street, she pushed the door halfway shut and contemplated the scene, revolted by the nauseating spectacle. As if unable to decide where to begin, she looked at the boy and suggested they wait until the rector was gone before setting to work. She then went through the kitchen and out to the backyard for another battle with the heat.

The castle, new to her from a different angle but so familiar to the boy, stood majestic in the hazy distance. Looking down at him she asked, unfairly she immediately thought, "what do you make of all this?"

He jumped at the opportunity to let her know about Snee, telling her with passion and conviction that he alone knew about Joe returning to the cottage. He used the word 'traitor' and 'culprit' and those words, so adult in their meaning, disturbed her. She listened, sceptically, and he saw it in her face, but he went on, anxious to be able to pinpoint so accurately someone who was responsible for all that had happened overnight.

The sense of outrage in what he said was not lost on her. She was sceptical of the involvement of the constable in setting up such a monstrous deed. But the boy's words piqued her curiosity.

The voices from the roadway had stopped and Joe could be heard coming through the house. For the boy this was a relief. He was angry with her for not believing him about Snee, he could see it on her face but also saw that she seemed to be puzzled as if trying to think of different things at the same time.

He never thought he would feel anything like anger towards her. That he could feel this way towards her seemed not to be wrong but beyond understanding. There she was in the sunlight, standing in the backyard of a simple cottage and he wondered what she thought of it all. Couldn't she see that with Snee against Joe and helping the League meant they were all against him? They had no one to look to now, no hope at all. Except of course, strangely, Field.

Joe's return meant the unwelcome job had to be faced. Part of it was unexpected and for the second time that morning he was given something to do that he did not relish. Joe asked him to take the donkey and cart, not to Mulcahy where it obviously belonged but to the barrack. Victoria was just as surprised as the boy.

"You don't understand. I just want to make a point," insisted Joe, when he saw the disbelief on their faces.

"Just tell Snee or Cleary that I found a stray donkey and cart in my house and the barrack is the place to bring it because I don't know who owns it."

This had the same effect on both and though the boy was apprehensive about driving the donkey and cart through the village, he saw the jest as a clear indication that Joe was not as beaten as they might think. And he was letting everyone know that. Victoria's scepticism vanished and she looked at Joe with a smile of complicity and turning to the boy said "don't you remember I told you how brave you are. I'd love to see their faces when you drive through the village and especially Sergeant Cleary's and the constable's. Just keep a straight face."

While she meant every word she said, she had her own motives for his being gone, for however short a time.

"Wait now," the boy asked, pointing towards the indoors, "will I say what happened?"

"No, just what I told you."

"And be careful to be polite to the constable if he's there. We know how you feel about him," Victoria added. Desperate to have him gone, she followed him round the side of the house.

Taking to his task with determination, he noticed, as he began to drive away, that the priest was attacking his garden with ferocity, despite it being the warmest part of the day. Had he seen Field coming across to Joe's, the boy wondered, hoping to get past the presbytery as soon as he could. He must have, and no doubt saw her as well. He was certain that the priest had to know about all that had happened the night before. By right he should be going the other way since Mulcahy lived beyond Woodlands down a long boreen. He would have preferred that as he saw the priest stop as he approached. Then he stepped belligerently out onto the road with a rake in his hand.

"Where are you going, my bucko?"

He straddled the road, the rake held like a spear. The donkey veered to one side and stopped at the boy's bidding. He didn't know what to say but gulped the words out that Joe had told him to say at the barrack.

The priest stood, sweat rolling down his face and through his white shirt from his exertions in the garden.

"Good God, child do you expect me to believe that rigmarole of a story? Do you know who you're talking to?"

Not knowing what to say after giving him Joe's explanation was seen by the priest as sullen insolence. He brought his face close and all the boy could see were the veins on his sweaty forehead. He had a vision of snakes swimming in a river as he watched the veins pulsating. Then he did the unthinkable. He laughed. Why he did not know. It had something to do with the image of thousands of snakes swimming down some river in a distant land. He must ask Joe if snakes could swim. He brought his hand to his face as if to cancel out the laugh. A sickening blow from the priest swung his head round before his hand got to his face, and he was spun off the cart onto the dusty ground coming to rest almost under the donkey's belly, still holding on to the reins.

He looked up to where the priest should be standing but the blinding sun caught him straight in the eyes. He was dragged out from where he lay. He waited for another blow. Instead, he was put standing against one of the shafts of the cart. Oh God. I will not cry. Not for him.

"Can I believe what I just saw right now?" A voice came from the other side of the cart. "Father, your emotions are running away with you and it's hardly the sun. You just knocked a child to the ground, something I never thought I would see someone in your position do."

Before he could turn, he realised it was Field. The priest looked more embarrassed than reprimanded for a moment, but then he pushed the boy aside and rounded on the rector.

"Mr Field," he thundered, emphasising the Mr, "it is my business to deal with my parishioners. You might be better engaged right now if you dealt with yours."

Quizzically, Field asked "and what do you mean by that?"

The boy still smarting from the blow to his face found himself like a spectator at a boxing match, like he often saw in the papers. The two men ignored him, the priest continuing to lecture Field.

"There are none so blind, there are none so blind, dear Rector," the priest sneeringly remarked, pointing at the same time towards the Protestant church. Only then did he realise that it was Joe's cottage that was being pointed at by the priest's stabbing, bony finger.

"What, Mr Field will be said when people, your people, find out that one of your revered churchgoers is at this moment alone in that shack with someone who is the personification of evil in this village and whose appetites are obviously varied. Indeed, what would her husband say?"

Field, dumbfounded, seemed lost for words. To the boy it seemed he was somehow in agreement with what had been said to him. Unprepared for what came next, he was to see a side of Field that he never thought existed.

Realising the full import of what the priest had said, Field looked for a moment in the direction of the cottage and then turned, coming round to face the priest.

"Rev Father, woe to the givers of scandal. To suggest, as you do, that any woman, never mind one of Mrs Sheldon's standing, is engaged in anything other than an act of Christian charity, which I might say, that unfortunate man would get from no one else around here, is outrageous in the extreme. In my years as a minister of the gospel I have never heard such an improper allegation made by anyone, let alone someone of your standing and calling. I will say again, woe to the givers of scandal."

He stopped to draw his breath and only then noticed the presence of the open-mouthed boy standing where he had been placed by the priest. About to continue, the rector obviously thought it better that the boy should not be privy to such a conversation. Neither he nor his clerical opponent were finished but they seemed to be at one on getting rid of the boy.

"On about your business, young man," Field waved.

Needing no encouragement, he jumped on to the cart, swollen-faced and bewildered, and urged the donkey onwards and up the street, out of earshot but in sight of those who were drawn to the sight of the two men of God, not exactly having a civilised conversation in the heat that engulfed everyone. As he got to Creighton's, he dared look back. There they were, more like Punch and Judy than two boxers. Behind them was the spire of one church and the squat cross that topped the other, all receding now as he rattled up the street. Two of Cremin's dogs lolled in the shade, too lazy to be coaxed into pursuit. Tying the reins to the pump and with the face of the traitor, Snee, in his mind he marched up to the open barrack door, stepped inside the musty hallway and defiantly shouted "Hallo". One of Sergeant Cleary's sons, known well to him from school, led him through the hallway out to the back of the barrack. Long and rectangular, the garden had trees at the bottom wall where a few more of the Cleary children played in the shade, watched by their mother who sat knitting in the corner. The garden, bathed in sunshine with the laughing children was very different to the musty interior of the hallway and the sombre, grey front that was all most people ever saw of the barrack.

Halfway down the garden sat Snee whom he recognised immediately though it was the first time he had seen him out of uniform. He slumped in a chair, stripped to the waist with a handkerchief, knotted at each corner, protecting his head from the sun.

Sitting up in the chair at the sight of the boy he smiled, thinly but welcoming. Not wanting to give him any satisfaction, Joe's message was coldly delivered. Snee, as far as the boy was concerned feigning surprise, asked him to repeat what he had said. Genuine surprise was his response, shaking his head in disbelief. But it was not enough to convince the boy.

The constable rose and put on his tunic jacket, leaving his shirt on the chair. He then beckoned to the boy and they went back into the hallway where Snee told him to wait for a moment. He was hardly gone when he was back with two glasses of water, one of which he gave to the boy. Reluctant to accept the gesture at first, he gladly swallowed it down, muttering 'thanks.'

Out onto the street he followed the constable, who before he looked at the donkey and cart, gave a practised look down the street. A learned routine.

"Hang on now, that's Jim Mulcahy's, sure the whole country knows that."

The glass of water was forgotten. Snee knew everything. But hiding it. That's probably because he is a policeman. Never giving anything away. No clues. Probably trained to be that way.

"I know a joke when I see one, you know, and what do you mean by saying he found the donkey in the house?

How was that supposed to happen? Does he think I'm a fool?"

Snee felt he was being made a fool of by Joe. The boy's dour, sullen face was not an answer. When he was told that Field had come across to Joe's to help get the cart out, and how it was done, Snee took on a much more serious though no less quizzical attitude to everything. That increased when the boy, pointing to his face, almost as an afterthought, recounted what had happened when the priest hit him, and the rector had intervened and "gave out to Fr. Kerley."

*

Desperately anxious to have the boy gone, she returned to the back door, too hastily she thought to anyone who might be watching. But she didn't care and was soon in his arms, madly wanting to say a thousand things, yet the good fortune of being alone with him and so unexpectedly, overwhelmed her. The morass around them was forgotten, the weight of fear and apprehension at being discovered was lifted, if even for a short while. Sensing that the front door might offer the most danger, he pulled her with him and kicked it close. Its closing darkened the room, full of chaos, and yet, gave all around them a sumptuous intimacy she could not have imagined.

The shout from the roadway catapulted them, their embrace freezing. Her first thought was that someone had seen them.

"That's Kerley," said Joe. They went to the window, and she stood with her arms around his waist as they watched the priest standing in front of the donkey and cart. The blow given by the priest made her cry out, as its force twisted the boy's face towards them as he fell to the ground. Joe tried to push her aside and of course she knew he was right, but she somehow held on to him, fearing that if he got out the door there would be serious trouble, which might now only make things far worse. He grappled with the door, dragging it open and was about to burst away from her attempts to hold him back when Field suddenly went past, half running. So intent was he that he never even noticed them.

"Wait, wait Joe, to see what happens."

The face of anger turned and the heaving, sweating body regained a degree of composure. Joe stood at the door while she huddled by the door jamb out of sight. He relaxed from his heightened, agitated state and she was glad that whatever happened, the rector taking Joe's place in dealing with the priest was a blessing. He still stood ready, if necessary, to do whatever had to be done if the boy was to suffer any further indignity.

An argument was in progress and try as they might, only snatches of what was being said were audible. The squabble continued as the boy was sent on his way. When Field turned to walk away, his head shaking with incredulity, she pulled Joe back inside. The priest stood as if to prove that a victory of some small proportion had been achieved. An impartial observer however, and there were few such in the village, might have concluded that the rector's intervention had stopped the priest in his tracks. Not only that, but it allowed the boy continue his journey unimpeded. Maybe it was just as well the intervention had taken place. Practically all of those watching had not forgotten the previous incident when The Pagan had not been as restrained with the priest as Field had been. But then, not everyone had heard what Field had said with such passionate intent.

Back inside now they slipped to the floor, holding each other in the stifling heat, their ardour diminished by what they had just witnessed. The scene around them didn't help. Sitting in sombre reflection, she could not get rid of the picture of the boy's head reacting to the blow from the priest. His plight, so caught up in a tangle of adults' rivalries, beyond his understanding, brought home to her why she had invited Joe to Woodlands in the first place.

The other image was of Joe's face, blazing with anger at the priest's actions. It was so unlike anything she had seen before; the dignified hopelessness the night she had seen him slumped against the wall in the rain, the look that first beguiled her, the face of passion she now lived for, all so different from what she had seen today. This naked anger was alien to her, frightening in its power. Where might it lead to, she wondered.

Now, with her hand languidly resting in his, a reassuring contact, there was so much she wanted to ask him, even of a practical nature as they both looked around the room. Even with so much needing to be done, silence and inactivity seemed terribly necessary now, a lull in a battle. She looked into his eyes and felt suddenly an uncontrollable urgency to cry.

She moved even closer, inching up to him and kicking away some of the rubbish at their feet to make more room.

"Don't ask why I cry, my darling," she whispered, stroking his face, "it could be for a thousand reasons. It's just everything, the boy, the priest, Field and of course you, everything. Do you know what Edward said to me once recently?" The mention of her husband's name brought another dimension into play to add to the knotted conundrum growing with each new happening. He just raised his eyebrows at the mention of Edward as a sign for her to continue.

"He told me that no one here could really be trusted, that if a problem does not exist then there will always be someone to invent one."

He smiled a dry smile and she continued, "I really didn't believe him, but am having second thoughts."

He shuffled to his feet, edging up against the wall and took her hand to help her up. They looked out the window onto the garden. Beckoning her to stay, he went out to where a coxcomb was still in bloom. Delicately he picked a flower, and came back inside.

"We have some inventing to do ourselves now, don't we?"

"Why, what do you mean?" she asked.

Thinking that he was referring to Edward, she waited. But it was not so.

"We must invent an excuse for himself when he comes back. He'll wonder what we've been up to when he sees the state of the place just the same as when he left."

Pushing him playfully, as if it was a reprimand, she was again in his embrace as he pulled her towards him. He dropped the coxcomb petal between her breasts and followed with a long, invasive kiss, rewarding her for her playfulness.

He was right. The sound of running feet came from the side path and he breathlessly presented himself and looked into the parlour, now in the very same state of disarray as when he had been sent on his errand. Bending towards him, she tenderly took his reddened face in her hands to comfort him where he had been hit. He didn't resist, even when Joe looked right into his face from where he stood behind her.

He did his best to reconstruct the confrontation between priest and rector, trying to explain the import of what had been traded between the two, emphasising that the rector had "given out". Being ignorant of what the priest had implied, he told them as truly as he could remember that Joe "was a person of evil" and "what would Mr Sheldon say?"

Both, visibly reacting to this, were momentarily stuck for something to say when Joe interjected.

"Nothing that so - called man of God says would surprise me. Alright then, that's what the church said, what did the law have to say?"

He began. She noticed that none of his suspicions about Snee had changed but it did seem that the constable had said nothing that gave any clear indication that he was somehow an accomplice in what had happened the night before. The matter of the donkey would take care of itself as Mulcahy would soon make his presence felt. Joe then remembered the night before, hearing Mulcahy go by but not returning. The amount of drink that the motorman and himself had taken might be a reason for that but he couldn't be sure. Mulcahy's side of the story would emerge in time, but Joe could not see how Mulcahy, "not mad but different," might be a willing henchman in what had happened.

Neither Victoria nor Joe was surprised at Snee initially thinking the whole thing was some kind of joke, until he heard that Field had come to the cottage to help, and then, as if from nowhere, appearing so suddenly to confront the priest.

With his story told it was as if a chapter was closed and they looked around again at what confronted them. A painful task it proved to be. She could not help but notice the many changes of expression on man and boy's faces as they retrieved simple objects, looking to see if they were beyond repair or beyond keeping. The boy looked with particular attention at Joe's two clocks, their soothing spell of peace and security, always present, now gone.

She noticed the picture of Joe's mother and stared through the broken glass into the depths of the sepia. Only the eyes she felt were not his. The other features, the cheekbones and high, proud forehead were there in the woman's fresh and candid features that eerily emerged from behind the shattered glass.

A few remnants were rescued, deemed without much discussion to be worthy of repair. The Coral Island was rescued in two parts. Even with the floor cleared and the table and chairs back in their place the room bore little resemblance to the tranquility of ordered chaos that the boy and Joe remembered it looking like. The terrible smell still lingered in the heat. New beginnings would, of brutal necessity, have to be made but, as with a violation, something was lost forever.

With a semblance of order gradually restored, she went out to the front of the house, surveyed the small garden and picked a bunch of hydrangeas from the corner near the gate. Finding a jar in the kitchen she placed them on the table. This gesture seemed to signal a new sense of purpose, the beginnings of a fightback, a retaliation in the face of what might be seen as insurmountable odds. But it was still dour, hard, and unforgiving. Those who had so wantonly impinged on the sanctity of the little cottage had made sure of that. They continued, sticking to their task until Joe issued a welcome command.

"Stop, we've done enough. It's not great but it's a start and I'll do a bit more later on at my ease; anyway, we're all starving."

It was then the reality of the shop boycott hit home. There was nothing in the house and a trip to town was out now with the bicycle gone. The obvious suggested itself to Victoria and again he was soon on his way with a memorised list of what he was to ask for at the kitchen in Woodlands.

He ran, taking the road's shorter route on Joe's instruction, remembering how determined they looked, walking down it a few hours earlier into the village, beholden to no one. Until reality coldly shattered their confident exterior.

My fault. Laughing at the priest. That's why he hit me. Falling into the dust. The donkey's belly. The cart shafts. Joe will come. But Field. Never expected that. Then Snee. Didn't believe me. A joke. Until I explained. Did then. And the cottage. Half an hour gone. At least. Nothing done to clean up. Why. They were together. The attack night. Joe's head. In her lap. Same now. Certain. Men and women. Some kind of mystery. Upsetting. Hurting. The Coral Reef.

What the priest had said, and the rector contradicted, left troubling questions, not about who Victoria was, or the priest hating Joe, but to them both being alone in the cottage. What the priest had said, and the rector's reply, now ran through his mind, addling his brain and torturing his body. The strange excitement of what the priest had said shut all else out. He arrived at the kitchen entrance of Woodlands hardly knowing what he had been sent to get.

Arriving back, tired with the weight of the hempen bag on his back, he found them at the kitchen table. The kettle was on the fire. Three glasses of water, a packet of salt and three empty plates decorated the table. In an atmosphere of sombre unity, the smell shut away by the closed door to the parlour, they ate in silence, savouring the best of Woodlands' food.

Lavishing attention on Joe, he saw her make sure he had enough of everything and forcing more on him to the point of irritation. She did the same with himself, but it was practical, normal, kind. With Joe there was something else.

He watched her eat slowly, daintily and with relish.

Sitting, drinking cups of Joe's strong tea in the oppressive heat, he longed to read their thoughts. Tea finished, they slouched on their chairs, tired, satisfied and postponing the future. Quite an unladylike pose in someone else's house. Looking at her, legs stretched out and crossed at the ankles made her seem like she had lived there all her life. A kind of harmony reigned, momentary but definite, blotting out the morning's events and what might lay ahead.

He noticed Joe too, battling with sleep, begin to doze in the chair. She too watched as he dozed, eyes leaden in the heat. She saw a man who sought little except to be left alone and whose guileless lack of sophistication had so completely shattered her world of complacency. But now his face was troubled, adversity and its consequences evident as his head tilted forward. The temptation to dispel this look of distress and what was causing it nearly overwhelmed her. She made no move though and drowsily watched the boy; legs pulled up under him on one of the roughly hewn chairs. Observing everything. He picked up the remnants of a magazine, one of a few rescued from the parlour floor and stacked near the fireplace. Lazily he paged through it.

The stillness and languor of the afternoon heat had overcome her too; she now closed her eyes, her thoughts drifting, basking in the presence of the man who had changed everything in her life and the innocent child who had led her to him. A line drawn from one to the other on the table would make a triangle. Conscious that she would never seat herself in this way in company, she did now; a riveting reminder of how unfettered she felt in the presence of someone, with the child as a witness, who an hour or two earlier might have left the priest of Shandrum seriously injured, if not worse, on the village street.

She would be forever grateful to Field.

*

He didn't think she was asleep like Joe. Whether or not, he now watched her as she had watched Joe. She was sitting sideways from him, and his eyes drifted from her head down to where her ankles were crossed. A dusty beam of the afternoon sun dwelt there. He was back taking her boots off where she sat on the step in the half darkness of Woodlands. His gaze grew more intense in the freedom her closed eyes gave him and he dared not move, in case the luxuriating feeling that swept through him might suddenly be snatched away if either of them spoke.

Maybe Joe feels like I do. How could he? No one could. And she. Does she feel anything? A woman. A man and a woman. A woman and a man.

The sound of a donkey cart dragged them from their slumbering solace and Joe woke up with a start, looking as if not quite believing what he saw was real. A knock at the door, a glance from Joe asking the boy to see who was there. In came Mulcahy to the parlour, a sheepish look of guilt across his face, shaking with apprehension. Joe left the kitchen.

"Joe, Joe…it wasn't me, I swear, I'd never do that. It was the boys in the pub…said they wanted it to get a small job done. I thought they were telling me the gospel truth, even though I wouldn't trust Maguire that much. They gave me a few bob there and then, and you know what happened. I had a few extra, a good few, before walking home. I'm here to tell you the truth."

His faltering words were genuine. They knew that. Victoria had heard of Mulcahy and his peculiarities. He occasionally passed her on the road, deferentially smiling. As she came into the parlour, his startled look said everything.

"Oh, Mrs Sheldon, I…I didn't know…didn't know you were here. Only the young lad I thought might be here but not you. Your husband's father, Old Sheldon, never did a thing wrong to us. In fact, he helped us like he did so many others but to hear them up in the Maguire's you'd think they all had short memories. Like they all playing below in the hurling pitch and going to matches. They've all forgotten where it came from. But they're like that, you know."

He stumbled through the words at the beginning but got into full flow when praising the Sheldon family name.

Victoria smiled and shook his shivering hand. Seeing Joe's relaxed attitude, he looked around at the three of them and continued as if his initial reason for coming was meaningless. Something else needed telling and he must have felt he had a willing audience.

"But the worst of it is that from what they're saying I won't be around much longer. They want me in the asylum above in Cork to see if it will do anything for my nerves. The brother, you know him Joe, he wants me out and he's in with the rest here you know. You know what they're like."

The last remark was directed at Joe.

He threw his arm in the direction of the village. "The rest" could mean anyone, but the three listening didn't have to stretch their imagination too far, to guess as to whom the image of distress before them was referring.

"The sergeant, Cleary above, told the brother that all he'd have to do was get a bit of paper signed if he had a witness

about me out at night and well, there's plenty of those."
He turned to Victoria, his embarrassed look appealing for some understanding.

"You see Mrs Sheldon, your husband told you I'm sure, but I get these turns at night, can't sleep and I roam the road talking to myself. They say I'm frightening the young ones with my roaring and shouting but all I do is sing the odd ould song or talk to myself about what's going on in the world. Sure we have great information altogether now with books and papers with all sorts of news. How could anyone be frightened of that? They're laughing half the time at me in Maguire's, and he doesn't like it since I told him straight out about this man here, Joe … that his money was as good as anyone else's here. He didn't like that one bit. No one else said anything except I heard one of them saying that the mad house would straighten me out."

Victoria struggled to make some sense of what was being said to her as it all simply added to the mire of subterfuge, suspicion and danger. The man before her had a look of despair in his simple face that clearly told her forces were ranged against him that brooked no opposition. She felt she had to say something.

"Mr Mulcahy, my husband did mention you to me but if I remember correctly, it was one day, we saw you passing by on the road and it was only to tell me where you lived, just beyond us at Woodlands. I know very little about this place and can only say I hope nothing will happen against your will. There's so much about everything here I just don't understand."

That seemed to soothe him to some extent, even though his face still told a story of apprehension and fear, and he jigged from one foot to the other. The boy recalled the day he had turned towards his father and himself in the chapel when nearly everyone else was nodding in agreement with the priest's sermon. Joe now put his hand on Mulcahy's shoulder and led him towards the door.

"Listen, ould stock, no need to worry about us. We're on the same team but for different reasons and we'll have to play the game as best we can, no matter what the other side throws against us. Some around here have more power than they should have and if they think it, they'll use it. And, by the way, if they send you off to one of those places above in Cork, I can guarantee you, I'll be up to see you with all the news."

She followed them out onto the roadside using the opportunity to make her excuses and go. She could see Joe was taken by surprise and both were disappointed that not even a few more moments could be stolen from the menaces of the day. The sun beat down and she felt exhausted from all that had happened. Joe had the answer to that and jokingly said to her, "no need for the motorman now, this man is going your way. Can't you take a passenger, Jim?" Mulcahy's face changed from hangdog and despairing to a throaty laugh at Joe's mischievous, yet practical suggestion.

Well, she could be just as mischievous while realising that she was giving those who wanted to vent their rage at herself, her man, the boy and Mulcahy even more reason to do so. Yes, why not, she thought. That will certainly give them something to talk about. Now she didn't care, not that she didn't have to but because there was something innocently inviting in Mulcahy's response to Joe suggesting she accompany him to Woodlands in the donkey and cart. The boy brought a cushion, worn out and frayed from the cottage and she took her place across from Mulcahy as he settled himself for the journey home. Joe told the boy to bring a basin of water for the donkey and off they went.

They left the village, both knowing the eyes that watched them were lost in disbelief. Field waved also, incomprehension etched on his now smiling face. It was a wave of collusion as if to tell her he admired her in her simple gesture of rebelliousness. The mistress of Woodlands, her parasol sheltering her and the madman of Shandrum were soon lost in a cloud of dust as the donkey picked up speed and the village was left behind. There was a belligerent richness to the scene that, even before they were out of sight at the corner, had tongues again wagging and heads shaking.

*

She had much to think on, too much when everything was considered. A hierarchy of problems kept her occupied. She was surprised that the boy's suspicions about Constable Snee should keep surfacing for the afternoon to the point of annoyance. It was a child's innocent interpretation of things and yet, maybe there was something in what he felt. An uneasy feeling played in her head at the thought that he might after all be right and if so, it was a grievous dereliction of duty and an appalling thing for an officer of the law to be guilty of, giving information that led to a man's house being ransacked and his personal belongings destroyed in such a novel, sinister way.

While she had an inherent trust in the officers of the law, her suffragette days had shown her another side of police work. She had always put that down to the law taking its course, but she had heard and seen enough as a suffragette to give her a glimpse of what the forces of law and order, either as a group or individually, were capable of and that was what she now recalled. Remembering the constable's parting words to her the day he called to Woodlands, she saw those words as perhaps offering an opening to discreetly pursue matters. He had said to call or send for him if he might ever be of assistance.

Walking back out into the sunlight she went round to where the motorman worked at ease, polishing the reason for his employment. The sudden interruption startled him. She asked him to drive her to the barrack but first she had something to tell him. Not aware of what had happened overnight and all morning into the afternoon, he was visibly shaken. Then she saw the anger rising.

Telling the story of events, starting from when she arrived, and conscious that she should present everything as objectively as possible, she was careful to be as clear as she could. She stressed Field's intervention and what brought it about, the chaos in the cottage. Field's second intervention with the priest had the motorman seething. His anger was palpable, understandably so when she told him the priest had hit his son. It was only assuaged to some degree when she praised his son for all he had done.

To lighten matters, she told him of getting a lift back with Mulcahy, but the angry look remained. Maybe he might well see her attempt at levity to be an example of just how naïve she was.

As they drove past the cottage nothing now seemed askew. The crowd had dwindled, the novelty of all that had happened earlier, now over.

She stepped out and was about to go in through the barrack's open door when she happened to look down the road toward the castle gate. There, sauntering away from her was the man she had come to see. He had obviously heard the motor and seen it stop but left whatever business had brought it there to be discussed in the barrack to his superior. It didn't quite work out that way and Victoria, with a word to the motorman, proceeded to follow Snee on foot. His slow pace meant that she had little difficulty in catching up with him just as he rounded the corner.

"Ah, Mrs Sheldon, a very good afternoon. A lovely day for a walk and no road lovelier than the one you are about to take, down to the bridge and along by the castle."

The trite remark annoyed her and before she had a chance to say anything, he continued.

"You know, the peace and tranquillity of the country is not found everywhere and with weather like this, who could ask for anything more serene?"

Growing more annoyed at this rambling piece of patronising rhetoric, she was not going to let such drivel go without a suitable reply. She would enlighten him on the level of supposed "peace and tranquillity" surrounding them.

"Constable, I would never presume to see myself as knowing more about things than an officer of the law, however I would enlighten you on a situation, about which you already know, where peace and tranquillity are not exactly flourishing in Shandrum. I refer to the dastardly deed perpetrated last night on Mr Golden's house and possessions. The fact that a dumb animal formed part of this deed is quite sickening. I had the opportunity earlier with Rev Field to witness the scene and it was far, far from serene and tranquil, I can assure you."

Her tone, scathing and deliberately sarcastic, brought little change to his blithe, matter of fact demeanour. He was again the policeman being informed of an alleged crime by a citizen. She might well have walked on or back to the village, but she thought that would be perhaps just what he might want. She would not give him that satisfaction. He looked round before responding.

"Forgive my flippancy just now. I was not aware you knew of what happened last night. As you suggested, I know most of what goes on around here and that has to do with the fact that I would far prefer to be elsewhere. If you hate where you are as a policeman, you surely are going to be far less inclined to turn a blind eye to things."

Intrigued by this rather perplexing reply and even more so by the personally confiding manner of the way it was delivered, she retorted, annoyed at what she thought was game playing.

"A blind eye, indeed. You may know what goes on but you and indeed, your superior, do precious little about it. Recently, the same Mr Golden was beaten senseless at this very spot, and nothing was done by you or your superior. Last night you know all about and are you telling me this sickening, grotesque violation of a man's home and possessions does not merit any action?"

He nodded gravely and seemed as if he were agreeing with the thrust of what she was saying even if it were critical of him, his superior, and the execution of their duties. What he said next did little to enlighten her.

"The only way, Mrs Sheldon, that we can talk about this is if you forget for a moment that I am a constable."

"What in heaven's name do you mean by that?"

"What I mean is that you are not now in England but in Ireland where the rule of law operates very strangely at times. Let me say that we have received no formal complaints about the two incidents you are talking about apart from a child's story. Now that is a policeman's answer to your question. And, yes, I can understand how exercised about it you are. Allow us, if you will, to first agree that this conversation is for you and me only, and if we are agreed on that then I will talk to you as Richard Snee."

Taken aback, her first thought was should she trust him? A conversation like this could be dangerous, yet it might also reveal some valuable information. She didn't rush in but left him waiting before giving him the opening to continue.

"You can trust my discretion."

He too, having been given this assurance, also took his time, and then proceeded to give her what she wanted to hear at one level, but which was to be deeply disturbing at another.

"First, let me say that I have spoken to your husband in similar terms, and I believe he knows very well the position he is in. To the stranger, yes there is peace and tranquillity here but it's the stranger who may be in danger. You are a stranger here, so is Golden, in a different way and for that matter so am I, and that's the problem. Even poor, mad Mulcahy. They want him out as well and they'll succeed and very soon because he too is different.

As for The League, it had all but died out here until the priest arrived, transferred from over near the Kerry border because he was a prime mover for it there. A transfer wasn't going to change that, because old habits die hard, and slowly. Over time, he mustered a few tried and faithful cronies to agitate and cause trouble for those they consider land grabbers first, and then anyone who dares stand for anything they see as different. It's only a small group but they have power and let all around them know that."

He paused there before imparting a chilling piece of information to her.

"The Sheldons fall into a certain category unlike some of the gentry round here because old man Sheldon was a gentleman, in the real sense of that word, and many here benefitted from him and your husband's mother and their way of doing things. But eaten bread is soon forgotten, that was then, this is now. And remember this, the self-appointed guardians of the law around here may well be more powerful than the law that I represent."

Trying desperately to absorb what she was being told she nodded at him to continue.

"I called to you some time back, you remember. The truth of course is, and your husband knows this also, that not just Golden trespasses on your property. Trespassing and all that goes with it is a second religion around here. They cannot, however, stomach his being allowed do it so freely and in a strange way do not blame him for that, they blame your husband. You know their motto, Ireland for the Irish."

"But why then perpetuate their barbarity on Mr Golden if we are to blame?"

She had some understanding of what Snee might say next, but she wanted him to say it aloud again, as if that would make more sense.

"Ah, there you have one other complication to the land one. Religion, or in Golden's case, no religion and that has a history too. Golden's mother left the cottage, locked it up and was gone. She arrives back a few years later with a son and no husband. You can see how that went down around here. One or two have said to me that the mystery was that she would have no bother getting a husband. To add another bit of mystery and make it harder for herself and her son, one of the sanctified tongues here let the rumour go about, that having gone to England, she probably didn't know who the father was anyway, probably some English pagan. She was a good-looking woman. Strong too, independent and only that she was strong she would not have survived. It wasn't from the wind, as they say here, that her son got it."

He paused for a reaction but the fact that Joe had let her know some of the details meant she wasn't in any way shocked.

"Your husband is well aware of all this and may have told you. Is this type of conversation upsetting for you?"

"It certainly is but go on."

"After that there isn't much to tell except that she lived her life in misery with her bastard son and wasn't let forget that. To add to it all of course was the fact that she had nothing to do with church, chapel or meeting and that's what rankled with the locals. When the priest came and marched up to her door, she gave him short shrift. You can imagine that was not forgotten. Young Golden had his miseries too but he upped and left when he could and only came back when she died. He'd have left again after she was buried only that the priest and himself had an argument; Golden dug his heels in and has since been a thorn in the priest's side and that of his allies. That's what has us where we are. As you can see the children won't even pass by his cottage without going to the far side of the road. They do the same with me now and then but for different reasons, though it wouldn't surprise me if a few rumours about me have festered in their little minds as well."

So caught up was she in what she was hearing that she wasn't even aware of the scorching afternoon sun, beating down on both of them, until Snee took off his helmet and dragged his hand across his forehead before continuing.

"My God, this heat. Will it ever end? But to get to the kernel of things. You see, there was a chance that Golden, and his opposition, might just have managed to live like two snarling dogs who never actually bite; but it was that young lad that made all the difference. In a way it was a double blow for the opposition because his father had been in and out to Golden's mother when no one else would bid her the time of day. She'd have ended up in the poor house only for your driver.

Victoria has no reason to believe this might be an exaggeration. He went on.

"She slowly wastes away and when she dies her son comes back and the child spends most of his time in his cottage. Whatever the priest wanted to brand Golden before that, the young lad's involvement allowed the priest to add another dimension. A pretty reprehensible one at that and the die was cast. Maybe what was and is just as important are the ramifications for others in all that."

"What others?"

"Well, anyone that is seen to be on Golden's side, like the motorman obviously but also yourselves because of who you are, what you stand for and the small matter of your attitude to his trespassing. In situations like this, anyone is fair game."

"Why are you telling me all this, Constable?"

"Because you for one and the boy for another expect me to be doing something to protect Golden and pursue those who are making his life here intolerable."

"That's hardly too much to expect now, is it? Who else can we look to for some sort of justice?"

"No, in normal circumstances it's not too much to expect, coming from where you do, and no doubt a child would see it just as simply as that too. Incomprehensible that a man in my position should stand by and do nothing with regard to what happened to Golden. But, let me explain."

She was impressed by his command of language and his appraisal of the situation, even if it made her more, not less, unsettled. The importance of what he was to say next was evidenced as he looked around again to make certain their conversation was not overheard. This seemed highly unlikely to her as they were, literally, away from everyone and outside of the village. The constable's fear that someone might be listening seemed absolutely groundless. Only then did she realise that Snee's demeanour had changed, and she was looking at a man barely tolerant of his situation. She could see it in his eyes, which had not betrayed anything in giving her the methodical description that she had listened to already.

"The truth is, Mrs Sheldon, that, strange as it may seem to you, I am for all intents and purposes, powerless to do anything. Outwardly, to the people of this village I am a policeman with all that word means. Behind that, where it matters, my hands are tied. There are two reasons for that, and one has to do with the other. I, like the priest strangely enough, was not sent here because I was a good policeman with an unblemished record. That, however, is another long and complicated story which my superior, Sergeant Cleary is well aware of, and I suspect one or two others of his cronies also, though none of them know all the details, at least I hope not."

"But neither you nor the sergeant should have 'cronies' in the positions you hold."

He looked her straight in the eye before replying.

"I won't offend you by saying I admire your innocence, but this is Shandrum. What you don't know, perhaps, and how could you, is that my esteemed superior's sympathies lie very much on the side of the priest and by extension, the League. I admire Golden, make no mistake about it, but my hands are tied, as I said. I take my orders from those I am supposed to and that's Sergeant Cleary. He dictates what I do, which for the purposes of this conversation, means that if you expect me to right the wrongs of this village in the name of the law you will, most definitely, be disappointed."

That the man before her, indeed any man, would be as open about themselves as Snee startled her, especially admitting to a not unblemished record and effectively being transferred to an out – of – the - way village because of it. On the one hand she felt sorry for his admission of powerlessness which in effect meant he was just a puppet of Cleary whose interests determined how the law was administered. Those interests, if what Snee was telling her was true, lay outside the law on occasion.

"Did Sergeant Cleary know that Mr Golden was returning to his cottage this morning?"

"I, as a good policeman, keep my superior informed of what I see and hear and I heard that, yes."

The boy was wrong even if his hunch was understandable. He was not aware of Snee's position as he had just outlined it to her, nor would he even understand it anyway. Everything now took on a different complexion.

Deciding that she had heard enough, maybe too much indeed, she reassured him of her discretion. Almost as an afterthought, she asked.

"Have you talked to Rev Field about any of this, any of what you have told me?"

"Him," he laughed in a way that verged on the scornful, "He wouldn't stand a chance. I know, just like you and a few others left round here, I am of the same persuasion, but no, I haven't. It would be too much of a burden to place on shoulders that cannot bear it. He's a man that's too good."

"Why did you tell me?"

He removed his helmet once more and moved into the shade where they should have been all the time. She followed.

"Frying pan to fire," he said staring through the branches at the sun, even though the shade did give some respite, "I told you because I felt I could, and perhaps knew I would have a willing ear because of what you know up to now. What I've told you may hopefully be as valuable to you as my telling it was to me. You know what they say, 'a problem shared,' even though I wouldn't be telling everyone round here about my situation. Strangely though, I think our friend, Golden, would understand but then, I can't be seen fraternising with the enemy now, can I?"

"No, you can't but you might at least let him know the danger he is in."

"No need to tell him because he knows it well without me telling him. Surely you know that?"

"Why did you come to the house about the trespassing?"

"Just like I've said, on instructions from my superior. Doing my duty, just being the good policeman."

She wasn't sure whether he was sneering or smiling as he said it. Summer sounds surrounded them, and she again took in the scene all around her. Steeple and cross away to one side with the castle, dominant symbol of another age, close by. Field joined field, a patchwork quilt of less than green now because of the drought, just like she had often worked into her children's stories in the hope that they would appreciate some of what nature had to offer.

"You know what you said at the very beginning?"

"Now that you ask me, what was it I said?" he replied curiously.

"It is indeed lovely around here, but it's also very…" she searched for words, "it's also wistful, so very sad."

"Indeed, not all it seems to be, right enough," he replied pensively, as if he wished he were far away from it all.

She moved back round the corner, waved to the motorman and the rumble of the motor saturated the burning, early evening heat. He arrived to fulfil his duty, but she told him she would walk back and asked him, instead, to go to town to meet the evening train to pick up a number of items due for Woodlands. She felt also, despite the grip of the heat on everything, that the walk might clear her head.

*

She formally bade goodbye to the constable and the motorman pulled away. On the one hand she was glad of all Snee had told her. Caught in a trap as a result of his previous actions, whatever they were, he seemed resigned to his situation though she felt it must be deeply unrewarding, for an intelligent man in his position, to feel he was a mere minion, duty bound but ineffectual. Interestingly, his ordered description of the situation he had outlined was fuller and more elaborate than what she had heard from either Edward or indeed, Joe. Both were sparing in their descriptions; Edward for his own noble reasons so that she would not be disturbed or upset by the undercurrents of life all around her; Joe, in their moments alone, gave her the simple background facts as if the present was all that mattered.

One thing was clear. The pleasant, slumbering village that both Edward and brother, Harold, had talked about in superlatives was all they had described. However, beneath the façade lurked forces sinister and menacing, led and supported by those who should be their very antithesis. Its very respectability was its energy and under that cloak it could flourish unhindered. The most unnerving and unsettling aspect of it all was the perverted involvement of the priest. She could, in some extreme sense, understand the rationale, indefensible as it was, that motivated the master, Maguire and even the sergeant. The thought of the priest chilled her and had her asking herself, what could lead a man of his calling to so obviously be its contradiction?

The street was not quite deserted. A few men lazed outside Maguire's and nearby a group of children played a game to some monotonous rhyme. Deliberately, the men slouched back into the shop at her approach. The children's game stopped and one or two shyly returned her smile and the rhyme began again after she had passed. Had she allowed her curiosity to get the better of her and look behind, she would have seen the men emerge again into the sunlight. Then it was on towards the cottage and her heart began to race. Aching to get some glimpse, some sense of him, she slowed somewhat as she passed. Just as she approached and glancing sideways but not turning her head, she heard a sound at the side of the cottage. She prayed it was him, an aching longing just to see him, even if she hadn't the slightest idea what might happen in broad daylight before the villagers' eyes.

The problem did not arise as she saw it was the boy. With two books in his hand, he jumped over the garden wall.

"I've it finished," he said with a smile of triumph, "you can have it back now, even though it's in two halves, but it escaped."

"Did you like it?"

He began to answer, shyly telling her the parts he most enjoyed. She listened and then his voice trailed off as he looked back up the street. The children's game had stopped, and the eyes of men and children were on the two of them, innocently standing at the Pagan's gate. The book was forgotten.

"They're all watching us," he said, nervously.

"Well, we can hardly stop them doing that now, can we?" she replied.

She was attempting to be matter - of - fact, to trivialise the whole thing, but she too was caught in a knot of apprehension. He began to shiver even though the heat was almost unbearable. Unnerved that she could not allay his fears, she looked back again to the shop. They were just too far away to see the expressions on their faces and certainly too far away to hear their talk. The strangest feeling gripped her. Entrapment, by the eyes of the adults and children. She felt naked and folded her arms in an instinctive attempt to protect herself. A raw, inhospitable chill in her bones banished the scorching heat. It was as if they were both stuck to the ground.

Then the trance was broken, unexpectedly for them both but by something that was least welcome in the circumstances. The priest emerged from the shop and the men moved and saluted him in deference. He responded by saying something and then turned to walk toward the presbytery and to where she stood with the boy. As he came towards them, she was propelled. A sick, unhealthy surge in her throat had her taking the boy by the shoulder and veer him away from the village.

"Come, we will go home," she said, her voice unsteady.

"Where is Joe?"

It was asked with a tinge of hurried annoyance, and she was suddenly sorry.

"Forgive me," she pleaded, squeezing him affectionately on the shoulder to make amends, "I'm just upset by all that has happened."

"He is gone to town to get stuff for the house. He wouldn't let me go as he said I'd done enough all morning. He went across the fields, but he wouldn't be back yet. He's still a bit lame."

Something kept telling her to look around again at the scene they were now getting further and further away from, but she fought off the temptation, anxious to get herself and her charge away from one of the most unsettling, indefinable experiences she had ever encountered.

They walked, quickly at first but when the corner was

turned, less hurriedly. He thought at one point she was going to cry and didn't know what he would do if that happened. The reassuring squeeze she had given his shoulder, while there had been a price to pay for it, left him revelling in its closeness and warmth. Maybe she would do it again.

*

At the lodge he made to go in after thanking her, only to realise he still had the two halves of the book in his hand. She must have believed him about enjoying it because she asked him if he would like to get another one. She wasn't sure if there was another he might like but they could go and see. Jumping at this unexpected treat, she could see the expectation in his face.

Walking up the avenue he noticed that she was now less anxious and serious looking than on their way from the village. He thought it must be because she was now in her own place and near her house where she could not be harmed. Joe and his house had been harmed of course. It was as if he were reading her mind, because just as she reached the door, she looked at him and he knew she had something important to say. He also knew it had something to do with Joe.

"Remember what you said about the constable, that you thought he told someone in the village about Joe coming back this morning so that they could do what they did."

"He did tell about it, I'm certain."

"Well, he did not. I have been talking to him on the road for a long time and I think he is not against Joe or on the side of those that caused all the trouble."

"But why doesn't he do something about it?"

"Listen carefully now. It's all very complicated, very mixed up, grownups and the way they are and that kind of thing, lots of which you can't understand now, because to children some things that grownups do are mysteries to them."

"Why is that?"

She had no answer to his simple question but told him that Snee hated being a policeman in Shandrum.

"He didn't tell me why. Again, it's very mixed up. Anyway, all that matters is that he is not against Joe and would never do anything to help others do what they did. He actually admires Joe. I believe him and you should too. Now enough of all that. We will find a book for you if it's the last thing we do."

The smell of the library consumed him once he followed in through the heavy door to a world of books. Dust covered many of them. Who read all these books, he wondered? Hardly Mr Sheldon, who was away in London so much.

She was flicking through the books in one of the corners from where she had got The Coral Island for him.

"Nothing here, I'm afraid," she said, regretfully, "but let's see, maybe here now," as she moved to another bundle on the floor, leaning over and shuffling through the different titles, which had dust rising in the sunlight. He watched her every move. She leaned further forward and just then the petal Joe had picked for her fell from the top of her dress onto the floor. She looked quickly to see had he noticed and of course he had. She picked it up and for a moment she was somewhere else. This momentary freedom allowed him to look to where the flower bud had fallen from and fix his gaze there. Then she looked across the bundle of books and their eyes met. He blushed and she smiled, guiltily, before picking up the flower bud and placing it on the mantelpiece.

"Oh, now wait, there may be something you might like but I'll have to get it. Wait for a moment, won't be long," and she curtly walked out the door.

He waited until her footsteps receded before slowly taking the flower bud and turning it over in his hand. The faintest scent of perfume and sweat filtered through the strong smell of the flower and he closed his eyes, almost swaying to the images that now pressed relentlessly in on him.

Her return found him red faced, standing to attention and clearly indicating something of his inner turmoil. Inviting him to look, she spread out four books on the table. The covers were gaily decorated; the titles stood out in bright green under the outline of a chimney with smoke curling to the clouds. Round the chimney was written "Chimney top Stories for Children." The titles jumped into his imagination: *The Lost Tiger, The Dying Swan, A Lamb Forever and The Queen's Secret.*

Then he noticed the author's name, Victoria Denham-Lynd. He put his finger on her name and shyly looked up at her, "that's you, isn't it? Can I have one?"

She nodded and then took *The Lost Tiger* and opened one of the desk's drawers. Taking out a pen, she opened the cover of the book and looked away into the distance before writing something. With impatient fascination he watched, but before he could read what she had written, she had covered the writing with a sheet of blotting paper and closed over the cover, before giving him the four books.

"They won't be as exciting as The Coral Island."

She led him to the front door and saw him off with a cheery goodbye. The door then closed. She was gone, locked away from him behind the walls of her big house. Clutching the books carefully, he walked down the avenue, now bathed in the darting shafts of sunlight that came through the trees. About halfway down he sat under one of the giant oaks and opened the book to see what she had written. There was his name and beneath it, in tall, angular script, the words *All these stories have happy endings. Victoria Denham-Lynd, August 1911.*

Again and again. The words. Happy endings. Tears. Why? All that had happened? Four special gifts. Her writing. There for him. Him alone. Sad and happy. All at the same time. Is that possible? Proud too. Her work. A writer. Her name. Oh yes, the coxcomb. She never knew. Never knew he smelled it. Grabbing something near his heart. At the edges.

Though tired and thirsty, the books buoyed up his spirits. It was just like the day he had gone to see the tangled remains of Joe's bicycle and found the bell. Finding it had rescued something from the grimness of what had happened. So had the books today, but that was because of the person who had given them. That made all the difference. Even if it were a stone that she had given him it would be a treasure.

Joe would not be home yet and that suited him. He would slip onto the pathway from opposite the lodge and make his way with the books to the cottage and he could read. Then the motor's sound. From force of habit, he swung back the entrance gates and waited. Dust rose round his feet as the car turned into the avenue. Instead of the expected nod or wave of recognition from his father, the motor stopped.

Looking across the seat the boy saw a troubled face. He wondered what else could have gone wrong to add to the mishaps and misfortunes of the day. What his father said began casually. He had met Joe in the town.

"Do you know what he's gone and done? Got a new bicycle in Rice's. I told him he was mad and that it would be another excuse for those against him. But he won't give them the satisfaction, he said. It's a dear one too and that will make them madder. I don't know what's going to happen, but listen to me now, whatever about the bicycle, listen to what I'm saying."

Leaning across the seat for emphasis, his father warned him to say nothing to anyone about who might have been responsible for what had happened to the cottage. Furthermore, here his father looked up the avenue towards the house, he should let no one know that Mrs Sheldon had ever come to visit Joe at the lodge while he was recovering. To the boy these warnings were unnecessary.

"Look, I'm only telling you for all our sakes. It's not that we don't trust you. Joe said you were a great help today in spite of what the priest did to you. I'm nearly sorry that the rector dealt with him rather than Joe as he would have got more than talk from him. And he'd deserve it.

Anyway, there are things you don't understand yet."

There again, he thought, just like she said, 'things you don't understand yet.' It had all to do with her and Joe, he knew, waiting in hope for some sort of further explanation. But his father's attention was drawn to the books.

"More books for you, isn't that great?"

Belying the thrill of getting the books, he answered, feigning disinterest for a moment but then, his resolve wilting, proudly showing what she had written and asking why he had never told him she was a writer. The question wasn't even heard as his father gazed at what she had written, his thoughts swaying in some other direction.

"They're lovely," he said, his voice not in sequence with his thoughts.

"They're something you can always keep, and Joe will be interested in seeing them, I'm sure."

Another flicker of unease evident on his father's face. Mention of Joe had him again shifting uneasily in the seat. It was a clear message, that the casualness of the mention of Joe's name, always understood and with no complications up to now, somehow took on other meanings for father and son, different for each but creating a perplexing embarrassment where it had never existed before. The boy was convinced that it had nothing to do with all that had happened at the cottage. Rather, it had to do with the conversation he had slept through the night before, when the voices of Joe and his father had wakened him, following their making quick work of the crate of porter.

Pointing to various items in the back seat of the motor, his father, glad of an excuse to go, left his son standing with his treasured books clasped to his side.

*

Joe sat, intently poring over the Cork Examiner and barely noticing his arrival. The paper separated them until Joe lowered it and saw the books.

"She gave them to me. She wrote them, they're for young children really but I'm going to read them, said I can keep them. Look what she wrote."

Letting the paper fall to the floor, he read her writing, lips pursed, face softening before commenting, "well she's right I suppose, children need happy endings. They'll have plenty time for the sad ones."

Giving a casual look at the titles of the other three books, he put all four together and handed them back to the boy before rummaging in the bag that he had carried from town. He held up two apples and pointed at a new clock on the mantelpiece that the boy had not noticed and said, "I nearly broke the bank today, that second clock isn't all I got. Three guesses and sixpence if you can guess what else I got. That'll make you rich. Away you go."

Knowing Joe was unaware that he knew, he played along as Joe put a sixpence on the table with a flourish.

"Maybe a new shirt?"

"No, one down, two to go."

"I'll guess you got something for me?"

"No, you're not even warm."

"Is it something that's able to move?"

"No clues: you have to guess it. I think I'll take back that sixpence, you had your chance."

Joe picked up the sixpence. The boy left him waiting.

"I'd say you got a new bicycle."

Joe's face fell.

"You blasted rogue; how did you know?"

"Just guessed, that's all."

Joe looked at the sixpence and then tossed it, twirling to where the boy caught it, a grin on his satisfied face. Solemnly, Joe marched him towards the parlour door. Inside the gleaming new machine stood amidst the cleaned-up room that still bore the smell of heat and dung.

"You should have seen their faces. Let them put that in their pipes and smoke it. The bastards. After all they did last night."

It was said with triumphal bitterness.

"Now let us celebrate. I'm tired after all that happened today and you are too, but we'll go over for a stroll."

That meant one thing. He begged a minute to examine the bicycle and his father's words came back to him, 'I told him he was mad.' Would this end up like the other one? Joe saw the question in his eyes.

"You're thinking you'll have another bell soon, I suppose. I can tell you one thing, I'm not going to make it easy for them."

They set off towards the castle, Joe's limp more evident, saying nothing but with spirits high. It was as if the day had never been as it had, a mixture of calamity and achievement.

Hauntingly, the castle rose before them in the lengthening rays of the evening sun.

He was always first to the top, leaving Joe to take one methodical step after another on the stone staircase. Slower this evening with the limp.

Here was a place where he felt nothing could touch them, a fortification that barricaded them from what lay beyond and gave a sense that they were in control. Spirals of smoke rose from the houses in the village and beyond as he scanned for familiar landmarks. Woodlands stood out, as always. This evening it looked as if whoever had planned it had stood where he stood now and sketched it so that the house appeared to drag the village behind it, moving inexorably through the landscape toward the river and the low hills beyond.

Stillness enveloped them as the sun began to dip, bringing to a close the long day that promised so much but left many more questions unanswered.

They stayed for another while, silent and at ease. As they prepared to leave in the twilight, the boy said to Joe that he had to go to confession.

"Confession, what confession. You didn't kill someone, did you?"

The boy smiled at Joe's intemperate question and then laughed.

"Father told me about the bicycle."

*

Seldom had he been as troubled or as dismayed as he tried to make some sense of the day's events. The plea for help from Golden now seemed so insignificant as he recalled his altercation with the priest in full view of all and sundry. A circus of sorts for the villagers but an unedifying spectacle, everything considered.

And then, The Pagan, after everything that had happened, parades down the village on the most up to date and expensive contraption one could find on two wheels. Field pictured it again as he idled near his gate. Instead of going into the cottage, he passed Field with a wave of his hand and went on past church, chapel and school. On the way to Woodlands? Getting to the dangerous corner, after which he would be lost to sight, he executed a spectacular half circle on the road and returned. Where does he get the money, he said to himself, curious as always. Those bicycles cost seven or eight pounds he had seen on the paper. You could pay by instalments, of course. Maybe that's how he got it? But he only has the odd bit of rabbit money. And how did he have the energy, after all that happened, to go to town and purchase what was bound to inflame his attackers?

The rector now became the first person in the village to inspect the new machine, an "All Steel 28 inch Raleigh," presented for his delectation by the proud owner.

"That must have cost a pretty penny."

His curiosity again got the better of him, but he was none the wiser with the answer.

"Well, Rector, and you'd know this better than anyone – God never shuts one door, but he opens another. Now, I'll be off. By the way, only for you today, Mulcahy's mode of transport would still be inside my door. I won't forget you for it or for rescuing the young lad from the other man of God."

The new bicycle, glinting in the sunlight, was wheeled to the cottage door. He didn't have to check if there were onlookers. There were, some curious, some envious and some rattled by the audacity of it all. Field, watching him go, was able to look beyond and see those who were being ignored by the owner of Shandrum's newest acquisition.

Aware that he still had a sermon to prepare, he gave a last look towards the village and went indoors. After all that had happened on that one Saturday, what would be his theme and what could he say to the dwindling, faithful band who would make their way to hear him speak the word of the Lord tomorrow?

He hadn't even sat at his desk when a verse from Ecclesiastes came to him: *There are righteous men who get what the actions of the wicked deserve, and there are wicked men who get what the actions of the righteous deserve.*

He gave it his full attention but wearied at the futility of his task and it making any difference. When finished, he had his usual temptation, to reconstruct it for more effect, but he knew from experience, that he was better off not doing so, as he was bound to feel the original was better. Tired after an eventful day, he sat back in the chair and dozed.

Having overslept, he woke to find it was his bedtime. In the stifling heat he tossed and turned knowing that sleep would now evade him. His thoughts returned to the street scene. He had no doubt but that he was justified in intercepting the priest after witnessing him hitting the boy. Violence in any form horrified him. Though he was aware of children being routinely beaten, to think that a man dedicated to the gospel would so wantonly strike a child on the public street, was for him, beyond comprehension.

And that was allowing for his temperament and his running battle with The Pagan, a battle with which he had been able to identify up to now. After seeing the destruction wrought by the cottage's late-night visitors, he now had an entirely different attitude. His eyes had been opened. The concept of The Pagan as the village ogre no longer had the substance it previously had.

Nothing compared, however, to the priest, with the boy present, introducing into the argument the outrageous and scandalous suggestion that Victoria Sheldon's intentions were anything but honourable in her being in the cottage. It had him searching for words at the time. Yet now, hours later, it left him questioning the priest's claim with less certainty, even though he hated admitting it.

Listening to his clock sound eleven from downstairs, he only then realised the darkness that had come down on his weary, muddled head gave no respite from the heat. Far from shutting out the day's events, an ever more relentless onslaught battered at his frenzied brain. Could there, after all, be something in what he so resentfully reacted to, the priest's allegation, delivered so emphatically? Could his assumption, so certain as it was, that this woman was responding in a Christian manner to another human being's plight, even an unbeliever's, be flawed? Thoughts and visions of the excesses of the flesh he had presumed distant from him now, crowded in on him, only adding to his dilemma.

The more he considered the priest's allegation the more he imagined the debauched scene that might have occurred in the cottage, somehow with his tacit approval. He found himself lingering on his imagination's meanderings as his conscience, without success, battled him back to the demands and strictures of the scriptures and his moral responsibility.

Not for the first time had he been reminded that the spirit is so often willing but the flesh, well, that's another matter entirely, he told himself. He would read a verse or two from the bible. It never failed to dispel the more insistent attempts of nature's more evil side to infiltrate the mind with the base attractions of the flesh.

This he did. Opening at random, his eyes fell on a piece from Revelations and as often before, the lines took on a relevance he might never have imagined.

I know thy works and thy labour and thy patience, and that thou canst not bear evil men; but hast tried them who say they are apostle and are not, and hast found them false.

And thou hast patience and hast endured in my name and hast not grown weary. But I have this against thee, that thou hast left thy first love ...

He who hast an ear let him hear what the spirit says to the churches; he who overcomes I will permit to eat the tree of life, which is the Paradise of my God ...

I know thy tribulations and thy poverty but thou art rich; and thou art slandered by those who say they are Jews and are not but a synagogue of Satan. Fear none of these things thou art about to suffer.

But I have against thee that thou sufferest the woman, Jezebel, who calls herself a prophetess to seduce my servants, to commit fornication and to eat the things sacrificed to idols. And I gave her time that she might repent, and she does

not want to repent of her immorality. Behold I will cast her
upon a bed and those who commit adultery with her into
great tribulation, unless they repent of their deeds. And her
children I will strike with death, and all the churches will
know that I am he who searches desires and hearts, and I will
give to each of you according to your works ...
He who has an ear let him hear what the spirit says to the
churches.

Scarcely believing what he was reading, he put down the
bible, overwrought by the words. A spectre was resurrected
of what the priest's words asserted. Maybe he was right,
maybe Kerley for all his irascibility and intolerance was
seeing things far more clearly than he. Why had he
allowed himself to be lured into the atheist's cottage and
then allowed himself to be flattered in the presence of the
woman. But no, that could not be right either and his
gaze rested again on the open bible on his lap. "Do unto
others," "the greatest of these is charity," all the familiar
strictures embedded since childhood flooded his mind to
counteract what he had just been reading. Had he, after
all, wronged Kerley?

Having walked away from the priest, disgusted at what
he considered salacious gossip, he was now torn by
doubt. The clock said nearly midnight and he could not
see himself sleeping with lurid images, the harsh words
of scripture and his wayward mind caught in a sea of
uncertainty.

There was only one thing for it. There was light shining
from the presbytery window. He would cross the road,
late though it was, have it out with the priest and resolve

the matter for once and for all, difficult as that might be. Doing so would mean that the sun would not go down on Kerley's anger, and both would be the better of it.

*

The heat of the day still lingered. Not even the hint of a chill was there at that hour to suggest a summer, the hottest he could remember, was any nearer in coming to a close. He raised his hand to the brass knocker and then stopped. From inside the house came the unmistakable sound of voices. His immediate instinct was to turn and come back in the morning, but curiosity, as always, had him by the throat. Who was in there? Though a light shone in the front room the voices were from further back in the house. Cautiously groping by the wall, he stealthily and nervously made his way round the back to where a sliver of light was thrown against the back wall and into the field behind it. His first thought was that the priest's back garden wasn't much better than the front. Extreme caution was called for as he got closer to the window.

Watching every step, he approached with inquisitive apprehension. He jumped, as the priest's cat, an overfed hulk, bundled past him from where he had been sitting on the windowsill. Distracted by this unexpected intrusion, Field clung to the wall praying he would not be discovered, bereft as he was of any excuse for being where he was at such an hour, indeed at any hour. He was spared as raucous laughter came from the room.

On closer inspection, he saw the two sides of the curtain were pinned together, with the light seeping through above where they met. This was too high to see through from where he stood. He went back to the garden wall and gingerly stood on it, hoping for a view of the inside. All he could see was the face of some saint disapprovingly staring at him from the far side of the room. There was only one solution, a dangerous one at that. He would have to stand on the narrow windowsill to assuage his curiosity. It was narrow and he was no nimble athlete, never mind his tired mind and body were after the exertions of the day. Having come this far he was determined not to be outdone by the mechanics of the problem that faced him.

Approaching the window from the side, he gingerly placed one foot on the sill. Helped by his being tall he was able to grab the underside of the top window sash and haul himself up. It was easier than he had expected but his balance was still perilous. He told himself to breathe easily and be patient. Otherwise, all would be lost. Edging his face along the glass he inhaled dust and grime. This window has never been cleaned, he thought. Moving towards the beam of light he settled his face against the grubby glass surface before looking.

He was to hear one sentence that made any sense as those inside seemed to be talking across each other and in good spirits. First, he saw the master, Slyne, glass raised in celebration, proclaiming loudly, "I'd definitely say his goose is cooked this time, Father, if what you say is true." The priest sat next to him, but the others' faces were obscured because their backs were to the window, shutting them out of Field's line of vision. By moving his face slightly to the right, he should be able to identify one or two more of them. The nearest I'll ever be to becoming a detective, he thought, feeling pleased that he had managed to become party to what was going on inside without those in the room being in any way aware of it.

It was at that moment, however, that he suddenly had an uncontrollable urge to sneeze, his nostrils invaded by the dust and grime. Raging at this inconvenience, he took his left hand away from the window sash in an attempt to smother the sneeze. Then he was falling, sneezing at the same time, twisting sideways, reaching out in the darkness for something to catch and then hitting the ground.

Dazed and bruised, his instinct was to call for help or wait for those inside to appear as they surely heard the fall. Miraculously, his glasses had not fallen off. Fear of discovery and pure animal instinct made him drag himself to his feet and get over the wall. They were at the back door but seemed to have difficulty opening it. That gave him time to struggle along by the wall, crouching as he went. Then they were out, voices raised in unison, at once threatening and perplexed.

"I'd swear 'twas him, who else could it be?" The voice was Maguire's.

McSweeney followed with "it could be that young fella, it wouldn't surprise me the tricks he'd be up to … and we know where he learned them."

A third voice interrupted, serious and conspiratorial. It was the priest.

"Come in men, don't let it worry ye, whoever it was couldn't see in anyway so no bother."

Beglin, as ever, backed up the priest's advice.

"You're right, Father, no bother, no bother at all."

Muttering at the vanished intruder, they moved back inside, and the door closed. Shaking, he sat against the wall, glad of the respite brought about by the intervention of his unlikeliest ally, the priest. Relieved too that he had been spared the indignity of discovery by such a group, formidable even when sober, never mind with drink.

Regretting the mishap, and madly curious to hear more, he had however, heard enough. All were there to celebrate something, and the single sentence meant the priest was the bearer of good news, giving them information that satisfied. He was certain it referred to The Pagan, though since those he had identified as being present were all League members, there was a chance it might be about someone else. The Sheldons? Maybe even himself? He swatted away the thought immediately.

A detour, taken hastily brought him to his own backdoor and into the kitchen. A hastily lighted candle allowed him search his features in the mirror. All in all, he was pleased to see that his face gave little evidence of what he had been through, though his arm and leg hurt. Worse in the morning, he surmised.

He poured a measure of whiskey, rare for him, but he judged it well deserved after his ordeal, and sat in his bed, knowing full well he would not sleep immediately. No, it wasn't Sheldon they were referring to, or himself, but the man whose house they had nearly destroyed. with their sick joke. How dearly he felt, as he supped his whiskey, would he have loved to have perched on the windowsill and heard more.

Over the course of the day he had seen and heard enough for it all to shore up a level of curious apprehension and precariousness that grew as he twisted and turned in an attempt to sleep. It came eventually but not until after he had heard the clock downstairs strike three. The few hours he got were far from peaceful.

*

August did not bring a longed-for respite. Despite prayers, predictions and rumours, every dawn brought the torturing rising sun. Thinking of the dreaded approaching schooldays again, his stomach churned with unease and foreboding. The grinning faces of his classmates and the steely, unyeilding posture of the master, conjured again all he had contended with last year. What new miseries would be hatched over the long summer days and nights now that the League had had its victories at Joe's expense?

News of what had happened to Joe was widespread, added to and exaggerated. How they laughed at Mulcahy, and his unfortunate donkey being dragged into the cottage and the cart harnessed. With a sinister, peculiar, twisted logic, it added further to the perception that Mulcahy was mad and not fit to be among them even though he had nothing to do with what had happened.

And then he knew she too would be dragged into the whole mess. The snide, unrelenting, swaggering insults would be thrown at him inside and outside the classroom. He knelt in the silent chapel which could be a refuge or a hell, like the hell it was as the priest told the congregation what he thought of Joe and how bad a man he was. He couldn't understand how Joe was a bad man and he didn't understand what the priest meant as he thundered from the pulpit. But the chapel, again ironically, was now, as before, an escape.

He was here now in the absolute quiet of the summer day with streaks of sunlight coming through the windows, throwing colours of every kind where they hit.

Dear St Jude, you are the saint of hopeless cases and I heard Mulcahy saying once that you helped him find his donkey when he strayed out of The Inch field. The mission priest told us you answer every prayer if it is meant. You know I mean it when I say I don't want all that to happen again when I go back to school. If Mrs Sheldon understands, then you, because you are a saint, must surely understand how I feel.

Yes, she had understood, the day school ended and the chance meeting when he cried as he confessed how school racked his mind and tortured his body. But as summer waned, would she understand how his anxiety grew as each day brought him nearer to what he detested?

The day of the coxcomb, as he now chose to remember it, despite so much else having happened that day, had she any idea of how he felt? He thought so, but a moment later he was back to believing no one could understand. He had tried since then to capture the feeling and maybe it might happen again soon. The thought, so gloriously uncertain, captivated him there in the chapel as he dozed in the heat of the afternoon, her image from different situations reaching in and out of his mind to tease him.

The new bicycle was something that invited consequences. How was anyone to know but they might again attack Joe and with greater ferocity. Not at all unlikely. At least he had the bell to remind him and only the books she had given him ranked higher in his list of prized possessions.

Joe was different now, he felt. They still did all the same things together, but Joe was a bit more careful about being seen going on to Sheldon's land. Maybe, the boy thought, it had to do with the posters with the stark words "prosecuted" there for all to see. At other times he noticed quite clearly that Joe's mind was elsewhere as the expressions on his face told a story, even if it were a hidden one. It might be a frown, a remote and distant smile, a passing puzzled look or a grimace that now and then took him away to what seemed like another country. The limp still hampered him, a stark reminder. Was it this that was responsible for the changing features on his face? That and all that took place in the cottage especially as he felt in his heart that simple homestead might never mean the same as it had before. Something had been torn away by what they had done and maybe that's what they wanted to happen for Joe and himself.

Long silences marred their journeys, and though this was often something he was used to it did seem different now. It was as if everything had somehow changed, and they both struggled to regain something that had been lost. Of course, he could not help thinking either, that maybe it was something else entirely that preoccupied Joe, as it did him, but she was never mentioned in conversation.

*

Field, almost back to himself after his fall, waited inside his front window for the motor to pass as the sound got nearer.

It grumbled to a halt, however. Edward Sheldon emerged. Why, why stop here before going on to Woodlands? Most unusual. Stranger still was the fact that Edward's usual calm, self-centred exterior was ruffled. He pushed the gate open, determinedly unhappy. Field, his curiosity peaked, met him on the doorstep. The wave of heat was the first thing that hit him even as the sky continued to darken, as it had from earlier in the afternoon. Maybe at last, rain. The possible change in the weather would have been on everyone's lips but Edward's demeanour left no room for such casual small talk.

"Edward, delighted to see you. I thought it was the weekend you were due, is something wrong?"

"I don't know how you can say you're delighted to see me. After all, it's because of you I'm here, so you can hardly be surprised."

Field, flustered now at this totally unexpected response, led Edward inside and proffered a chair.

"Edward, quite frankly, I don't know what you are talking about. I have no idea... Pray, explain. I am completely at a loss."

"Rector, please. I have been travelling all night and most of today. Your letter reached me yesterday afternoon and I dropped everything, at great inconvenience, I might add. I had to get back. Surely you understand my position."

"What position? What letter? Here, let me get you a drink."

"No, that's not necessary. I'm tired and I want to get to the bottom of this as quickly as possible. Surely you know my reputation, indeed my future, is at stake."

There was no mistaking the plea, the appeal in Edward's eyes for sympathy to his plight, whatever it was. Field had never seen this side of Edward but plainly now he was a man in a bind.

"Edward, please start and explain to me what you are talking about."

"What do you think I'm talking about? I'm talking about this."

Impatient now, Edward dragged a letter from his pocket and waved it in the air between them. Field took it and before opening it looked at the address. In neatly written script, bearing Edward's name and London address. "Private and Personal, Addressee only" were written at the top left-hand corner of the envelope.

Edward sat back in the chair, exhausted. Field sat forward; disbelief etched all over his face.

The Rectory,
Shandrum,
Co. Cork.
22/8/'11

Dear Edward,
It is with the utmost sadness and haste that I write. I will be as brief as possible in bringing to your attention the following disturbing information which has come my way from a trusted source and with which I feel I must acquaint you.
Your wife appears to have formed an illicit liaison with one of the village's most undesirable individuals, Joseph Golden, The Pagan, a man you know well. He visited Woodlands on

foot of an invitation from your wife and I confess I have seen the note which confirms this.

She recently spent a day in Golden's cottage where an impressionable child, the son of your motorman, was also present. You may be aware that this child is considered by many of the most upright citizens of the village to be at the risk of grave moral danger. I see no need to elaborate.

You will be aware that the said Golden was recently attacked by persons unknown and convalesced in your gate lodge.

I feel it imperative, as your rector, that I bring this disturbing information to you and know, from the papers, that your work is occupying most of your time at the moment. However, you will appreciate my concern as I fear for the scandal that such a licentious and possibly corrupting relationship may have for all involved. I echo the concerns of my RC counterpart in all of this.

I am,
In trusted loyalty,
Reginald E. Field (Rector)

A signature was entered above his name.

Field's reaction was a consolation of sorts to Edward in that he realised, from his expression as he read, that the letter had not been written by him. But was this despicable hoax, or rather its riveting, devastating message true? Field, for his part, felt he could go some way in putting a context to the letter's details, unequivocal in their intent to cause grave and possibly lasting damage to Edward, his wife and his short-lived marriage.

On his journey back to Shandrum, Edward had more than enough time to ponder the possible consequences of Field's letter, as he then believed it was. Now, realising the sophisticated nature of the hoax he was left in no doubt as to what his social and professional career might be subjected to if word spread and there was even a scintilla of truth to what was alleged.

"Rector," Edward responded as he looked again at the letter which Field had handed back to him, "forgive me, how could I have been remiss and not check my files for some previous correspondence from you and compare the writing? But be that as it may, how could I fall for a ploy like this and more so what has been going on? Is it the League and what are they up to? Are the usual suspects behind this? The worst thing one can do with something like this is give it credence, and they will be aware of my return. In other words, they have succeeded."

Field poured the drink that had earlier been refused. Then, he concisely outlined for Edward the happenings of recent weeks without giving any hint of his own suspicions. That would be fuel to the fire. The innuendo of Golden recuperating at the gate lodge was not lost on Field but he made no reference to it. The recent Saturday and his and Victoria's presence at The Pagan's cottage was the culmination. He stressed, however inadvisable it might have been for her, that it was her compassionate and Christian attitude that had her in the cottage in the first place. He instanced her arriving the very same time as himself and seeing the damage done. She had done no differently than he had. Simply helped.

Giving his version of events to Edward and speculating as to the possible consequences, he wondered, curiously, if there was some way, no matter how unorthodox, of finding out who the accomplished author of the letter was. How had the letter E in his name been found out? He then realised that it was written in plain English on the church's notice board.

Edward had long been immune to what might happen in a place like Shandrum. Unsigned letters, some vaguely threatening were not new to him or indeed his father before him. Though Field had assuaged his fears to some extent, he was furious at Victoria getting so publicly involved against his express wishes in the vagaries of the village scene, even if Field now pleaded it to be something she could hardly have avoided. Anyway, the consequences were evident.

Though mutually distant from each other Edward found a certain reassurance his reasoned and dispassionate appraisal of the situation. That, he might gratefully hang on to when he faced Victoria.

"Edward," Field leaned forward and again carefully chose his words, "it is not for me to advise someone of your standing on how to deal with this but as your rector, and friend of the family since I came here, can I say this is the work of people who will seize on any opportunity to make life awkward for you? Whoever wrote this poison, is, I venture to say, also intent on making life as miserable as possible for The Pagan and I just told you what they have visited on him recently. He's lucky to be alive. Now, the object, as I see it is to set you at odds with him and is there anything, I ask you, as despicable as involving your good wife? I will say no more than suggest you ignore this vile allegation. Contempt is what it should be met with, I am not in doubt."

"I am extremely upset and annoyed at this but your suggestion - well, that's my intention as long as nothing else emerges to build on this. Golden will certainly bear the brunt of the abuse and will continue to be so treated as long as those whose duty it is to protect him fail to do so."

He shrugged, Field readily agreeing.

"An appalling state of affairs that a citizen, whatever his persuasion, can be so treated, and insinuations made at will about my motorman's boy. It would turn one's stomach that such gossip can be tolerated. I must say, much as I appreciate your concern, I think it was ill - advised of you to help perpetuate that when you spoke at service about it."

"Indeed, I was misled into thinking there was some unmentionable activity in our midst. My counterpart convinced me that a united front was needed, and goodness, did he get his way? As for the law, that sergeant creates a bad taste in my mouth and as for his constable, well, one need hardly wonder, though it's not for me to judge."

By now, a very tired Edward had little inclination or energy to get into any further discussion and he was too much of a pragmatist to believe that anything other than the status quo would continue. And pragmatism now brought his upcoming meeting with Victoria to mind. It would, no doubt, be an ordeal.

"I must be off. I wonder if it would be better to ignore this altogether and say nothing to Victoria. She will however want an explanation for my arriving as I do seeing how I emphasised the importance of giving time to this damned commission once the term ended in the courts. Always something, isn't there?"

As his words trailed away it seemed as if he was talking to himself as he wearily got up from the chair and walked out to an ever-darkening sky. Rain was imminent.

The motorman waited, impassive. Edward looked towards the sky and spoke.

"Well, maybe some good news, at least. London has been a furnace and the continent worse, I believe."

He felt a twinge of sorrow for Edward, a man of power, influence and wealth. He was on the verge of saying "if it was only the weather we had to worry about," but he thought better of it.

*

The thought that, without notice, her mother must be coming after all was the first thing that entered her head, throwing her into confusion and anxiety, because of what would be an added element in an already fraught situation.

But no, stranger still was the telegram's message that Edward was on his way with no elaboration, just the train's arrival time. It had, however, to be serious if he was to abandon his work on preparing for the new commission even for a few days. She knew when first approached by No. 10 to head the commission, he had, despite the prestige of such a request, pleaded the promise made

343

to his new wife, of time to be together when the courts closed. When the Prime Minister intervened however, he simply could not refuse.

One thing the unexpected telegram gave her was time. Edward had somehow faded from her routine thinking into some sort of blur. A replacement had wrenched him, subtly yet powerfully, away from her and her husband was no longer the preeminent man in her life. The telegram starkly shook her into realising that Edward had to have a more than important reason for dropping everything.

The inner and palpable conviction that her husband was not the prime focus of her thoughts and certainly not of her feelings, made her strangely detached in a way she would never have anticipated. It had, when she reflected on this contradictory frame of mind, to do with Edward himself, as much as the man who occupied her waking and her sleeping.

Remembering his visits to Eastleigh and the night he proposed to her, she felt she somehow always had the measure of him, a man whose approach to her hinted strongly of a certain desperation. He came, after all, not in passionate pursuit but in a spirit of business-like practicality with what he - and of course Harold in the wings - thought of as a jolly good proposition. He got what he had asked for and she, by becoming his wife, had got much more by fate and circumstance.

It had been nearly a week since he had gone back to the cottage and the miserable, sick welcome that awaited him. She ached for the closeness that his being in the lodge convalescing had afforded her. Danger there was, but had

Edward's arrival not been imminent, she would have had to manufacture some excuse, plausible or otherwise. It was if they were oceans apart rather than a mile down the road.

The boy was an obvious, malleable link, but every time she thought of him the raw edge and depth of his look that day in the library came back to haunt her. She had been unwittingly trapped into some acknowledgement, that here she was witness to the boy grappling with the man, and it had to do with her. There was a frightening, forbidden appeal in that and she dared not harbour it.

It was now a downpour, ferociously hitting the front of the house but who could complain about it? Respite at last. But Edward should have been here by now and all the usual reasons came into play, late train and the like. She began to worry that something might be wrong as the sound of the motor, dulled by the force of the pouring rain, quickly brought her to attention.

She greeted a haggard and irritable-looking husband who pushed past her deliberately, or was pushed past her, as the rain swirled at the open door. His rather ungracious entrance was not lost on the motorman as he huddled against the elements before depositing Edward's meagre luggage in the hallway. The essence of discretion, as always, he turned quickly and bade goodbye with a minimum of fuss.

A hasty, superficial kiss was his only greeting before he began pacing the floor, his face a picture of barely concealed disgust and resentment. She immediately thought he knew everything but then surmised if he did know he would hardly have kissed her, superficial and dispassionate though it was. His first words gave credence to her suspicion.

"I have been made a fool of," he blurted out, "let us go upstairs. I am dog tired after a useless and wasted journey. And to think I left the work of such an important body because of some despicable genius from the village who made a fool out of me."

It was the first time she had ever heard him admit to being bested in any way and would have made some comment had he not been halfway up the stairs. Still afraid to hope that some errand other than what she suspected had brought him, she followed. A window had been left open and the effects of the rain were visible. He closed it with a bang and threw his coat on the bed, sitting next to it, running his hands through his hair and rubbing his face in exhaustion.

"This is a complete surprise, Edward, what is the matter and who has made a fool of you? How? I thought something had happened to you when you were not here at the expected time."

"That's all part of it. I had to call to Field as he's tied up in this mess also. Here, this will explain and by the way, Victoria, and be in no doubt about this, you are not completely blameless in all of this. I warned you about entangling yourself with anyone but our own around here."

He threw the letter on the bed and sat back to rest his head on the pillows before closing his eyes. Had he noticed, he would have seen the colour leave her cheeks. It was as if every detail had been revealed and yet it could have been so, so much worse. She knew the writer was not Field and also knew that if he were to compose such, he would have come to her first, long before informing Edward. He was not someone who rushed into things but then she thought of how quickly he had confronted the priest in the street. Yet that was understandable.

Opening his eyes, Edward watched her fold the letter and the drained look on her face was answer enough for him.

"Edward," she said, surprised at her calmness, "you know this was not written by the rector, I'm sure of it. What did he say?"

He was already nodding in agreement.

"Just that really and obviously, there are those in the village intent on making life as miserable as they can for me – for us. It does seem too that you are part of their plan to achieve that. Before you say anything, I know it's only a few fanatics hanging on to some glorious ideal of patriotism mixed up with religion, but they have influence."

"Yes, I know what you're saying and whoever wrote this scurrilous rubbish is right in one detail."

Here she hesitated, a sudden surge, pushing her to tell everything there and then. She drew back, however, not out of fear but some instinct. If all was to be revealed this certainly was not the right time either for her or her husband. Again, she thought, when would there ever be a right time?

"Golden did come to see me here and at my request. I have told you that I could not continue seeing the motorman's son, an innocent, being compromised. The boy has told me, in tears I might add, that his life is a hell, especially at school because of his friendship with Golden. He hates every day of it. I just felt that, as an outsider, I might be able to convey to the man the misery for which he is responsible. Foolish, perhaps but that's the way I felt."

"And?" said Edward, a frown of annoyance creeping across his weary face at the introduction of another element into the whole sorry state of affairs.

"And he came here and gave me another side to the story."

"Yes?"

"Well, it wasn't very much different from the one you had given me about the villagers."

She was incredulous at her composure and her ability to so casually and conversationally recount her first meeting with Joe. How she hated to call him Golden when referring to him by name. It then struck her that it was a small price to pay in view of the circumstances.

"And what had he to say about them?"

"It was more about his position here and I'm surprised you never told me about him."

She stressed the *you* and imperceptibly noticed that he was for a moment taken aback, as if stung by her remark.

"What do you mean by saying I never told you about him…there isn't very much to tell, is there?"

"That probably depends on what you mean by 'very much.' He told me a number of things about his background here and about his mother. He suffered much as the motorman's son does now but for different reasons. This, as I'm sure you know, had to do with his illegitimacy and the position of his mother who had to brazen it out until she died. He also told me, again as I'm sure you know, that only for the motorman and latterly his son she would have had no human contact, an outcast, ignored and scorned by those who somehow thought they were her betters. That's why her son is so resolved not to allow priest or people determining for him how he should live his life or what friends he should choose, young or old."

Edward's discomfiture as she spoke surprised her and he kept his face on the window, not meeting her eyes. Yet, he was fully aware, obviously, of Joe's position. He swung his legs off the bed complaining again of his tiredness and said he would wash before catching up on his sleep. Was he so tired though that he would make no reference to other parts of the letter, for example, the 'illicit liaison" and the implicit interpretation put on her being in Joe's cottage for 'a day' while the boy was there? Maybe Field had dealt with that? Maybe, but something she had said, some snippet had perturbed Edward. She might have let matters rest there, but she wanted Edward to give some response to how Joe had been treated, and Snee's expressed inability to do anything that might not be agreed by his superior, effectively no law and order in Shandrum.

He cut her short quite curtly by saying the rector had told him about the events around Joe and that he understood how, in the circumstances, she saw it fit and necessary to get involved, even if he wished she had not. When she mentioned Snee he wearily shrugged and replied with a half-hearted sneer.

"Victoria dear, these are the Irish. If you had any idea of how the majority of my friends in London see them and their Home Rule demands, then it might enlighten you somewhat. You suddenly seem to have gained an inordinate amount of interest in matters taking place in a remote corner of the Empire."

"But that is just not good enough, Edward," she haughtily retorted, "how can a man in your position, a man at the heart of the law, not see something wrong with the wanton savagery taking place here? Are you trying to tell me, that if he had been killed the night he was attacked, then nothing should have been done about it because of some peculiar aspect of life in this part of the Empire? Surely things are not as bad as that here and don't forget it is completely at variance with the rosied picture you painted for me when you asked me to marry you."

"But you see, my darling, he was not killed, was he? Please don't misunderstand me. It was disgraceful and it was terrible but maybe, as my friends say, when they get their coveted Home Rule, they will work out some better way of dealing with things, though I would not for a minute bet on that."

Furious at this weak and facile attitude, she glared at him and shouted with a conviction she never thought she possessed.

"Edward, you are a disgrace, as are your so-called friends. Did I ever think I would see you compromising your principles simply because the Irish are the Irish? And in case you've forgotten, you are bloody well Irish too, you know."

He had moved towards the door, then turned, his haggard face and bloodshot eyes telling their own story. Nothing had gone right for him today and he would not be dictated to by his wife and her new-found interest in the Irish. He tried to be measured.

"Victoria, my affairs are my own. How I conduct them as they relate to the people among whom we live is my business. I do not tell you how to write your books and you will not tell me that I am responsible for everything that goes on here. I can and will deal with my own affairs as I see fit."

He was almost out the door and then remembered something.

"And by the way, you seem to have ascertained what Mr Golden's reasons are for associating with the motorman's boy. I suggest that satisfies you. We can all see what the consequences of your actions, honourable though your intentions were, have been. I need hardly say more."

Then he was gone. She expected the door to bang closed, but it was not so. It was closed gently as if all was well and matters were sorted, sorted by him of course, she thought. Arms folded, she moved towards the rain spattered window, having picked up the letter from where it lay on the bed. She smiled as she read about the 'licentious and corrupting relationship' with 'one of the village's most undesirable individuals.'

Edward had shown, that though the letter writer's intention had been realised, he was prepared to bite his tongue as it were and accept Field's assurances. It was his attitude when she had mentioned Joe visiting Woodlands, and what he had to say, that intrigued her. Edward's troubled look had as much to do with what she had said as did the letter.

The rain obscured her vision as she vaguely looked into the imagined distance, the avenue, the lodge, the village and him. She left the muggy atmosphere of the bedroom and went downstairs to the library. That wasn't much better but was neutral and afforded her a chance to escape Edward's proximity and be alone. Her work had suffered in recent weeks and the promised deadlines, kept to so methodically in the past, were now practically ignored. Not that she was not writing. She was, but it was now exclusively confined to the world of adults and driven by her fantasies, her way of surviving when she couldn't be with their object.

She looked back over what she had written but never sent. Glad now she hadn't, who was to know where any written communication might end up and be used? One piece jumped out at her. It referred to her great aunt once telling her that heaven and love were wonderful but not easily attained. To Victoria, heaven was now somehow a bland goal compared to what she felt about love, caught up as she was in its honeyed trap. Her writings now were far from children's fables, beginning and middle leading to a happy end. She could argue, imagine, accept, deny and wish in any way she liked. She could look ahead and do the same with the future. All the possibilities could be looked at and pondered. The range was endless, at times confused, even bizarre but always bringing them together in interludes of unspoilt intensity.

The boy was always there too, though, as if a shadow to remind her of the stark reality. Right here in the library she had witnessed the beginnings of the decline of innocence.

Whatever happened between Joe and herself had some balance, a grownup equality. The child was different. A transition had been made and she had been completely at a loss. His look had reached somewhere inside her and secured an admission that childhood was fading and might not linger for very much longer. And she had no control, no power or for a moment, no inclination to shout stop. That unforeseen change, summed up when their eyes met, had irrevocably altered the trust that makes innocence a victim for one unforgettable moment that then becomes forever.

That searing, delicate affirmation – coming together in the mind's eye and then the heart but drawn apart just as quickly because convention so ordains, would surface she was certain, again and again. It frightened her because he was her main contact with Joe, but it was now much, much too dangerous with all that had happened. She must avoid involving him in the jealous uncertainties, the intrigue and the consequences. And then he was just the child again to her, the angular frame, alone with the tear-stained face and the fear, of not just the adults but those among whom he should be happiest and most at ease, his classmates.

Now her thoughts ran on and on, sometimes terrifying, sometimes subdued, always returning to the prospect of the next meeting. He had warned about contact too soon but her mind raced deliriously, gathering momentum as the rain's incessant beat continued.

*

He desperately needed time. Things as serious as this could not be decided on the spur of the moment. Appalled that his name had been linked with the infamous letter, indeed used to perpetuate the whole hoax and making Edward Sheldon to look like a fool, he could not get the priest out of his mind. Pondering the details, he became more and more convinced that his counterpart was the brains and the move behind the operations. This conclusion shocked him, shocked him in that he would think of a fellow clergyman as capable and willing of initiating and driving such a slanderous, devastating campaign. He thought again of the eviction photo and how what it portrayed had made the priest what he was today. No matter, how could one's past, however terrible, be allowed to rule one's future? Maybe easier said than done!

Now, he knew a lot more. But what was he to do with the different scraps of information he now had accumulated? The letter was one. Then his knowledge of those who had frequented the priest's house and the unsavoury conclusion of someone's, The Pagan's, 'goose being cooked.'

Had he not been in the cottage that day and seen the destruction, along with what he could only interpret as The Pagan's resigned affability, he would, no doubt, agree with the priest. The scandalous suggestion greatly disturbed him and try as he might, he was incapable of expunging the seductive image of the mistress of Woodlands in the arms of The Pagan. It had all the makings of a penny dreadful.

His conclusions changed again and again, with varying degrees of uncertainty. Thinking again of the day at the cottage and the practicalities of getting the donkey cart outside, he did notice what might best be described as a certain familiarity between the two of them. Were he asked to put it into words, he doubted he would be able. Something in their subtle absence of reserve, their lack of ceremony, maybe familiarity, best described it. Yet even his conscience could not oust the terrible cliché that now pounded at his brain, one that his very calling should, without question, ever resist, "no smoke without fire."

Then Sheldon's return. He wondered how matters with his wife were when they both had to confront the reality, that where Golden and the young boy were concerned, they, the Sheldons, were now fair game. Whether they liked it or not, they now were being dragged into a situation where it seemed they could only end up as losers.

His old bete noire, curiosity, took hold of him again. What had transpired when the tired and dispirited Edward faced his wife at Woodlands? How might she have reacted? Only one way to find out.

Making his way along the road, the summer sun, a feature of so many weeks, now struggled to make an appearance. Mulcahy, rattling out the words of some street ballad, came towards him in the infamous donkey and cart as he reached the gate lodge. He merited a greeting, a nod and the wave of a blackthorn stick. Here was one without a care in the world it seemed, thought Field. Yet he was in danger too here in his own village.

Mounting the steps to the front door of Woodlands, he went over again what he should not say. He would try to play the detective. Ushered in by one of the servants to the drawing room, a large photograph of Old Sheldon had him recall the many conversations he had there with a very different man to his son. Then of course there had been no woman in the house, Edward's mother having died many years before her husband. Now there was evidence of a woman's touch. It was an observation he often made on entering a house, knowing immediately if a woman's hand was evident. Never having married, he wondered now if the same might be said of the rectory which he was at pains to always have looking its best. But a woman's hand? "It is not good for man to be alone," came to mind as the approaching footsteps came closer.

A sombre Victoria entered, followed by her husband, now looking much smarter than the day before. Greetings over, Edward immediately spoke.

"I am not at all surprised to see you. You are lucky to catch me as duty calls and I'll be on my way shortly. Affairs of state, as they say. No, it's that infernal letter that brings you?"

Taken somewhat off guard by Edward's almost cheery opening, Field coughed as a distraction and then felt he could quite appropriately refer to the letter as Edward had mentioned it. He began, shakily.

"Well, you will appreciate that, thinking of the ordeal you both have suffered as a result of this dastardly trick, I thought it incumbent on me to visit. I am appalled, as you indeed are, by the sinister insinuations made. It must be extremely distressing. To be quite honest I came to seek your advice even though I do know Edward that I gave you some yesterday. Can anything be done, or more to the point, should anything be done if it simply perpetuates the upset already caused?"

"Victoria and I have discussed the matter in great detail this morning. She believes nothing should be done to pander to the baser instincts of those who are determined to do their worst. I, for my part, am inclined to agree but there is one thing I might be able to do which could, possibly, yield some degree of evidence."

"And what might that be," asked Field, intrigued.

"Edward has decided to turn detective," interjected Victoria, speaking for the first time and Field thought he detected a note of barely concealed derision in her voice.

"And what would you do if something were to surface, something whereby the script could be traced?"

"Haven't thought that far ahead and I certainly haven't forgotten how I felt yesterday, as you so clearly saw, when I realised I had made an ass of myself by reacting as I did. The trouble with using the law in such a matter as this," and here he looked towards Victoria, "is that every jot and tittle becomes fodder for public gossip. How the press would love something like this, causing irreparable damage to my reputation. All in the public interest, of course, as our so-called best newspaper editors say. You haven't forgotten Parnell, have you?"

"No indeed, most reprehensible the whole affair, can we ever forget it, despite the passage of time?" Field answered. He wondered if there was any point in pursuing matters any further, since Edward's intentions were clear, in so far as whatever transpired would not lead to getting the law involved. Victoria would not be side-lined.

"Whatever has to be done about this should be done. I have emphasised to my husband, and I presume you agree, the extent to which Mr Golden's safety is in jeopardy. The letter is all part of it, to build a case where if anything untoward were to happen to him or indeed the boy - let us not forget about him - there would be some warped justification to it. In that regard, perhaps, I should acquaint you with a conversation I had recently with the constable."

She gave the full story of what Snee had told her, adding decisively that there appeared to be people in the village, those of standing, who were content to accept such a system almost as an endearing Irish trait. Field was left in no doubt that he was included.

Edward, who had enough of this discussion from the evening before and earlier this morning, attempted to come to Field's rescue as well as his own.

"On this particular subject, let me be clear. My wife and I differ quite strongly on many aspects of this wretched situation and now is not the time to go over old ground again. Suffice it to say that what Golden has been subjected to is deplorable. For me now to react retrospectively as it were, to what has happened, would, I am certain, be seen as a further reaction to the cursed hoax. Whatever else happens, I am not going to make a fool of myself twice in as many days, especially when I know that very little, if anything, would be done."

He had come, curious as to how Victoria might deal with the troubling implications of the letter, in so far as it involved herself and Golden, hoping that something more concrete might emerge. Snee's position, which understandably troubled her so much, was not news to him and members of his own congregation were quite open in surmising the basis on which he had found his way to Shandrum. These ranged from the salacious to the comical, with women and vice at the core for some and with others believing that he was really a German spy in a policeman's uniform. What interest, Field often wondered, would Berlin have in Shandrum?

Despite their best efforts to maintain a degree of marital harmony about the situation, Field could clearly see that although a truce of sorts had been arrived at, husband and wife were not really at one. He found himself in one of those positions that he dreaded, not wanting to offend either but conscious that whatever he said would offend one.

"I have to agree with Edward," was his reluctant reply. "You are aware of my knowledge of The Pagan's – I must avoid using that term, I now realise - plight, witnessing as I have the devastation visited on his home. His singular attitude toward the conventions of church and state, never mind his involvement with your good motorman's son, has drawn the suspicion and wrath of both sides of our community on him. Let Edward do his detective work as you refer to it and then see what emerges."

He hoped, rather than anticipated, that Victoria would leave it at that but her reaction as he spoke made him realise he would have been better to have said nothing. He knew immediately that what he had said, appeared to Victoria as condoning the situation Golden found himself in. Her nostrils widened in contempt, and he braced himself for her reply. Fingers apart, she placed her hands on the table and they were pointed towards him. Suddenly he was mesmerised by the stark beauty of the woman he suspected of being in thrall to The Pagan, the very last man in the village he would have thought of or suspected. The ferocity of her stare added rather than detracted from her allure and he felt she almost knew what his thoughts were.

"Rector, I am learning very quickly that those in this unfortunate country who are best placed to change the rot with which it is infected are the very ones who seem intent, by doing nothing, to ensure it continues. Who then are the victims? Those like the boy, an innocent who happens to spend his leisure time with a man who happens to be different and rejects what you and I believe in. Why shouldn't the boy visit the house he always visited when an ostracised woman lived there up to her dying day and no one except father and son visited? And yet, because of the sordid suspicions of those with little to do, that boy's life is a misery, and the attitude of the grownups feeds the canker to their children and they, because they are children, do everything in their power to act like little savages and revel in it."

"Victoria," Edward interjected, feeling things were getting out of hand. But his wife was in full flow and would not countenance interruption. Her eyes veered back from Edward to Field.

"What I cannot understand is the attitude people in your position and my husband's take. Wring your hands, decry and denounce but then do absolutely nothing. And I am expected to give my consent to more of the same. I cannot and will not."

Field opened his mouth to say something, but he knew he would be foolish to continue a battle where the hope of winning was nil. Edward, with a look of resignation that might be reserved for his worst day in court, sat drumming his fingers on the table.

"Please Victoria, the rector is our visitor and while we understand your view, you are an outsider. I told you that things would be different here and they are. If you, the rector or I can succeed in turning the law-and-order system here upside down to what it should be, you can be assured that they will come up with some other connivance that will be just as exasperating. You will learn in time."

She didn't answer and was clearly stung by being treated as a child who needed educating. Field, lost for words now and feeling sorry he ever let his curiosity get the better of him, saw that Edward's patronising attempts to placate his wife were simply making things worse. However, she remained silent, folding her arms and standing up while they remained seated. For her the conversation was over.

Standing over them, she steadily focused on something unknown and unknowable to them, indeed beyond everything, leaving Field with a jittery feeling that she had her own mind made up, lawyer husband and village rector notwithstanding.

He realised he was simply an intruder into a domestic dispute at this point. His presence had exacerbated matters rather than leading toward any kind of solution. He rose, muttering something about things having a habit of working out for the best sometimes, only then recognising the silliness of what he had said. Husband and wife made no effort to detain him.

They were both sullenly glad to be alone with each other without the distraction of Field's presence, whose only contribution to the situation was to inflame matters between them. Their disagreement, not as might be suspected about the letter, had been down to Victoria's incredulity that Edward would be so blasé about what was going on in the village. The previous evening over dinner their exchanges had been furious, eventually with more heat than light. She recalled one of Edward's more scathing remarks, "who or what have I married?" To be answered by two words, "a woman."

Her lingering look into the distance, that had so taken Field's attention, was toward the cottage and the man who seemed destined to be harried and pursued almost at will by the forces ranged against him. That's where she wanted to be now, not with her husband in their ornate surroundings, but in the simple cottage and in the arms of the man who was now more than an obsession.

She saw little benefit in prolonging the argument with Edward and felt it might be more productive to give an impression that she was content to let matters rest. Thinking over what had happened since he arrived back, one thread seemed to run through all their differences and bickering. Edward, whenever she brought up Joe by name and talked about his visit to Woodlands, or his mother, was suddenly withdrawn, almost uncomfortable, tending toward deflecting the conversation.

In all that was said or unsaid, he left her in no doubt at any stage about his displeasure at her involvement with what were, as he put it, 'matters best left in the village' even if he did admit to understanding her motivation. Even this had grown more grudging as the previous evening's dinner went on.

*

He might have stayed longer had a telegram not arrived seeking his return as soon as possible so that the commission he was chairing could get on with its deliberations and report by summer's end.

Showing her the telegram, he did try to patch things up by saying that he would ensure the work of the commission would be complete by the end of August, allowing them as agreed, go to the south of France for their delayed honeymoon in mid-September. She reacted with little enthusiasm, hoping he took it as a reaction to the strained atmosphere created by their disagreement.

The motor had hardly gone through the gates of Woodlands when her thoughts, not for the first time that morning, turned to Joe and how a meeting might be arranged. There was now greater danger than ever, with the contents of the letter and its success in getting Edward back undoubtedly common knowledge that would be gossiped and gloated over by all and sundry. Evidence of this came quicker than expected with the arrival of an invitation from Lavinia Chapman to lunch, "to see out the summer in style." They would again be joined by the Bressingtons and Kingston-Halls. All an excuse, Victoria surmised, to ply her with drink and quiz her for their satisfaction.

Rather than hinder her, the danger, precariousness and intrigue associated with planning how to get herself into

Joe's arms as soon as possible infused her with an energy and determination, even if further moral condemnation might ensue. Effortlessly lured into the outcast's unconventional world and in so short a time, had her single-minded in determining to outwit and defy anyone who might deny them what was now theirs.

The chilling looks of the villagers and the strides of the priest, that bore down on her and the boy that day as they left the cottage to go home, came back to her as if to halt any further thoughts of her grand plans. She cast the feeling aside as if with scorn as her new-found sense of purpose grew. Never had she thought that her writing would be unimportant, that her editors' pleas would go unanswered. Her writing now was what she was compelled to commit to paper, couched in an intensity unknown before, as she scribbled every thought, every feeling she would have shared had they been together.

What would he think of the letter that had brought Edward hotfoot from London? Would he shrug and smile, just laugh it off as no surprise to him or dismiss it with indifference? Or would it bring the flash of anger she had seen the day the boy was on the street and at the priest's mercy? How was she to know if there was no way of seeing him?

In the drawing room with Edward and Field, both babbling to keep her in her place, she had decided it was pointless to continue and the conversation died, allowing her to look away in the village's direction where he might then be. The recollection of what he had endured would not be pushed aside by Edward's stony silence or Field's embarrassed shuffling in the chair before he had left.

Now Edward was gone and would be of little help. The rector was only down the road and might yet prove useful. Blushing at her convoluted rationale she would give him a chance to do something about what he and her husband claimed they were incapable of doing. She would give him an opportunity to redeem himself, a concept she had heard him refer to from the pulpit once or twice since she arrived.

He had left chastened, conscious that once again he had allowed his insatiable curiosity to get the better of him. Now he was back in haste following her note which the motorman had delivered, in the absence of his son. She was as glad the boy was not at home when she called as she was unprepared for any awkwardness that might ensue if she were to ask him to be messenger boy again.

"Rector, I need some advice on the matter recently discussed with my husband," was the note's, terse, intriguing message.

His sense was it had to do with the letter but that was yet to be seen. All he was interested in was in some way making amends for the debacle in the drawing room when he ended up feeling like a fish out of water, upbraiding himself for his ability to be more a nuisance than a help. He had left the house feeling utterly foolish, thoroughly unworthy of his calling. That morning, caught between husband and wife, not for the first time in his life, he found himself agreeing with one side but unable to disagree with the other. He took Edward's side, conscious that his wife's indignation and reasoning was the morally correct one. Nothing was simple anymore, he thought to himself.

Edward's view of Shandrum was more secular and because of that, more objective, he felt. As a man of the law, highly respected because of that and someone whose opinion, as a consequence, demanded serious consideration, he just couldn't be dismissed out of hand and certainly not by his wife.

Yet, Field could not deny that the livelihood, indeed the physical safety of The Pagan could not be guaranteed with alien forces determined to do their worst. It was, he had to admit, Victoria's righteous anger that had brought the whole thing into sharp relief.

As he was ushered again into the drawing room, the last thing he wanted was another show of that righteous anger from a woman as formidable as the one he was now about to face again. Her sultry, imposing presence, when he had found himself caught between her and her husband, was what made him most uncomfortable when his opinion was sought.

He sat opposite her facing the window, immediately feeling at a disadvantage with the sunlight in his face. She wasted no time with niceties apart from thanking him for responding so promptly.

"The facts are, whatever has been said or discussed between us and my husband, that the person most completely maligned by the letter has no idea of its existence, though most of the village probably does. I know my husband and I are mentioned, and you realise we are less than happy with such slander but it's not us I am talking about now. We can and will take care of ourselves."

"I agree entirely," Field replied, not yet certain what way the conversation might go. He would watch every step and avoid falling into any traps that might leave him again at the mercy of her considerable ability to gain the upper hand.

"I don't believe Mr Golden should be left in the dark, as it were, about this latest insidious form of attack, hoax or no hoax. It's another step in what I, whatever you and my husband think, believe is a carefully orchestrated campaign to further ostracise him, as if enough damage has not been done to him already."

Victoria, her scheme concocted in passionate anticipation of success, now felt it less plausible, facing the one who might bring it about. It was not a time for dithering, and she ploughed ahead with was after all, a tenable ploy.

"I believe I should tell him on Edward's behalf and my own what has happened over the last few days and how it's another example of the contemptible aggravation to which he has been and will continue to be subjected. You could tell him on our behalf but that would be weak and a dereliction of duty on our part. I do not want you to be a go-between."

In fact, that was exactly her intention.

"So, you plan on visiting him for this purpose?"

"That indeed would be the most forthright thing to do – Edward, if he were here or myself calling - but I do not intend to put on a show for the villagers merely to have a personal visit gossiped about and exaggerated to suit the needs of those who, as we well know now, might well use it for their own purposes."

"I cannot agree with you more," Field answered, anticipating that at some point he might well be part of whatever plan the woman before him had hatched.

"And this, I presume, is where I come in," he added, smiling for the first time, almost conspiratorially.

"Yes, I think it quite in order, having assisted Mr Golden before," she almost said Joe, "that you should call on him and inform him that there are some matters I wish to discuss with him."

She felt herself redden but if he noticed he gave no indication. The smile was gone now, and she was again tight lipped and grave. As if to chide him for what he might be thinking she quickly added to what she had said.

"Of course, and this is really where you can be of enormous assistance, I am suggesting that you accompany him from his cottage so that it will be noted in the village. I would have the motor collect you both, but I want to keep things as separate from Woodlands as possible even if it will be known that he comes here with you. Your accompanying him might, hopefully, offset him being exposed to more venom and innuendo. In fact, it would show the letter writer and his cronies that whatever they had intended to achieve, it had one definite effect, that those blackened in it intend to stand together. You are extremely important in that respect."

Again, he was back to a sea of uncertainty and unable to be decisive and he knew she noticed it. Not surprised by her proposal, he was troubled by it. He ventured a trite reply that might be to his advantage.

"That may be the danger; don't you suppose that they will see it in the opposite way, that it is evidence their plan has had an effect?"

Fearing he might desist, she rounded on him decisively.

"Let them think what they will, we must do what we see as fit rather than try to figure out their views or intentions. You must play your part."

Fearing that she might continue more aggressively he immediately piped up with feigned gusto.

"Yes, yes of course. I didn't mean to be awkward. As you say, they will draw their own conclusions. And I must emphasise that, while this is a rather unusual request, I will do whatever I can to be of assistance to one of my own flock. I have been used as a pawn in all of this and I fear for what the future may hold."

"I know what fear is, Rector. Emeline Pankhurst said to me once as we faced a hostile crowd on one of the occasions I was part of a public demonstration with the suffragettes, that if fear dictated how we might act then we would never act at all."

"Brave women indeed but their battle is an uphill one still, isn't it? Now to the present, when do you want us to come, assuming that he's available and willing to accompany me? With this new bicycle he might be out and about at all hours."

An inward smile was her thought, he will be, don't you worry.

"Anytime this afternoon. The sooner he is aware of all this the better. We know what they have already done and of what they are capable. After all, religion and patriotism are a strange and powerful mix, don't you think?"

Ostensibly he agreed but as he began his walk down the avenue, he was overtaken by a sense of dissatisfaction verging on despondency. She had the upper hand all the way through and really, without an objection, he had agreed to her plan which, he now saw, was using him to give a modicum of respect to a possible rendezvous with The Pagan. He had become party to a very dangerous and questionable plan. Again, images of Golden with her surfaced and it was those images that led him to the next conclusion.

As he passed by the gate lodge and onto the road it was as if a flash of enlightenment hit him. The Pagan suited her better than the staid, respected King's Counsel she had been wife to for a few months, just a single summer. But he shuddered at the consequences, while marvelling again at the complexities of human nature where men and women were concerned. Something in The Pagan's blunt, uncompromising defiance rested easily in this woman's searching and fiery soul. She might have left the suffragettes behind but not their spirit.

Almost by chance he had stumbled on the truth. Everything he had stood for and preached in relation to the sacredness of the marriage vows was jettisoned where this man and the wife of the master of Woodlands were concerned. He would grapple long and hard with this painstaking fact that seemed to sweep aside in an instant one of the most sacred tenets of the faith he professed. This was one secret he would not be sharing. Who would agree with him on such a fundamental principle?

Then his mind turned to the mental and moral mess that he was tied up in, with the latest turn of events quickly making him an accomplice. The letter proved one incontrovertible fact – from where the League stood, the occupants of Woodlands and The Pagan were interchangeable, depending on circumstances.

As for the Pagan - he again determined not to use the term - he knew least of him even though a neighbour. Only for the attack on the cottage he would never have been inside the door and yet, even in the midst of chaos that day, he did get an impression from the atmosphere in the room of a house of books, newspapers, magazines, all of which told him that here was a man of intelligence, indeed learning in the broadest sense of that word. Because of all he stood for otherwise of course, no woman, least of all Victoria Sheldon, a married woman of status, would have anything to do with him. Yet that is what had happened. Man, though a little less than the angels was still man and for every Adam there would be an Eve. In the circumstances he thought the comparison appropriate.

Where did all this leave the innocent, the child left to the mercies of adults' machinations? He would still be pilloried because of his association and the idea of his being in moral danger, clearly alluded to in the letter, would let no one forget the priest's diatribe. He, his counterpart, had played no little part in perpetuating what he now considered to be a convenient myth. A myth, indeed, but a very dangerous one.

And there was another thing about him. The evening of the bicycle accident, when they all ended up in the gate lodge, he had felt threatened by his composure and saw in that an arrogance bordering on contempt. No sign of subservience was evident toward him as a man of the cloth or Victoria Sheldon. Now, after all that had happened, he had a different view and that evening now seemed like a very long time ago. There was something wholesome, natural about this man who every day he had lived in Shandrum was seen as a pariah, of questionable morals. That wholesomeness signalled for Field the antithesis of immorality and depravity where the boy might be concerned. However, he admitted to himself that his wholesome image might be tested again and again because of the ebb and flow of events.

He was back at his own gate before he knew it due to the jumble of thoughts that swirled in his mind, competing for answers, since leaving an expectant Victoria Sheldon on the steps of her home. Now he had to keep his promise. He also had to somehow square a circle. How could he be party to something which flew in the face of all he believed in and which he was in no doubt about, contributing to whatever consequences might ensue? A tightness in his chest told him he was getting into deep water.

*

The familiar, acrid smell of rabbits being cleaned seeped through the kitchen from the backyard and into the front room where he lazily lolled in the streams of sunlight that came through the two windows. Looking out towards the road all he could think of was the school, standing sombre and empty waiting for the return of the village scholars and himself in ten days. Each passing day brought the wrenching terror, and his nights were no different, with no escape from the sinuous dreams that permeated his sleep. The holidays were rushing by with ever increasing and ominous foreboding.

So engrossed was he, that he hardly noticed the rector come to the front door and knock. He shouted at Joe, immersed in gore and grime. What could he want? Maybe something to do with his previous visit?

"Oh, it's you again, is it? I hadn't expected to find you here but then I should not be surprised, should I?"

"You want Joe?"

"Yes, I won't keep him very long."

"He's outside at the rabbits, I'll get him."

He found Joe methodically washing his hands in an enamel basin with very little water in it. He motioned to the boy and Field was asked into the room where he had first been on that fateful day.

"Certainly, a big change from the last time I was here," he said, taking a seat while he looked round and took in what he could.

Joe casually ambled in and Field made as if to get up, but Joe gestured and he sat back in the chair.

"Sorry to take you from your duties but I am on a mission of some importance."

He looked toward where the boy stood, clearly a hint that whatever he had come for it was not for the boy's ears.

Joe noticed and said, "can't you finish the rabbits? There's not much left to do."

He went to the yard to do a job he detested but it was the rector's visit that now occupied him. That was until Joe shouted from inside, telling him to bring two of the best. This he did and Field accepted them with some embarrassment. Jauntily he bade Field goodbye adding, "about four then." This suddenly alerted Field as to why he had come in the first place.

"Of course, I'd almost forgotten, four then."

He was almost at the door when he turned and handed Joe back the rabbits.

"Might be better if other eyes didn't see me with those, but leave them over after dark, will you?"

They watched him through the door, sauntering back across the road with a nervous glance toward the village.

In the front room, the sounds of time had always dominated. That was until the League had its way and the two clocks were smashed on the floor. Joe, not to be outdone, had replaced the one beyond repair. It read half past two and over the next hour and a half the boy noticed how furtively Joe looked towards the mantelpiece.

"What did he want?" the boy asked with as much lack of interest as he could disguise.

"I have been summoned to the hallowed walls of Woodlands, in Shandrum in the county of Cork to discuss a matter of international importance with grave consequences for King and Kaiser. I will let you know the outcome."

Try as he would, with the time nearing four, Joe was unable to strike a casual pose and the boy knew why.

He was anticipating his visit to Woodlands for the same reason the boy would. He would see her, speak to her, be near her, able to watch her and think about her while in her presence. The fact that Field would be there made some difference, he supposed, but that was all.

As Joe's whistling became more animated, the streak of bitterness and resentment hit home again. Behind the pages of a magazine, he pretended indifference, but he resented and envied Joe because of what lay ahead for him.

He recalled the scene here in the kitchen the day after the attack as they rested after eating and how Joe looked at her and how she returned his gaze, almost as if they both thought they were not being observed. Joe had been so different with her, different than he had ever seen him. He would be that way today and it was wrong because Joe would have something that he desperately desired. Hadn't he met her before Joe, talked to her before him, welcomed her to Woodlands with his memorised words? It was he who had first told Joe of how beautiful she was.

Whatever she wanted him for might have to do with Mr Sheldon's departure that morning, looking gaunt and dissatisfied as his father drove him through the gates.

Now it was five minutes to four and he watched Joe and the rector get ready to head out in the same direction. As Joe met him at the door and they set off, he noticed how nervous Field was and how Joe still limped. He wondered would he always be that way from the savagery of the attack. Even with the limp, Joe's forward stride contrasted sharply with the slight stoop of the older man who had to hurry to keep up. Moving from the door into the garden where some of the summer flowers were fighting for survival, he leaned over the wall to watch. They reached the dangerous corner and were gone.

Looking back towards the village he soon realised he was not the only one watching each step of the two unlikely partners. The usual faces were there, so familiar and so grimly interested. He hurried back inside.

He sat back in the chair, uncertain as to what he would do. The photograph of Joe's mother, it too not unscathed by the attack, caught his attention. It was Joe's dark, lush eyes that now looked out at him. He remembered the woman and his memory was of a slight, emaciated frame in the bed, dignified still in her isolation and pain. He remembered visiting her before she died with his father with food from Woodlands' kitchen meant for themselves. It did not leave them short however, as she barely managed to eat a few meagre scraps.

He was only five when her death brought her son back from some faraway place and into his life and that of the village. After the funeral he recalled Joe, standing on the floor of the gate lodge, saying to his father, drink in both their hands, something about blood being thicker than water and that the priest would find out it was. Drunk or not that night, Joe kept his promise.

*

Field is no fool. The phrase, for some reason, had caught her imagination and would not go away. Now, as she waited for them to arrive, it began to irritate her. Like a nursery rhyme that cannot be kept from the mind, it kept going round and round in her head, drumming away at its self-evident truth as if to warn her that she should not forget what it told her. It was a message not to be dismissed. Behind his rather bumbling exterior he was not a man to be underestimated. His curious, piercing eyes looked deeper than most.

His insistence on agreeing with Edward annoyed her, but she could accept that. His actions, especially in confronting the priest on the street, were not only necessary but noble. And his intervention meant that Joe had not got to the priest first that day, with consequences she didn't want to contemplate. And he had not baulked at being a willing messenger even if she suspected his insight might well lead him to draw certain conclusions.

She kept looking towards the avenue; it did not escape her that whatever conclusions Field might draw, she was shamelessly using him and his position to give some semblance of propriety to her meeting Joe. This was not the time, however, to argue with her conscience. It hadn't made her reveal all to Edward. Why? She had come back to the question a number of times, wondering what things might now be like had she taken what many might see as the honourable path and told him the truth. Honour and truth, however, can easily fall victim to other forces and she was the perfect example.

For Field, she had dressed demurely, even if every item of clothing she put on was for the man coming with him. The flowers on the drawing room table, arranged and rearranged, were for him too, even if he never noticed. The tea offered, were it taken, would be from the best china and it would be for him. For him she was creating a world within herself and her home. Never before had the commonplace taken on such importance.

Everyone she knew, including Field, would consider her behaviour outrageous and obsessive, not worthy of the mistress of Woodlands, her family back in Eastleigh and certainly not her husband. Here she was, a woman that wrote about the black and white of truth for children, always with some kind of moral in keeping with the norms and demands of polite society. Now, her mental and physical obsession, with consequences yet unknown, would be understood by no one. Yet, anytime such sobering, predictable reasoning gnawed at her she was swept back to a deeper, more invigorating reality. The threads and strands that he had unearthed in her body and her mind more than adequately contradicted the staid, standard, accepted reasoning that sought to be heard but without success.

There it was again, Field is no fool. She still couldn't resist the childish rhyming intrusion that penetrated and nagged at her even as she wished it banished. Banished, along with anything that might make her feel ashamed or embarrassed at using a man in Field's position to get what she craved.

The hands of the clock led the afternoon towards evening and still they had not come. Her impatience and apprehension grew only to be subdued by her desire. Every time she made her way to the window the only reward was the mocking stretch of avenue and then doubt became fear. Had something happened, something untoward that would deny her?

Field is no fool. There was something about his position as rector, that she felt gave him an objectivity lacking in others.

But where was he? Her impatience gave way to apprehension each time she went to the window. Doubt mingled with fear. Might something have happened to deny her what she craved? So much had happened in this place that anything was possible.

*

Her musing had carried her away and they were halfway up the avenue before she saw them. Field animated, Joe more sombre with eyes fixed on the house. Now they halted. Field listened. Her eye, catching the side of Joe's face with its delicate, diffused potency, enraptured her.

They were on the steps, and she didn't wait for the knock. The faintest of smiles crossed Joe's lips as their eyes met. Faced with Field's disarming look, she could not respond, desperate though she was to do so.

They eased into their chairs, she sitting at the top of the table with Field, settling in as if disinterested, between Joe and herself. She would not be fooled by the casualness of the rector. This was not a man to be underestimated. He had proved that the day he had confronted the priest.

A servant arrived with a tray and placed it on the table before leaving but not before she gave a quizzical look at all three seated round it. Victoria poured and then sat forward in her chair, business-like and direct. Inside she was shaking but she had experience in situations like this from her time with the suffragettes when she faced politicians, lawyers and the police when the cause had to be advanced. And no greater cause than that of now, with all at stake and every step had to be taken with an outward show of formality.

"My thanks, Rector, for being so kind in prevailing on Mr Golden to come and for accompanying him."

Field nodded, waiting for her to go on.

"I assume you have given Mr Golden some idea of why we thought it so necessary that he come here?"

"Not beyond explaining that it was a matter of importance,

and I would not presume to pre-empt what you might have to say."

A game was being played and including him was evidence of it.

She turned to Joe, acutely conscious that in addressing him Field would study every gesture. In a measured tone, she felt as she spoke that she could well have been Edward at his most serious at the Old Bailey.

"Mr Golden, my husband was recently the recipient of a letter purporting to come from Reverend Field. The letter makes a number of scandalous and outrageous allegations about you – and indeed others. Some of what the letter says refers to you and the motorman's son and this may not be news to you. Put simply, the letter reflects most unfavourably on your character. I might add, of course that the perpetrators' plan worked, to the extent that my husband dropped everything in London to return when he got the scurrilous piece of trash."

Joe's eyes never left her face as she spoke, though he deferred to Field's presence when he was mentioned. She felt he was teasing her, facilitated by the man who sat between them. While maintaining her tone and composure she luxuriated in his attention as his eyes moved over the contours of her face. They would, she knew, have strayed further had the rector not been a barrier.

"Reference is made in this letter to my presence in your house and my visits to you when you were recently recovering from your injuries. The letter writer's purpose is very clear. Though it pains us all to respond to a well contrived and calculated hoax, we feel it needs to be brought to your attention. It proves, as if it were needed, that there are people here whose purpose is obvious. The law, as I have quickly come to understand, operates selectively, if at all, which means we must all be very careful. Your attention has been brought to your trespassing on our property and I am repeating that now." She waited and the longer the pause continued the more uncomfortable she became. Perhaps Joe saw that and responded.

"Mrs Sheldon, I must remember that, but I must say what I think I've said to you before. Nothing that happens in the village surprises me and I can say the same about what you have just told me."

Then, as if to bring Field into the conversation, he continued.

"There is no mystery here. What they are doing is casting the net wider at a pace and dragging in people like yourselves. They don't want me here but, just in case it hasn't occurred to you, they don't want you here either. We know the ringleader and we know his followers. I've good reason to know the whole lot of them and what they slyly preach by day they put into action at night. Very brave men in the dark of night but then they have God on their side."

He grimaced in disgust as he turned away from them.

Field, feeling he should contribute something, jumped in, taken aback to Joe's reference about God on the side of evil, true though it was, as he grudgingly admitted to himself.

"Are we making too much of all this?" he asked, looking out the window as if addressing the world outside rather than those on either side of him. Hardly were the words out of his mouth when he realised that his question was not only foolish but naïve. He knew more than anyone who was involved. Not wishing to be too far removed from reality, he hurriedly attempted to redeem himself.

"No, I suppose we're not. It all really is outrageous."

He wondered if he should tell them about those he saw through the priest's window. No, he would not. Being privy to that information gave him a certain protection. Were he to tell them might result in him having to get further involved in some way. He wished for nothing more than time now. Lamely, like a traitor he thought, he went on.

"Now that we know what's afoot we have to be far more vigilant."

"Yes," agreed Victoria, patronisingly. It signalled the end of the conversation and she stood up. Ostensibly, the matter of the letter and its content - though not all the content - had been brought to Golden's attention.

As Field and Joe readied to leave, Victoria dwelt on the farcical nature of what had just taken place. She had little doubt that Joe thought as much also. What of the rector? Joe was the last to get up from his chair, and she thought he was going to say something. Her heart pleaded with him to let Field have the final word. He did not disappoint her and rose slowly. Field was not so easily read but that did not worry her now. His summary, weak and watery, that finished the conversation suited her. Only one precise move now needed to be executed.

Both men looked at each other and Field thanked Victoria and made towards the door. Victoria got there just before him, opened it and stood back to let him out. Standing now between both men, Victoria casually pressed a piece of paper into Joe's hand as he passed her by. She would have prolonged the momentary touch but would not now tempt fate, having achieved what she had planned.

Field, standing on the steps and anxious to preserve proprieties, bade goodbye to Victoria. Joe had not spoken since the conversation at the table had ended, but now, looking away into the soft, hazy distance, he turned to Victoria.

"The rector here is right. We must be more careful."

The simple words could have a thousand different meanings, she thought, but what he said was all she wanted. She closed the door, easily and patiently, as if closing the chapter of a book and waiting for the next one to begin.

From the drawing room window, she watched them go down the avenue, one slightly bowed, as if dismissed, the other exuding an animal suggestiveness with every limping stride. Now all she had to do was wait.

*

"By the orchard wall at nine. I will be waiting for you. V. x."

He looked briefly at the handwriting he had last seen on the cover of the book she had given him. Now, as he dwelt on the short, simple message, its powerful meaning brought a strange and shivery feeling. It was as if the message was for him and not for Joe.

He had discovered the note by chance. Joe had come back, and they had eaten a simple meal together. Then, he stood up, took off his shirt and carelessly threw it aside on the chair at the table before going out to the yard, whistling a familiar tune. The note had fallen on to the floor and as Joe went through the back door, the boy had pounced on it, read it and then put it back into the shirt pocket.

Seldom had he seen Joe wash himself twice in the same day although he had a habit of splashing a handful of water over his face if he was going to town sometimes. But this was different. Joe seemed to be taking more care as the razor was meticulously guided across his face and not with the usual hurried pace.

The boy watched him as the words jabbed again and again. He recalled the day they had both seen her asleep by the orchard wall and he had noticed the look on Joe's face. Now, at nine which suddenly seemed such a magical, suggestive hour, Joe would be with her again. Jealousy, fiery and hateful streaked through him.

The man now so jauntily shaving into the cracked mirror had to do nothing and she was there for him. The words on the book cover she had written for him made him proud but now something completely different bubbled inside him. "The orchard wall at nine. I'll be waiting. V. x." It would be alright for them in the long run. A wretched swell of hopelessness churned in his stomach, almost like the way he felt about returning to school, but this time compounded by a lingering loss, something out of reach. Something was slipping away. He didn't know how or why, but it was.

Standing, as if to attention, Joe performed the final ritual, as with accustomed ease he drew what remained of a comb across his thick, dark hair.

The boy wondered what excuse he would make. Would he tell him a lie? Taking the basin to the back door Joe scattered the contents in all directions. Turning back to where the boy sat, he seemed now less certain, as if something had broken a spell.

"I can't take you with me tonight because I'm going to meet someone, it's Mrs Sheldon. It's because of today, being up at Woodlands with our friend across the way. It's hard to explain it, it's grownup stuff and hard to understand for you. But I won't always be seeing her, and we'll still be able to do all the things we do, you and me. You can do the snares tomorrow and we might get a decent catch."

He had stumbled awkwardly through the words, and it seemed as if he wanted to say more. He didn't and the boy was glad. He wished him gone.

All he would remember from Joe's explanation was "It's hard to explain it." That was something he could understand and more so now if Joe, always having a way, some way, of explaining things, couldn't explain now. Maybe, some things can never be explained.

Joe glanced uneasily around the room. The sounds of children playing with a barking dog came from up the street. Though wishing Joe gone he knew he would have to be careful. Would he go by the path, their path trodden so often in fair weather and foul? That way he would surely be safer. He was going to say something about the path being the safest way but that would be helping Joe and now that was the last thing he wanted to do. The back door latch fell into place, he was alone, and Joe was gone. He took a mouthful of water and left by the back door just as Joe had earlier.

*

Angels and saints looked solemnly down as streamers of the sun's dying rays filtered through the stained-glass windows, catching specks of dust drifting aimlessly through the dry air. The stations of the cross, each telling their sad story as Jesus stumbled and faltered towards Calvary, dotted the side walls, too high to be caught by the slanting sun's rays.

His impossible prayer began.

Dear Jesus, you can do anything. Keep her for me and not for Joe … the prayer was from the heart but the fact that he was praying for two non-believers choked the words as his lips attempted to form them. As if the two he prayed for were hopeless cases, he tried again and begged that the school be burned down. The absurdity of that was not lost on him either. God could do anything but he had no doubt that the school door would be opened again at summer's end. And that would come too soon. Kneeling, looking beyond the light of the sanctuary lamp, he grasped for words to change his world.

The sound of a door opening made him soon forget his praying. It was the door from the sacristy to the altar and through the rays of sunlight now came the priest, a bunch of keys jangling from his hand. As if caught in some terrible act, the boy stiffened, like the rabbits he had so often seen when the lantern light caught their eyes.

Throwing a cursory glance around the chapel, the priest came to the altar rails, opening and closing the golden gates before stepping on to the aisle.

Crouching lower in the seat, his knuckles were white.

Hoping against hope that the priest would turn left or right, but no, he came towards him, head held high, moving in and out of the sun's rays and back into the shadows again. As he got closer, jumbled excuses came racing into his head for being where he was, but just like the prayers earlier, nothing made sense.

Anticipating that he would be yanked out of the seat, he waited, ready for the scrawny hand to fall. Miraculously, it never did, and the priest passed by, his swishing robe and keys almost catching the side of his face. How could he not have been seen? Maybe it was the sun that blinded him. Maybe some unuttered prayer had been heard after all. Then another thought. Had the priest seen him and deliberately left him where he was, now to be locked in for the night? But no, maybe after all it was a miracle. Thank you, Jesus.

The door banged and the keys rattled, shutting him in as the sun slipped away, leaving him alone with angels and saints for company.

All again was silence, a sombre stillness descending. The sudden change of atmosphere shook him into realising the dilemma he was now in. Having escaped the clutches of the priest he was now imprisoned within the very walls that so often offered him respite. Maybe one of the side doors might be open? He left the seat and checked. No luck there, no miracle this time. He looked round the walls at the windows. High up was an opening in each one for air but even a cat would have trouble getting out there were it even able to reach. Patrick and Brigid looked down at him, uncompromising and rebuking. Joseph and Mary, from the windows behind the altar seemed no different. All around him were the stations of the cross, telling their sorry, despairing story.

He sat and thought of what he might do. Twilight faded with unexpected haste, as if to seal his dilemma, and now he was shivering, not with cold but fear. His father would assume he was at Joe's and Joe would assume he was at home. How quickly he had forgotten about Joe and his rendezvous at Woodlands as a more immediate problem took his attention.

He sat at the altar rails where the glimmer from the sanctuary lamp shaped the altar itself, the cross high above it and the tabernacle underneath. God was there but that conviction was not enough to keep away the chill that had his teeth chattering even though the heat of the day lingered everywhere. Looking down from the altar he realised how small, how unimportant he was, dwarfed by the ceiling that seemed to get higher and the walls that seemed to be closing in more.

Would he be better off in one of the confession boxes? He wasn't brave enough to move from the outside to a deeper darkness and dismissed the idea with a shudder. He could shout out, but no one would hear him and after all you should not shout in the house of God. Peering down the aisle towards the locked front door another spectre grabbed at his imagination, that of the coffins left there overnight before a burial. A prickly fear numbed the back of his neck, and he uttered a "Lord have mercy on their souls." He remembered those who had recently died and imagined their gaunt, lifeless shells lying inside the long boxes. Two, Jack Dean and Helena Mason, had died from the deadly heat of the summer, found alone, shrivelled in their little cabins across the river, with no one interested or worried enough to look in and see if they were alright. Their names had been in The Cork Examiner as if a warning to others.

How many others had spent their last night in the darkness at the door, their life's journey now over, ready for the journey to the graveyard, as the chapel bell tolled, telling all that one day it would ring for them too? How often had the master told the class this, his face dark and solemn? Coffins, bells, funerals suddenly brought an outrageous idea to mind. But no, the consequences would be too great, a triumph for the priest and those who would revel in such a sacrilegious act.

Aided, perhaps, by the deepening darkness and silence the idea kept pestering at his brain gaining more credence the more he thought about it. To succeed he would have to venture down towards the front door, lost now in blackness and far away from the dimming sanctuary lamp light. Old ghosts lingered there, names he had heard from the time he could remember. Some familiar, others long before his time, names entangled in old stories, told and retold. Ghosts or no ghosts, it was his only chance.

A look back at the tabernacle, another mumbled prayer for help, he edged to the very first pew and then the next, heart beating as sweaty hands held on for some kind of support that would aid his plan. He guessed he must be five or six rows from the back door and the phantom coffins. Knees together, he clung to the solid support of each pew and forced himself to move forward to the door. He mistook how near he was and bumped into it, the sound, like thunder echoing down the aisle and back to the altar.

Jesus, help me.

At least he knew where he was. Now he moved to his left, reaching out for the banister he knew would lead him up the wooden stairs to the gallery. He knew no one could hear but he made as little noise as possible. Propelled by the ghosts around him and grasping the banister he plunged upwards. Forgetting the turn, he hit the wall, screaming fitfully but clambering forward until he stood where he guessed the rope might be.

Pawing the air and whispering hoarsely to himself that it must be there, his left hand suddenly found it. Discovering gold would have given him less satisfaction, as for a moment he recalled a saying of Joe's, "hitting gold dust."

Hauling with all his strength the first peals of the bell frightened him. He had never been so near the sound. The silence was broken and each peal gave him renewed courage and although there was no rhythm at the beginning he soon concocted a measured pattern as the rope brought him off the floor and back again, beads of sweat running down his body. Exhilaration took over and he recalled another saying of Joe's about being hung for a sheep as a lamb. It made exciting terrible sense now and he was lost in sustained defiance and heady freedom. Arms tiring, he kept going.

He didn't expect an immediate response but suddenly there were footsteps on the stairs before he knew it, lost as he was in the task at hand. An urgent angry sound came from below and he stopped, lathered in sweat. The lantern's flicker came ahead of its carrier as did a cacophony of sullen, outraged mutterings. Frozen now in reality, any sense of the momentary power he had felt evaporated. Voices, shadows jumped from every crevice, crowding in on him. He hoped it might not be the priest first but who else could it be?

He was grabbed by the arm as a look of grim satisfaction covered every feature of the priest's face who brought the lantern close, detective like, to identify who had roused the whole village.

"I had to ... I'm sorry ... I was ... you locked me in."

The priest was not about to countenance the garbled expressions of regret, contrition or explanation. Dragging him down the stairs, he displayed his prize catch to those below, now moving backwards out the door to the yard, swinging lanterns casting eerie shadows as they moved.

He saw no point in struggling as his feet barely touched the steps of the stairs before he was thrust forward into the middle of the crowd. The priest, out of breath from his exertions, blurted out to the onlookers.

"Look at this brave man, hah ... another trick of you all know who ... Only someone like The Pagan would come up with a trick like this to be carried out by someone caught in his evil clutches. I've never seen anything like it."

The bystanders nodded energetically at the priest's words, as he turned and slammed the doors shut. God was safe again from the atheist's wiles. He waited, thought about running but the crowd imprisoned him. Propelled to offer some explanation, he began again, pleading his case to the crowd as much as the priest.

"I … it was locked. 'Twas the only way out … Joe had nothing to do with it."

"I'll Joe you", the priest spluttered, incensed by the familiar reference to someone so reviled. He plunged forward and the boy, with the agility of youth, bounced backwards, surprising those behind him for a moment, who broke ranks. He might have got through but the chance was gone and the crowd regrouped.

I'm done for. That's it now.

He said the words to himself with an air of dejection and finality. The priest came towards him, and he tensed his body for what he knew would be some kind of onslaught similar to that previously on the village street when he was saved by the rector. But no rector now even though he must too have been roused by the bell ringing.

Just as the priest reached out to grab him the scraping sound of the chapel gate's rusty hinges immediately swung the crowd round to see who was now arriving. They waited, lanterns held higher for a better view. The word "motorman" was mumbled by those who caught the first glimpse of his father who strode towards the crowd with an easy determination. A few among the crowd drifted back into the darkness while the others, far from being afraid in any way, saw the arrival of his father as a novel extension to what would be played out in front of them, their eyes darting from the priest to the motorman. There was to be little satisfaction for them.

Ignoring the priest his father came forward and placed a reassuring hand on his shoulder.

"What happened to you?"

The words were gentle, not perhaps what the crowd might expect from a father to his son who again had disgraced him and his dead mother.

Before he could answer, the priest launched forth again.

"I'll tell you what happened and it's nothing to be proud of for you or him. He was put up to this vile act, this blasphemy, by you know who. We all know who."

Murmurs of assent came from the crowd. Emboldened, he went on.

"He must think the people of this parish are fools. Well, we won't stand for it any longer and if he hasn't learned by now, he soon will. God is not mocked, you know."

He felt his father's grip tighten as the priest spoke. He felt foolish now, a laughing stock but it was more for his father, dragged before the villagers for another free show. The grip relaxed, as his father cut short the priest who was about to continue.

"I'll find out what happened, Father."

"So you should, these good people deserve an explanation. But I think we all know who is responsible for this outrage."

A large black rosary beads appeared from his pocket, and he informed the crowd that a decade of the rosary would be rendered to offer some atonement for what had happened in the house of the Lord. Before he began, however, he repeated the biblical warning about those corrupting the young deserving of a mill stone about their necks and their fate then sealed.

The prayer began as he found himself being guided through the crowd by his father and on to the welcoming darkness of the roadway. Different voices, most recognisable, muttered as they passed by to the gate. Turning for home, they noticed someone moving in the other direction. It was Constable Snee, walking back toward the village as the drone of the prayers sent him, the boy and his father on their way.

Reaching the beginning of Woodlands' wall he thought of saying something by way of explanation. Neither spoke, as if there was little need for elaboration. It was as if both just wanted to be away from what was happening in the church yard and from the sting of the priest's wrath. Just ahead a sudden thud made him cling in terror to his father. As if by some magic, Joe was suddenly there, having jumped on to the road from the wall of Woodlands.

"Oh, it's yourself," said his father with a mixture of annoyance and relief. "It's a good job you're not back there. They're praying for you."

"Again?"

Joe's laugh, hearty and irreverent, lightened the mood. He too had come running, roused by the untimely ringing of the bell. However, he had made his way by the path and observed the goings on in the churchyard from across the road. He saw the father and son emerge and unknown to them he followed inside the wall until they were out of sight of the village. That's when he jumped over to join them.

Though neither father nor son had spoken since they left the churchyard, both men now stood by the wall as the boy recounted the saga from the time he entered the church until he was dragged out of it.

"Do you know something, I'd say he saw you and took the chance to lock you in. How could he have missed you if he walked down past you?"

Joe's words made sense now, and his father nodded, before adding.

"Sure with all he's done, that wouldn't be beyond him now, would it?"

*

She had been early, anticipating, hurrying the late evening forward, while again assessing her situation with whatever objectivity she could muster.

Her writing had practically ceased, and she had cited "exceptional circumstances" in the last letter of apology to her publishers, waiting in vain as they did for a draft of her book needed for Christmas and promised by her.

Edward, still conveniently absent, never seemed so irrelevant and his sudden dash back on receipt of the hoax letter was proof beyond doubt of it. She had no problem understanding his fury at being made a fool of and could readily appreciate how he must feel about the implications of what the letter said. But it was his attitude toward the spirit and letter of lawlessness in the village, "let sleeping dogs lie," that really infuriated her.

The present soon asserted itself with the thought of the illicit tryst leaving her staring into the distance to catch a glimpse of his arrival. The setting sun had the top windows of the house on fire, and coupled with the balmy breeze from the hills, added to the fever of the clandestine. Everything falling into place, she thought only to counter with, can this be really happening? Dragged up from the past, from the deep and never forgotten recesses that passion never allows die, came the thought of a similar summer evening, when she had waited for Nathan and what would prove to be one of their last meetings. What had brought it all back now, she wondered, chastened by the power of suggestion and the power of the past to absorb and spurn the present.

His loping movement, warily making his way toward her, made all her brazen optimism return. The evening's atmosphere, recollection of past passion and the man approaching her, limp still evident, had her hungry with anticipation. The limp brought unwelcome images back until she had her arms around his shoulders, taut and muscular. He stepped back, a warning to them both, his eyes scanning the landscape.

"But Joe, who would see us here?"

She pulled him back and though her question, once asked, appeared to tempt fate, it seemed to satisfy him. Safe in his embrace and keeping to the orchard wall they made their way towards the house, both conscious that while it gave them some privacy, they were not immune to being seen. Foolishly perhaps, their warm embrace reassured them, caught up as they were in the moment.

"Follow me," she said as she stepped ahead of him, and he entered the house for the second time in the same day. This time, however, it was by the back door and soon they were climbing the stairs, their pace increasing as they neared her bedroom door.

Later, she realised that more passion was experienced in her husband's bed in an hour than in all her time as a married woman. In the arms of the atheist she was locked into a depth of confidence and abandonment that pushed all other considerations aside.

He cradled her head and she laughed, recounting the afternoon's fiasco in the drawing room. Joe laughed too but confirmed her suspicions about Field, telling her that he had no doubt but the rector knew what her intentions were.

"We won't talk about the rector now. Keep religion out of it, that shouldn't be too hard for you," she answered, teasingly, with a roguish glint.

She wanted that thought away too even though it was she who had brought the subject up. Running her hands through his hair, she attempted to give it some semblance of order.

"You should see your own."

Joe countered, joking as his hand now ran through what she could only imagine was her wildly dishevelled hair.

A silent moment and then from somewhere inside her came the question, unannounced and beyond her control. "Joe, what are we going to do?"

It was a stab at an inevitable reality, to which a few hours before she would never have admitted. Now the question came from something that intruded in their moment of relaxation and untrammelled satisfaction that followed on what they both had experienced in each other's arms. Now, the intense, exhilarating freedom to be herself had also brought the question to her lips, the question she had been for so long unable to ask herself.

Its asking made them huddle closer, to escape whatever the answer and its consequences might bring. It was also an attempt to freeze the moment so that, somehow, an answer might not be necessary. But once uttered, a despairing vista opened up and they were both left hanging on to the little they had of themselves.

The staggering spectres of doom, facilely dismissed a few hours ago, now loomed large. A surge of fear, naked and uncompromising, made her repeat it.

"What in the name of God can we do?"

"If I knew the answer to that one, girl, I'd be over in London now instead of himself and he'd be here with you, his wife."

His answer, so jokingly glib, should have annoyed her but it didn't. Something in its colloquial simplicity, said everything. And no one had ever referred to her with such commanding familiarity as "girl."

Slowly and sensually, they came together again. Not for long, as the chapel bell pealed out in the night.

"There's something wrong."

"Has this ever happened before, the bell ringing at an hour like this?"

"Not that I can ever remember. You never know what's going on. I'll have to go, it must have something to do with the priest. Maybe there's a fire or something. Don't be afraid, they won't destroy anything we have."

His parting words, followed by a kiss, convinced neither of them, and were certainly said more in a wild, hopeful stab than in anticipation.

"We can only hope, Joe. I love you, go on and see what's happened."

*

Pulling the bed clothes round her, she waited for the ringing to stop. The silence descended as the pealing faded and she could hear herself breathing. She had read one time that no matter what we think, we have only one thought at a time but that could not be true. Myriad thoughts, conjecture, fear, hope, all fought for attention. She got up and went to the window. The trees impeded her view of the village; she scanned the night sky for some evidence of a fire as she was now convinced that this had to be the reason for the bell ringing. Whatever the reason, it had cut short her time with Joe after all the meticulous machinations she had gone through to get him to be with her. Maybe someone was dead, burned alive, she thought guiltily.

Would she go as far as the village if the lodge was empty? Would that be wise, she wondered, but her mind was still a jumble.

By the time she had dressed and got to the lodge about fifteen minutes had elapsed. Arriving at the door she noticed candlelight and knocked, certain someone was inside if there was a light. But no answer. She peered through the window and saw a newspaper scattered on the floor.

Stepping out onto the road and just outside the gates she paused, wondering what next to do. Then the sound of voices approaching made her go back inside the gate and hide discreetly behind one of the piers, lowering the light in the lantern. As the speakers neared, the familiarity of the voices eased her apprehension. The motorman and

Joe appeared to be arguing. His words were now distinct, and he chuckled.

"You'll have your name in the paper, one of these days."

"Joe, this no laughing matter. We'll be the talk of the place again, as if things weren't bad enough. You didn't hear what Maguire said as we were leaving. He said you had put him up to it to get the priest out of bed."

"Wouldn't it be the crime of the century if that was the case. That puts a few ideas into my head alright."

Joe laughed uproariously and she stiffened at how jokingly he was treating something that had taken him from their bed such a short time ago.

"Maguire wasn't the only one who had a go at you, I might add. They were all convinced you are the prime suspect and with no light in the cottage they were more certain."

They were now nearing the gate and she moved out from behind the pier. The lantern light stopped the talking. Only then did she realise that the boy was with them. He was first in the gate, and she saw that his face was red and tear stained. She addressed him rather than his father.

"Why, what happened, is everyone alright? I thought there might have been a fire."

The motorman stepped forward but before he could speak, Joe jovially answered.

"We have a new bellringer for the chapel. He decided to get a bit of practice."

Joe's making light of things again got no response from her.

"It's a long story. He found himself locked into the chapel by Kerley, accidently I'm fairly certain, though this man would not agree. When he couldn't get out and it got dark, he thought he would spend the night in the confession box. You know what that is? Anyway, as it got darker, he got more frightened and decided that the best way of getting out was to ring the bell knowing it would bring someone. You know who came of course and half the village was there as well in tow. I was reading the paper and got to the chapel as quick as I could and found this fellow getting another taste of the priest's medicine. Now I think he should be in bed."

"Sadist," muttered Joe, his joviality nowhere evident now. The motorman and the boy moved toward the gate lodge door. She put her hand on the boy's shoulder and brought the lantern close to his face, looking into his large, helpless eyes.

"Do you know what," she said, glancing at the two men as if addressing them as well, "I think you have done one of the most sensible things I've heard of since coming here. I think I'd have done the very same if I'd been locked in a church too."

He smiled up at her as she added, mischievously, "especially if it were a Catholic church with all those pictures and statues I've heard about. Don't tell anyone I said that though."

Her light-hearted remarks brought a certain ease and the motorman seemed less agitated than when he had been trying to convince Joe of the animosity felt by the priest and people in the chapel yard, all of it directed at him.

"Well, we won't keep you. It's getting late. I'm off to Cork bright and early in the morning."

"You're right," replied Victoria, "I'll have the list ready first thing. You could take this brave young man as helper if he's awake that early. Well goodnight then and goodnight to you, Mr Golden."

She could not resist singling him out.

"Goodnight," answered Joe, affecting a casual tone as he spoke from the shadows.

She left the two men and the boy watching the sway of the lantern as she walked up the avenue until she reached the turn.

Without a word being spoken, as if the lantern light now gone was a signal, the boy opened the door and the two men followed him inside.

He lit a second candle as Joe settled at the fireplace and his father got two bottles out from under the table. Then he got ready for bed. He would leave them, knowing that their voices would quickly lull him to sleep as so often happened. Yet it was a night, after all that had happened, that begged a few final words before bedtime.

"You'll be the talk of the place, you might even get into the Examiner, who knows?"

Joe grinned as he raised the bottle to his mouth. His father sat back as if wishing to ignore what had just been said.

"Wait till I go back to school, I'll know all about it then, won't I?"

The old familiar grip of fear caught in his stomach again. Going back to school was always going to be an ordeal but now the bully boys would have a new, exotic reason for targeting him. This would be based on whatever embellishments were added to the night's events when the parents who had assembled in the chapel yard got home and spun the story of his embarrassment. He waited for either Joe or his father to say something that showed they had some small understanding of what he had said.

He had never told Joe about all that went on at school beyond a casual remark now and then, though he had often told him that he hated the "sight and light of school." Yet he had told one grownup, that day on the side of the road when she had found him in tears, as she caught up with him. Maybe someday he would tell Joe all about it.

"Well, whatever about me, you'll go down in history. People will tell the story for years to come and you might even become a hero as time goes by, someone who had the guts to do something that many others, even grownups, wouldn't. Of course, they'll all say I put you up to it. Sure, let them … it won't be the first lie told around here about me, will it?"

He nodded in agreement and looked toward his father who had the fire going at this stage and a kettle on the crane.

"It's time you were off to bed, I'll bring you down a drop of tea when it's ready. We'll see about you coming to Cork in the morning but if you're asleep when I'm going, I'll let you be."

His father's words, coming from a man now at ease before his own fireplace with a bottle in his hand, made him feel better and he took one of the candles and made his way to the bedroom door.

He was nearly asleep by the time his father came with the tea and he gulped it down. He handed the cup back and his father leaned over and tucked in the blanket around his shoulder. That was unnecessary because the night was hot. A whisper in his ear about the trip to Cork being a certainty and the cup of tea lifted the still gloom. One simple treat followed by the promise of a trip to Cork had him sink into the bed before his father had even closed the bedroom door.

But he couldn't sleep. He remembered the last night Joe had been drinking with his father; missing out on the conversation and Joe's raised voice in disbelief, at whatever he had been told, and him waking with a start in the corner.

Taking all the time he needed and easing himself out of the bed, he crept along the floor to the door. Another advantage he saw was that his father had not fully closed it. He saw his father and Joe settled at the fire, two more bottles opened.

"I didn't tell you what his lordship asked me that last day I drove him to the train. He asked me did I know who attacked you that night on the way from town."

"That's not so strange, I suppose, is it?"

"No, but then he asked me about the young lad and the priest and if I thought the priest might be right in you having anything to do, with as he put it, 'an innocent child.' You know what I mean."

"Oh, indeed I do. And do you know what I would have said to him if he asked me the same question? I'd have said what I said to Kerley that day on the street, that he's a lot safer with me than him."

Joe laughed and the boy could not understand why.

"Why do you think he asked me though?"

"Why do you think now?"

"Because he may be afraid that someday the truth about you and him will come out, I suppose. We went over all that the night of the last supper you were here, and we weren't sober at the end of that conversation, were we? But I've never seen you as shook by anything. You still were able to say he had more to lose than you. But think of him, his position, his house, what many would see as his good name and how he is looked up to in London. And then there's herself."

His father's tone changed now. Joe, as if to evade some problem beyond solving, quickly replied.

"Look, you're right, sure enough. Don't you know, now that I think of it I still find it hard to believe, but didn't it make perfect sense for my mother to leave when it all happened? She'd probably have ended up in one of those places in Cork with other girls like her. She wouldn't have got much comfort here although the priest at the time, what was his name again, oh yea, Gunnery, he wasn't the worst, but he'd have had to toe the line as well. To think she did that and then came back with me long before I can remember."

"Joe, I saw your mother here. She was too proud a woman to stay away but didn't she pay a price? By Christ, she did. She stood up to the whole lot of them by hardly saying a word but just standing her ground. And you were the apple of her eye, oh indeed you were. I've little time for those, priest and people, who made her life so miserable, but I'm not as brave a man as you. But you too have paid a price, you haven't got off scot-free, have you?"

"No, I haven't, but they can all go to hell, the whole bloody lot. But, come here to me, go back to Sheldon. What else did he say?"

"Ah, he was in very poor form. And I think it had something to do with herself. They were very civil when saying goodbye. It was only when we drove out the gate here that he started. I think he's afraid that the League will have a go at them if they get any excuse. I suppose, when he was on his own he could put up with something happening, but now with his wife in the house it's a different kind of cross to carry. And then, as he was getting out of the motor, you'd never guess what he said? Watch yourself too."

"Why?"

"Ah, he mentioned the motor and that it would be an easy target if they wanted to give him and me a fright. He could be right, you know. But really, it's herself that's his worry, I think."

"Do you think so?"

"Well, maybe I shouldn't say this, but I will. As I was about to leave him in the waiting room, he said he'd a favour to ask of me. I didn't know what he was going to say, you know he's always so serious, but he wasn't himself at all."

"Go on, tell me what he wanted."

"He said things were bad with what happened to you and the fact that the wife had helped by getting you in the motor that night. And he said he feared for the youngster. He just asked me to keep an eye out for 'any suspicious activity around Woodlands.' He saw I wasn't sure what he was getting at, and then do you know what he said. 'Ah, you know what I'm getting at.' And Joe, he left me in no doubt what he meant. He might have said more only for the train arriving. But he didn't have to … I knew what he meant."

"What are you saying?"

There was a pause and movement. He heard two more bottles being taken from under the table and he shifted slightly behind the door to make himself more comfortable.

"Well, he was talking about you."

"Well, that's the best yet, don't you think?" Joe replied taking the proffered bottle and continuing.

"Why do you think he was back home out of the blue? He got a letter in London from someone claiming to be Field. You can imagine what it said but we all know with her in the picture now it's a different story. And so it should be. Wasn't I up at the house today with Field and she said I had been mentioned in connection with herself and the young lad. Sheldon should hardly believe that sort of thing, with the way things are. Sure anyone could write that sort of rubbish."

"Joe, I'm not blind, you know."

The silence that followed only made his father's words more intriguing. What did he mean by saying he wasn't blind? Blind about what?

"What do you mean by that, man?"

"Joe, I know where you were tonight. Don't ask me how and it's not as if I'm spying on you. And if I know where you were and I'm minding my own business there's plenty others who won't be. Now, don't get me wrong, I'm not going to run to Sheldon telling what I know. It's simple, Joe, you're getting into something that will bring us all bad luck in the heel of the hunt. That's all I'll say about it. Christ above, have you any idea what would happen if, maybe I should say when, they find out where you're spending some of your nights? No light in the cottage will get chins wagging, I'm certain of it. And it'll be another excuse to add to all the others and they'll come up with some other scheme to ensure you and the Sheldons get their comeuppance. Can you imagine Kerley up on the altar with the bit between his teeth? Anyway, I'll say no more. Maybe I've said too much but, for the sake of all of us I had to say something."

He had never heard his father speak like this before. There was fear and warning in his voice, fear for all of them. Perplexed and disturbed by what he had heard, he felt sorry for Joe, but only for a second; he couldn't forget that a few hours before he had felt so differently. He still did. 'Seeing herself,' as his father put it resurrected the jealousy that plagued him because of Joe's privilege, so easily gained even if it all was dangerous, as his father said. A lull followed. Maybe Joe would say he wouldn't go near Woodlands anymore and that would satisfy his father. The answer, when it came, was definite and clear.

"Look, I know you had to say something but it's no one's business but hers and mine. And whatever about me I'll kill any bastard who harms a hair of her head. Now that's all I'll say about it and we'll leave it at that, just like I said now, our business and no one else's. These things happen."

Silence again. The kind that said both men had said their piece and that, for the time being anyway, was the end of it. His aching body had stiffened from sitting in the one position. "One for the road," his father said as two bottles clinked. About to steal back to bed, he almost missed what his father said next.

"Here, throw that back. Of course I can't say I blame you, you boyo you. She's a smashing woman alright, any man's fancy, sure, the whole place is agreed on that."

"Well at least that's something to drink to, Shandrum is agreed on something."

Both men laughed. Of all the things that he had heard said, it was his father's reference to her as 'a smashing woman,' uttered so casually, that struck something deep inside him and which he couldn't understand. He could understand Joe being referred to as a 'boyo' but his father's recognition of how beautiful she was and the whole village being of the same mind was like what it must feel like to be stabbed. What he thought was his and his alone, was not the case. He knew now that others might well feel the same way.

The sound of the empty bottles joining the others on the floor brought the night's events to an end. He made his way to the bed as the front door opened and Joe prepared to go. His ordeal in the chapel all now seemed like an age ago. All he had heard from the kitchen was now uppermost in his mind, leaving him confused as he slipped into an uneasy sleep. The candle still burned.

*

"What's wrong, what's wrong? You're alright, I'm here." Shaking convulsively, he felt someone's arms around him.

The candle still flickered on the windowsill.

"Put it out, put it out. Put out the fire."

"It's only the candle, it's not a fire."

With a soothing, firm embrace his father brought him from the bedroom, out through the front door and stood him on the flagstone doorstep. Standing on the cold stone he was suddenly fully awake and aware of where he was. The sky was shot through with stars. but it was a different kind of light that caught his attention. Through the trees, from an upstairs window in Woodlands a light still shone, and he wondered if his father had seen it too. He began to shiver before being guided back inside.

"It was only a nightmare; you'll be fine now."

He was walked back through the kitchen, where the empty bottles stood like soldiers. He recalled what had made him wake in terror. The school was in flames, and he was perched on the school chimney, holding on to the rope of the chapel bell which stretched endlessly up to the sky from where he stood. Down below he could recognise the faces that peered up at him, faces grinning, sneering, shouting at him to jump. Joe was there, as was Field and the priest, all united for once to try to save him. He couldn't jump because there on the edge of the screaming crowd she sat in the driver seat of the motor. She seemed to be attempting to drive through the crowd, but they seemed unaware of her. If she got through, he could jump from the chimney into the seat beside her. He kept pointing at where the car was as the flames leapt higher all around him and it was at this point that he woke up and saw the candle.

*

His father moving about the kitchen woke him. The trip to Cork beckoned and he was only too happy to be away from the village. A day in the city was always an exciting luxury and he was the envy of every child that heard the motor speed away on its journey.

On those city trips his father stuck to a rigid routine, methodically collecting what had been ordered for Woodlands first. This meant going to different shops where his father was instantly recognised, and bits and pieces of news were shared with the weather inevitably being mentioned. His father mentioned Nurse Prout's assertion that the men in Ballyhooly were shaving with lemonade and again the retort often was that they'd soon be on to "the hard stuff" when the lemonade ran out.

A more leisurely tour of the shops was then made as the city's sounds and smells invaded his rural senses. The unattainable and unaffordable were all around them and they had to settle for what could be managed. Magazines and papers for Woodlands, which would eventually find their way to the lodge and Joe's, were selected. His father pressed a few coins into his hand, and he eyed the large array of comics lined up in one of the newspaper shops. Then his favourite selection, with "Illustrated Chips" first because it had one of his favourite characters, Homeless Hector, in it. Hairbreadth Harry was next and then Happy Hooligan. His father always got Ireland's Own to be read first by himself and then passed on to Joe.

With everything carefully checked off on his father's list the ultimate treat awaited. This always brought to his mind the story of the Wedding Feast at Cana and the good wine being kept until last. The welcome musty smell of a public house brought respite from the heat and a chance to rest his tired feet. A large bottle of lemonade invitingly fizzed before him and he took as long as ever in selecting a bun from the countertop of the little shop that was part of the public house. Just like Maguire's. His father had a bottle of stout and they listened to the chatter of the men at the bar with their strange city accents.

The weather was still the main topic of conversation with predictions as to when a desperately needed break would come or not. The priest's prayers for rain to help the harvest and the farmers were not yet answered in Shandrum his father told one of the men. He replied that if it was down to prayers "we'd all be drowned by now."

Near to where he sat, the boy could not help overhearing two men in animated and deep conversation about another subject. One was saying that Cork could win the All Ireland football final now that they had easily beaten Tipperary and Kerry had been beaten by Waterford. His companion was less certain about Cork's chances, saying that it was over fifteen years since they last won, and that beating Waterford should not be taken for granted.

The conversations fascinated him and sitting with his father he savoured every drop of lemonade until it was time to go. Not a word was spoken on the way home, and he was alone with his thoughts. His outing was over, and it was back to the routines of home in the waning days of the summer holidays. As for the routines, things were now taking on a different complexion and the predictability of the evening's snare setting, and the night's collection of the catch somehow seemed uncertain.

Back at the lodge he jumped out with his bundle of comics and a few items his father had got for themselves and Joe. The motor continued up the avenue and leaving all but the comics on the kitchen table he set out along the path for cottage, not knowing what might lie ahead.

The cottage was empty. And again, something told him that before he reached the back door. The snares were gone, but he now saw that as Joe's excuse to meet her even if he didn't want to admit it to himself. The comics always took him away into another world of fun and adventure, but he struggled to reach such a welcome escape now. Joe not being there and the implications of that, was a stark reminder that nothing was the same anymore; the familiar, the normal that had made things so simple were now gone.

She had changed everything and now, with Joe, they had ensured that he was pushed out on the edges, dangling uncertainly and so unsure of what lay ahead. Just a nuisance. That day in the library. Her glance. Tingling desire. All that Joe's now.

Putting one comic aside he picked up Happy Hooligan and began to read. The next thing he knew was being woken by the sound of another Saturday evening ritual, that of the villagers passing by on the way to confession. He must have fallen asleep, worn out by all that had gone on the night before, his nightmarish dreams and the trip to Cork. Their voices outside told him the time. The first thing that came to his mind was that Joe would definitely be home well before confession time if he simply had been setting the snares.

As if an answer he heard the thud of Joe's boots as he jumped over the back wall into the yard. The door opened.

"Well, are they all alive in Cork?"

The casual question seemed forced, and the usual ease was absent as Joe hurriedly set about lighting the fire and issuing another familiar cliché.

"The troops must be fed."

He turned back from the fireplace before continuing.

"The snares are down but I won't be able to go tonight."

Their eyes met and what he said next made him interested and suspicious.

"I thought that maybe you'd do the round yourself since you've always said you could do it on your own. Now here's your chance if you want to take it."

He was trapped. He had often boasted to Joe that he would be well able to do the rabbit round on his own, a chance he would normally relish were he not aware of the reason. He could hardly say no now, even if it meant giving Joe the freedom to make his own plans, plans that both knew were already in place.

*

A poor start in the moonlight. A few empty snares at the beginning of the round was, according to Joe, never a good sign. Dejected, he climbed over a fence into the next field. This route would take him towards the river with the castle away to his right, Woodlands to his left and the dim lights of the village behind him.

His luck changed and by the time he was halfway round he had five rabbits hanging from the stick on his shoulder. Their weight slowed his progress as he swung back towards home where he would leave what he had caught. Joe often did this if they had a good catch halfway through.

His father, sitting by candlelight reading a newspaper, barely recognised his good fortune as he left the rabbits with the used snares just inside the door. Waiting just long enough to say that he was on his own tonight, he saw his father's expression change as he turned back to the paper. The clock said eleven. In a little over half an hour he should have the round finished and that would be that for the night.

The second round was not a success, yielding just one rabbit when he thought his good luck might continue. He collected the last empty snare and headed back uphill towards the orchard wall of Woodlands which he would skirt on two sides before getting home. He passed by the spot where Joe and himself had seen her sleeping by the wall in the shelter of the parasol in one of the summer's hottest days. All so long ago now.

Rounding the wall and moving away towards home he turned back and saw Woodlands outlined against the sky. He had quenched the lantern light as he had so often done with Joe. So familiar were they with where each pathway around the fields of Woodlands and beyond led, there was no need for light. Light shone however from one of the upstairs windows, her bedroom window. A lump caught in his throat as his imagination carried him away in a jealous rage. He watched, unable to drag himself away from where he stood. Were a stranger to observe him, he seemed like a boy in an old rustic painting, caught in time with the soft glow from the window of the great house on one side, the river on the other and the shadow of the village away in the distance, steeple and spire barely visible in the moonlit sky.

Convulsed by where his imagination had taken him, he wanted to move but couldn't. But now something else caught his attention. He crouched, dismissing the thoughts that had so consumed him. Three figures slinking in unison came from the side of the house, across the grass, making for the riverbank. If they kept coming in the same direction, they would pass within a few yards of where he was. Dragging snares, rabbit and lantern, he crawled to the relative safety of the nearest oak, trying to blend into its enormity, fearful that he might be seen in the moonlight. He heard Maguire's unmistakable voice, first.

"Jesus, lads we have them all where we want them now. Wait until Fr Kerley hears this. The whole bloody lot are finished now and good riddance. Who does The Pagan think he is, anyway? In bed with the gentry if you don't mind. Can you beat that?"

Another voice.

"Who does your one think she is, for that matter. If only Sheldon knew what she's up to and by God, he will. The shame of it will drive the whole lot of them out and their fine motor with them."

It was the master. Adding to the fear of discovery, his sneering voice only brought the prospect of school back to the boy's mind and all it meant.

"Do you think we should have taken down the ladder? It might be better if we did."

"No, no. We're not going back now and anyway it will soften their cough when they find it. It'll show we're not the fools they think we are. Doesn't he beat all. And you know, I always thought he wasn't up to it and he so interested in the youngster. Well, he better make the best of it."

McSweeney then threw in his few words, bringing a raucous laugh from all three.

"Aha, wouldn't any man be up to it with a woman like that? Didn't ye see the cut of her in the bed and that was only half of her we saw."

Maguire had the final word before they moved on. It was directed at the master.

"Not a word to anyone until Fr Kerley knows. And John, you were right when you said there was no smoke without fire. Isn't the education a great thing after all?"

There was a satisfied chuckle from all three and they made their way home by the line of trees that reached the wall.

Relief at not being noticed was the first thing he felt, but only for a moment. What they had said beat at his brain. He remembered that McSweeney was the one who told Joe the night he was attacked that he should "get a woman" for himself. He still did not understand what that meant, but what was certain now, was that Joe had indeed got a woman, his woman, for himself. The master being one of the three did not surprise him. Hating him as he did, made it easy to align him with anything even remotely unsavoury.

Moving out from behind the tree he looked toward the house and the lighted window. What had Maguire,

McSweeney and the master been up to and what had they seen that had been so worth their while? Clearly from the conversation he had overheard they had stumbled on something that would as the master, full of confidence, said "drive the whole lot of them out and their fine motor with them." Were he and his father included?

With frightening eagerness, he left the rabbit and the snares at the tree and made his way towards the house. He suddenly saw what they had been talking about. A ladder reached the windowsill. Without an instant's hesitation he began to climb, taking each step with patience and care, uncharacteristic of youth.

Nearing the sill he paused and looked back at the expanse behind him, soundless in the moonlight. Then, almost afraid of what might happen next, he peered through the opening in the curtains that had been carelessly drawn. Her head was what he saw first as it rested against Joe's shoulder, her hair wild as he had never seen it. He flinched. She's looking at me. But no, she was asleep. As he moved his head slightly, he saw that Joe, however, was wide awake and again he thought he was looking straight at him.

Captivated, he gazed, shivering with a feeling that made him grasp the ladder with a grip he thought himself incapable of, a grip that might never be broken. She moved and threw back the sheet, edging yet closer to Joe. The sight of their nakedness seeped and churned inside him. He moved his head a fraction so that only she was visible. Transfixed, he now savoured what at other times he had only envisaged in his blurred, confused imagination.

He thought of the day in the library; now here was the languorous provocativeness of her body.

She stirred again and Joe's powerful arms tightened around her. As if a signal, she woke, smiled lazily at Joe and opened her mouth for his kiss, before drowsily falling back to sleep again.

Joe looked towards where the light split the curtains. He's looking straight at me. But no, his eyes were looking through him, not at him, as if brooding on something that had no answer, even in the arms of the woman he now held.

But no answers for me either. Tired trudging the streets of Cork. The rabbit round. Move a step higher. Elbows now on the windowsill. Head in his hands. Staring. The three. They saw this too.

How long he stayed there he did not know but he never wanted to leave. He hated Joe for what he had, just a few feet away from where he watched. And he hated her for what was not and could not ever be his except in feverish dreams. He found himself sobbing, silently, not knowing why. The echo of the men's laughter came back to him and a savage reality shook his tired, cold limbs. He must go home. With a final glance at those he loved and hated, he stepped down the ladder, less cautious now, as if nothing really mattered.

Foolishly, he decided he would manage to get the ladder back to the shed from where it had been taken so that his secret would be preserved. The fact that the secret, deliberately unearthed by the three intruders, would then also be preserved had not yet occurred to him, so fraught was he with conflicting emotions.

As his grip on the ladder loosened, he descended, hurriedly, step by step waiting for what he thought was the last rung and then the solid ground. It wasn't. He had, in his hurry, miscalculated, stepping from what he later realised was probably the third or second rung. He felt himself falling backwards, pulling the ladder with him, shouting in surprise, splitting the silence of the night. His shout turned to a scream, as one of the rungs of the ladder hit him on the head, while the frame cut into his shoulders and pinned him grotesquely to the ground.

*

She was standing on the floor before she realised where she was. The boy's screams and Joe's swearing woke her.

"Stay here, there's something up. Just our luck."

Short, garbled sentences, uttered as he struggled into his clothes, brought her quickly to the dread reality of being caught. Paralysed, she obeyed his command as he bolted for the door, trundling down the stairs. Hurriedly drawing a sheet around her she went to the window. With some difficulty she opened it and peered into the moonlit night. Late August's chill and Joe's voice, at once disbelieving and exasperated, greeted her.

"Christ Almighty, what are you doing there.? Why aren't you at home? What's going on? What's that ladder doing here?"

His voice quickly changed however when he realised the agony being experienced by the child, trying to extricate himself from the rungs of the ladder and not succeeding. Despite the pain, something underneath him dug into his thigh. He brought his hand to remove whatever was there and grasped the object that was causing him further pain. It was a pen, which he pushed towards Joe.

"Wait, wait, I'll get you out. Just don't move, do what I tell you."

She leaned further out on the windowsill.

"What's happened? Who is it?"

"Quick, come down and see for yourself. He's hurt I think, bring a blanket."

Dressing quickly, she arrived to see Joe cradling the injured, whimpering body. She looked at the scene around them and wanted to ask all the same questions as Joe. He was wrapping the boy, shivering and embarrassed, in the blanket and moving past her towards the front door.

Once inside, he waited at the drawing room door for her to open it. Hardly glancing at the door, she told Joe to bring him upstairs. Joe hesitated, but she was bounding up the stairs before him, conscious of the state she had left the room in and not wanting the child to notice anything untoward. If she had only known.

The incongruity of what was happening was not lost on any of them but for very different reasons. Vaguely aware of where he was being taken, pain careered through his body as Joe took each step. He felt a terrible desire to tell Joe everything by way of explanation but how could he account for the ladder falling on himself and having to admit to what he too had seen.

She scurried back after failing to close the window as they entered the room. The hastily arranged bedclothes were drawn back and, at her direction, Joe eased him into the bed. A strange, transfixing smell met his nostrils and for a moment his pain was gone, revelling in the sensuous intimacy that the smell suggested.

"Are you alright, why are you so still?" she asked.

Looking into her eyes, the words were uttered before he knew it.

"It's just the smell."

He couldn't help saying it. As if he had committed a mortal sin, he quickly turned away to avoid their eyes. Had he not turned away, he would have seen their eyes meet as what he had so innocently and with such childlike openness, said, sank home.

"We'll have to see your injuries so here, try to sit up."

She put her arm under his shoulder and slowly lifted. Joe removed his sweaty, soiled shirt to reveal hunched shoulders and arms, scraped and bruised. He sat defenceless on the bed, waiting for whatever attention he might get, knowing that at some stage the questions would come. She drew her breath in at what she saw and said she was going to get some kind of dressing before he got notice of what was coming.

"You'll need a doctor, I think, but that will do in the morning. I'll be back in a minute and then we'll hear what's been going on."

He heard her footsteps on the stairs and alone with Joe, he waited.

"C'mon, out with it. What were you doing with the ladder? You were supposed to be on the rabbit round. Out with it now, you were caught red-handed."

As he began to tell what had happened, he realised, that even if he had succeeded in getting the ladder to the shed, he could not let it go unknown to Joe what the Master, Maguire and McSweeney had been up to and that they knew as much as he did. He would simply tell them that he saw the men leaving and would not say all of what they said, because he wouldn't know how.

He had barely begun when her footsteps were heard again. Joe signalled to him to wait, and she came into the room armed with a roll of bandages, a basin of water and a small, coloured bottle of Lister's antiseptic. Joe signalled again and between sobs, embarrassing hesitations and eyes turned away, the story of the night's events unfolded.

Each snippet of revelation had the same effect on Joe and Victoria as the full extent of their passion and their predicament was stumbled over by the now shivering boy. His story came more slowly as he got to the part where he told them he too had climbed the ladder.

"Stop, please, that's enough."

She had heard enough but Joe persisted.

"And what happened with the ladder, sure you'd never be able to carry that to the shed."

"I wanted to take it away so that you wouldn't know anyone had seen anything."

He turned towards them, searching for some understanding of what had been his foolish, well intentioned plan.

Close to tears, she heard his childish concern for their right to go on, for a time at least, with the illusion that what they had together was known just to themselves; foolish, silly optimism, she thought to herself.

"But you would have had to tell us sometime, and sooner rather than later, after all we would all have been in danger if we had not been told," she replied, a hint of annoyance in her voice now.

"I know that, I know now … it's just I was all mixed up, didn't know what to think. You were just asleep. Joe awake…"

"Alright, alright…"

The words had given her some respite and she was suddenly reaching out to him in comfort. An absolution of some sort. She realised that his aching body would be caused more pain and pulled back.

The caress of the treatment, even the stinging of the antiseptic, fought and won the fight to turn the pain into a searching pleasure and made all that had gone before worthwhile. Finally, anointed and bandaged, he lay back on the bed to again absorb the lingering smell of man and woman, Joe's familiar smell mingling with hers. It was hers he relished.

Arms folded, Joe stood, looking out into the moonlight. She tidied up. Afraid to move with the pain, he felt himself drifting into sleep. He watched, half asleep, as she moved to the window. With nothing to hide now she took Joe's hand and the last thing he remembered before his aching body finally slept was a blurred picture. Two profiles, two ghosts, side by side, hand in hand, looking way beyond the walls of Woodlands, searching for some kind of answer to all that had gone before and what lay ahead.

The only answer they got was the forlorn bark of a dog somewhere in the distance.

Cremin's, he thought.

*

Leaving him to sleep, they went downstairs. She took his hand and led him to the drawing room, where their first embrace had taken place.

"Let's have a drink and see what must be done ... rather what can be done, I suppose is the best way to put it."

"I'll move the ladder first, so it won't be seen in the morning. Be back in a minute."

She went to the cabinet and got out a bottle of whiskey and a rounded bottle of amontillado. Setting two glasses on the table she poured the whiskey and then the sherry. She was not ungenerous in her portions, truly a sign that this night - it was after twelve - had thrown up its share of ecstasy, agony, confusion and most of all, fear.

Joe came back in and was about to speak when she motioned him to sit and pushed the glass towards him. He needed little encouragement. It could have been a celebration, a fitting end to a night of passion and a future maybe, however impossible. But the mood was sombre. Funereal, she thought.

He drank, slowly and deliberately. Then he put his hand in his pocket.

"See what he found when he fell. At least it's proof we know one of them, not to say I'm in the least bit surprised."

He slid a pen across towards her. Fascinated and repulsed, she took it. It was expensive. She saw the engraving and looked back at Joe. PJS 1903.

"Whose is it?" she blurted, putting it away from her as if it were a disease.

"The noble schoolmaster, Patrick Joseph Slyne. He wears that pen like a badge of honour."

She waited for him to go on. When he did, she could not understand how this man could commandeer any shred of optimism after the night's events, knowledge of the intruders or not.

"At least we have time on our side, even if it's not much. They'll let the hare sit for a while."

There was conviction in his voice, not some vague false hope that things might work out. He knew well of whom he spoke and their methods, new and shocking to her, were understood to the bone.

"But Joe, everything is running against us now. The boy, his father, the schoolmaster and the others. That boy is in serious pain. He can't go back to school, and I fear after what he's seen tonight will only create more problems for him. You understand don't you?"

He finished the whiskey. With ease and precision, he placed the glass on the table.

"He could have seen worse, maybe."

"He's only a child, Joe … a child," she argued, incredulously.

"All he saw was us asleep in bed together. Anything wrong with that? In the heel of the hunt that may the least of his worries. It's what they'll make of it."

Aggressively, he pointed to the village.

"How are you going to explain his injuries? It will land him in deeper trouble."

She realised she was searching with questions that were followed by more. A complicated, twisted dilemma. The composure of the man sitting before her was one of those questions.

He picked up the bottle and poured himself another drink, He drank, pushed the half empty glass aside and leaned forward towards her. The assured, composed face now lit up with more than mischief. His eyes were on fire, and she waited on the chair's edge.

He held up the pen.

"Maybe this is mightier than the sword, after all. We could turn the tables on them."

The words, tantalising, begging certainty of some sort, rolled off his tongue. He took back the glass and tipped it back.

"But by Christ, if it's a fight they want, they'll get it," he said, hammering out each word with a hate filled assurance.

"But Joe, we are trapped, what can we do? And what do you mean 'turn the tables on them?"

The apprehension she had felt before, the hope that they could somehow defy the curse that dogged all love affairs, that of being discovered, was now turning to fear. But for the man sitting opposite her, what had happened tonight, was not an end but a beginning. Something drove him, something that had enabled him to be different through his years in the village, even if the consequences of that were isolation, intimidation and physical attack. Maybe it had come from his mother's angry pride before him, defying the odds and ploughing her own lonely furrow.

The cunningly conceived plans to make his life unliveable, rather than making him retreat, simply bolstered him and the night's events had instilled a relish to play a game, more effective in the long run, to the one those who hated him played. But what was it?

When he had outlined his plan, he reached for the glass.

Pausing before he drank, he leaned across to where she sat and kissed her, long and full. Then, raising the glass he laughed and said, "here's to law and order," before gulping down the drink.

The clock said one as he left, leaving her no less afraid and uncertain about what he had outlined to her and of which she would be an integral part.

*

Before long, he was dragged from sleep, his aching limbs defying each attempt to move. Without opening his eyes, he knew there was someone else in the room.

"Don't move, here, let me help."

His face turned to where she stood, and it seemed she had not left the room all night. Maybe she hadn't. She helped him sit up against the bank of pillows and he was surprised by her dexterity. Happily, he was powerless to protest or resist.

Feeling he should say something, he searched for words, but she told him not to say anything, yet. She would be back with something for him to eat and then they would talk. About what he didn't know.

The extent of his injuries became more apparent, and he was riddled with aches from head to toe, the ladder having landed with maximum force pinning him to the ground. He wondered what his father would say.

The smell of toast arrived before she did. Cat-like, he watched, fascinated, as she poured and sugared the tea, made especially for him. Placing the tray on the bed near him, she broke the slices of toast into small pieces. Aware of the difficulty he had in moving his hands, she motioned him to be still and brought the first mouthful of toast to his lips. Obediently, he took it, as he did the mouthful of tea from the cup that she raised, carefully, to his mouth. His initial awkwardness and embarrassment at his inability to feed himself gave way to a different feeling, akin to that of the previous night when she had soothed his wounds, and every touch, instead of deadening the pain, resurrected a more pleasing sensation that more than made up for it. The same, delectable agitation enmeshed him in a swirl of pleasure and pain.

With each piece of toast her fingertips brushed against his lips and soon the food became irrelevant as he waited for her touch. Anticipating each movement, he leaned forward. It was then his eyes, up to now watching her take the toast from the plate, were drawn, imperceptibly, to hers. Her hand stopped in mid-air, the piece of toast suspended. In an instant they were back again that day in the library, telling each other wordlessly what they both knew in different ways. The result was the same. She stopped as if struck and moved back, spilling the tea she held in her other hand in the process. The mundane practicality of dealing with this mishap broke the spell but not the reality of its happening.

Trying to lean forward and somehow help, the pain thwarted his movement and he whimpered. She rose, leaning toward him and bringing her arm round his shoulder to settle him back in the bed while her other hand cradled his head. Settled against the pillows he expected her to move away. She didn't. He felt her breath and she started to say something, only to stop before the words came. Then she was weeping, crying uncontrollably, which left him helplessly upset and totally at a loss.

"What's wrong...why are you...?"

"It's nothing, forgive me," she sobbed, trying to regain her composure, "I'm tired and worried and it's just everything is becoming so difficult. I don't think you understand but someday you will."

"Is it about ... Joe and all that?"

"Joe and all that. Indeed, Joe and all that about sums it up," she said with solemn deliberation and then, drying her eyes, she sat back and looked at him.

"Yes, Joe and all that means you have to listen to me very carefully. Your father knows of course you're here. Mr Golden ... erm, Joe, has told him. We will get you home this morning, and we'll see about the doctor. If needed, I will tell him you were trying to help with a ladder, and it fell over on you, the same story I'll tell those here in the house. The less anyone else knows, the better. By the way, you are a very lucky boy. You could have been killed."

She picked up the tray and what was left of the breakfast and made as if to go. At the door she turned and pleading for some understanding, spoke to him slowly, choosing her words.

"About last night ... and what you saw."

He blushed furiously and wanted to be anywhere but here now as the events of the night before were back. Waiting uneasily, he fidgeted.

"You should not have seen what you saw but because you did you should not think it all nasty and wrong. there will be plenty of others to think that. It happened because Joe and I are ... very lonely, very lonely and I am very afraid. He is brave and is the only one I have here now."

A pang of jealousy ripped through him throwing him into turmoil, pushing at him to say something, something that would let her know that she had him and that while Joe meant the world to him, he hated him for what he seemed to have got so easily. Her.

"Your father is on the way. Remember, you will have to trust us and do what we say."

He would always remember that morning as the toast and tea day.

*

Waiting for the boy's father, she again went over the detail of Joe's plan, alternating between false hope, utter despair and question upon question.

The motorman striding purposefully up the avenue brought her back to the present. Had Joe placated him? that would be an unfair expectation to place on either of them. She had the door open before he had time to knock.

"I know you are worried, we all are, but there is nothing wrong that can't be put right with rest and Dr Lehane's advice. Come on up and see him."

In taking the initiative, she thought it would fend off some of the many questions that showed on the face of the faithful servant of Woodlands. One of the first things Edward said to her about him was that he could be totally trusted.

"Mrs Sheldon, I just can't believe this. After the ruckus in the chapel and now he is going to miss school, though that won't worry him. Questions will be asked no matter how we try to cover this up. If Prout, the nurse, gets even a jot of information she'll have her own story on what happened, and it will have legs by then."

She struggled.

"Yes, there are so many aspects to it all. Joe ... Mr Gol ...,"

Joe explained how he was injured. He really was trying to be helpful, never realising that in trying to help us by taking the ladder away he was also helping those who were here earlier. Yet I think he did know that at some stage he would have to tell us about the men since he witnessed them leaving.

"That was not all he witnessed," he replied, his tone more of fatherly concern than reproach.

She blushed. With contrition and embarrassment in her voice, and assuming that Joe had told him of all that had happened, she saw no point in some long-winded justification of an answer.

"For that, Mr Go ... Joe ... and myself take full responsibility."

He had every right to be aggrieved but if he was, he didn't show it, simply looking away for a moment and then motioned towards the stairs.

Joe had warned her that it was important to take early advantage of the little they had in their favour if the advantage the night intruders thought they had might be offset. Letters, important though they were, that she had intended writing - to her mother, her publishers and Nathan's parents on the anniversary of his drowning - could now wait. She opened the drawing room door and then it hit her. There was Joe, the motorman and then Nathan in her mind this morning. Edward, her husband, barely crossed her mind, embroiled as she was in the heady immediacy of what was happening all round her. From what she understood, his work as head of the commission in London might finish sooner rather than later with him arriving home once that was done. He might never exist, she thought, as she opened the drawer and gingerly took the pen, examining it again with a mixture of fascination and disgust.

Placing it in an envelope she put it in her bag and went back upstairs. The motorman, sitting on the bedside, turned as she came in. She was about to say that the boy could stay as long as necessary, despite her thinking at the same time that it might not be a wise thing to do at all. Her problem was solved.

"He's shook enough and I'm no doctor, but I think he'll survive without seeing Lehane. It might be better too and also I'll take him back to the lodge; you know what wagging tongues there are here, just one or two, but they can do damage."

The boy's disappointment was evident but perhaps not to his father, she surmised. She suggested that if they got him down the back stairs and into the motor it just might go unnoticed. She would help settle him in at the lodge. The motorman nodded and turned back to where son lay. "C'mon me bucko, it's back to the little grey home in the west for you."

With that he lifted him from the bed, gently as he could, she noticed. Though the movement brought whimpering protestations, he settled into his father's arms, and she led the way to the motor. She sat into the back seat and soon he was settled, with his head on a rug, in her lap ... the very same way she had sat the night Joe was attacked. He had hardly time to reflect on what was happening now and what had happened then, as the motor came to a stop at the lodge door.

She eased him out towards where his father stood. Soon they were inside; he was back in his own bed in surroundings far less lavish and imposing than those where he had spent the previous night.

Looking at his shrivelled frame in the small bed, she could not but feel a pang of compassion. But she had to go and promised she would bring whatever was needed to help him get better. As a farewell greeting, she paused at the little bedroom door and smiled at him for a moment before adopting a more serious tone.

"You have been a great help and only for you we might all now be in far greater danger than we are."

His father followed her out the door and they were on their way to the village. Field was at his gate, but it was the cottage she had her eyes on, so overwhelmed with a sense of being possessed, permeated with his presence. The few short hours recently spent together had shaped a familiarity within her that was only nudged to one side when she considered again the complete incongruity of it all.

He would have heard the motor, she surmised, but would not have ventured out, cautious of drawing attention to himself and a further connection made in others' eyes with the woman in it. Maybe her mission this morning might have some effect on the perceptions of others? Or was that a vain hope?

The motor stopping at the barrack's door already had faces at doorways. Children who would daringly race alongside to examine the gleaming machine of their betters were today pulled back in line and the motorman sat alone at the top of the street. He looked back over the seat and noticed that a group of the regulars stood outside Maguire's, laconically looking in his direction.

Expecting Snee, she was surprised to be greeted by the station sergeant, Cleary. More surprising was his presentation. He was dressed as well as his slovenly frame allowed, squeezed into his uniform, appearing somewhat comical to her. Yet, here was a man closely involved with those who had attacked Joe and who was a support and a cover for their activities. A valued ally to those who were now, no doubt, plotting their next move.

Rising awkwardly from behind a cluttered table she saw that he had once perhaps been quite an attractive man. What followed surprised her even more. Coming to the counter that divided them, he leaned forward and in a tone that dripped solicitude, addressed her.

"Mrs Sheldon, I believe. You have been here all summer and this our first meeting. A pleasure to make your acquaintance. Constable Snee, though, has in the course of his duties reason to have met you."

This was nothing like she expected. Taken aback for a moment by the introduction, she was rescued from an unexpected quarter. Two of the sergeant's children, ill dressed, came tumbling down the stairs. Their giggling, childish cavorting stopped instantly. She wasn't sure if it was because they saw her or their father.

"Children, how many times must I tell you, you walk down the stairs, not run. Now, outside, and don't disturb us."

Then they were gone but not before they had furtively taken in every detail of her clothing. This simple domestic incident allowed her time to regain her composure.

"Beautiful children, Sergeant. Yes, as you were saying, I have met Constable Snee."

Bent on avoiding any familiarity following her remarks about the children and particularly in light of the sergeant's disarming attempts to be friendly, she slowly opened her handbag. As if for effect, she hesitated before taking out the envelope. Without opening it, she placed it on the counter, halfway between them.

"This, Sergeant Cleary, was found last night outside one of our windows at Woodlands," she began, waiting for some reaction. She got none, and his friendly demeanour was maintained. "It leads me to believe that the owner must have lost it there while trespassing on our property. You are no doubt aware that there are signs clearly evident noting that trespassing is forbidden on our lands, signs that even a child can understand, never mind their betters."

Expressionless, he took the pen from the envelope. In an instant, his expression changed, indicating he clearly knew to whom it belonged. Feeling she had some advantage gained, she made ready to leave. With a deliberate edge to her voice, she looked him straight in the eye, waiting for a moment, before she continued. It wasn't the first policeman she had faced in a similar manner.

"I trust this matter will be dealt with, Sergeant. Thank you for your time and good morning."

"Good morning to you, Mrs Sheldon."

Emerging into the glare of sunlight, with some degree of satisfaction, she looked down the street. Twos and threes outside Maguire's observed her. At another time this might well have been just innocent curiosity, she thought, as the motorman opened the door and she got in. Back down the village street. She looked straight ahead glancing sideways at the cottage with her heart thumping. Field was still at his gate and she gave him a cursory greeting while the motorman raised a finger.

To Field, her greeting was an improvement on the blank, straight ahead, imperious expression on her face when she had passed on her way up the village. After his messenger duties he expected some obvious sign of recognition from her. Rather churlish of her, he thought. Women, he surmised, recalling his father's words to him which over many years had proven to be true. To a man, two plus two is four but to a woman it can, somehow, be five.

She was under Golden's spell and with hindsight that was evident from the day of the bicycle accident. Most definitely from the day he had been called to the cottage by the boy to witness the sick joke so expertly engineered. For all her sedateness, as Edward's wife and mistress of Woodlands, there was about her an air of worldliness, and for a woman, an unusual confidence, not flaunted but imperceptibly challenging. The night of the party confirmed that she was the perfect hostess, but on her terms. His visit with Golden, ostensibly under another guise, confirmed his suspicions. Added to it all was her stark attraction which would turn the head of any man. Even his. All this seemed to crystallise into something else as the street scene before him seemed caught in time. All about her gave off a whiff of danger, moral danger, a characteristic, he had concluded a long time ago and not just now, so all consuming, that it very often saw consequence as alien.

With the motor now gone, he waited to see if there might be any reaction, anything at all that might give a hint of how the visit to the barrack might be seen. The presbytery door opening and Kerley emerging gave him his answer. Though only a few yards away, the priest ignored him and made his way, with purpose in his gait, to where the crowd stood outside Maguire's. Anyone in his path moved aside, saluting deferentially, and they sauntered after him, one by one, into the shop. No one doubted that the priest going to Maguire's had to do with Edward Sheldon's wife going to the police.

The crowd that had followed the priest inside emerged almost immediately. That, Field surmised, left only the priest and Maguire inside and that told its own story. It wasn't to hear Maguire's confession that brought the priest to his shop.

Whatever was in train did not take long and the priest came out onto the street and made his way home. Again, he ignored Field - it had to be deliberate - and this time it rankled. It could have nothing to do with what he had learned a few nights before when he had the unfortunate fall from the windowsill. Or was he just being dismissed? An irrelevant nonentity. Suddenly, he felt very much alone. Alone and more tellingly, afraid, as he looked up at the searing sun and walked to his own door. As he did, The Pagan came round the side of his cottage, stood for a moment inside the wall, arms folded. Field noticed him as he turned at his own door and was rewarded by a friendly wave. Interesting, Field thought, greeted by The Pagan but not by the priest.

*

His father brought him a cup of tea and helped him up to a sitting position in the bed.

"We can get the doctor if you want to, but I think you'll manage without him."

"No, I don't want him."

What was said next was with difficulty and embarrassment but there was no rancour, only a sober assessment. It was as if the words had been rehearsed.

"What you saw last night when you climbed up that ladder was not right. It's their business and we'll just leave it at that. One good thing is that you also saw the three brave buckos. There will be trouble about it when they spread the word, but you, you just keep your mouth shut. You won't see much school for a while and maybe that's just as well."

The reference to school seemed an afterthought. The reprieve was a price worth paying for, even if it was a painful one. He shifted uneasily and felt he should say something. Words did not come easily. Mumbling, he told again about the ladder and his reason for trying to remove it, "so they wouldn't know anyone saw them."

Hands on hips, his father listened, gravely shaking his head.

"The bastards will stop at nothing now, you know."

The crisp, despairing comment said all they both needed to hear.

*

Every twist and turn of events she pondered, one overtaking the other. The child's knowledge - the fact that he had seen them naked together - disturbed her. Not as much though as the three trespassers, who so easily and no doubt, with relish, had intruded on their intimacy. She felt violated, something that was hers and hers alone had been taken away, made public. She couldn't get the thought out of her head.

Something in Joe's defiance had seemed to offer some consolation the night before, as he sat opposite, with glass in hand and fire in his eyes. Now, in the clear light of day she wondered if his words "turn the tables on them" bore any resemblance to reality. Would presenting the pen at the barrack have the effect he so defiantly predicted? Should she doubt him? She desperately wanted not to and hoped, against her better judgement, that the three who had witnessed what they had the night before, might be somehow dissuaded by her gesture in presenting the pen to one of their cronies at the barrack. Joe was certain, at least last night, that shattering the anonymity of those who had put the ladder at the window, especially Slyne, the master, would be their undoing.

Yet she knew in her heart and supposed Joe felt the same, that even if it gave a few hours' respite, it would not keep their sneering lips shut. It was too good a story to keep hidden. More dangerously, other plans were no doubt being made to reap the greatest possible benefit for their cause. Would another letter, carefully constructed and with such damning news even now be readied to wing its way to Edward in London? Or would a different course be taken?

Even as the possible consequences of that thought went round and round in her mind, the more she returned to more pleasurable sensations, reliving the night before. She remembered a line from a school poem, "What though the field be lost, all is not lost ..." Joe's assurances, weaker now and perhaps made in a fit of rage the night before, she wanted to cling to and believe, even if it offered the merest, slender thread to hold on to when all around seemed to be falling apart.

She must visit the lodge at some point and see how the boy was. Was it just to salve her conscience? How and what was the effect on him and had she not been concerned enough? Again, Joe's words came to mind about him 'seeing worse.' She consoled herself with that, conscious again of how willingly she accepted his view of things. In other circumstances she would dismiss them as nebulous meanderings to pacify her.

Yes, no sense of guilt or outrage enveloped her about the boy, even if what had happened was clearly her responsibility. Had his innocence been trampled on? Remembering Joe's comment, it was as if she felt the opposite to what she, as an adult and a woman, should feel. Her mind wandered and she smothered the thought. Why, he is only a child, something briskly and abruptly chided her. Strange, provocative thoughts engulfed her, and she tried, but failed, to unravel what might be wrong and what might and should be right with any certainty.

Trying to counteract where her thoughts were rambling to, she thought again of how the three villagers must have gloated at their discovery and how their reaction would have been so different from that of the boy. Somehow that thought led to another one, for the second time in a few hours. Nathan's face was there again, clear as if it were only yesterday; her shouting "Why?" as her last look caught his tangled, golden hair askew, drooping across his forehead.

This latest image, why now, why in the midst of all that was going on around her and beyond her, why should Nathan so suddenly jump to the forefront of her mind?

*

Field watched the Mass goers through his window. He had just come back from opening the church door for early arrivals. The calendar on his wall showed the last Sunday of August and he mused again on a question that baffled him since childhood. Was August still summer or the first month of autumn? Whichever it was, the clothes worn by those outside were still those of summer, as the heat, merciless for weeks and weeks, still persisted.

The Pagan's cottage still got a wide berth. Such a demonstration of abhorrence mystified Field. How quickly, he thought, one can be made a pariah and superstitious ignorance be perpetuated, simply on the word of one man, in this case, a man of God.

As the last straggler hurried towards the chapel gate the pariah had wandered down his pathway and back again. A trial run for when the Mass ended when he would lazily move about his small garden doing his odd jobs, servile work on a Sunday to the priest. Field thought of the commandment, 'thou shalt keep holy the Lord's day.' Then it was time for himself, always alerted by the first predictable arrival of the Bressingtons with Lavinia Chapman in their horse and trap. Others arrived and he wondered what he would say to them today. Apart from the one time he had followed the regrettable agreement made with the priest to refer to Golden from the pulpit and his undesirable effect on those around him, he always tried to imbue his sermons with some element of goodness and patience. More bees are caught with a spoon of honey than a barrel of vinegar. Very different from the thunderous denunciations from his counterpart. Today, his theme, as worked over last night, would be on the good suffering and the wicked prospering. He often wondered if what he preached, prepared so meticulously, had any effect as he scanned the often drooping eyelids of his staid and stable flock. Never was that more true than over the summer, when the stultifying heat beat in through the side windows, allowing little respite to those few who came so faithfully every Sunday. Another predictable sound, telling him it was almost time to begin, was the sound of the motor. The early summer, when Edward was at home, saw husband and wife arrive five minutes before the hour. That, of course, changed as summer wore on and it was she, the only Sheldon attending, that maintained a long tradition. Field recalled old Sheldon, dismissing horse and trap and walking in fair weather or foul, to Sunday service. He admired that.

He had to make a conscious effort to avoid looking in her direction, especially during his sermon, where he always made an effort to address all those present rather than looking vacantly into the distance, as if addressing the church's front door. Engagement. It came from his early years of training and the oft-repeated piece of advice: 'if you don't engage with the congregation they won't engage with the words you preach, even if those words are those of the Lord.'

He let his guard down somewhat during the final hymn, *Come Thou Fount of Every Blessing.* By some strange coincidence it was at the line, *Prone to Wander, Lord, I feel it,* that he looked deliberately to where she sat. Clearly and lustily, she sang but her thoughts were elsewhere. And why wouldn't they be? he thought. How easily can woman be the sublime image of unsullied beauty and the temptress at the same time? His mind raced to the visit with The Pagan to Woodlands and he felt again that he was used, as he had been by the priest. By the time the line *Take my ransomed soul away* was reached, he felt alone again, cut off, even with his congregation around him. Looking away from her, the man who should be by her side came to mind. Edward Sheldon, even now and without his knowledge, was totally alone also, his marriage of a few months surgically torn apart.

The hymn ended and they stood, bringing his thoughts quickly back to his final duty of the morning. With more than usual haste he made his way down the aisle to the front door to greet his congregation as they emerged from the stuffy interior to the stultifying heat outside.. The simple ritual, mundanely monotonous, gave him a certain satisfaction as if a connection had been made, however tentative. The terrible surge of loneliness that he had felt during the hymn was gone for a while as small talk took up his attention.

Snee was always first away, as if escaping from something. With a cursory greeting she passed him by as a few others paused a little longer and he listened to what they had to say. In many cases it was predictable - 'wonderful preaching, rector,' 'the singing was heavenly' - and then they were gone. Back to their civilised, monotonous lives. All, except Victoria Sheldon.

It was back then to his own abode. Crossing the street, he looked beyond Maguire's where two boys were playing and the men sat watching. A few women stood talking outside the post office. In the distance he noticed Snee ambling toward the barrack's door. A very normal Sunday midday in Shandrum. A nagging sense of unease playing on his mind, he walked slowly to his front door. Something in the air belied the tranquility of August's last Sunday.

*

September's first day passed. They met later that night. Joe left the light burning in the cottage and then took the pathway until he arrived at the wooded area by the river that afforded some privacy. Passion unabated, they ended up, despite the risks, going back to the house. With him she felt almost invincible. On her own each day it was a different story.

Each time they met she had begun again out of sheer necessity to engineer some hope, to place some faith in the ploy that Joe had concocted. Maybe the pen did have some effect in stalling the plans of those who might so easily and grimly use what they knew. In his presence, in his arms there was something that buoyed up her spirits. Her implicit trust in him convinced her, crazy though the thought was, that somehow, in spite of all the barriers in their way, they could be together, eternally caught up in their grand passion.

She even found herself basking in his jaunty defiance. They were two against the world and this only intensified their need for each other. Their clandestine meetings and her trust in the object of her desires were too much to give up and question too soon. The light in her bedroom window burned late as did the light in the cottage, both for very different reasons. Joe got home to the cottage to find a bare flicker of lamplight in the parlour.

Monday morning came. With apprehension and anticipation, she opened Edward's letter. It was apologetic but the facts were "the damned Irish question" and the commission's deliberations had dragged on way beyond their deadline with some important members absent due to holiday commitments made for months. He wanted the job finished as parliament awaited its outcome. His solution, practical and formal. She should come to

London. He would get a suite in Hazlitt's and she could visit her mother in Eastleigh.

He went on with details of the Parliament Act which had been passed earlier in the month depriving the House of Lords of its absolute veto on Commons' legislation and this, he said, could well have implications for the work his committee was involved in so diligently. Furthermore, and more importantly, perhaps, he stressed that this might well have serious implications for the Home Rule question and for Ireland. Only time would tell.

She barely read the detail but his closing words, *Only time will tell,* reverberated. Pithily, they summed up everything. Another problem adding to those already facing her, Edward's invitation to London. The silver lining was that he would not be coming back to Woodlands in the immediate future. This gave her time. She would appreciate the invitation but point to the unending summer heat; being stuck in London, even in Hazlitt's, was not her idea of a holiday. A simple, effective excuse.

She had begun with her reply when she was summoned to meet a visitor.

Snee's expression, usually laconic, told her something was not quite right. Without hesitation she ushered him into the drawing room. Carefully placing his helmet on another chair, he sat where Joe had sat just the other night. Whatever familiarity had been built up in their previous conversations was less evident now. She wondered had he forgotten their earlier meetings when he so clearly confided in her about his position in the village.

Taking a notebook from his pocket, he shuffled through

it. For affect, she surmised, impatient for him to begin, as if a sentence was to be passed on her. Coldly and formally, he began.

"I have been sent by my superior following your visit to him on Saturday. About a pen, a very valuable pen, as it turns out. He has confirmed that the pen, as the initials note, is the property of Master Slyne. That pen has been missing since before the school holidays. The master's suspicion is, as conveyed to Sergeant Cleary, that the pen was taken from his desk and he strongly suspects, indeed he is certain that he knows the culprit. He cannot believe his luck and is not prepared to let the matter rest now that the pen is back in his possession."

She was about to shout stop, at the implication of this lie, when Snee, noticing her agitation, gently raised his hand, a signal to let him continue.

"Just let me finish. The sergeant wishes to convey his thanks to you for returning the pen which is now with its rightful owner."

He paused then, as if relieved that his duty was done. He managed a smile, strained, almost apologetic.

"I had to put it like that to you. For me, mainly, but also for you, with the way things are going."

"Go on," she said, depression starkly evident in the two words.

He pulled the heavy chair forward a little, as if playing for time.

"You're surprised, you're shocked. I can see it but I'm not. So, before you begin to counteract what I've just told you, let me tell you in my best policeman's voice what the situation is. Whose story will be believed in the village and even further afield if this goes further? Not the child's. I know that, you know that. They have done their homework and I can see the smugness of satisfaction on their faces. They are not going to let all they know go unused."

He leaned forward and brought his right hand to his chin. "You should have been more careful."

This ticking off annoyed her but that soon turned to embarrassment when she realised that he knew about Joe and herself and if he knew the village knew. Wondering what might be said next, or what she should or should not say, she sat, red faced, struggling to maintain her dignity.

"Is there something wrong with the young lad? He's not at school, the holidays are over. This gives credence to the master's story."

"You should ask his father that. How should I know?"

Her reply was terse, defensive and she knew it showed.

The constable, a disarming smile on his face, offered a mild rebuke.

"C'mon, Mrs. Sheldon. Surely you haven't forgotten what I told you a few weeks ago. If I'm here as a policeman, it's because I'm doing my duty, which is another way of saying I'm doing as I'm told. I've no say in that. They know a certain amount about you down below there in the village - those who matter do anyway."

His manner was now familiar, fatalistic and confessional. He had made a similar remark to her the day he had enlightened her about what was going on all around them. On that occasion the opportunity for elaboration, perhaps the fact that somehow here was a kindred spirit, made her ask the obvious question.

"What do they know about you? Your situation can hardly be much worse than mine, can it?"

Inevitable though such a question seemed, he was surprised and looked towards the window out into the sunlight.

"Ah, if you only knew."

She waited for him to elaborate as the clock struck midday. He waited.

"They know enough. Don't think I'm saying something I shouldn't but there may be little time left so I'll say this. I'm condemned to Shandrum because of a woman and the complications that followed. Looking back, I consider myself lucky. That doesn't mean I'm happy here but it's better than what might have happened. I was first in my class the day I passed out, but I'll only ever wear a constable's hat. And luckily so. Do you know what the Inspector General said to me that day as he singled me out? He put his hand on my shoulder -'you'll be a credit to the force, Snee, you'll go far.' Yes indeed, as far as Shandrum."

He laughed, somewhat sadly she thought, before continuing.

"Whatever about me at this stage, you as a woman and as mistress of all this, stand to lose a lot more. Because of a man, a man I take my hat off to for different reasons. But the two of you are in their sights now. With knowledge they could never have imagined having, even in their wildest dreams."

Though she followed exactly what he was saying, she asked him anyway.

"And what's that?"

"What's that? You, an ... adulteress and The Pagan your lover. The village atheist, from village cottage to Edward Sheldon's bedroom. What more do they want?"

Adulteress, atheist, lover, bedroom, Edward. The constable's crisp analysis shocked her. How dare he, she thought stung by the savage reality of what he had said. Yet there was something decidedly honest, even honourable about his view and how he expressed it.

"But ... I, I lo ... love this man, I love Joe and I don't care what names they call him, or me for that matter."

Her voice trailed away in a tremble. He was momentarily taken aback by her candid admission, delivered as it was with quivering certainty. Grateful that someone she could talk to was listening when she had no one else in whom to confide, she continued, fully aware that she hardly knew this man, yet his story couched in mystery meant a connection of some sort, again, a kindred spirit, as it were.

"It's all terribly complicated. I know about Edward, of course he's my husband, all that and what it means but ..."

Reaching for his helmet he stood up and made ready to go.

"You have said nothing that surprises me. Love may not be something you'd associate me with, but I know a bit about it. Yes indeed. You heard our rector a few Sundays ago preaching about the Lord and telling us how incomprehensible his judgments are and how unsearchable his ways. Well, let me tell you, where men and women are concerned, the Lord is lagging far behind." Before she opened the library door to let him out, he stopped.

"Whatever about men and women and even the Lord, what I do know a lot about is the danger you and those who mean most to you are in. No one down there is going to listen to you like me. You won't get an inch and as for The Pagan, God only knows what's in store for him."

"But what can we do?" she pleaded.

"Go, before you end up like me, hounded out."

"Go? How can you say that? Look at what they've done ... but ... but let me get back to the pen. The pen was not stolen by that boy. He would never do it, he's inherently honest. That pen was found by him the night they came. How dare they, and the teacher one of them? The child saw and heard them, what about that?"

Trenchant though her argument was and the truth of it, the fatalism on the constable's face quickly brought her back to reality.

"This is Ireland and this is Shandrum and no one will believe the child. And now they have the other trump card for the League. I won't tell you what I've heard some of them say and I've heard a lot in my day."

The relentless midday sun greeted them as they came out onto the steps and observed the sleepy calmness that permeated everything away beyond the river and the wood and right back to the village.

He went, almost jauntily and as ever, she was left to herself with far more questions that before he came. Yet one incontrovertible fact now brought everything into focus. Joe's plan had not worked, in fact it had probably made things far worse. She went back inside, sat at her desk and took out a sheet of paper. It was headed in a sloping scroll: Woodlands, Shandrum, Co. Cork, Ireland. She began, "Dear Mummy."

Then she paused, realising that a letter would take time, and there was precious little time now left. Of this she was certain and Snee's stark advice, at which she had so instantly reacted, only confirmed that.

Summoning the motorman, she asked him to take her to the post office in the village, but on arriving there, she said she would go to the town post office instead. The telegram's content to her mother, were she to send it from the village, ran the obvious risk of what it had to say getting into the wrong hands, a vital advantage lost. Crotty, a quiet, retiring man who ran the post office seemed aloof from what went on around him and she felt guilty for not trusting him. But better safe than sorry and using the town post office gave a greater guarantee. She could not be too careful.

*

He spent most of his days alone. She came to see him only at times when his father was present and as time passed, he knew this was deliberate. She was different, hurried in her manner and her face told a story. Things were not right and that was not a surprise for him. Joe was the cause of it all and it was useless denying that. He came with papers and comics, and square blocks of toffee from the town. Try as he might to jolly him along, Joe could not hide the difference between before and after - before 'her' and after 'her' - so dramatically coming into their lives. He too was elsewhere, distant and preoccupied.

School had begun and the footsteps and idle chatter of a few scholars as they passed on the road coming and going made him realise what he had been spared, thanks to his injuries. The longer they lasted the better and his plan was to give an impression that he was actually worse than he was. How could he ever face back there?

He read the papers, avidly searching for stories that interested him. The Mona Lisa had been stolen from the Louvre museum in Paris; temperatures had reached nearly 98 degrees as the long summer was set to continue well into September according to experts; the richest prince of the Indian Empire had died leaving millions of pounds; the New York Times had sent the first round the world cable which took sixteen minutes to get back to where it had been sent from in the first place. These news stories and more kept him occupied and intrigued. How could someone steal a big painting from a museum and how was all the money the Indian prince had left counted? Would something happen if the temperature reached 100 degrees? And how did that cable telegram go around the world? Joe usually had some kind of answer to those imponderable questions.

By the time he had finished reading, a splash of early evening sunlight made its way through the bedroom window, falling on the papers scattered on the floor. His shoulder and knees ached when he moved. Somewhere in him was the faint hope that she might walk through the front door on some excuse.

In a half dream his thoughts flitted through all that had happened since the first April day he saw her. Fleeting images flashed through his mind reawakening the now familiar desires that she had been responsible for and that she alone could somehow satisfy. Even those thoughts were brushed aside every now and then by more turbulent, darkening impressions of past dangers and the certainty that the future would be little different. Another phrase of Joe's came to mind - no rest for the wicked.

For some reason, the new bicycle came to mind. Joe was a fool to have bought it.

*

Never had she seen such uncontrolled rage. He sat upright in the bed when she told him Snee had visited. The concocted story about the pen and its being stolen from Slyne's desk incensed him, not because he didn't think them incapable of coming up with a lie. It clearly dashed any hope he had of it, somehow, stopping them in their tracks. His pride was hurt. Presenting the pen at the barrack and formally complaining about the trespassing - his master plan - would, he thought, so incriminate Slyne that the League might be forced to desist, at least for a while.

For how long they lay in silence she did not know but then, anxious to tell him what else Snee had said and its importance, she told him everything, begging him to let her finish before saying anything. His breathing, his clenched fists, the way his body tensed as she went on, told her that whatever consequences they had anticipated had been overtaken by starker choices to be made.

Somewhere in her she knew there would be resistance.

It was part of his very nature, nurtured by all he had to endure as much as by his ability to refuse defeat. And that was to be clear in his reply. He leaned forward and his arm came round her shoulder as she nestled against it, waiting for his latest analysis.

"Isn't Cleary the right bastard sending him here with a barefaced lie? I can see them now, wherever they worked this one out. I can just imagine it. The master, delighted to have his valuable pen back but wondering if his blunder might have him in some sort of trouble, being rescued by Maguire, most likely. I can see him, the cunning bastard, less intelligent than the master but cuter, putting a plan in place. I can hear him - *don't worry about the bloody pen. Say 'twas lost weeks ago, no, wait, here's something that will stump them all. Say 'twas stolen from the school before the holidays and you had your suspicions, but you wanted to wait until after the holidays to give him a chance to return it, the way 'twas taken in the first place, from behind your back. But now your suspicions are confirmed and you're going to take it further. That young brat needs to be taught a lesson and it's up to the sergeant now to come up with the best way to do it.*"

Joe's mimicking Maguire had her shivering against him as he painted a picture that, while supposition, was most likely, true.

"Well, that leaves us all at their mercy doesn't it?"

Looking into her eyes, he answered.

"Don't talk like that, girl. They don't know everything that happened the night the master lost his pen, do they?"

"What do you mean, everything?"

"They don't know the young fellow saw and heard them…"

"Joe, Joe … they won't believe him, you know they won't. I have been in courts with suffragettes and their children, and I can see how a child's voice is ignored and their innocence turned to the advantage of those who claimed their mothers were unfit to look after them. He's not had a happy summer, has he, brought face to face with things he can't understand about love and hate and our parts in all that? Yes, the League will have its sleazy triumph but at what cost to him … and us?"

They were silent now as she inched closer to him, before they lay down again, their closeness a despairing escape.

*

Field, his reading done, quenched the light. Then, out of years of habit, he pulled aside the curtain to give a cursory glance at the moonlit sky and then the street. His line of vision was to just beyond the chapel in the direction of Woodlands to his left and to his right toward where the first houses on the village street began.

The light burning in the cottage did not mean Golden was always there as he had begun leaving it on at night since the cottage was ransacked, a deterrent, more as hope than anticipation of nothing else happening. Latterly of course, Field surmised that the light might well be on, but no one at home. He grappled again with the vision of Edward Sheldon's wife, one of his parishioners, and the powerfully persuasive Golden. Yet, this led him not to condemnation but to somehow see, if not accept, the naturalness of it all.

Their earthy magnetism he had seen in other relationships, indeed in a few marriages. That however was as far as it went and he had no doubt but that other forces, sinister and determined, would exact retribution.

About to turn away towards his bed he was alerted by a movement. The priest's door opened and one by one he counted the shadowy figures that slinked along by the wall entering quickly, the last one glancing behind to confirm that there was no one about. Of the five he could only definitely identify three, the master, Maguire and McSweeney, because of his size. Sorely tempted to eavesdrop, as he had done previously, he decided against it. He wouldn't tempt fate a second time. Pulling a chair across to the window, he settled himself to see what might ensue, preparing for a long wait.

His head drowsily fell against the windowpane rousing him from his descent into sleep. Fortunately, it was at a waking moment that he was rewarded. They were leaving, less conscious of being seen, fortified, he mused, by the demon drink. They were in high spirits. Five had gone in but only four came out. They were quickly gone, lost in the sombre darkness of the village street, Maguire crossing the road to his public house and the other three waving goodbye, as they headed up the street.

Doubting now that he had actually seen five, he continued to wait. The door opened again and the fifth figure came out, cautiously looking about him. He had in his hand what looked at first to Field like a small Gladstone bag. He appeared to be taking some instruction from the priest, nodding in agreement with what was being said to him. Then, closing his door he raised his hand, either a farewell or a blessing, and sent the man on his way.

Or so Field thought. About to finally turn for bed he suddenly saw that the figure was not heading in the direction the others had but halted in front of the cottage. Bending low on the roadside he seemed to begin some sort of ritual. Leaning closer to the window, Field then realised what was happening. The man had begun to paint on the wall and Field realised that what he initially thought was a small suitcase was a gallon of paint.

Perplexed and perturbed, he swallowed, as the figure, on one knee, bobbed his way along by the wall in the village's direction, occasionally looking over his shoulder. Another dastardly deed to get at The Pagan - there again Field winced at the phrase and determined he must not think that way again. Should he interfere? He went over what he might or might not do. Before he could decide on anything, the figure had risen, stood back on the roadway to contemplate his handiwork and then breaking into a trot, he was shortly lost to view.

Relighting the lamp, he found himself shaking. He could not remember himself ever being witness to such an antisocial act in progress. Not so much witnessing it perturbed him, as its origin and the fact that it symbolised another, this time rather novel, cycle of hatred in action.

Safer to wait for a while as the clock neared two. His curiosity grew, but he would leave nothing to chance. Coming downstairs he went out his back door, down the garden, over the low bramble covered wall and into Flynn's field and turned right. The moonlight helped him and soon he emerged onto the road below the chapel.

Mindful that being out for a walk at two o'clock in the morning would be highly unusual, he tried adopting an air of nonchalance and came past the chapel and towards his own front gate. Then, as if noticing something untoward he crossed over to the cottage where he was met by a strong, deep smell of lavender from the little garden.

But it was what was scrawled on the wall that he had come to see. He scanned the undulating, hastily painted letters - ADULTER. The blue paint stood out against the whitewashed wall. The first thing was the incorrect spelling, then, that this wretched appellation attributed to the man who lived in the cottage was also incorrect, as the term applied only to someone who was married. The word itself, and its implication, did bring all the moral condemnation he could muster, and his imagination jumped to the other party involved. The term could well and truly be applied to her. Maybe that was the intent, an indirect but obvious slur on the mistress of Woodlands for all in the village to see.

A sound behind the cottage put paid to his moral meanderings. His first thought was that someone else, maybe more than one, was coming towards the back of the cottage from the castle field to visit some other retribution. But no, it was The P…, it was Golden coming back from his night's tryst. The back door opened, and the lamp was relit.

Pondering what to do, Field then heard a burst of song from inside the cottage and a strong, measured voice rang out with *Oft in the Stilly Night*. He listened, assuming the first verse would finish it but Golden was only getting

into his stride, beginning the second verse with gusto.
It was a song Field particularly liked and when Golden
came to the words

I feel like one,
Who treads alone
Some banquet-hall deserted,
Whose lights are fled,
Whose garlands dead,
And all but he departed …,

he felt they applied as much to himself as to the man
singing them.

Whether or not the scrawl on Golden's wall had some
connection with the singer it certainly wasn't making an
unhappy man of him. The song ended and Field opened
the small gate and knocked, rather timidly, to acquaint
the singer with one of the less romantic facts of life.

The door eased open. The first thing he noticed was a
large fire tongs raised in protection and anticipation.

"What's wrong, come in, come in."

"No, you come out," replied the rector, with
uncharacteristic decisiveness, "wait till you see this."

He followed, tongs still held in readiness.

"They never swallowed a dictionary, anyway," was the curt
summary.

"Don't you think this is a fairly tame one after all, knowing
what they do now. After trying to wreck this place and
half kill me this looks a bit childish."

"Or calm before the storm, adultery involves two. What
do they know?"

Field surprised himself with the level of confidence he

brought to the directness of his question. Before waiting for a reply, he asked "it is true, isn't it?"

They looked again where by now long dribbles of paint had reached the bottom of the wall but the message was stark and clear.

"It doesn't have to be, man. Sure, weren't they calling me a degenerate up to now? What more can I do to surprise them? The night they nearly killed me do you know what their answer to that was. Go away and get a woman. Well, that's what I've done, and she's a damn fine woman too."

The last few words, spoken with an air of triumphalism, were directed more in the village's direction than at Field. He was taken aback at this public confession but found himself full of admiration for The - Golden - even if it went against everything for which he, as a clergyman, stood. After all, he thought, it is written, indeed commanded, Thou shalt not commit adultery. Was something happening to him at an hour of his life when the tenets he had preached throughout it might be resting uneasily with him?

Golden had bent down and was tapping the outer layer of whitewash.

"A few minutes will fix this, hang on there now 'til you see."

Field waited for him to return and stared again at the truth about one of his parishioners and not just anyone but Edward Sheldon's wife, George Sheldon's daughter-in-law. My God, what would he say were he alive?

Golden was back now with a trowel, brush and bucket. Beginning with the letter A he deftly sliced away the outer layer of whitewash. Working at speed he soon had the letters removed, leaving a roughened rectangular outline. Then, with deft, downward strokes of the trowel, he removed the streaks that had made their way to the ground.

"Here, do your bit for Ireland," he joked, giving the brush to Field. Seldom spoken to so familiarly, he swept what had been scaled away from the wall into a heap and though he struggled, he got everything into the bucket just as Golden re-emerged from the back of the cottage. Now he had a half bucketful of whitewash. With a certain relish he soon had the small wall looking pristine white and for good measure he gave the wall on the other side of the gate the same treatment.

Adversity turned to advantage, Field could not but admire how quickly it had happened. Merely a pyrrhic victory, though, he thought. Yet, better than the whole village and more especially the innocent children seeing the crude handiwork that they would struggle to understand.

Gathering up the bits and pieces, Golden stood back and admired his handiwork while Field decided that the night had seen enough and turned to cross the road. He was halted by what came next.

"Do you know something, Rector, you could be next."

"How next, next for what ... what do you mean?"

"If anyone sees you here with me, I could be knocking on your door some night for the same reason as you did on mine tonight."

"Well maybe, but they'll hardly be scrawling the same word on my wall now, will they?" Field said, with a laugh.

"Ah now, you never know," Golden replied, his tone conspiratorial, "don't you know what Jackie Mulvey said to your co-partner here when he came next door to tell him that he was getting married?"

Even though he did not know what was said to the priest, Field knew the reference, a man who had married very late in life after courting a local girl for nearly thirty years. Curious now, as always, and drawn in by Golden's confidential, man to man manner, he listened, eagerly.

"Not a word of a lie this, he told your friend that, at last at the age of sixty-eight he intended getting married and wanted to talk about the arrangements for the wedding. When it was suggested to Jackie that he might be a bit advanced in years to be taking on such responsibilities, do you know what he said? 'Well, Father, I wanted time to think about it and now I'm fit for anything. Sure she'll be able to answer the rosary for me anyway.'"

Giving Field a playful punch to the shoulder, Golden giggled, "It might be the same with yourself. Better late than never."

Normally embarrassed by such talk and somehow feeling he was party to some implied impropriety he felt himself at ease with Golden in a way he never really had with anyone. A barrier of some sort had been breached the day he helped out at the cottage. Here now was further evidence that the man he was standing in the street with at this hour could so easily bridge a gap and draw him into an atmosphere of collusion at a number of levels. Maybe it was the night, party to the sharing of so many unimaginable secrets.

"The next thing you'll be telling me is you have a prospective wife for me," Field laughed.

"Well now that you mention it, you could do worse than inveigle Nurse Prout, that fine upstanding woman, into your affections. You'd never have to open your mouth."

"Oh no, stop!" Field replied, seriously and decisively, shivering at the thought. "I better go before you corrupt me. If my bishop only knew what I'm doing here and talking about."

To bring some seriousness to the conversation and maintain some deportment in the face of Golden's disarming and devil-may-care attitude, he thought he should mention what he had been privy to earlier in the night. He wondered why he had not thought of it earlier. "There was some sort of meeting next door to you earlier. It was after that this job was done," he said, pointing to the wall.

"How many?"

"Four or five."

"The usuals?"

"I only recognised a few."

The flirtatious camaraderie was over and Golden stood, sombre and deflated, muttering something like 'at least I know.'

Field, now sensing that he had some advantage, decided to put matters into what he considered the proper perspective.

"Before I go, I must say this. The situation between you and Victoria Sheldon will have dreadful consequences. In my position I must say that to you. Tonight is only another episode, as if they hadn't visited enough callous barbarity on you."

"Well, sir, you have said it. Now consider your duty done. We've thwarted the boyos on this occasion anyway, thanks to yourself, so we'll leave it for the night."

The temporary advantage Field felt was suddenly gone again and the other man was in command, simply by uttering a couple of words. He was glad to go, unsettled at the thought that he was an accomplice of sorts now. The effortlessness of Golden underplaying not only of danger but of sin had him envying, for a moment, the priest's no-nonsense attitude. That too was temporary when he reminded himself of what he had witnessed.

Grappling with forbidden images of what was taking place in Edward Sheldon's bedroom he cursed the night and what it had brought, knowing full well it was just a harbinger of what was to come. The village slept all round him. In the candlelight he scanned the holy book, not seeking solace but censure.

*

Something was wrong. It was just after eight. The normally staid, sober face of the motorman couldn't hide it and his efforts at description floundered in genuine embarrassment.

"It's better that you come with me, and quick."

He drove at speed down the avenue and through the gate, turning not toward the village, but toward the hills, by the river and the wood. In a few seconds he brought the motor to a stop. Huge letters stalked the wall, hurried and uneven. The first word she saw was HERE, then WHORE, then ENGLISH. ENGLISH WHORE HERE.

A sickening convulsion surged inside her. He kept moving in the motor, turning at Mulcahy's boreen and sweeping back the way they had come. Each letter jumped out at her again and the motorman simply shook his head.

"I don't know what this means."

Neither did she but his words did nothing to obliterate the grotesque imagery they had left behind. She was now the focal point, the daubed epithet menacingly making her responsible for sin and sinners.

Never had his father driven so dangerously. Or so it sounded. His face pressed against the kitchen window gave him a glimpse as the motor slowed for a moment before going out onto the road and turning right. A minute later he saw her again as she was driven back up the avenue, her hand to her mouth, her face transformed. Struggling into his clothes, with more ease than he would have his father witness, he made his way out onto the road. Pretence had worked well allowing his absence from school to be prolonged. He was careful but curious as to why the motor had gone such a small distance and then turned back. Nothing untoward was noticeable and he crossed to the other side to get a better view as the road rose up in the direction of the hills. Then the letters on the wall came into his line of vision, the last word HERE first and he had to walk a few yards to see where the writing began.

Not immediately was its import understood. WHORE was a word he'd heard casually thrown away in conversation among some of the villagers. Then he stumbled on what it meant as written on the wall. The stark, harsh implication did not fit the image of the woman who had just also seen what was written. There was something hostile and contradictory in what he now looked at. Then he realised his presence on the roadway might be noticed. But it was more than that, he recoiled from what he saw as sullying what he treasured. The blunt, unadorned message pointed too at him, putting him on display, making a show of him.

Hurrying back to the lodge he dreaded being seen, being caught where even his secrets were displayed. Back inside, he realised that her hand to her mouth said everything, the perfect picture of what the latest twist had thrown in her face. But why did he feel found out? Why did he somehow feel naked? Why was this feeling so different from the other times he had been caught, the night he rang the bell and even the day the priest had collared him for all to see on the street? It was that word. Why?

The motor was coming back again along the avenue, and he positioned himself behind the curtain. Unexpectedly, it stopped. Guiltily, he jumped into one of the chairs at the fireplace as the doors slammed and footsteps sounded. Solemn faced, his father opened the door and stood aside to let her in, her eyes full and her face drained.

"Are you well enough to do a message," she said, more a command than a request.

"You can be sure he is," his father answered and at once he knew he was not fooled by his acting worse than he really was. He was on his feet in an instant, any semblance of pain or injury hardly noticeable.

"What is it?" he said even though he knew that it had to do with words on the wall.

Her face now close to his, she placed her hands on his shoulders. He thought she was going to cry but he was wrong. She gave him the message, repeated it and he nodded. Then he was away, taking the familiar path.

For a terrible moment he thought Joe was not at home.

"Easy on there, I'm coming."

Barefoot and sleepy eyed, Joe emerged from the bedroom, showing no great surprise at his visitor.

"What's up?"

"Go in quick. Wait 'till I tell you. There's a terrible thing above on the wall?"

"What wall?"

"Sheldon's but listen, she sent me with a message."

Joe was reaching for his boots.

"You've to cycle out to Casey's crossroads and turn down to the clearing near the gate at Woodlands' inch field. She'll meet you there and you're to hurry on."

As an afterthought he added, "sure you'll see the writing then on your way."

"Go in and wheel out the bicycle. I've to spruce myself up a bit."

He grabbed the bike roughly, pulling and pushing out the backdoor, then going to the parlour window to watch him go. With a typical sweep of the eyes Joe gave a glance of subversion in the direction of the village before cycling off towards his third meeting with Victoria in less than twenty-four hours.

He was back for a moment at the riverbank the day

Edward had cantered up on his horse and beckoned Joe across to talk to him. He now had them in his mind's eye, detached from river, fields and low hills away in the blue distance.

They were easy in their conversation, heads nodding in agreement, equal in each other's presence even if it was the master conversing with the commoner, one a man of land, power and influence, the other with just as much influence but in a very different way.

Lost in that memory, he was aroused by the banging of the presbytery door and as if transfixed he sprung to rigid attention. The usual sneering eye thrown at the cottage was, this morning, for reasons the watcher inside could not understand, directed at the low cottage wall. There was the slightest slowness of stride, the cause of which was not clear.

Then the priest turned towards the school as the last stragglers hurried in. The boy expected him to go in as he often did, unannounced and without knocking. Not so today. He stepped inside the door but quickly stepped out again, the master following.

The conversation was serious. Their faces turned to the cottage and the priest's head shook in disbelief at whatever the master said. It ended with one going back inside and the other setting off on his daily walk, checking his watch as he went. The boy hoped he would come back into the village and take the castle walk as he sometimes did. But no, today he went the other way which would take him away from the village, through the forest across from Woodlands where he would eventually come up Mulcahy's boreen and come back by the wall of

Woodlands. He would certainly then have something to stare at just before he came to the lodge. Would he meet Joe by chance?

*

The motorman had walked along the wooded road following Joe's arrival. He arrived at the bridge over the river that entered Woodlands at that point. Standing for a while he then planted his elbows on the bridge, leaned over and peered in, waiting for his next instruction. Not once did he look back to where they sat in the motor.

Seeking Joe's silence until she had finished, she spoke calmly but definitely. Joe's plan had backfired. Were he not to accept what she said to him, then she would; she would not satisfy the mounting desire for the consequences of her love for the man sitting beside her to be satisfied. Nor would she allow the boy, his father willing, to be caught up in the consequences of what his elders were involved in and about which he had so little understanding. He was being forced to grow up long before he had a chance to be a child.

Despite the revolting scar the ominous daub of paint had left, she, strangely, felt a new strength and objectivity that saw and went beyond the lurid message. She had spent an hour thinking, once she had recovered from the sickening shock of what she had seen.

"Jesus, Victoria, what are you asking me? I don't have the answer but is it this one? Can't you see their faces?"

From the back seat of the motor, he stared into the trees, his expression twisted in the face of what he thought he would never have to stomach. Defeat.

"What about the boy? His father won't agree, I'm certain of it."

"Don't talk to me about that child. I've tried to protect him in my own way, maybe not always the best way but you know what his life here is. He hasn't one and so will it continue to be. Maybe his father doesn't see it, maybe you don't. Soon they will use what we thought would stop them for a while, the word will get round that he stole the master's pen. Where will that leave him? Worse off than ever, one of the things that is singular, his honesty, so much a part of his innocence and his character will be set at nought. A thief."

"And what about himself?" Joe gestured in the motorman's direction.

"I haven't said a word to him, but he must know something is going to happen. He is not a stupid man and I've felt since I came here that he knows a lot more than he lets on he does."

"You're certainly right there. Indeed you are."

He was still looking into the trees when she drew his head towards her, placing a kiss on his forehead. Looking into his eyes she slowly assured him that they were right to risk all.

"You have been fighting all your life and maybe I have too in a different way. But for you and me now, it's a new fight and if you do what I think we should do we can face it together. It will be our fight, not on the terms set by jealousy and bigotry. It will be on our terms and the first step towards that is to take away what they most want here, what they are feeding off morning, noon and night. You, Joe. You with the child and myself part of it all too. With us gone they have nothing, only bitterness and defeat, even if they don't see it that way. But we have ourselves."

His face changed, dissolving into a softness, not unlike the precursor to passion, that so intoxicated her at other times. Now that softness did not presage passion. Had something in her carefully crafted plea appealed to his sense of the natural, that in beginning anew, past battles are not only forgotten but even won?

She was about to suggest that enough was enough for the moment and they should go. He began as if to speak, then stopped.

"What is it?"

"There is something I have never told you. I will now, and it may change everything, but I can't keep it from you."

She listened.

"Only for him I would never have known it and it's only a couple of weeks ago when I was getting over the business of the attack. I never asked him how he knows, and I probably never will."

Wide eyed she had listened. He finished what he had to say, nodding in the direction of the motorman, still statue-like, gazing into the river. The day he had told her he was a bastard child now seemed long, long ago. She had tested him just now with her proposal, but this was a test for her, perhaps a test that if failed, would add another imponderable to where they and others found themselves. His reluctant decision to agree with her would, after all, come at a price.

Edward's father was remembered as a man who had the interests of his workers and indeed that of the broader village at heart. He had not been wanting in that either, where Joe's mother was concerned but she, independence in her bones, had lived a life which was the very antithesis of life in the big house down the road. Vilified and ostracised, because she dared live with her bastard son in the shadow of church and chapel, she had taken on the village in her way and so would her son in his. Ironically, the food that kept her alive in her final years had come from Woodlands' kitchen through the motorman. The money that came regularly from George Sheldon, who had fathered her son, was sparingly spent. It would in time provide that son with a tidy income, never flaunted, that helped preserve his independence, when others perceived him to have nothing apart from what he got from his rabbit hunting and fishing.

"We will talk of all this again but that's all you need to know now because it's enough."

He had barely told her when she saw the resemblance, the high cheekbones, the eyes. Why hadn't she seen it before? Maybe because apart from the physical likeness that's where it all ended. Her husband and the man sitting with her in the early morning sunshine were chalk and cheese.

"It's from your mother then?"

"What, from my mother?"

"Where you got the difference from, you are so unlike … you are a completely different man to Edward, in every way. It was she who made the difference, all the difference in the world and, you know, that was Edward's loss. Only for her we wouldn't be here today trying to salvage the present and whatever there is of the future."

"She lived the way she wanted. If they only knew, that as a result of that, what I live off was and is Woodlands' money."

"Forget about money ... why do I want you? Why does all I have here mean so very little to me if I look into the future, no matter how uncertain and don't see you there? Edward Sheldon never made me feel that way. He's not a bad man but he never was the man for me, and mother knew that but wouldn't stand in my way. She said it could be a stepping stone. Yes, I married him and had I not, I would never have met you and never known he had a half-brother. It would make you believe in fate."

The motorman, for the first time since they had arrived now lifted his head and looked in their direction before settling himself again, elbows on the bridge.

Joe's disclosure should have ripped through her already battered mind and sickened soul. Yet, it didn't. Curiously, all at once it had closed and opened a chapter. Maybe at another time in some distant place she would ponder it all, the strangest of strange alliances. Now she would only see it as making some unknowable sense in the midst of mayhem and threat.

"I'll try but I know he won't agree. It's hard to blame him, you know, but look, I'll try."

She watched him walk to the bridge. At the sound of the door opening, the motorman looked up. He listened, shaking his head. Joe's gestures were in the direction of the village. As he had predicted, the motorman would not agree. Joe persisted, but in a few minutes they were both back at the motor, the motorman decidedly unhappy.

"Maybe you'll talk to him," Joe said, with little conviction. They were his parting words to her before wheeling the bicycle away from where it stood and making ready to leave. The motor started and soon overtook Joe. The motorman waved and she looked through the window at the man who had changed her life. As they approached the gates of Woodlands the motor slowed. A donkey and cart was in the way, the donkey grazing at the roadside, while its owner, Mulcahy, stood with hands on hips looking at what was written on the wall. He seemed not to have heard the motor, absorbed as he was by what he saw. Then with a hurried, apologetic wave at the occupants, he moved the donkey and cart further to the side and the motor edged past.

*

They both climbed up the front steps. She wanted to wait until they were inside but broke the awkward silence with a cliché.

"This heat, will it ever end?"

How could she not have noticed? They stood in the grand hallway and his eyes followed, to the portrait. The father of the two men in her life. He seemed slightly ill at ease as she surprised him with a question while gesturing in the direction of the portrait.

"Would you ever have told me?"

"It crossed my mind but look at the trouble it would cause you, not to mention others. And won't it cause trouble now? I did think that at some point, Mrs Sheldon, your husband, might have told you. Of course, one is never sure what husbands and wives tell each other."

The mention of Edward brought her quickly back to the task at hand. She beckoned toward the drawing room where the first thing her attention was drawn to was a large photograph of Edward's father. Again, it was only now she saw what had passed her by so often since she had arrived. Imagine, she thought as she sat down, only a few nights ago she had sat here with Joe and the photograph, on a cabinet, stood right behind where he had sat.

He waited, tensely drumming his fingers on the table. She was about to begin and then changed her mind. Two glasses, the whiskey bottle and what was left of the amontillado were quickly on the table, much to the motorman's surprise. She poured the whiskey and he reached to indicate that she had been too generous. With the sherry in her hand, she began, repeating what Joe had said to him. He raised his hand.

"I made a promise to my wife before she died that I would always look after him until he was able to look after himself. That promise won't be broken. And by the way I can't believe that Joe will go along with your plan in the finish. He's much too proud a man."

Admiring his honesty and loyalty she went on to lay the facts before him even if he was not to be swayed.

"Well, maybe this can be your way of looking after him. You know much more of what goes on here than I do but that boy of yours is miserable. Maybe in spite of all you know, you can't see what's right under your nose. He's an isolate, he has no friends and the very people who should be offering him something, his priest and his teacher, are perpetuating the misery he suffers every day. Is that what you want for him? And soon he'll be regarded as a common thief when the master's story gets about."

"Maybe so, but I will fight my own battles for him. We could talk about this for hours, but I won't break my promise."

Slowly finishing the drink and thanking her, his solid answer stood. She felt she had betrayed the boy, consigning him to a life she would not wish on anyone. The last part of the jigsaw, which so consumed her, had not fallen into place.

"I'll get Meaney to help and we'll do something to try and get the paint off the wall. It won't be easy but at least it won't look like it does now. We should have done it earlier. If we don't do it now, you'll have a procession out of the village all day to see the work done by the brave boys. Some are probably doing that now. I'll run into town and get a can of that new stuff they have for cleaning floors. It might work. They say it's great, from Germany."

"Thank you. And please think about what I've said."

Disconsolately he shook his head as if he wished he could please her. She walked him out to the front steps and waited until the motor pulled away on its way to the town to find some magic formula that would obliterate the three stark words from what now defined her in the eyes of the villagers. She thought of Lavinia Chapman.

*

Back at the cottage, he saw the postman return, having finished his round. He saw the rector come and go from the church. Sounds of the first playtime came and went from the school yard. He saw the priest return from his walk and call again at the school door. This time it was a shorter, more agreeable conversation which ended with both laughing at whatever had been said last. A shout from the master towards the classroom and Maguire's son appeared, obsequiously saluting the priest and waiting to know why he was summoned. Behind the curtain, he waited and watched young Maguire, one of his main tormentors, go back inside. He guessed what might happen. Occasionally, young Maguire was put in charge while the master was away. He revelled in this role, treating his fellow classmates on the basis of whether he liked them or not.

Priest and master came out onto the road. Still chatting, they began walking towards the village. He shrunk back just to be certain he would not be seen. The gold top of the master's pen glinted in the sunlight. From habit they moved away from the cottage as they approached it but neither could resist looking at where the handiwork from the night before had been removed and the new whitewash gleamed in the sunlight. Both looked at each other but nothing was said and then they were in the presbytery door. He wondered why they had given the wall such attention.

Why was Joe not back? Maybe he was helping to clean the Woodlands' wall.

Hearing the presbytery door slam after a few minutes, he was quickly back at the window. The master came out onto the road reading what appeared to be a letter.

He veered to the opposite side of the road at the cottage and continued towards the school completely absorbed in what he was reading. So intent was he on watching the master that he never noticed Joe arriving. Intensely annoyed at this intrusion, the master set his face to avoid the bicycle. Joe veered in front of him, causing him to come to an embarrassing halt, and jumped off the bike as if to block his path. Whatever Joe said to him clearly flustered him. For a moment it seemed as if he considered replying, but he stormed round the bicycle and into the school.

"What did you say to him?"

"I asked if he teaches painting as well as spelling to the scholars."

The remark made no sense, but it was Joe's sombre face that claimed his attention. He must be mad because of the words on the wall at Woodlands. Not knowing what to say next he started the fire, assuming Joe would want tea.

"Did you see the writing?"

It was awkwardly asked and Joe, who had been standing between parlour and kitchen as if looking for something, replied briskly.

"I did indeed, yerra, what would you expect from the likes of them. A lot they care about anything but their own twisted ideas. Their best work is done in the dark, as you know yourself. What's done during the day is by the man next door."

He hesitated before continuing, "maybe if they didn't have us they'd have nothing to do except turn on themselves.

We're their sport - anyway, don't worry about them, what about putting down a few snares tonight, you'd never know it might be a lucky one."

"But I'm sick, I'm supposed to be sick."

"Sure your father knows you're better, how could you have come down here with a message otherwise?"

He baulked first at this piece of news about his father and then smiled.

"We all know you're better even if you still have a few scratches and scrapes. Your father knows you hate the blasted school. Every cloud, as they say, has a silver lining. You'd never know what might happen yet."

He was about to say more but he leaned over to put the kettle on the crane. So, his father knew about school. The fact that he was keeping him at home gave him a warm glow. The suggestion of the rabbit run brought back the old surge of jealousy; he would have the rabbit round, but Joe would have her.

"What's that thing about a silver cloud and the lining?"

Without giving an answer, Joe instead said, "your father might want to talk to you."

"About school, is it?"

"Ah no, wait and see, be off with you now."

He collected the snares from the backyard shed and took the path home. The motor was parked just outside the gates, and he peeked around the corner. His father and Meaney, the gardener, with buckets and brushes were sweating in the heat as they tried to banish the message. He watched, wondering would they succeed. After a while they stood back and seemed satisfied that they had.

"The best we can do," he heard his father say, "it's blotchy I know but at least it can't be read. We might it give another run over tomorrow. That's great stuff, isn't it. It takes the Germans, you know."

He pointed to a bright yellow can as they collected what they had and carefully placed them in the back seat of the motor to be driven back up the avenue. The boy nipped back inside before they could see him and waited for his father to return. What time depended on what he was required for at the house and as he often said on returning to the lodge, "there's always something."

*

She thanked them. Meaney looked sheepish and embarrassed as he unloaded the buckets and brushes to bring them round to one of the sheds at the back. The motorman told her that they had been able to make a good job of the words on the wall and that she shouldn't be worried. He praised the concoction he had got in the town, adding "I wonder what they'll come up with next." He should have gone to the train station to pick up materials Victoria had ordered when he was in town. So anxious was he to get rid of the words on the wall that he postponed going to the station. It was to there he now set off.

She watched him go, this solid servant who would turn his hand to any job that needed doing and do it well. Watching the motor drive away she was certain his mind could not be changed.

On the motor's return, and not waiting to unload what he had collected, he sought her out.

She knew there was something wrong. What next, she thought, apprehensively.

"Do you know what I saw at the station? You won't believe this. Poor Mulcahy was taken off to the asylum on the up train. He was there between Snee and Cleary and do you know who was there as well, in her element? Blabbermouth Prout pretending to be there on some kind of nursing duty. Mulcahy, the poor bastard, didn't seem to know what was happening and he seemed half asleep sitting on the bench with his brother next to him, his brother who has been trying to get rid of him for years. And what has he ever done except shout at the moon about what he's read in the papers; he's never harmed anyone, even if they do say he's mad."

She remembered only this morning seeing him looking at the words on the wall and listened now to the motorman's tale of woe, his garbled outburst such that she thought he might even cry. So much happening so quickly.

"He noticed me when I collected your items from the office and I went and shook hands with him, though Cleary wasn't too happy with that. Snee looked troubled, as if not wanting to be there. All Mulcahy said was, 'we never died a winter yet.'"

He told her about Mulcahy being the only one in the chapel the day of the priest's thundering sermon who looked towards himself and the boy as if disagreeing with what was being roared from the altar.

"Now they're happy, another scalp under their belt. Get rid of what you can't put up with."

Suddenly realising he had gone on, he looked at Victoria

and made to return to collect what he had brought from the station. Regaining his composure, he turned and said, "I often wonder who is mad and who is not in this godforsaken place."

*

"Reginald,"
Knowing from whom the letter was before he opened it, Field was not prepared for the greeting. Never had Sheldon addressed him as anything other than 'Rector.' It was, he felt a cry from the heart, a man to man expression used by someone at his wit's end.

"What in the name of God is happening? Another damned letter, scripted in the same hand as the first one. I would be happy to treat this contemptible narrative as another damned hoax, but I can't. The detail has me totally unnerved and devastated.

This can't and won't be ignored and its consequences are too serious to even think about. When my bedroom in Woodlands is described in detail, that is shocking enough but can I believe that in that very room my wife of a few months is unfaithful? It's something out of a penny dreadful. If this gets out, and I've no doubt it will, it will put the Hampton case in the shade and that's saying something. My reputation is on the line here, Reginald. Can you imagine the scandal that will ensue?

Find out as much as you can and don't be afraid to confront Victoria. I know now why she had no interest in coming to London to be with me. I cannot leave London because of this damned commission and Parliament is screaming for it to finish but a number of the most influential members are only just back from holiday. There's even talk now of the Americans and the French wanting to meet us and submit something.

Please believe me when I say that my work has been affected and every waking moment is misery.

I await a reply, before the 15th inst. as I have to go to Paris for a few days to meet a French delegation, an arrangement made without my advice but something I have to honour; an ill wind though as it's an opportunity to meet with Harold, Victoria's brother, who will be holidaying there.

Ever grateful,

Edward G. H. Sheldon."

Finished off with Edward's flamboyant signature, the letter merited a second reading by Field, because of its content. There was no doubt the words were those of a desperate man, dragged between duty and his marriage. Duty had clearly won out, something that did not, for some reason, surprise Field. The letter now placed him in an unenviable situation, a dilemma that had many ramifications. Distracted as he was, he almost overlooked the second letter from the morning post. Not recognising the handwriting, he read the few lines it contained, puzzled by its content and never realising that there might well be consequences to what it too portended.

Rev Field,

I need to meet you. I have walked by the rectory a few times in the last day or two hoping that we might meet, as it were, casually. But our paths did not cross, so I write this. I will not call to you. If you take an evening walk the day you get this at about seven I can arrange to meet you near the mill bridge, as if by accident and no suspicion will be aroused. Further

oblige by consigning this note to flames.
In anticipation,
J Arthur Snee
Const.

Totally at a loss as to what this request was about, Field determined, aided by his insatiable curiosity, that he would oblige and take an evening walk and 'accidentally' meet the constable. No suspicions would be indeed aroused if church and state met on an autumn evening. For what could Snee possibly want him?

He held both letters as if balancing the importance or not of one over the other. Should he visit Woodlands and face Victoria with Edward's letter? The man's cry of desperation left him with little option. What did Snee want and why was it so serious that he could not or would not call to the rectory? Something told him to wait and in so doing he gave Snee's request priority over Edward's doomed marital situation and all it involved.

That evening he set out at precisely six forty-five and walked into the setting September sun. A hurling match in Sheldon's field meant there were few about and shouts from that direction peppered the evening air. Not wanting to appear to be on some kind of mission, he ambled through the village, past the barrack and onwards down the hill past the castle gate corner and on to the mill bridge. He fully expected to see Snee at any moment but was disappointed. He waited, looking as casually as he could over the bridge before retracing his steps. Snee was coming towards him, down the hill. He went back to the bridge and waited.

Both men stood, their backs to the bridge, the castle in full view, towering over all. To anyone watching or coming upon them they had met by accident, not design. In fact, and this gave Field some assurance, it was not at all unusual for them to stop and chat were their paths to cross and they often did. After all, Snee was one of his congregation.

"Did you burn it?"

"Your letter, oh yes, it went up in flames as I boiled my kettle for a cup of tea after lunch. I must say it intrigued me. I'm all ears."

"I am breaking every rule in the book, let me say first. Were the reason I'm meeting you here known, I can bid goodbye to my career, such as it is and my meagre pension. I do not want to be seen approaching any of the parties involved officially. I am alerting you to a situation that has developed quite rapidly over the last day or so. It has serious consequences. Let us not pretend that tongues are not wagging. You know why and so do I. Never have I seen Nurse Prout smile so much and that says something. You know about the walls of Woodlands and the Michelangelo job done there."

Field was about to tell him about the painting on Golden's wall but thought better of it for the moment, so intent was he on hearing what Snee had to say.

"The League is in its element - you know why - and a plan has been hatched using two fronts. The master has made a formal charge to the sergeant – and we know whose side he's on – about the pen, noting its value, both financial and sentimental. He had his suspicions but when he learned that the motorman's son had supposedly found it in Woodlands his suspicions were confirmed. That's his story and it will stick. The sergeant will summons the motorman on Monday morning to have his son appear before the magistrate in the town next week. I can tell you now, without a shadow of a doubt, that his son will find himself transported post haste to one of those industrial schools in the city. That's only half of it even though it's certain that theft of the pen alone would merit being sent away and children are sent to those places for less.

To copper-fasten their case I saw the priest and my sergeant, poring over a new Act of Parliament. So great was their excitement that they shared a gem of information, as the priest termed it, with me. According to this Children's Act that only became law three years ago, in 1908, if a child is, wait for it, I wrote it down…"

Snee pulled a jotter with a small pencil dangling from his pocket and went to the last entry.

"Yes, here it is, chapter and verse as you'd say yourself, 'Section 58 …' Children liable to be sent to industrial schools."

Snee straightened himself, looking up and down the road and then back over the bridge along the riverbank. Presumably, Field thought, this was to exclude anyone who might possibly hear what was going to be said next, though he thought Snee was rather overegging the pudding. Was it to give what he was about to say more weight? In view of what he did say that thought proved to be true. There was however an interruption.

The sound of a pony and trap rounding the bend from the town side had Snee quickly putting his jotter out of sight.

Oh no, thought Field at sight of the passengers who were the last three he wanted to meet. The two Bressingtons were penance enough but when he saw the third as Lavinia Chapman, his heart sunk.

*

The sweating pony stood, vainly trying to swat at the flies in the evening heat with tail and mane. Field tried to maintain a charitable attitude and greeted all three while Snee was less effusive and simply nodded at them, with a simple, "Evening, all," maintaining his formal pose.

"My God, Rector, you no doubt have heard the news about that mad and dangerous man that we finally are rid of, Mulcahy. As well as his brother we can sleep easier at night now that his caterwauling won't be heard again at all hours. Truly frightening, I have to say."

It was Lavinia, sitting regally in a floral summer dress between husband and wife. Her flushed cheeks told Field she was well fortified and the other two were little better.

Constance Bressington then had her say.

"Constable Snee, do convey our gratitude to the Sergeant for expediting this matter. It does enhance one's faith in the law."

Bressington himself was not going to be excluded from the conversation. Pointedly looking at Snee, he said with a barely disguised sneer.

"My faith in the law would certainly be enhanced when those who defaced the walls of a neighbour's residence are apprehended. As for the so-called madman, I say live and let live. I won't go over all that seeing that I've made my case to these two fine ladies for the best part of an hour in the hotel. It left me exhausted, quite frankly and we will push on."

Field could not believe his luck that he would be rid of the unwelcome intruders so soon. Wishful thinking of course, as Lavinia would add fuel to the fire, before Bressington set the trap in motion and the pony braced itself for the uphill slog away from the bridge and into the village.

"One problem solved, Rector, but what about the rumours I'm hearing? Utterly shocking and the involvement of the lower orders, an untouchable, is a diabolical addition. The sacredness of the marriage vow being sorely tested, I believe. And by whom? What is the world coming to? I can tell you, old George Sheldon must be turning in his grave."

Bressington's annoyance at what Lavinia said made him ready to move away. She lurched sideways, almost into Bressington's lap, as the trap set off. He unceremoniously pushed her away while leaning back toward the two on the road, throwing his eyes skyward. He made sure he had the last word as he raised the whip in farewell.

"Let he who is without sin and all that is what I say."

Field and Snee looked at each other.

"Are you thinking what I'm thinking?" Field asked.

"Neither of us got a word in and even if we had, there was no chance of an answer being listened to by the two women anyway."

Snee, smirked and replied, "a bit like listening to your sermons on a Sunday morning. We can listen but no chance to answer back."

He quickly reverted to the seriousness of what had brought the two of them together and referred to what Lavinia had said. "That", he said to Field, "shows you the whole place is awash with rumour."

"It's like food and drink to them. They're talking about the papers, even."

"Get back to what you were saying before the invasion."

Snee got the jotter out again and solemnly read from it.

"If a child is 'living in circumstances calculated to cause, encourage or favour the seduction or prostitution of the child' - that's the legal bit but it's the consequences that are important. 'The child can be sent to an industrial school.'"

He closed the jotter. Field flinched at hearing such language and immediately retorted, "but that's not the case with the motorman's boy, he comes and goes to Golden's place. That's all."

"And he stays there overnight now and then. Forget the prostitution piece, it's the seduction part that they think will clinch it for them if the pen doesn't. And can you imagine what the gutter press will say when all this gets out. The safety of a child being questioned, and Edward Sheldon being cuckolded by the same man."

"My God, can I believe that what's being said here, or will be said before the magistrate, that Golden has other motives for the boy staying in his cottage? I know it has been said but in a court of law?"

"Well, Rector, if the sermons of our two esteemed ministers of religion are to be heeded then that has already been alleged. The master will obviously testify and will be believed. They're planning on you and the priest possibly being called as witnesses in view of what you said once from the pulpit and what the priest said more than once in his church and publicly. I don't know about you, but he'll have no problem in taking an opportunity he thought he'd never get. The magistrate will be impressed."

Field felt affronted as well as deeply worried.

"Why are you telling me this?"

"As I've said, I will not be seen approaching any of the parties involved because my sergeant and those around him will immediately suspect me if those other parties, and you know who they are, manage somehow to outwit the League. You, on the other hand, will not be suspect but you'd just better be discreet, all the same, when you inform the others of the danger, not that they might be in, but are in."

Field tried desperately to make some sense of this turn of events.

"Your task may be easier if you talk first to the lady at Woodlands, though I'm not sure that's the name she's being called around here at the moment. And if I were you, I wouldn't be seen talking to either Golden, the motorman or his son. Every move is being watched, as you can well imagine. That's the policeman in me talking and it is advice I think you should take."

"This is most alarming. Why are you doing this? You are breaking a confidence, giving information, that you came by as part of your official duty. Maybe you are in as much danger as they are?"

Snee smiled and made ready to leave.

"Ever since I came here, I've had to watch myself too. My official duties, as you say, have made me privy to much more than you'd ever believe. The fact is the law is broken in this village more than it's observed. I've been aware of a number of things in my time here that turned my stomach but this I can't let go. If the worst happens then at least I can tell myself that I tried. They may suspect me anyway by reason of letting me in on their master plan but if they do, so be it. If you play your part, they may not be able to prove it."

Snee headed off in the village's direction leaving Field looking over the bridge at the trickle of water that passed for a river after the summer drought. When would things ever be the same again, he wondered?

Edward's letter posed a substantial problem, but so did the startling news Snee had given him. They will stop at nothing. The more he thought of what now faced him the more dangerously complicated it all seemed. As he made his way back toward the village, he concluded that a rift between himself and Edward was inevitable. Nor did he relish facing his wife, but Snee's advice was sound, foolproof. Making his way down the village street towards Golden's cottage it again struck him at the outrageous connection, the vilest he could think of, about to be made in a courtroom. The papers would be full of it, no matter what the outcome. And to think that he might be forced to obey the law and publicly admit that, yes, he had warned his congregation about the whole matter.

Even more frightening, if that were possible, was the fact that an innocent child would be taken from his father. Taken on the premise that he would be safer in an institution than his home or shared home as the case was. Field knew little of the vagaries of those who preyed on children, but he now was certain that Golden wasn't one such. He would hardly be in Victoria Sheldon's bedroom if children were his interest. He recalled his father often commenting that the law does not mean justice. That such a concoction would be engineered by those whose sole purpose was to put Golden, and anyone connected with him, in their place, literally as it were, enraged him.

Inside his own door he made supper for himself. His visiting Woodlands would cause little suspicion and believing there was no time like the present, he wolfed down his meagre meal. Then, putting Edward's letter in his pocket, he set out to meet the one who would now find herself with not just her infidelity as a problem but, increasingly, her having put her own safety as well as that of others in jeopardy. He was not hopeful as he walked up the avenue.

His arrival, with the September sun in its decline behind the low hills, was not particularly welcome, he felt. She blushed and so did he, knowing that matters of the flesh had brought him. But that was only half the reason.

She showed him in, and he again took his seat. Maybe it was on instinct, as a precursor to some difficult talking, that she automatically went to the drinks' cabinet.

"What's your fancy, Rector?" she asked, almost gaily.

"I'll have whatever you are having ... you make a very good choice, no doubt."

Her choice on this occasion was wine and when she had poured her own, she raised the glass.

"To all our futures."

He felt it was a fitting toast in the circumstances and hardly had he taken the first sip when he again marvelled at the beauty and bearing of the woman before him.

"This is not going to be easy," he sighed and raised the glass again.

He pushed Edward's letter towards her, believing it was better that she saw its contents and its import rather than his trying to explain it. She scanned it, took another sip of wine and handed it back.

"The world of men, Rector, is what I see in that letter. I am obviously second best. Affairs of state take precedence over affairs of the heart."

He quickly saw that appealing to her on Edward's behalf was not going to be successful and he swallowed the whole of what was left in the glass before realising that he had emptied it. She replenished it against his remonstrances.

"So, there is no hope?"

She shook her head, her magnificent head of hair swishing from side to side.

He saw the decision was final and wasn't surprised by it. He had made his plea on Edward's behalf and had got his answer. No haggling, no tears, no justification, just a mind made up. He thought of Lavinia's insult about 'the lower orders.' A mind made up. Is that what love does, he thought, or is it lust? Knowing no answer would come to that, he pressed on.

"You are in danger, Victoria and so is your lov… so is Joe Golden and so is the motorman's son."

"Well, after the literary display that adorned the walls for a few hours, I daresay I am."

"Well, there have been developments even since then and I have information of a most serious nature on good authority."

He told her about his meeting with Snee and what he had learned. She winced at the suggestion that Joe's interest in the boy had been interpreted, for advantage, as being improper and worse, but listened closely. Far from getting agitated she took a moment when he had finished and looked out the window across the front towards the hills, now in twilight's glow. She then leaned forward, topping up his glass and then her own.

"Well, Rector, that's the best piece of news I've heard in all of this. The hypocrisy of moral righteousness has come up trumps for those presumed defeated. The very trap their scurrilous minds have invented is to my advantage."

Field was aghast. What was going on? Had the wine affected his comprehension as the woman he thought would, if not a shivering wreck during his visit but at least perturbed, seemed suddenly to have got a new lease of life.

"What, I don't understand…"

"Maybe you will in time. Now I would never be so discourteous as to hurry you out of this house, but I need to meet the motorman. You and indeed your source have been invaluable and that won't be forgotten by me."

She raised the glass again and he had little option but to do the same.

"As we said when we began, Rector, here's to the future."

He shuffled to his feet, slightly unsteady, not knowing whether to say more or not. They left the drawing room and in the great hall Field looked up at old George Sheldon's portrait. Lavinia Chapman was right. He surely must be turning in his grave.

He hadn't been in the house more than half an hour. He had arrived consumed by uncertainty and apprehension. He left, feeling that somehow and for reasons he could not understand, the forces ranged against the mistress of Woodlands had somehow met their match. 'Frailty thy name is woman' had the backing of the bard, but Hamlet would have been wrong when it came to Victoria Sheldon. Golden, you cad, he thought enviously.

Since it was Friday night, he turned his thoughts to his Sunday sermon, always preparing in time. Tonight would be different and his writing would be to Edward Sheldon in the first place and then on to the sermon. The letter to Edward was short and to the point, the essence being one of regret and one of fact - he was sorry to be the bearer of bad news, but his cause was lost. His wife was not for turning. He added that he would apprise him of more details when they next met.

Then to the sermon and he pondered for a moment on a suitable theme. Then, shaking his head rather wistfully, he began his introduction, remembering Bressington's parting words at the bridge, "Let he who is without sin…"

*

"That part is easy but what will I say to Mr Sheldon? He'll just see me as helping you all against him. I'll lose my job."

Even in saying that, the motorman's objections evaporated. He had no qualms about his boy and his being part of Victoria's plan when she starkly explained the alternative.

"Hard as it may be for him to be sympathetic, when Edward realises, what was in hand to get at us and the future for your boy he will understand, he will have to. In any event he will have my mother to contend with but that's a whole other long, long story. Now do you want to tell him or will I?"

"No, I'll tell him. Joe will back me up, not that it's going to be a problem. Jesus, what would we have done only for Snee? To think I'd lose that child after losing his mother. The bastards."

The words were said to no one in particular and Victoria was neither shocked nor offended. She nodded in agreement and laid out the plan with added emphasis.

"Everything must be normal, no indication in any way that any plan is in train. That's absolutely essential."

There was much to be done under the guise of normality but only so much could be done in the time available, especially if discretion was to be maintained. They had literally a single day.

*

Using the cover afforded by the path, Joe and the boy made numerous trips to the gate lodge on Saturday. The items carried were of sentimental or practical value and, on setting out with what they carried, they scouted meticulously to make sure they were not being observed. The pathway had been their saviour in the past and now it was invaluable. The last two items carried from of the cottage were the clocks and the bible. Joe carried the bible, the clocks being lighter.

She wrote to Edward and her publishers that morning. She wondered what next might be in store, when just before lunch, a sweaty, red-faced boy appeared at the door, having run all the way from the village. With a handsome reward for his efforts, he skipped down the avenue as she read the contents. For a moment she hesitated, wondering if the telegram was from Edward. She hoped not.

Not a problem. Am on your side. Harold subdued. Mother.

She had told Joe that the motorman would meet him in the town hotel at five on Saturday afternoon about a matter that Joe had not even thought of but one that made absolute sense. Joe cycled, again something that would raise little suspicion. Meegan, a local solicitor, not guessing or interested enough to think that anything untoward was in the offing, signed appropriately where Joe had transferred his cottage and the quarter acre on which it stood to the motorman. With the solicitor gone, they had one drink before Joe discreetly left the hotel by the way he had come in, the back door. He visited a few shops on pretence and then cycled back to the village and the cottage, now looking barer and bereft of most of what made it a home.

The boy was there, waiting for what he did not know. He kept saying to himself what she had told him to remember when she had sat down with himself and his father.

"Trust your father, trust Joe and trust me. We have to act quickly, there is not a whole lot of time for explanations. Your father has told you what's happening."

Joe didn't bother bringing the bicycle around to the shed. He took a wrapped package from one pocket and opened it on the table. From the other appeared two bottles, one of porter and one of lemonade. They both ate the few slices of ham and then Joe threw two toffee bars on the table.

"The last supper. Another one."

"Yes, I suppose it is," the boy replied, taking a lingering look around the kitchen and out into the parlour where the evening sunlight caught the dust in its track. He thought of the Last Supper picture that hung in the school classroom.

"What about the bicycle?"

"Instead of one mode of transport your father will have two from now on. Not many around here can match that."

*

The boy got up, saying he'd be back in a while. In all the complications of what faced him, there was something drawing him toward the simplicity of the familiar. Out the door, over the low back wall, through the two fields, leaving cottage and village behind. Every step familiar, every twist and turn trodden in rain, sun and snow. Just ahead, the blunt towering outline, solid, majestic. Just like another home. Quickly through the door, low and arched.

Again, every step ordinary, intimate. Two at a time, he took them with ease, spiralling toward his object, the open sky above him. Up and up and up, yet hardly breathless.

Now at the very top, unhindered by that familiar caution of "be careful." The air of the autumn evening still in summer's stubborn hold, gently wafting, as if in time with the flow of the river below, welcome after his exertions.

Placing his elbows on the parapet, he slowly, almost reverently, looked into the distance at what had been his life so far. High up and alone he felt again the heady excitement that he had so often felt here with Joe. The lofty walls, victim to the last streaking rays of sunshine, supporting his perch, had pushed everything away, as they so often had. He was untouchable, basking in the joy of childish freedom and Joe's rueful claim. "We are lords of all we survey."

*

Another blistering Sunday morning. The bell rang out for mass and the villagers assembled. The chapel was full, in anticipation of what the priest had in store, now that Nurse Prout had predicted fire, brimstone and more, "on good authority." Missing from the congregation were three regular attenders, the motorman, his son and Mulcahy.

The clock said a quarter past the hour as Victoria settled into the front seat next to the motorman who seemed more anxious than she'd ever seen him. She noticed how he had managed to pack the essentials. Then to the gate lodge where the boy waited. He hopped into the back seat.

The motor pulled away as she took one look back up the avenue.

Even the priest stopped to listen. Too early yet for the motor to bring her to church, everyone thought. Thoughts turned back to the man on the altar. They waited for the sound of the motor to pass. It stopped for more than a moment and quizzical looks were exchanged. Then it was gone, and the priest stood and looked over his congregation, in preparation for the sermon he was about to deliver.

Joe had said he would wait for them and "walk out his own door." That he did, turning to give a last look inside. The three in the motor could not believe their eyes. Nor could Field believe his, peering through his front window, and it dawned on him that he would have one less worshipper at his service that morning.

What had taken all their attention was how Joe looked, dressed as never before, wearing the suit the boy had brought from Woodlands in the parcel. The limp still evident, he closed the cottage gate, slowly and easily. Then, without a word and Victoria watching his every move, he took his place next to the boy sitting in the back seat, holding the bell rescued from the bicycle.

Driver and passengers looked out onto the sun-struck street, occasionally glancing left and right, as the motor moved away from the cottage and up the empty street. It slowed to let one of Cremin's dogs cross. Then the turn, as usual, at the barrack and down the hill, past the castle gate toward the mill bridge. The barrack door opened. Snee emerged, just too late to see the motor pass. He followed its sound, nodded to himself and set off for his customary walk before Sunday service.

The castle, tall and stately, loomed on their left. Victoria turned to the man and boy in the back seat.

"Let me see, yes I've written it down here. Train is at twelve thirty from Cork, we'll be in Dublin by five and on the boat at nine. Everything will be fine."

They nodded.

The motorman, duty bound, stared straight ahead, impassive and resolute.

Looking back at the castle, the boy then remembered what Joe had said about the suit.

"It might come in handy for some state occasion."

Acknowledgements

Over thirty years ago, my late wife, Maura, no stranger to the vagaries of village life as a child, read the first draft and commented, in her own inimitable fashion, on how she saw it. Her objectivity convinced me this was a story worth the effort.

Gratitude to Lucy Weir, who proofread the penultimate draft and made appropriate suggestions. Thanks again to Lucy for the cover picture and to Declan Howard for the finished product. Suzanne Winterly's advice was extremely helpful as were the views of Phil Ryan, Colette McGee Kerr, Eilish Barrett, Gillian Cussen, Colm Madigan and Des Derwin.

As ever, Orla Kelly, of Orla Kelly Publications, brought her professional publisher's eye to bear and her advice was invaluable.

My children, Rachel and Mark, encouraged me over many years, to take up what I had started when they were leaving childhood behind, and finish it. At last, here it is.

Please Review

Dear Reader,

If you enjoyed this book, would you kindly post a short review on whatever bookstore where you purchased the book or on Goodreads? Your feedback will make all the difference to getting the word out about this book.

To leave a review, go to Amazon and type in the book title. When you have found it and go to the book page, please scroll to the bottom of the page to where it says 'Write a Review' and then submit your review.

Thank you in advance.

Lightning Source UK Ltd.
Milton Keynes UK
UKHW041522131121
393911UK00002B/201